Without warning, Dr. Bryce Miller, a young doctor from Boston, inherits a large, historic ranch in northern New Mexico from a wealthy uncle she barely knew. She flies out to sell The Sun to the highest bidder but things get complicated when a body is found murdered on the ranch. Is it a warning meant for her?

Meanwhile, she must choose among a colorful cast of suitors who want to turn the working cattle ranch into either: an upscale housing development with golf courses, an oil-and-gas field, a nature preserve, a casino resort, the underground home for a doomsday cult, or the plaything of a shadowy business mogul. Each is willing to pay a large sum of money - and maybe do anything - to get the ranch.

She has seven days to decide.

PRAISE FOR J. COURTNEY WHITE

"Hope in a book about the environmental challenges we face in the 21st century is an audacious thing to promise, so I'm pleased to report that Courtney White delivers on it."

– **Michael Pollan** from the Foreword to *Grass, Soil, Hope*

"Courtney White's experience with the Quivira Coalition has made him master of two indispensable truths: people of different and apparently opposing interests can work together in good will for their mutual good; and, granted their good will and good work, a similar reciprocity can be made, in use, between humans and their land."

– **Wendell Berry** from *The Age of Consequences*

"In a time when environmental reporting has become justifiably gloomy, this book is a refreshing breath of pragmatic optimism. White's vision of stewardship, openness to new ideas, giving as well as taking, and flexibility will inspire anyone who loves humanity or the great outdoors."

– **Publishers Weekly**

"White strikes a refreshing tone that will resonate with readers turned off by the superior or condescending attitudes of some environmentalist writers... Throughout, he balances abstract questions and ideas with tangible life experiences...[R]eaders will be engaged by his frank and thoughtful discussion of our modern environment."

– **Kirkus**

"Courtney White employs a masterful blend of storytelling and science to communicate a most hopeful message: that building healthy soils – in some surprising and creative ways – can help solve our food, water, and climate challenges all at the same time."

   – **Sandra Postel**, National Geographic Society

"The solutions Courtney describes are not just ideas but are demonstrated strategies already being implemented by creative farmers, ranchers, ecologists, and designers. This book is a must-read for anyone interested in practical ways to restore the planet's health while experiencing a flourishing life."

   – **Frederick Kirschenmann**, author of *Cultivating an Ecological Conscience*

"The problems that humanity faces today are the sum total of billions of small missteps. Courtney White focuses on the solutions that will arise from billions of small right steps... We can reforest our world, restore grasslands, build soil, purify water, provide wildlife habitat, feed humanity, and improve health and nutrition while creating the ecological abundance of the future. Bravo!"

   – **Mark Shepard**, author of *Restoration Agriculture*

"Courtney White chronicles a new and critically important sphere of knowledge: a world of soil, sun, sky, and animals where good people regenerate the earth in ancient and novel ways. Reading about the environment rarely brings one as many smiles and as much joy."

   – **Paul Hawken**, author of *Blessed Unrest*

BOOKS

Fiction

The Sun: a Mystery (volume I of the Sun Ranch Saga), Early Hour Press.

Consilience (to be published in 2019)

Nonfiction

The Age of Consequences: a Chronicle of Concern and Hope with an Introduction by **Wendell Berry**, Counterpoint Press.

Grass, Soil, Hope: a Journey Through Carbon Country with a Foreword by **Michael Pollan**, Chelsea Green Publishing.

Revolution on the Range: the Rise of a New Ranch in the American West, Island Press.

Two Percent Solutions for the Planet: 50 Low-Cost, Low-tech, Nature-based Practices for Combatting Hunger, Drought and Climate Change, Chelsea Green Publishing.

Grassroots: the Rise of the Radical Center; and The Next West, Dog Ear Publishing.

Knowing Pecos: a Small History of a Big Place, Dog Ear Publishing.

BOOKS

Photography

The Indelible West: Photographs 1988-1998 with a Foreword by
Wallace Stegner
published as an e-book at www.indeliblewest.com

THE SUN

A MYSTERY

J. COURTNEY WHITE

early hour press

To my family

This book is a work of fiction. All characters, organizations, locales, plots, and events contained in this novel are either products of the author's imagination or are used fictitiously.

No part of this book may be used or reproduced in any form without written permission from the author except in the case of brief quotations in articles or reviews.

To contact the author see: www.jcourtneywhite.com

THE SUN: A MYSTERY. Copyright © 2018 by J. Courtney White. Published by Early Hour Press, Santa Fe, New Mexico. All rights reserved. Printed in the United States.

The Sun Ranch Saga © J. Courtney White.

Sun Ranch & Early Hour Press logos © J. Courtney White

Logos and Map Concept: J. Courtney White

Logos and Map Illustration: Jone Hallmark

Cover Concept: J. Courtney White

Cover Design: John Tollett

Library of Congress Control Number: 2018910646

ISBN: 978-1-7327561-1-3 (ebook)

"The care of the Earth is our most ancient and most worthy and, after all, our most pleasing responsibility. To cherish what remains of it and foster its renewal is our only hope."

– Wendell Berry

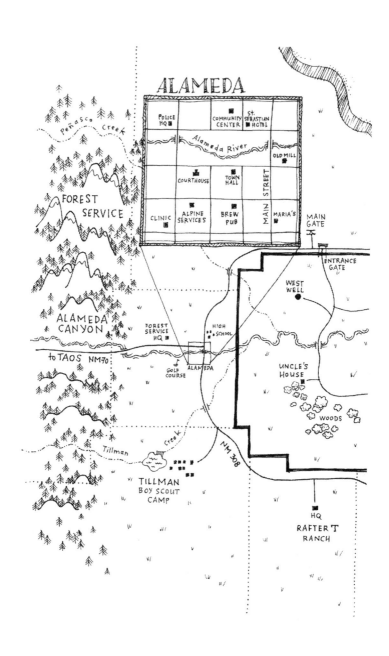

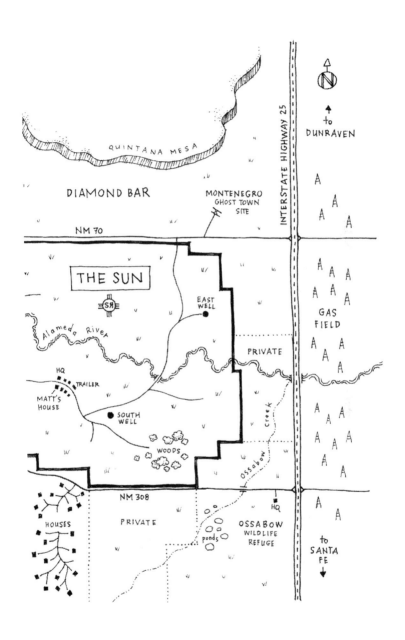

MONDAY

Doctor Bryce Miller hated making wrong turns and by the time she reached the ranch foreman's little house she had made three.

She developed a nose for directions at an early age, much to her father's exasperation, mostly because he was forever taking the incorrect street over her protests. "Precocious," he called her once after she untangled a complicated set of his wrong turns while visiting New York City on a rare family vacation. She took it as a compliment. Years later, she astonished a boyfriend by marching him right across Venice to their hotel using only a paper map even though she had never before stepped foot in the famous sinking city. Finding her way around became a point of pride, especially when navigating the labyrinths of unfamiliar hospitals. Once, she had the nerve to gently correct the trajectory of a conceited, highly accomplished colleague who had turned into the wrong hall in his own medical clinic, earning veiled expressions of outrage from his acolytes in tow. To everyone's surprise the famous physician took the correction gracefully, prompting a small, mental fist-pump on her part.

This morning, however, she made three wrong turns in a

span of fifteen minutes, two at forks in the ranch entrance road and the third when she mistakenly turned onto the paved driveway that led to her uncle's home. The last one irked her. Did she do it to be on asphalt again? Was she that much of a city girl? The dusty road wasn't rough, just unfamiliar, as was almost everything on the three-hour drive north from the airport in Albuquerque. A native Bostonian, she had visited the Southwest a few times, mostly for medical conferences, but this was her first trip to New Mexico. Perhaps the long drive made her impatient. A similar journey back home would have taken her across three state lines by now! Besides, driving wasn't her thing. She decided early in life to avoid sitting behind a wheel as much as possible, partly out of a sense of environmental responsibility but also because she hated traffic. Specifically, she hated getting *stuck* in traffic and for the same reason she hated making wrong turns: she had work to do. "Life is short and getting shorter," her father liked to say, needling her affectionately. It was also his cheeky way of pushing back against the world's nonstop madness.

Of course, he didn't make that joke anymore.

Despite the wrong turn Bryce kept driving, curious to see her uncle's home. The driveway entered a stand of trees before looping upward steeply, climbing a hill. Rounding a bend, the car exited the woods, arriving dramatically in front of the house. She couldn't stifle a gasp. Stunning views radiated outward in three directions across the ranch. She let the car drift to a stop at the edge of the parking area, killed the engine, and lowered the tinted passenger window. Grasslands stretched away like a stilled sea, interrupted only by small islands of trees looking like they had become unmoored from a nearby forest and drifted across the green vastness. To the north, she spied the Alameda River, which she had crossed on the entrance road, meandering eastward across the ranch toward the plains. In the distance beyond the river loomed a long band of flat-topped hills and above them a dark mass of forested mountains, looking like a lost continent, she thought. Her gaze dropped back to the green sea. On the drive from the airport, she had been mesmerized by the rich colors of the high desert, full of yellows, browns, and purple-reds, but this was different.

This was grass country.

Bryce followed the vista west through the windshield. A belt of tree-dotted foothills rose purposefully until they became forests and mountains, split by a deep canyon from which the Alameda River emerged. Snow glistened on tall peaks on the horizon. She leaned forward and stared upward. The sky was piercingly blue and vast, speckled with puffball clouds. It was so close she felt like she could touch it. She never felt that way about the sky in Boston, a consequence of sea salt in the air, she supposed. Here, the sky was pure crystal. It felt like an image from a dream. Or a mirage. No wonder her uncle picked this spot for his home – the view alone was worth the fortune he had spent!

Lowering the driver's window, she studied the house. It looked like a fancy version of a Lincoln Log cabin she built once as a child. It was a square, two-story structure built with golden-brown logs, topped by a steep roof and a stone chimney. A short, handsome wooden stairway led to a porch and a front door flanked by two large windows. The roof extended over the porch, supported by four wooden posts. To the right, on the north side of the house, was an observation deck. She could see patio furniture and a huge BBQ grill sitting near a railing. The parking area appeared to continue around the corner of the elevated deck, following the curve of the hill. There was a hot tub somewhere, Bryce remembered, as well as a Swedish sauna, a small gym, and a large wine cellar – not things one normally found on a working cattle ranch, she suspected.

A light breeze tickled her face, carrying hints of grass and earth. As she took a deep breath, a tingle ran down to her toes. Why did that smell seem so familiar? She had never visited a ranch in her life. She stopped at a dairy farm in Vermont once out of curiosity. It was pretty, she recalled, but smelly. A few years ago, she drove from Chicago to St. Louis to visit a college chum, slicing through farm country, but all she saw were rows of green corn as high as the car. That was the extent of her agricultural experience. True, her mother and uncle had been raised on a farm in Nebraska, but her grandparents sold the property shortly after Bryce was born and retired to Florida. Neither one of their children wanted to farm. Bryce's mother moved to Boston to attend college, married her father, an impertinent high school science teacher, and became an accountant. Bryce's uncle went west and grew rich. When her mother became ill a few years ago, Bryce broached the idea of visiting the family homestead, but she refused and the subject wasn't mentioned again. She closed her eyes as the fragrant breeze tickled her face. The air was incredibly dry. Bryce heard chattering bird sounds in the trees behind her uncle's house. Why did she feel so at home here, thousands of miles from her deeply urban life, six thousand feet high under electric blue skies?

Bryce's phone rang suddenly in the fleece vest she wore, breaking her reverie. She glanced at the rental's clock as she pulled the phone from a pocket, hoping the call came from the ranch foreman, Matt Harris, who she was due to meet right now. Instead, the call came from a medical colleague, undoubtedly wondering if she had time to discuss another urgent case. She smiled wanly at the phone. Her crazy life followed her like a bloodhound. It didn't matter if she sat in a rental on a remote ranch in New Mexico or went surfing on her occasional week off. On the drive from the airport, she answered a dozen calls, including one that required a quick exit from the freeway so she could concentrate on the conversation. Frankly, the good cell coverage surprised her – maybe she expected more primitive conditions in New Mexico? She hated thinking that, though she felt relieved when the signal finally faded away as she drove past Santa Fe.

Wait. There was a strong signal here! Bryce tapped the fore-man's number and held the phone to her ear as it rang. Hope-fully, he was waiting at his house as planned. He had called her last week anxious to talk as soon as she arrived at the ranch, though he wouldn't say what it was about. It sounded important. Over the years, she learned to read voices like she could read faces and the foreman sounded agitated. Was he worried about losing his job? Why had he been so guarded on the phone? And why did he insist on meeting at his house and not at her uncle's? That seemed odd, though life was full of little mysteries. There was a click. An answering machine came on. "Hi, this is Matt..." the message began. She lowered the phone. Why hadn't he picked up? Maybe there was a ranch emergency – some cow thing.

Bryce tapped the phone off with a finger and returned it to her vest.

She started up the car and turned around in the parking area slowly, giving the grass sea another look. It flowed endlessly to the eastern horizon. What was her uncle up to here? She knew he had purchased a large ranch called The Sun four years ago, in 2004, with the profits from the sale of his successful marketing firm in the Bay Area. Assuming it was an investment, it surprised Bryce to learn he moved to the ranch lock-stock-and-barrel almost immediately. What possessed him to abandon the bustle and sophistication of San Francisco, where he lived for decades, for a lovely backwater like New Mexico? Was it a Wild West thing? She imagined him in a cowboy hat. It was possible. Although she had only met her uncle eight or nine times over the years, she knew he possessed an eccentric streak, as well as a killer instinct for making money. She also knew he had died suddenly, unmarried and childless, while staying at a winery in France, leaving his extended family to speculate about the fate of his valuable ranch.

But why in the world had he willed it to *her*?

At the bottom of the hill, Bryce guided the car back onto the dirt road. At a fork, she spied a weathered sign low to the ground. *Headquarters* it said simply, pointing right. Following it, she casually wondered where her uncle's cattle were – off in a field probably. The large herd came with the ranch and the smug probate lawyer told her the animals were almost as valuable as the house. When she expressed skepticism – they were talking about *cows* after all – he handed her the valuation sheet. She nearly stopped breathing. Looking up, she saw a smirk on the lawyer's face. There was more. What she didn't inherit, he said slowly for effect, was a mortgage – on anything. Her uncle paid cash for the land, house, animals, and everything else, which made her wonder what he did out there in California to earn so much money. Clearly, he was shrewder than people gave him credit and buying a 140,000-acre ranch may have been his best move of all, though she suspected dying early wasn't part of his plans. The upshot, said the lawyer, was that the ranch was hers, free and clear except for taxes and fees. Toss in cash from a bank account for the ranch's operation and here's what the inheritance is worth. He handed her another piece of paper.

She took one look and nearly fell out of her chair.

Bryce could see a cluster of buildings under two rows of tall trees up ahead, looking like a leafy oasis in the sea of grass. Headquarters, had to be. The foreman's house should be the first building on the right she recalled from a map. She slowed the car as she approached a small brown house. Near it stood a tall windmill, its heavy gray blades making a screeching sound as they turned slowly. It looked like it came straight from a western movie, Bryce thought – or a museum. Behind the house was what appeared to be a corral. What really caught her eye, however, was the silver pickup truck parked in the driveway. The foreman was home! She parked behind the truck and pushed up her sunglasses as she stepped out of the car to get a better look at the house. It was a simple, cinder-block thing fronted by a white fence. Behind a gate sat a small, thirsty-looking lawn. It was late May – shouldn't the grass be greener? She waited. Where was the foreman? Napping? She honked the rental's horn, surprising herself at its loudness in the quiet air. Nothing. She walked to the gate in the fence, opened it, and crossed to the front door. She knocked once and waited. The windmill screeched again. She knocked a second time.

"Mister Harris?" she called loudly. "It's Bryce Miller."

Nothing. Feeling slightly annoyed now, she cupped her face with her hands and peered through the living room window, whose curtains were partially open. Dimly, she saw a light-colored sofa, a stuffed chair, and a pair of mostly empty bookcases against a far wall. There was carpeting and possibly a stereo system on a wooden console, though she couldn't be certain. A laptop sat on a coffee table in front of the chair. She could see a closed door in a hallway and what looked like the entrance to the kitchen.

No foreman.

Bryce pulled her phone from the vest pocket, but there was no signal at all. Maybe he was out back. She crossed back through the gate, leaving it open, and turned to her right. Rounding the corner of the house, she had to side-step a rain barrel that had fallen over. Behind the building was a miserly backyard with two neglected-looking trees and a peeling bird bath. She noticed a pile of cigarette butts near the back door. No foreman. She crossed to the corral. It was empty except for piles of horse poop. There was a small wooden structure at one end of the corral, probably for horse stuff. Its door was padlocked. Bryce folded her arms across her chest in frustration. Where was he? Uncertain if she should continue to feel annoyed or begin to feel worried, Bryce turned a half-circle, peering around. The silver pickup sat quietly in the driveway. Something didn't feel right. She decided to hold her breath and listen. Other than the screeching windmill and a few distant bird calls, everything was so... quiet. There was no background noise, she suddenly realized. The steady urban hubbub that she had known all her life was gone.

At the sound of another metallic screech, Bryce walked toward the windmill, shading her eyes against the bright sky as she traced a spindly metal ladder to its top, not entirely sure why she thought the foreman might be up there. He wasn't. Was there an outhouse? She surveyed the grounds. No. Indoor plumbing, right. Perhaps the pickup in the driveway didn't belong to him after all. Maybe the foreman was busy at one of the other Headquarters buildings. Maybe they had a more relaxed attitude toward keeping appointments here in the country. Perplexed, she began walking back to her car. She glanced at the silver pickup as she walked past.

A dog suddenly lunged at her from the bed of the pickup, snarling and snapping its jaws. Bryce recoiled, tripping over a tree branch that lay incautiously along the side of the driveway. She recovered quickly and spun around athletically, but the dog had disappeared, no doubt lurking in the truck's bed waiting to attack again. She could feel her heart beating fast. She approached the pickup cautiously, rising a bit on her toes in order to peer into the bed without getting too close. It was empty at first. Then she saw a black tail followed by a black-and-white body, then a head, pointy ears and brown eyes. Reflexively, she pulled back, but the dog didn't attack. She peeked again. The dog stared back.

Its eyes were sad.

She leaned closer, ready to jump at the slightest twitch of the animal's muscles. Growing up, she had always wanted a dog but they were strictly forbidden by her mother who considered them to be too much like farm animals, preferring fat, lazy cats instead. In college, Bryce intended to visit the shelter to find a canine companion (the human varieties weren't working out so well) but never quite found the time. Then came the crush of medical school, where it was almost impossible to take care of herself much less a pet, followed by a highly coveted residency at a major research hospital in New York City, another round-the-clock commitment. Hard on its heels came the big job – the same job she held today as a pediatric oncologist at a major hospital back home in Boston. She settled into a brutal routine with the occasional week off which she used to go surfing some-place tropical to dissipate stress and recover her sanity.

No time for dogs, as it turned out.

She smiled at the baleful animal in the truck. "Hey there," she said soothingly. "Why the sad eyes?" It didn't move. "Where's your person? Did they go away somewhere?"

The dog continued to stare at her.

"Are you hungry? You look hungry."

To her surprise, the dog wagged its tail – but just once.

"Well, that's progress. What's your name? Are you a him or a her?" she asked, trying to see under the dog, but without success. "Who do you belong to?"

The dog stared back – but less sadly now, she thought.

"Do you know where the foreman is? Mister Harris?"

The dog wagged its tail again, twice this time.

Bryce peered through the open passenger window into the

cab. She saw a travel mug in a cup holder, a water bottle next to it, a pair of work gloves on the passenger seat, and a magazine on the floor with a cow on its cover. Did that mean the truck belonged to the foreman? Maybe everyone here had cow magazines. There was a CD on the seat next to the gloves. She reached through the window and picked it up. *Loyal Brigand*. Hard jazz. Not what she expected a ranch foreman to listen to, but you never knew. She dropped the CD back on the seat and pushed off from the pickup with both hands as if she were in a small boat leaving the dock. Maybe she was supposed to meet him at one of the other buildings? She climbed into the rental, shutting the door harder than she planned. The dog appeared in the back of the pickup, his ears alert. Bryce gave him a wave, but he vanished again.

She swung the car back onto the road and drove slowly through the Headquarters looking for a sign of the foreman, or anyone, in the leafy oasis. On her left, she saw a brown, rambling, one-story building, looking historic. A sign stuck in the ground said *Office*. Next to the house, a sprinkler sat quietly in the middle of a large lawn. A trampoline stood beyond it, waiting for children. A hammock hung motionless between two tall trees. Beyond the lawn, grasslands. On the right, she passed a double-door maintenance facility of some sort, looking new. Its doors were closed tight. A yellow tractor sat passively beside it, near a pile of large rocks. As the building slid by, she caught a glimpse of three tall, cylindrical containers on thin metal legs behind it. Hoses hung down from each one. There were other structures, including what Bryce suspected was a barn, but they began to blur together.

A little farther on, as the canopy of trees began to thin out, she spied a short road on the right leading to a large circular structure. It reminded her of the corral back at the little house. It was empty as well. On the left, under the last row of trees, was a trailer. It was long and narrow, its silver metallic hide pocked at regular intervals with windows, each closed with curtains. A solitary door occupied its middle, connected to the ground by a short stair. She slowed down. There was evidence of tire tracks in the semi-circular driveway, she thought, but no vehicles. It looked lifeless.

A small chill tingled her spine.

Bryce hit the brakes, stopping the car in the middle of the road. She had reached the edge of the sea of grass and didn't feel like venturing any farther in fear of getting lost. She drummed her fingers impatiently on the steering wheel. Where was the foreman? Did he forget their meeting? Unlikely. She pulled her phone from her vest but it still utterly lacked a signal. She tossed it onto the passenger seat in exasperation. Honestly! What sort of foreman skipped appointments? The missing kind. The chill returned. She pushed it away, feeling faintly ridiculous. They had crossed wires somehow, that's all. She decided to go back to her uncle's house, feeling certain he went there looking for her.

Bryce tugged on the steering wheel and stepped smartly on the gas, forcing the car into a tight U-turn, tires crunching loudly on the gravel. She had miscalculated. The car rocked side-to-side violently as it left the road, tossing Bryce around in her seat. The steering wheel slipped from her hands briefly. The wheels made a straining sound in the grassy dirt and the car slowed to a crawl. She prayed it wouldn't get stuck! Fortunately, the vehicle kept going but rocked again as it reentered the roadway. Finally, everything settled down. Bryce took a deep breath as she gripped the steering wheel firmly.

No more wrong turns, she promised herself.

THE FOREMAN WASN'T WAITING at her uncle's house.

After parking, Bryce fished her phone from the passenger

well, where it had fallen during her little driving adventure, but none of the messages waiting were from him. She tapped the foreman's phone number only to be rewarded a few moments later with the click of the answering machine. "Hi, this is Matt..." She sighed and turned the phone off clumsily, still uncomfortable with these new-fangled touch screen devices. She missed her well-worn Blackberry. She reluctantly made the switch last year only because her father gave her the new phone for her thirty-fifth birthday, only two weeks after its official debut. He was always doing things like that. An early and enthusiastic tech head, he had an uncanny nose for spotting trends before others. Years ago, he was the first person on their block in South Boston to bring home a pocket calculator, causing her frugal mother to grumble at its cost (though she quickly began using it for work). When Bryce was thirteen, he surprised the three of them by bringing home a personal computer – a shiny Apple II – changing their lives forever. Predictably, her mother declared the machine an indulgence they couldn't afford. Her father gave Bryce a wry smile. "What good is an indulgence if you can't afford it!" he protested. Then he winked at her.

Life was short.

Maybe the foreman had left her a note. Getting out of the car, Bryce climbed the brief flight of stairs to the front door. No note. She turned to her right and walked along the porch to the observation deck, connected at the corner of the house by an archway. Stepping onto the spacious wooden deck, she saw a sliding glass door to her left that led inside. There was no note stuck to it either. She walked to the center of the rectangular deck. The eight-chair patio set and the large BBQ grill looked expensive, she thought. In the far corner was an elevated hot tub. A peek inside revealed it to be dry. *Where was the foreman?* Frowning now, Bryce punched his number again and lifted the phone to her ear as she walked toward the railing. She suddenly spied a vehicle traveling toward her on the entrance road, trailing a long plume of dust. She shaded her eyes against the bright sunlight. It looked like a pickup. Finally, the foreman! Wait. What about the truck at the little house? Maybe this was someone else. There was another ranch employee, as she recalled. The answering machine kicked in. "Hi, this is Matt," she heard again. His voice was calm compared to the conversation she had with him last week. "I'm not available at the moment, but thanks for calling. Please leave a message at the..."

Bryce stabbed her phone with a finger, ending the call, feeling more worried than annoyed now. Maybe he couldn't answer because he was driving the truck. Reaching the railing, she saw another wooden stairway, narrower and steeper, heading down to a second parking area just around the corner from where she had left the car. She lifted her eyes to the entrance road, shading her face once more. The approaching truck appeared to be in no rush. She felt like waving to catch the driver's attention and speed things up a bit, but she decided to wait instead. She took a deep breath. The wide grasslands in front of her made it feel like she stood at the prow of a golden boat in a vast green sea. It was a comparison that came easily. Her father had been a sailor nearly all his life. As a teenager growing up near the ocean, he saved enough money from his many odd jobs to buy a used but sturdy catamaran which he sailed energetically during his meager spare time. There was something about the sea that grabbed him by the throat and never let go. Even the political turmoil of his college years, followed by his hectic life as a public school teacher, never deterred him from finding time to sail his beloved boat. He felt at home on the water, a feeling he eagerly shared with Bryce, who just as eagerly soaked it up. She learned her life-long love of maps from him. She could remember the excitement she felt when her father spread a new nautical chart across the dining room table. They would pour over the map together, their fingers hunting among inlets and islands, making plans. She loved to watch her father during these moments, his eyes sparkling with possibility. Of course, the irony was incredible. Why was he such a wizard on water but so incompetent with directions on land?

It was a mystery.

A white pickup truck suddenly emerged from the woods on the driveway. Bryce crossed the deck and headed down the porch toward the front door. As the truck pulled into the parking area, she could see an older man behind the wheel, debonair in a trim beard, a grey cowboy hat, and a blue kerchief around his neck. His hands held the wheel comfortably, she noticed, as if the vehicle were an old friend. He sat erectly, which in her experience meant he had either served in the military or grew up in a family that valued good posture. Parking next to her car, he opened the truck door and climbed out stiffly. He wore brown boots, jeans, a large belt buckle, and a plaid, snap-button shirt with the sleeves down. He was lean and white-haired. As she reached the bottom of the porch stairs, Bryce could see that his face was smooth above his beard, though by the look of his weathered hands he had to be seventy. He had lively blue eyes in an otherwise serious face, suggesting he was mischievous or stubborn – or both.

"Doctor Miller, I presume?" he said in a courtly twang. He stuck out a hand. "Earl Holcombe. Welcome to The Sun. It's a pleasure to meet you."

She gripped his hand firmly. "Nice to meet you too."

"I'm your neighbor to the south, one of them anyway. The Rafter T Ranch. It's just a little, bitty place compared to this operation," he said, nodding at the vista. "I was sorry to hear about your uncle."

"Thank you. It was a shock to everyone."

"I bet. Hoo boy," he said, shaking his head.

He was sizing her up, she knew from experience with older male doctors, so she stood her ground confidently in her casual but upscale outdoor clothing, a pair of trendy sunglasses sitting comfortably on top of her well-cut short hair, feeling every inch the urban-dwelling, New York Times-reading, latte-drinking, East Coast liberal that she appeared to be – and was.

"Did you know you'd be inheriting the ranch?" he asked.

"Not a clue." Her phone suddenly rang in her vest pocket. "Sorry," she said, pulling it out. After a glance at the number, she silenced the ring. "I thought it might be the foreman."

"Matt?"

"He called me last week. He wanted to meet at his house as soon as I got to the ranch, but he isn't home. I saw a truck in the driveway though."

"Silver? That's his," Earl said. "Did you see the quad? It's a four-wheeler. He uses it to check on cattle and fix fences."

Bryce shook her head. "No, I didn't see anything like that."

"He's been having trouble with a well in the south pasture. Maybe he needed to run down there."

"Does he own a horse?"

"Yes ma'am," Earl replied with a nod. "Brunhilda. She's quite a gal."

"The horse wasn't there either."

Earl wrinkled his eyes at her. "Not there? That's odd. He doesn't usually use her for ranch work. Were there any other trucks?"

"I didn't see any."

"Well, I'm sure there's a logical explanation. Matt's as good as they come. Did he tell you what he wanted to talk about?"

"No. But he sounded anxious. You have any idea?"

"No ma'am. I know he's worried about his brother, who's a

Marine over there in Iraq. Went in as part of the surge last year. But he's not going to bother you about that."

Which was perfectly fine with her. In March, she attended a peace rally on Boston Common to mark the fifth anniversary of the start of the never-ending Iraq War but it had turned ugly when a small gang of pro-war antagonists crashed their quiet protest causing bad feelings all around. It was a sign of the times, she supposed.

Earl nodded his head approvingly. "That's a good fight, I'll tell you."

Not wanting to be discourteous, Bryce decided to change the subject. She glanced up the entrance road. "I'm curious, how did you know I was here? I didn't tell anyone I was flying out except the foreman."

"He told me," Earl replied. "And I knew you had arrived because of the sensor on the main gate. Your uncle had it installed so he could tell when someone came on the ranch. He insisted it buzz at my house too. And he put up a surveillance camera."

Bryce frowned. "A camera? Why?"

"No idea. Maybe your uncle was worried about all that wine in his cellar." Earl shook his head. "You a wine fancier?"

"Only when I'm not too tired," she replied with a smile.

"I hear you," he said, chuckling. "I did some research on you last night, by the way. That's an impressive list of credentials. You're a children's doctor?"

"That's correct," she said, knowing what was coming next.

"Bone cancer," he said admiringly. "That's got to be tough."

It was a familiar compliment. "Some days it is," she said quietly, not knowing what else to say.

Earl took the hint. "Did you know your uncle well?"

"I didn't know him at all," she replied. "Well, hardly. I met him maybe ten times, mostly while growing up. He and my mother were twins, but we lived in Boston and he lived on the West Coast. I knew he bought a big ranch in New Mexico though." She turned her head to study the sweeping view. "This place is amazing."

"She's a beaut alright. One of the last of the old frontier ranches," Earl said following her gaze. "Do you know your plans yet?"

"I do," she said firmly, still surveying the vista. "I'm going to sell it."

"In that case, here comes your first suitor."

He nodded at the entrance road where she could see a large red SUV traveling fast toward them, a dust plume rising high into the sky.

"That's Doreen," he said, squinting. "She sells big real estate. Watch out, she's something else too. There's another one," he said, nodding at a white truck on the road, not far behind. "That would be Bill Merrill. Smoothest talking SOB in a cowboy hat I ever met."

"It's Memorial Day. How do they know I'm even here?"

Earl chuckled. "I think they spy on each other. Here comes someone else!"

He nodded at a shiny sedan speeding behind the other two.

"Who's that?" Bryce asked.

"Frank McBride, I bet. He works for Nature Unlimited, that big national outfit that buys land for conservation. Their office is in Santa Fe so I wonder what he's doing here." Earl pointed. "Here comes a fourth one!"

A black vehicle emerged from the dust behind the sedan, moving at a slower rate. All four vehicles were now filling the air with a great deal of dust.

"What's going on?" she asked, amazed.

Earl's eyes twinkled at her. "It's The Sun, my dear. You have it and they want it. And I suspect they'll do anything to get it too."

Bryce watched the four vehicles race down the road. "Mister Holcombe, do you have any idea why my uncle willed me the ranch?"

"No ma'am. He and I talked a lot about his plans, but not that."

"You knew him then?"

"I helped him get started here," Earl said. "He didn't know which end of a cow got up first. Fortunately, he hired Matt. Your uncle was an odd duck, as anyone around here can tell you. But I liked him and we got along even though he was a Democrat."

"I'm a Democrat," she protested.

"And that's fine," Earl said with a nod. "I won't hold it against you either."

Bryce laughed easily. A moment later, she returned her attention to the oncoming vehicles.

"I was sorry to hear about your mother as well," Earl said solemnly.

Bryce was silent. "Thank you," she said finally.

"Your uncle didn't seem the same after he came back from her funeral. You said they were twins. They must have been close."

"Not really. I think they had some sort of falling out." She turned to him. "That's why this is all so strange. Other than her funeral, the last time I saw my uncle was during a trip I took to the Bay Area five years ago. We had lunch and chatted. And now this."

She indicted the sprawling grasslands.

"He must have seen something in you," Earl said.

"I don't know what." She gave him a look. "Which end of a cow gets up first?"

Earl chuckled. "You're going to have to figure that out for yourself." He nodded at the vehicles, now approaching the hill. "Want any background on your suitors?"

"Please."

"Alright. Doreen in front represents a developer who wants to build two golf courses on your ranch, one there, and one there," Earl said, pointing. "Plus a mess of fancy homes in between. I've seen the plans. Hoo boy. The developer's got the support of the Mayor and the Alameda town council, just so you know. Most of them, anyway."

Bryce nodded.

"Bill in the white truck," Earl continued, "he's oil-and-gas. They've got a bunch of wells to the east of you. Something called hydraulic fracturing. Apparently, it's a new way of getting at gas deposits. I guess that means there's one here on The Sun. Anyway, he's got the backing of our county commissioners. He's going to tell you we can get along with industry, but don't believe a word of it."

"Don't worry. What about the other two?"

"Frank, the Nature Unlimited feller, can be a bit touchy. Your uncle outbid them for the ranch and he's been sore about it ever since. I think he wanted your uncle to will The Sun to them, so he might doubly grouchy." Earl looked at her. "His outfit is not a fan of cattle, by the way, despite what they say. Word is they want to put bison out here."

"Is that bad?"

"To cattle ranchers it is," he replied. "I can't quite tell who the fourth feller is, but it's likely Mister Nibble. The electronic book things? Don't ask me. I think his real name is Kenneth or Keith. The owner of the company he works for has more money than God and bought all the land north of you."

He nodded at the dark escarpment and the forested hills lurking above it.

"Used to be the old Circle A, but he combined it with a couple of other ranches and renamed the entire outfit the Diamond Bar. No one knows what he's up to," Earl said, his tone taking on an edge of warning. "But I can tell you his property is shaped like half a donut and the Sun is the hole in the middle."

After giving Bryce a knowing nod, Earl redirected his gaze to the road just as Doreen's SUV disappeared below the hill, followed shortly by the white truck.

He turned back to her. "Your uncle had a different vision for The Sun, which I guess he didn't share. He wanted it to be a model ranch. Healthy land, healthy food. I liked it and we talked about it a great deal, at least until he'd get going on one of his liberal rants about climate change or something and that would be the end of the conversation." Earl shook his head. "Maybe he thought you'd keep his vision going."

Bryce was silent for a moment. "Not possible, I'm afraid. Is there anyone else? What about you? You want to buy this place?"

Earl's eyes widened. "The Sun? Absolutely. But you know what it's worth. You can't do that with cattle, not anymore, and cattle's all I got."

Doreen's SUV burst suddenly from the woods. It came to a hard stop next to Earl's truck in the parking area. It was followed closely by the white truck. The other vehicles appeared in short order, parking smartly. Doors opened and people climbed out, the air thick with competition.

Earl caught Bryce's eye. He chuckled. "This should be fun."

Doreen rushed at them wearing a flowing red dress over a plump frame with big, unnaturally dark hair and maybe too much make-up on her round face, Bryce thought. She wore embroidered cowboy boots on her feet, a heavy silver Navajo concho belt around her middle, an ornate silver necklace, and multiple silver bracelets, looking like the model in the airline magazine ad for New Mexico that Bryce had read on the flight out. Her eyes were different, however. They had the hungry look of a carnivore.

"Doctor Miller! My name is Doreen Wainwright, it's so nice

to meet you," she said in a noticeable southern accent as she thrust a business card into Bryce's hand. "I tried to give you a call last week."

"Nice to meet you too. Sorry. I'm hard to reach when I'm working."

"Such an important job too," Doreen said unctuously. "Taking care of kids with all those cancers. Must be so fulfilling. My heart goes out to them."

Her smiled vanished. "Hello, Earl," she said, her voice dripping with disdain.

"Ma'am," he said, touching his hat.

"How long are you here?" she asked Bryce.

"Until Sunday. It's my week off."

"You go surfing normally," Doreen said. "What fun! You took second place at Waikiki last year in that amateur contest. You would have won too if someone hadn't hidden your board and caused that time delay. It was probably that brute Manolo. He's always doing things like that, stretching the rules, probably sleeping with the judges. I did a little research."

"I guess you did," Bryce replied, blinking.

Doreen cast an evil eye over at Bill Merrill who had reached them. Bryce noticed he also held a business card in his hand.

"I have the perfect client for you," Doreen said to her. "His name is Mark Sampson. He pulled himself up by his bootstraps just like you and has an incredible vision for this beautiful ranch." She glanced at Bill. "And by that I mean real jobs for real families."

"Real jobs driving golf carts and flipping burgers at the country club, you mean," Bill said smartly. "Allow me to introduce myself. Bill Merrill."

He handed Bryce a business card. *Alpine Services. Working For Tomorrow Today.* He wore boots, jeans, a big buckle on his belt, a bolo tie around his thick neck, and a white cowboy hat on his head. None of his clothes had a speck of dirt, Bryce noticed. He had an open face, blue eyes that sparkled, and very white teeth. Underneath his cheery exterior, however, was a cockiness that signaled a man used to getting his way.

Bryce turned to Doreen. "Mister Sampson wants to build a country club here?"

"Just a small one," Doreen replied. "He's very community-minded. Children! Lots of them will be living here. Think of the fresh air they'll have!"

"Ask her how many homes they plan to build," Bill said.

"Just a hundred," Doreen said smoothly. "They'll be done very respectfully. He's ecologically-minded."

"That's just Phase One," Bill said.

"There's a Phase Two?" Bryce asked, alarmed.

"He'd rather see a bunch of oil wells," Doreen snapped, nodding at Bill.

"You'll hardly know we're here," Bill replied.

"Until there's a spill," announced Frank McBride, who had arrived. "Or the local water supply becomes contaminated."

"We have an outstanding safety record, Doctor Miller," Bill said calmly.

"If you don't include the accident in Canada that sickened three hundred people," Frank countered.

"I heard about that accident!" Bryce said, alarmed again.

"That wasn't us," Bill said defensively.

"Does it matter?" asked Frank, an edge to his voice.

"We provide good paying jobs," Bill said smoothly to Bryce.

"We're building homes for families," Doreen interjected.

"Full of cats and dogs," Frank said. "Studies show cats are the number one menace to songbirds. They're furry murderers."

"What a terrible thing to say about someone's pet!" Doreen exclaimed.

Frank shrugged. "At least they keep the coyote population healthy."

"This is getting good," Earl said, chuckling.

Frank extended a card. "Frank McBride. Nature Unlimited." He was tall, thin, tanned, and neatly bearded with intense brown eyes. He wore hiking boots, tidy beige slacks with a belt, and a green, golf shirt with a *Nature Unlimited* logo on the breast. The neat, dark hair on his head, unprotected by a hat, sported a subtle shine, as if glistened lightly with gel.

"Did you know," Frank continued, "that The Sun is home to an endangered fish? It's called the Alameda chub. It looks a little bit like a trout. Unfortunately, its habitat has been reduced ninety-five percent in the grasslands around here, thanks mainly to oil-and-gas development." He directed a slight nod of his head at Bill.

"So why then does your organization want to put buffalo out here?" Bill replied. "Won't they step on the fish?"

"They're called bison," replied Frank, sounding as if he's had this conversation too many times before. "They don't step on fish."

"Don't you environmentalists say cattle step on fish?" Bill countered.

"Some make that claim, yes." Frank replied tersely.

"I guess buffalo are more careful," Bill said to Bryce, almost winking.

Earl chuckled again.

"I greatly admire the research work you're doing with children," Bill continued, efficiently changing the subject now that he held the stage. "The daughter of a colleague of mine has osteosarcoma, which is one of your specialties if I'm not mistaken. She's in a clinical trial at the Stimson Hospital in Dallas. I know doctors are waiting for FDA approval of that new drug. I can't make any promises, but we might be able to help out with that."

"Did you just try to bribe her?" Frank declared.

"No sir. I'm just trying to help sick kids. We know some people, that's all."

Bryce pointed a finger at him. "And I'm going to take you up on that regardless of what happens with the ranch."

"Yes ma'am," Bill replied, showing his teeth. "In any case, we would like to meet with you at your earliest convenience."

"As would I, Doctor Miller," Frank said. "I was very sorry to hear about your uncle's passing," he added. "He and I had many productive conversations about the future of The Sun right up there on the porch."

"If they were so productive," snapped Doreen, "why did he will the ranch to her?"

A pained expression crossed Frank's face. "I also applaud your work," he said, "and I wanted you know that we'll have a robust educational program here on the property for children, making sure they get outdoors and enjoy nature..."

"Are you going to teach them how to not get gored by a buffalo?" interrupted Bill.

"Bison," Frank said, trying not to clench his teeth. "They'll be perfectly safe."

"The buffalo or the kids?" Bill said, half-smiling.

"Honey," Doreen said, touching Bryce on the arm, "don't you think the world has enough snakes and bunnies?"

"But not enough McMansions for the rich?" Frank shot back.

"And you'd rather see oil wells?" Doreen retorted.

"Of course not," Frank replied tartly. "They're foul, evil things."

"I see. So, what's in your gas tank over there?" asked Bill, jerking a thumb in the direction of Frank's car. "Vegetable oil?" Frank looked uncomfortable again. "We have a robust renewable energy program at our company, Doctor Miller," Bill continued. "We know where the future is headed."

"You ought to know, you're the ones screwing it up," Doreen interjected.

"Remind me again how many solar panels they're planning to put on the roof of that country club?" he said to Doreen, showing his teeth.

"None," she replied curtly. "We'll have lots of recycling though," she said to Bryce, holding up a finger. "Mister Sampson doesn't like to waste anything."

"Is that why he wrote all those fraudulent checks," Frank retorted.

Bryce raised her eyebrows. "Fraudulent checks?"

"Those charges were dropped," Doreen said quickly. "He had a misunderstanding with a contractor, that's all."

"Mark Sampson isn't even his real name," Frank said to Bryce.

"It isn't?" she replied.

"And he's wanted back in Greece for tax evasion," Frank added.

"He's never been convicted of anything," Doreen said, shooting Frank a deadly look. "Unlike that Board member of your organization." She leaned toward Bryce conspiratorially. "Insider trading on Wall Street. Can you imagine?" she said in mock shock, eyes wide.

Frank grimaced as Bill showed his teeth again.

Earl grinned. "I love it."

"I understand you're a jazz fan," Doreen said to Bryce, leaning in. "I can't wait to tell you about the music festival Mister Sampson wants to start."

"It'll be held right over there too," Frank said, pointing at an expanse of grassland. "Just beyond the shopping mall."

"Shopping mall?" said Bryce, alarmed once more.

"Boutique shops only," Doreen reassured her with another friendly pat on the arm. "They'll be very tasteful."

"Only if you think tourists from Texas have any taste," Frank said.

"And you like your jewelry made in China," Bill added.

"Tourism provides clean jobs," Doreen countered. "That's why we have the support of the Mayor and the town council. We all think *it's* the future."

"I can sum up their vision of the future in two words..." Bill started.

"Healthy living," Doreen interrupted.

"Fur coats," Frank cut in.

"Minimum wage," Bill finished.

Bryce furrowed her brow at all of them, feeling dazed.

"Are you aware, Doctor Miller," Bill continued, "that this county has one of the highest poverty rates in the whole state? Not to mention a serious drug problem."

"I didn't know that," she replied.

"Not like the clean-and-sober oil industry," Frank said, rolling his eyes.

"How many people will you be hiring?" Bill asked. "Two or three bird watchers? We'll be hiring dozens of people," Bill said to Bryce.

"For just a few months," Doreen announced. "We call them "thank you ma'am" jobs. Here today, gone tomorrow." She leaned forward. "Not to mention all the brothels that come to town," she said confidentially. "Being a doctor you know what that means."

"Don't forget the meth labs," Frank added. "This place is perfect. I bet there'll be two or three right over there." He pointed toward the river.

"I see," said Bill, sounding irritated at last. "We don't tolerate that of course."

Doreen leaned toward Bryce, giving her a look. "What's that new show on TV about the high school chemistry teacher? Isn't it set in New Mexico?"

The fourth person had come up. He stood apart from the others, his hands clasped behind him patiently. He was small and thin with a sallow complexion and pale blue eyes. He was dressed in a dark, generic suit with a red tie and black loafers, looking more like an accountant than...what?

"And you are?" Bryce asked.

"Kevin," he said pleasantly, nodding his head slightly. "Kevin Malcolm. I represent your neighbor to the north. I'm here to pay my respects as well."

"Did you know my uncle?"

"I did not."

Bryce frowned. "Are you a real estate agent?"

"I am not."

He didn't unclasp his hands, she noticed. "Do you have a card?" she asked.

"No, I don't. We think they're environmentally wasteful. We'll contact you."

Bryce noticed that the other suitors were scrutinizing Kevin with expressions that ranged from awe to fear. She shot a glance at Earl, but he was squinting at the odd-looking man as well.

"Do you live in Alameda?" she asked Kevin.

"I do not."

Bryce waited for him to say something more, but he just stood there silently, hands still clasped behind him. "How did you know I was here?" she asked.

A shadow of unease crossed Kevin's face. "How did they know?" he said, nodding at the other three.

Bryce sighed at him. "What's your vision for The Sun?"

"It's confidential," he replied coolly. "The owner will be here later this week. He would like to talk privately with you."

"The Big Kahuna himself?" Earl said, impressed. "This is getting serious."

"Alright," Bryce said with an impatient nod. "I'm happy to meet with him. Do you want my phone number?"

"We already have it," Kevin replied.

"You do?" she said, astonished.

"And they've probably read every email you've ever written," Frank said darkly. "Not to mention every web site you've visited."

Kevin shook his head. "I'm afraid that's not allowed, as you know."

"Well, that's reassuring," Bryce said, not sounding reassured.

She noticed that the looks of awe and fear had returned to the faces of the other suitors. Was it just his boss's money or did the odd man in the red tie represent some sort of threat? When no one broke the silence, Bryce stuffed the business cards she had been holding into her vest and pulled her phone from the other pocket. She needed this to be over.

"I have to call the foreman. Nice to meet everyone," she said in her best doctorly voice. "Thank you for driving out. I'll call you tomorrow to set up appointments. Mister Nib..." She caught herself. "Mister Malcolm. Call me when you're ready."

Bryce turned around to indicate that the meeting was over, feeling for a moment like she was back in the hospital. She punched the foreman's number and lifted the phone to her ear. She glanced over her shoulder. The suitors were heading back to their vehicles.

She caught Earl's eye. "Those are my only choices?" she whispered.

"Afraid so."

She tilted a chin at Kevin's back. "Do you think he really has my phone number?"

"Yes, I do," Earl replied ominously.

The message machine came on again. "Hi, this is Matt..."

She could hear car doors slamming behind her. She waited impatiently for the message to finish, drumming her fingers against her thigh. There was a beep.

"Mister Harris?" she said into the phone. "It's Bryce. It's about four. I'm up at my uncle's house, standing here with Mister Holcombe." She paused as a car honked angrily in the parking area. "We're just wondering where you are. I hope everything is alright. Give me a call as soon as you can."

She hung up and tapped the phone thoughtfully against her palm. *Where was the foreman?* Missing? It felt that way. In seventh grade, a classmate of hers disappeared one morning while walking to school. The teachers thought she had stayed home sick while her mom thought she was safe in class. It was lunch before an alarm was raised and general panic set in. Police arrived. Fortunately, the girl was quickly discovered at a local video arcade eagerly neglecting her education.

Bryce's thoughts were interrupted by another honk of a horn as the cars jockeyed to leave the parking area.

"Does the foreman smoke?" she said suddenly.

"Cigarettes?" Earl replied. "Not that I saw."

"There was a pile of butts outside his back door. There was a dog too."

Earl turned his head sharply to her. "What dog?"

"In the back of the silver truck," she replied. "Collie, I'm pretty sure. Black-and-white?"

"That's Matt's dog," he said, now alarmed.

"Is that a problem?"

"That dog never leaves his side. Something's wrong."

THEY PULLED up sharply at the foreman's house in Earl's truck, kicking up a small cloud of dust. On the drive, they speculated about his disappearance, settling on the theory that he was on the ranch somewhere with the quad, possibly at the South Well, and had misplaced his radio. It didn't explain the dog's presence in the truck, however, unless the animal had been chained to prevent him from following Matt, Earl said. The two were inseparable, having gone through rough times together over the years including a bout of homelessness. Raised in Michigan, Earl told her, Matt quit college to cowboy on cattle ranches out West but became disillusioned with the traditional way of doing things. He was looking for an operation that was kinder to the land and its animals which made him the ideal foreman for her uncle, who wanted to do something new on The Sun.

"Is he afraid I'll cut him loose right away?" Bryce asked as they came to a stop.

"No, I think he expects to stay on for a little while."

"Then why did he want to speak with me, do you think?"

"No idea. Let's ask him when we find him," Earl said as he opened the door of his truck and began to climb out. "I'll check the house. You look in on the dog. See if he's chained. His name is Seymour."

The dog suddenly appeared in the back of the silver pickup, his ears alert. He looked happy to see Earl, Bryce thought.

"Seymour?" she said, opening her door.

"Don't ask me," Earl replied. "I think it has something to do with Matt's sense of humor. Like his horse, Brunhilda."

Earl headed toward the house. Bryce shut the truck door behind her as she scanned the area. Nothing had changed as far as she could tell. The corral was still empty. Beyond it a narrow dirt lane crested a low hill before disappearing. She turned to the silver pickup.

"Hello Seymour," she said cheerfully as she approached. "Remember me?" The dog wagged its tail. "Are you here voluntarily?" she asked while surveying the truck bed. The dog didn't appear to be connected to it by a chain.

"Looks like you're free. So, where did your person go?" she said kindly. "Not telling? Maybe there's a clue here somewhere."

She inspected the truck's cabin again through the open passenger window but nothing new stood out. Wait. Something caught her eye near the steering wheel. There was a key in the truck's ignition. Actually, it was part of a clump of keys that hung down, suggesting there were a lot of locks on the ranch. Locks to what?

A door slammed. "The house is empty," Earl called loudly. "Is Seymour still there?"

"He is," she called back. "And he's not chained."

"That's not good," Earl said as he passed through the gate in the fence. "It means they got separated somehow and he doesn't know where Matt's at. Is the horse still gone?"

Bryce nodded. "Yes. So is the quad."

"Hoo boy," Earl sighed as he reached her. "I couldn't tell you why exactly, but I got the feeling Matt hadn't been home for a while."

"When's the last time you spoke with him?" she asked.

"Two days ago."

"Did he sound anxious to you?"

"No," Earl replied, squinting at the corral. "He sounded like Matt. I wonder what happened to his horse?"

Bryce followed his gaze. "Is he attached to her too?"

"Not like Seymour. Actually, Brunhilda was owned by your uncle. That means she belongs to you."

"Is she valuable? Could she have been stolen?"

"She's a champion roper, so that's a possibility. Or maybe she got out somehow." Earl squinted at Seymour. "But if Matt went looking for her why didn't he take his dog?"

Seymour flattened his ears under Earl's squint as if he had done something wrong.

"What's a roper?" Bryce said, feeling sheepish.

Earl squinted at her now. "Do you know what a rodeo is? Brunhilda's part of the team that ropes cattle. Her and Matt."

"Oh," Bryce said with a nod, realizing she had never watched an actual rodeo in her life – or ever wanted to. "Is it important there's a key in the ignition?"

"No. I do it too," Earl replied as he peered through the window. "But it does mean he can't get through any of the perimeter gates, so he's likely still on the ranch as we thought. I tell you what, I'm going to run down to the trailer and see if the Mexican knows anything."

"Pardon me, the Mexican?" Bryce said, offended.

"Yes, the Mexican," Earl replied, sounding annoyed. "Don't go and get all liberal on me. He's the ranch hand. Estevan. From Mexico. Which makes him Mexican." He turned toward his truck. "I won't be gone long. Maybe find Seymour some food."

He ambled to his truck, climbed in, and fired it up. As he drove toward the other buildings, Bryce turned to the dog.

"Looks like it's just you and me, handsome. Are you hungry?"

He wagged vigorously.

"Alright, let's find some food. What sort of name is Seymour anyway?"

As she pushed off from the truck, the dog rose to its feet and jumped to the ground.

Approaching the little house, Bryce heard the windmill screech again. A sense of foreboding washed over her. The foreman sounded worried on the phone when they talked last week, but there was nothing unusual about that, right? Life had thrown him a huge curve ball. His employer had died. She was going to sell the ranch. Where would he go? Or was it something else? The possibility of foul play crept into her mind, but she pushed it away, blaming the notion on the collection of Sherlock Holmes stories on her bedside table though she rarely found time to read. She turned the doorknob and entered the house, Seymour close on her heels. Earl thought Matt hadn't been home in a while, why? Was it some ranch thing – a missing cowboy hat or boots in the wrong place? Perhaps it was the stuffy air she sensed as she entered the living room!

A flashing light caught her eye. Bryce crossed to the coffee table and peered down at the laptop. A red light blinked slowly along its lower rim – the signal that the battery had drained. It was unplugged from the wall. Had it been left on? If not, how long would it take to drain on its own? There was a pile of papers next to the laptop. She peeked at them. She saw the words "Bull Sale" at the top of an article featuring a handsome animal. There was also a magazine about organic wine-making. She heard a small whimper behind her.

Seymour sat patiently in the kitchen doorway. "Sorry about that," Bryce said, heading toward him. "So, what does he feed you?"

In the kitchen, she saw two bowls resting quietly on a dirty dish towel at the foot of a counter. One was a large dog water dish, but the other looked like a breakfast bowl for cereal. On the countertop sat a bag of cheap dog kibble. Seeing no other source of nourishment, she grabbed the bag and poured kibble noisily into the empty bowl.

"Here you go," she said hopefully.

The dog continued to sit and stare at her, almost reproachfully, she thought.

"No good?" she said in surprise. "Does this stuff go bad?"

As she inspected the bag for an expiration date, the dog came forward a few feet and sat on its haunches again – staring straight at the cupboard above the counter.

"December 2008," she said to Seymour with a shrug. "So, it's still ok."

She put the bag of kibble down and nodded at the cupboard. "Let me guess, the good stuff's in here."

The dog wagged as she reached for the handle on the cupboard. Opening it, she saw dozens of cans of tuna fish, neatly stacked. She opened the other door, revealing more tuna. She blinked. There were forty cans at least. She could hear the swish of the dog's tail on the floor as it wagged energetically.

Bryce pulled down a can. "Tuna? That's what he gives you?" She checked the ingredients and then shrugged. "Dogs eat fish, right? Dogs eat anything. Alright, tuna it is."

A quick scan of the countertop failed to produce a can opener, however, so she pulled open a drawer. It was full of spoons, forks, and knives, all tumbled together. The drawer below it had what she wanted – lots of utensils – but not a can opener. She checked a third drawer, which was empty, before returning to the utensil drawer, which she now searched carefully. Still no can opener. Frowning, she crossed to the sink, discovering a church-key bottle opener near a forest of empty beer bottles along the sink's edge. She searched the dishwasher. Nothing. She peered into the beer bottle forest, checked three other drawers and another cupboard, all without success. She searched the kitchen table and the refrigerator next before returning to the tuna cupboard for another look.

"Where's the can opener?" she asked the dog.

She surveyed the living room briefly before opening the back door and examining the area surrounding the pile of cigarette butts. There were two empty power drink containers she hadn't noticed before, but no can opener. Frowning deeper, she returned to the kitchen. Something wasn't right. A can opener for so much tuna should be easy to find. Seymour continued to wait patiently, tail wagging. Unconsciously, Bryce began to tap the can of tuna against her palm thoughtfully as if it were her phone.

"Curious," she said to the dog, who cocked its head slightly.

She glanced down at the bowls on the ground, trying to make a decision about the kibble, when she noticed something odd about the water dish. She reached down and lifted it up slowly – and then turned it over.

It was dry.

Bryce drew a sharp breath. "What happened to your water?" she asked Seymour as she stood up. "Were you shut inside?" How long did it take a dog to drink all its water, she wondered? A day? Two? As long as it took a laptop battery to drain?

"He left you behind, didn't he?" she said to the dog. "To go somewhere."

She looked at the front door. Earl hadn't unlocked it when he entered, she realized. He just walked straight in. She remembered the keys in the truck's ignition. Nobody probably locked their doors on a ranch. Anyone could have entered the house.

She studied Seymour. "So, who let you get out?"

Suddenly, the house felt ominous. Had she overlooked something important? She surveyed the kitchen from where she stood. There was an empty cork bulletin board on the wall that she hadn't seen before. Five photographs were pinned to the refrigerator door. A smiling young woman. A Marine in full uniform. An older couple. Two of Seymour. There was a wall calendar nearby, two years out-of-date. She backed into the living room, holding the water dish and the tuna can. Nothing new. She stepped into the narrow hall to her right. There were four doors, she saw, three of them closed. The one at the end of the hall was partially open. She could see a sink, a bathroom rug, and a small window in the far wall.

Earl said the house was empty – but did he check all the rooms?

Cradling the water dish in an arm, Bryce opened the nearest door, exposing an unmade bed. Entering the room cautiously, she saw a modernist night-stand next to the bed and a new-looking chest of drawers along a far wall. IKEA, she suspected. There was an empty set of book shelves on a wall. Crossing the room, she peered at a desk under a window dimmed by heavy curtains. Banking-type papers and receipts sat on the desk, which was missing its chair. There was a closet in a corner. Its door was ajar. She approached it slowly and then hesitated. She pulled the door open swiftly. The closet was bare except for a string of nearly identical western shirts on hangers, an old suit-case on the floor, and a few boxes on a shelf. She exhaled.

Bryce suspected the second door led to a second bedroom. It was barely shut. Pushing it open gingerly with a finger, she saw a single, sheetless bed against a wall, a small pile of clothing in the middle of the floor and not much else. A peek behind the door revealed a fat-tire bicycle leaning against the wall. Did ranch foremen ride bikes? There wasn't a helmet, she noticed. Nothing stood out among the clothing, so she worked her way toward a closed door near a thinly curtained window. Surely another closet, she thought. She paused in front of the door. Why was it shut? She gripped the handle and pulled, but it refused to budge. She tried again with similar results. The handle turned easily in her hand, so why was it stuck? She lowered the water dish and the tuna can to the floor and gave the door a hard, quick jerk with both hands. It opened with a loud creak. Bryce stepped back quickly. She saw... nothing. The closet was empty except for two dusty mousetraps in a corner, one of which appeared to be sprung.

There was one more door in the hall. She yanked it open unceremoniously. Towels on shelves. Toilet bowl cleaner. A bucket and a mop. She caught Seymour's eye as he sat patiently at the end of the hall. He cocked his head at her.

Bryce walked rapidly through the fence gate, Seymour close behind. Earl was waiting for her in his truck, the engine running. She carried the water dish and the solitary can of tuna.

"What took you so long?" he said loudly.

"I couldn't find a can opener."

"Can opener? Are you talking about tuna?" Earl said as she approached the truck. "I told Matt a hundred times to stop feeding Seymour that stuff. Dogs don't eat tuna normally."

"It's all he wants," Bryce replied, holding the can up. "Did you find the...Mexican?"

"No. Estevan's not home and his truck is gone, but that's not unusual. He might be out moving the herd, though that's usually Matt's job. Anyway, I thought we'd run down to that South Well in case someone went there to fix it."

He whistled to Seymour. "Let's go," he ordered, but the dog jumped into the bed of Matt's truck instead. After giving them a sad look, he disappeared.

"That's not good," Earl said.

"Seymour didn't have any water in his bowl. I think he'd been left inside."

"I do it," Earl said with a shrug. "Sometimes you have to leave them. Especially with a dog like Seymour. He'd follow Matt anywhere. I'm sure he had a good reason."

"But I found Seymour in the truck," she protested. "Someone let him out."

Earl thoughtfully stared at his hands on the steering wheel.

"I think something's happened," Bryce said.

He looked up. "I do too. Come on."

THE DRIVE to the pasture took less time than she expected. After passing through the Headquarters, they turned right at a fork in the road, leaving the grove of tall trees behind and confronting Bryce with another sweeping view of the grasslands.

To keep their minds off the foreman's mysterious absence, they chatted about their lives. Raised in the oil patch of eastern Oklahoma, Earl earned a degree in economics, he told her, thinking he might go into business. After completing a stint with the Army, however, he decided to try his hand at cowboying for a while to see what it was like. His first job, as a wrangler on the legendary Spur Ranch in eastern New Mexico, brought him to Sun country. Other jobs followed. The work suited him but he didn't much care for the rough way the land or the animals were being treated on these places and because he was a contrarian by nature he told his bosses so. Eventually, he took up a dare from a rancher he respected to put his money where his mouth was and purchased the Rafter T in 1964. Wife? Widowed. Kids? None.

What about herself, he asked? Bryce shrugged. No husband. No kids. No squeeze at the moment. No time. She grew up in South Boston as an only child. Sailed a lot with her dad. Had good grades, but focused on athletics in high school and planned to try for college on a sports scholarship. Changed her mind at the last minute, opting to become a doctor instead after a good friend fell ill. Figured it was a long shot, but to her surprise she was accepted to Columbia, then Harvard Medical School. Now the hospital.

"That's my story," she said. "Such as it is."

Earl gave her a look. "That's a pretty good story," he said. "Were you part of that bussing nonsense that took place in Boston back in the seventies?"

"My father was," Bryce replied. "He taught at South Boston High, which is where I went. He was right in the middle of the desegregation fight. It wasn't nonsense, by the way. My father said it was the right thing to do."

"It was nonsense if it was just poor people that got bussed," Earl insisted. "Or did they bus the kids of white, wealthy liberals to black schools?"

"No, I don't think so," she conceded.

"Then it was the wrong thing to do," Earl declared. The truck suddenly clattered loudly across a cattle guard.

"Tell me about The Sun," Bryce said, changing the subject.

"Well, it's got a long history, that's for sure," he said with a nod. "In the 1700s, it was owned by a wealthy family, the Quintanas, who supposedly had roots in Spanish nobility. Back then it was called *Rancho Corazon del Sol*," Earl said in twangy Spanish. "Heart of the Sun. And it's been coveted for just as long, I suppose like any heart."

He was quiet for a moment.

"Unfortunately, the ranch became the focus of a dispute among Quintana family heirs," he continued, "a brother and a sister. According to legend, it was so bad their father decided to hide his wealth in a strong box and bury it in the mountains to keep his children from fighting over it when he died. Buried Spanish gold." He shook his head skeptically. "It's brought a lot of crazies to the area over the years to search for it."

"Any luck?"

"None. That's because it's bunch of hogwash. No historian believes the story but that doesn't seem to discourage the crazies. Anyway, the Quintana feud ended tragically."

"What happened?"

"The brother inherited the land and decided to sell the ranch," Earl recounted, "but the sister opposed it. One of them died, I forget which."

"How?"

"Murder, I think," he replied.

Bryce held tightly onto the arm rest as Earl suddenly made a sharp turn to the left. "What happened to the ranch?"

"It ended up in the hands of their rivals, the Mirabals," he continued. "Not sure how it happened. In any case, ol' Diego Mirabal secured a grant from the King of Spain for most of this country after Comanche raids drove a lot of the settlers out. Things were calm for a while after that but blew up when the area became Mexican territory after the Revolution. It was a mess. People squatted on deeded land. Property titles were fought over for years in court. Fortunately, your ranch was kept intact because Mirabal's grandson made a fortune trading with the Americans. Did you know a branch of the Santa Fe Trail crosses The Sun?"

"I didn't!" Bryce exclaimed.

"It does, though it's not much to look at," Earl said with a shrug. "Anyway, in 1856 the ranch passed to Eamon Fitzgerald, an Irishman who came here to trade. Rumor is he won it in a card game from the Mirabal heir, but I don't believe it. People are always making things like that up." He shook his head. "However they got it, the Fitzgerald clan made out like bandits selling beef to the miners up in Dunraven during the gold boom. But then the veins ran out and they had to sell parts of The Sun to keep going. That's how it got down to its current size. Later, they sold the whole place to a disreputable Anglo lawyer from Santa Fe."

"What happened next?" Bryce asked.

"After World War I, it was bought by a New Yorker and became a dude ranch. It was quite the destination, apparently. Some famous people stayed here, including a writer from England. I forget his name. And some archaeologist. By the way, the old homestead is near the wildlife refuge." Earl nodded to the east. "The Depression put an end to the dude business and the New Yorker got embroiled in a scandal back home involving a young lady who wasn't his wife. When he went bankrupt the ranch was forfeited to his insurance company. After the war, they sold The Sun to a Texas oilman named Lloyd Talbot who was married to a Hollywood movie star. They didn't come to the ranch much and when he died she sold it to a guy who made a fortune selling popsicles."

"Popsicles?"

Earl shrugged. "Unfortunately, he let the ranch run down. His cattle kept coming onto my place and a neighbor's. Some animals got hit on the highway. There were a series of owners after that, including a big shot businessman from Denver. But no one was serious about keeping The Sun as a viable cattle operation until your uncle bought it." Earl turned his head to her. "And now it belongs to you," he said with finality.

Bryce nodded, not sure what to say. Suddenly, they hit another cattle guard hard, rattling the truck. Up ahead, she could see a large, dark cylindrical structure.

"What's that?" she asked, pointing.

"That's the South Well tank," Earl replied. "Your uncle had it custom-made. It can water the whole thousand-head herd at one time." He eased up on the accelerator a bit as they approached the tank.

"I don't understand," Bryce said, peering around. "Shouldn't there be a windmill?"

"Your uncle tore it down. Put in a solar pump. See the panels?" He pointed at a small structure to the left of the tank and a bank of solar panels beyond it. "I advised him against it. There was nothing wrong with the windmill. Anyway, the pump keeps acting up. It's been driving Matt crazy. We're going to go around this way to get there."

He guided the truck to the right. As they bounced across a rough patch of ground, Bryce noticed that the grass had been replaced by dried mud pocked with holes and ridges. Cattle tracks, she supposed. She spied a metal trough at the base of the tank, encircling it. She could see sky reflected on liquid inside.

She studied the structure, but it had no other features except for a skinny metal ladder attached to the side that rose to the top of the tank.

"How often do the cattle come here to drink?" she asked as they rounded its side.

"About once a week. Pipes run water to the pastures from here. Matt can pretty much manage the whole southern half of the ranch from this well. That's why it's bad when it breaks down. I tried to warn your uncle..."

Earl fell silent suddenly. A green all-terrain vehicle had come into view. It was parked close to the dark tank. And it was empty.

"Is that the quad?" Bryce asked.

"It is. And that's not where Matt usually stops," Earl said, his voice quiet.

He pulled up to the quad and shut off the truck's engine. They climbed out. To her surprise, he walked past the four-wheeler, apparently wishing to see around the big tank. Bryce headed for the quad, her stomach tightening. It looked like a supersized golf cart, she thought, but with fat tires and no top. Reaching it, she leaned over its side. She saw a solitary key in the ignition, a walkie-talkie radio attached to a spot below the dashboard, a red bandanna hanging from a knob, and a tube of sun screen in one of the cup holders between the two front seats. On the passenger seat sat a dirty towel and a pair of sunglasses. On the floor were a pair of mud-crusted work boots, an orange-handled hammer, and a pair of pliers. On the floor in the back rested a pair of heavy-duty wire cutters, a roll of gray wire, a short, sharp shovel with a red handle, and a large amount of steel chain, uncoiled, both ends of which held metal hooks.

No can opener.

"Find anything?" Earl said, giving her a start.

"What's that?" she said, pointing at the chain with the metal hooks.

"Tow chain. There can be a lot of mud out here. Wait a minute." Earl frowned and leaned over the machine. He pointed at the radio. "That's not where it should be."

"What do you mean?"

"When he's driving, Matt keeps the radio in one of those." His pointed at the cup holders between the seats. "It fits pretty good and doesn't bounce around."

"Maybe he put the radio back when he parked here?"

Earl made a face. "Maybe. But he wasn't that tidy. You've seen his house." He turned to survey the area around them, hands on his hips. "Something's not right," he said.

Bryce felt the sense of foreboding again, deeper this time.

"Stay here," he ordered.

He walked to the left, disappearing around the side of the large tank. The air was completely still. Bryce couldn't even hear a solitary bird singing. Where was the foreman? The quad had the feel of being hidden behind the tank, it seemed to her.

Suddenly, she heard a muffled, clanging sound that echoed dully through the tank. Then a 'ping' pierced the stillness as metal struck metal. It came from the other side. What was Earl doing over there? Was he hurt? She decided to find out. Rounding the tank quickly, she saw him climbing the narrow ladder. She slowed her pace. Why would he go up there? Reaching the top, Earl ceased climbing. He stared at something in the tank. Then he removed his cowboy hat and held it to his chest, bowing his head.

"Hoo boy," she heard him mutter.

Bryce inhaled sharply as she recognized the melancholy slump of his shoulders, a sight she had seen too many times. "What's happened?" she asked, coming forward.

"I found Matt," he called down quietly.

"Are you sure it's him?"

"I am."

His meaning was clear: the foreman was *dead*. How could that be? They were in the middle of *nowhere*. She exhaled slowly. "I'm sorry."

"I am too. He was a good kid," Earl said from the top of the ladder.

"What happened?"

"I'm no expert, but it looks like he was hit on the back of the head."

"Murder?" Bryce asked, incredulous.

"It looks like it," Earl said as he replaced the hat on his head. "We need to call Dale." He began to climb down the ladder. "He's the Chief of the Police department in Alameda. I've got a radio in the truck."

Chief of Police? Murder? Bryce felt dizzy. Earl reached the bottom of the ladder. His face was grim.

"Why would someone kill him?" she asked.

"I have no idea," Earl replied, shaking his head and sounding depressed. "Matt could be a hot head at times, but never enough for something like this. I'm going to go call Dale."

He began walking back to his truck, limping slightly, she noticed. He seemed to have aged ten years since their arrival at the tank.

"I'd like to go up and see for myself, if that's ok," she called.

"Suit yourself," he replied without turning his head.

Bryce climbed the narrow rungs of the ladder easily, slowing her pace only as the top approached. The tank was nearly full, she saw, the water reflecting the clear sky above. Not far away, a body floated face-down. The striped pattern of his light-colored western shirt was visible above the waterline, as was the back of his head. It looked like a bloody mess. A black lump floated nearby. His cowboy hat, she assumed. She couldn't see anything else in the water near the body. Bryce lifted her eyes. There was a round object on the tank wall directly across from her, extending over the water. What was it? She climbed up another rung to get a better view. A pipe. To fill the tank with water. She saw a few leaves floating. But where were the trees?

She leaned heavily on the ladder for a moment. How did the foreman's body get up here, she wondered? She looked at the ground, far below. Had the foreman been killed down there or did someone chase him up here? He was probably struck on the ground, she decided. But how did the killer get the body up the ladder? She studied it as it floated in the water. The foreman must have weighed at least two hundred pounds, she calculated. Carrying him would not have been easy. That suggested a man, but not necessarily. A strong woman could have done it too. Bryce suddenly realized her fingerprints were all over the ladder. So much for crime scene integrity.

Right, *Murder*.

Feeling wobbly suddenly, Bryce gripped the sides of the ladder firmly as if afraid she might slip and fall, though she knew she wouldn't. How could such a terrible thing happen in such a beautiful place? A puff of air tickled her face, smelling of earth and grass. Then it faded away to stillness, as if the ranch had decided to hold its breath. Lifting her head, she saw that the view from the top of the tank was extraordinary. She climbed up another rung on the ladder, its second-to-last. She could see the dip where the meandering river crossed the land. There was a low row of hills to the east and blue sky above it all. Somewhere out there beyond the grass was the oil-and-gas field that Earl mentioned, though it was hard to imagine. From where she stood, it all looked so pristine and peaceful.

Where was Earl? On the other side of the tank, hidden from view. Were the police on their way? The puff of air retuned. Bryce balanced her herself carefully on the rung, feeling a little bit like she stood on a surfboard. She decided to twist around to see the western half of the ranch. She touched the top of the ladder lightly with her right hand as she turned to her left. She could see the ranch Headquarters not far away and beyond it her uncle's house on the hill. She traced the entrance road to its source at the gate on Highway 70. Then she followed the river upstream as it passed through a compact cluster of buildings, which had to be the town of Alameda, before disappearing into the deep canyon. Among the buildings, she could see two church spires and six or seven two-story buildings. Twisting her body a bit more to the left, Bryce followed a ribbon of asphalt south from the town to a small huddle of structures fronting a bright lake. Farther to the south was more open country, though she could also see a swath of houses, loosely packed, in the distance.

Bryce turned back to the grasslands surrounding her, feeling now like she had climbed the tall mast of a boat. The sea of grass seemed just as deep and unfathomable as any ocean she had ever known. And just as marvelous. She spotted a dark mass in the distance. It had to be the cattle herd, grazing a few miles away. A breeze touched her face again. How did Earl describe the ranch? *A beaut.* Indeed.

She took a deep breath.

For the moment, The Sun was all hers – dead body and everything.

TUESDAY

ryce stood in the living room of her uncle's house sipping a mug of coffee when a famously jaunty bit of classical music suddenly filled the air.

Where was it coming from? She raised her eyes to the vaulted log ceiling, two stories above her head. Up there. The musical fragment faded, replaced by silence. Mozart, she was pretty sure, though the bewigged maestro wasn't her style. Why had it played? Was it a kind of cuckoo? She dropped her gaze to a wall clock nearby. In the semi-darkness, she could just make out its numerals: *6:19 am*. Maybe her uncle had an odd sense of tracking time? It was possible. She scanned the interior of the house, recognizing its open design and tasteful western décor from the night before, including the many bronze sculptures of handsome men on horses. The walls of the living room were covered with Western-themed paintings, some residing in thick golden frames, looking a little spooky in the half-light of dawn. She kicked herself for not turning on more lights upon emerging from the guest room. It had been a long, restless night, full of shadows and creaking wood. A strong wind came up at one point, rocking the house. Eventually, she gave up on sleep altogether and rolled out of the bed, feeling ill-at-ease – a stranger in a strange place. To her relief, she found a large container of instant coffee in the back of the refrigerator. It was a start, at least.

Lifting her eyes again to the ceiling, Bryce took another sip from the mug. She tried to imagine a snippet of a Count Basie tune or a Charlie Parker sax solo filling the air among the timbers. Her uncle would not have been pleased, she suspected. Her eyes drifted down to the magnificent antler chandelier hanging over the living room table. Did he invite his friends to eat here, she wondered? Did he invite anyone from the community? Maybe the antlers weren't supposed to impress. Maybe he just wanted the room to look pretty. Suddenly, the merry Mozart tune chimed again in the air. She froze. It repeated a third and a fourth time.

It wasn't a cuckoo clock at all, she realized. It was the entrance gate alarm.

Bryce headed for the sliding glass door that led to the observation deck. Outside, she quickly crossed to the railing at the far side. In the dim light, she could see four sets of headlights moving slowly along the entrance road toward the house, one farther ahead than the others. Police cars, she was certain. Last evening, one had arrived at the water tank carrying a tall, stone-faced young man in a gray cap and uniform. After calling in the discovery of the foreman's body, Earl had sat in his truck, saying very little. He seemed profoundly shaken by the foreman's death, she thought, not unlike how a family member would behave. She learned years ago not to underestimate grief. Maybe he had been like a son? Leaving Earl to his thoughts, Bryce went for a short walk on the ranch road, thinking about the conversation with the foreman the week prior. Why hadn't she pressed him for more details?

And now there was going to be a murder investigation.

The early morning air was cooler than she expected. She gripped the mug with both hands, waiting for the small armada of police cars to arrive. Earl said her uncle installed a surveillance camera at the entrance to the ranch. Why? She was pretty confident it wasn't to protect the valuable wine collection because the probate lawyer had given her a key to the cellar door. How much was his western art worth? Lots, she bet. Did he have expensive jewelry? What about the cattle herd? Was there cattle rustling anymore? Or was her uncle worried about something else valuable on the ranch – a concern shared by the foreman?

She recalled what she knew about her uncle. He left the family farm in Nebraska at eighteen and moved to the Bay Area to go to college, where he majored in marketing. After graduation, he entered the budding tech industry and had the great good fortune to meet a now-famous founder of a fast-rising company. He parlayed the relationship into a highly successful career, becoming part of a pioneering group of marketers who helped make tech sexy. He grew rich. Later, according to his sister – her mother – he became highly nostalgic about those early years in the industry, describing them fondly as a "Wild West" minus the six-shooters. Maybe that's why he collected western paintings and bronze men on horseback, Bryce thought. The historical fascination with the Old West mystified her. What was the attraction of an era defined by racial prejudice, economic exploitation, and environmental abuse, not to mention the suppression of women? Why were *those* the good old days?

She took another sip of coffee from the mug. Despite knowing the outlines of his life, her uncle had been an enigma to Bryce. Perhaps that wasn't surprising. He was a professional marketer after all, relishing the ambiguous persona that he created as part of the job. Even at her mother's funeral he remained distant, though she was too grief-stricken to take much notice. He asked her a few questions about her job and life, but that was all. So, why install a surveillance camera on a remote ranch in a place where doors weren't locked and keys were left in trucks? Did it have something to do with the rapid expansion of his wealth in recent years? There had been family rumors. "Behind every great fortune is a great crime," her mother declared once over supper in response to a wisecrack by her husband, who didn't suffer the lack of scruples among the rich very well. At the time, Bryce thought her mother had invented the comment, but learned later that a novelist had said it first in reference to the mafia. Was she implying her brother had done something illegal?

The police vehicles vanished below the hill.

Bryce placed her mug on the railing and headed toward the porch and the staircase that led to the main parking area, sinking her hands into her vest's pockets against the cold. She wondered how Seymour was faring. After interviewing Earl and herself at the well, the police officer told them not to touch the foreman's truck or go inside his house. She had tried to talk Seymour into coming back to her uncle's home but he refused to leave the truck. Repeated attempts with a tuna can didn't help. Earl tried rousing him too, but the dog refused to budge. He lay immobile in the back looking sad – as if he knew what had happened. In the end, they put bowls of water and kibble in the pickup bed with him. Earl drove her back to the house before heading home, looking as glum as the dog.

A vehicle suddenly appeared in the parking area. It was an old model Ford Bronco with a solitary driver behind the wheel who waved a friendly hand as he navigated the vehicle to a stop near her car. In the rising morning light, she could see the words *Alameda Police* stenciled on the door along with an attractive logo of a river flowing through green mountains. Bryce raised a hand in return. No other vehicle appeared behind it, so she assumed the convoy headed to the crime scene. As she headed down the stairs, the Bronco's engine shut off, filling the air with quietness – and a sense of foreboding.

A door slammed.

"Doctor Miller?" said the man as he rounded the front of the truck.

He was smaller than she expected a rural policeman to be, though she didn't know why she thought that. He had a stocky build, thick, dark hair and a kind face with impish brown eyes that she liked right away. He wore a light blue business shirt tucked neatly into new jeans, a black belt, and a pair of casual hiking boots. He was missing a tie and the shirt was unbuttoned at the neck. It was a practical wardrobe, she supposed, for the job. He was also missing a firearm, she noticed. His body language was friendly – a natural condition, she decided, despite the intimidating words on the side of the Bronco. His pleasant demeanor reminded her of her freshman roommate in college, an unrepentant gossip who also earned a notorious reputation as a campus prankster. The lively eyes were the same. The wrinkles on his face suggested he was in his late forties, she thought as he approached, though he might be younger. Maybe the dry air and high altitude etched a face faster here.

He extended a hand to her.

"Dale Archuleta. Chief of Police. It's nice to meet you," he said in a lilting but firm voice that carried a trace of an accent, she noticed as she shook his hand.

"Bryce Miller."

"I apologize for not calling you last evening, but I was in a meeting in Albuquerque all day that went late."

Bryce nodded. "It's alright. I was kind of in shock anyway. The deputy said your meeting was called by the Department of Homeland Security. Is everything ok?"

"Yep. You probably heard about that attempted bombing in Exeter, England, last week. DHS decided to quickly organize statewide meetings of law enforcement as a result."

Bryce frowned. "Isn't it rather remote out here for terrorism?"

"You'd think so," Dale replied, shaking his head. "I don't know who would put Alameda on a target list. But when the Man tells you to go, you go. It gave me a chance to talk with the state police forensics team. That's how they got here quickly."

He nodded at the empty ranch road.

"I was sorry to hear about your uncle," he continued. "I only met him a few times, but I liked him. He was quite a character, even for around here."

"That's what I hear," Bryce replied.

"I'll never forget the day he came into police headquarters to complain about Sasquatch," Dale said, chuckling at the memory.

"Sasquatch?" Bryce said in surprise. "You mean Bigfoot?"

"The same. There are folks around here claim that the Big Guy lives up there in the mountains." He tilted a chin to the west. Bryce followed his gaze. "They also think we have evidence confirming his existence but we're in a conspiracy with the Forest Service to cover up the truth." He rolled his eyes.

"What truth?"

"Exactly. Anyway, the Mayor took advantage of the controversy and announced that she was starting an annual Sasquatch festival in town." He shrugged admiringly. "Pretty clever, if you want more tourists."

"And my uncle..." Bryce prompted.

Dale chuckled again. "He went ballistic. *Loco.* He tried to complain to the Mayor about her idea, but she refused to see him. Wasn't he in marketing?"

"He was. You think he'd like the idea."

"I thought so too, but he raised a real ruckus, especially on social media or whatever it's called. I never quite understood why he got so upset."

Dale glanced at the road again.

"Any idea yet who killed the foreman?" Bryce asked.

"Nothing for certain," Dale replied, shaking his head. "But we're looking for the ranch hand. Estevan Gutierrez. He's missing. Deputy Sandoval went to his trailer after speaking with you and Earl but it's been cleaned out and his truck is gone."

"Cleaned out? You mean he took off?"

"It looks like it. But he won't get far. There's a full court press on to find him." Dale nodded at the highway.

"Do you think he killed the foreman?"

Dale made a face. "Earl doesn't. He said Estevan's not a killer. Apparently, he and Matt got along well. Earl called him a hard-working Mexican."

He gave Bryce a wry look.

She grimaced. "Is he here legally?"

"He is. I checked his papers, twice," Dale replied. "I don't think your uncle liked my asking, though. He was touchy about his privacy. He was a funny dude." His tone became serious. "I understand that Matt wanted to speak with you."

Bryce nodded. "As soon as I arrived. But when we talked on the phone last week he wouldn't tell me what it was. I think it was something he had to say in person. Do you have any idea?"

"I don't," Dale said with a sigh. "Matt was a friendly guy but also kind of secretive."

"Do you think Mister Gutierrez killed him?"

Dale put his hands on his hips thoughtfully. "I think the missing horse makes him a suspect."

"Brunhilda? There's no sign of her?"

"None. And her tack is missing too. Her saddle and bridle," he added helpfully.

Bryce's phone suddenly began ringing in her vest pocket. She pulled it out quickly and squelched the device in mid-ring. "Sorry. Work. Do you think he stole her?"

"Estevan? It's possible. Trouble is you generally need a horse trailer to steal a horse, but Earl says both of The Sun's trailers are still here. He has some other concerns too." He fell silent for a moment, looking thoughtful again.

"The odd placement of the quad?" Bryce asked.

"Yes and the radio," he replied quickly. "But they're just Earl's gut feelings. Until we have hard evidence, I'm keeping an open mind. Anyway, please keep Matt's death quiet until I contact next-of-kin. Go about your regular business until I make an official announcement though keep your eyes and ears open. Ok?"

Bryce nodded absently, feeling bewildered.

"The deputy told me you think someone let Seymour out?" Dale asked.

She focused. "He was in the back of the truck. I think someone went inside the house. Could it have been Estevan?"

"Possibly. I need to go there and look around for myself." He checked his watch as if he were about to leave.

Bryce snapped a finger. "Oh! I forgot to tell the deputy that when I tried to feed Seymour I couldn't find a can opener anywhere."

Dale narrowed his eyes. "Is this about tuna?"

Bryce nodded. "I thought it was strange."

"The tuna?"

"No, the can opener. I thought it was strange that it was missing."

Dale scrunched up his face doubtfully. "Ok. We'll look into it. I've got to go catch up with the guys. We'll talk later." He waved and turned to walk back to the Bronco.

"One more thing," Bryce said suddenly. "Which end of a cow gets up first?"

Dale paused, cocking an eyebrow at her. "The rear end. Does this have something to do with the murder?"

"No," Bryce said quickly. "I was just curious."

Dale nodded and resumed his walk to the Bronco. "Any idea who you'll sell the ranch to yet?" he said over his shoulder.

"You want it?"

Dale laughed easily. "Is it free?"

"I'm afraid not. Anybody you'd recommend?"

"Have you talked to the Mayor yet?" he said loudly. "Because if you haven't, she'll tell you exactly what to do!" He opened the Bronco's door. "By the way, the body will be moved to the clinic later today. Doc Creider will be out in the morning to do a preliminary examination. You're welcome to join us."

"Thanks, I'll try to be there, though I'm not much of an expert in that department."

"That's alright, neither are we!" he said, preparing to slide behind the wheel.

"Hey!" she called suddenly. "Did that Sasquatch festival ever take place?"

"No," Dale replied loudly. "Whatever your uncle did, I guess it worked!"

AT THE RANCH'S ENTRANCE, Bryce turned left onto the highway and pushed hard on the accelerator. Although Alameda was only fifteen minutes away, she suspected it would be bad form to be late for her appointment. Actually, the secretary implied it would be bad form to be merely *on time*. Her Honor was busy. This was fine with Bryce, who wasn't in the mood for a lengthy sales pitch anyway. She had meetings scheduled with Doreen, Bill, and Frank, commencing with the unctuous real estate agent who insisted they meet in the Mayor's office. All Bryce wanted from each of them was a brief pitch and a formal bid. Assuming she would hear from Mister Nibble eventually, she'd announce her decision before she departed on Sunday to go home. Jeffrey, her lawyer, could handle the negotiation and the rest of the legal paperwork related to the sale. She wouldn't need to return and if she was lucky she would be able to quickly push the image of The Sun's lovely grasslands out of her memory.

The foreman's dead body too.

As she passed a slow-moving delivery truck on the highway, she recalled the first dead person she ever saw. It happened when she was twelve. She had gone for a summer sail on the catamaran with her father among the islands in Quincy Bay when she spied someone in the sea. At first, she thought it was an athlete resting face up after a long swim from the shore. But the water was so cold! He would need help, surely. She urgently signaled her father, who nodded and steered the boat toward the swimmer. It wasn't an athlete, however. The man in the water had a grey beard and wore a dark suit. His eyes were half open to the sky. He floated motionlessly, except to rise and fall gently with the swell. She shot a querulous look at her father but was met with a grim shake of his head.

Holding a safety rope, she leaned over the edge of the boat as they drifted close to the body, not the least bit afraid. He looked so peaceful, she thought. Did he fall overboard? Was someone searching for him? She scanned the surrounding sea, but there was nothing close at hand except a weathered buoy bobbing a hundred yards away. She glanced at her father again, who had a pen in his hand as he wrote in a waterproof notebook that he always carried. He was forever taking notes and measuring things. As she watched, he lifted an electronic instrument to his face – to take coordinates, she realized. After a moment, he lowered the device and made a careful note. When he looked up, she was surprised by his expression – a weariness he only showed in rare moments when he let his guard down, usually when he thought no one was watching. She didn't understand why he wore it now. He caught her eye and something in her heart sank.

"Suicide," he said simply.

She refused to believe it. The boat came close to the dead man. She leaned farther out, gripping the rope. The lower half of the body rested below the water's surface giving her the impression that he was only half a man. He wore a nice coat, a blue vest, and a white shirt with a tie, as if he had walked into the water directly after work. As his face drifted by, however, she could see its discoloration – a ghastly shade of gray. She anticipated a shudder of revulsion, but it never came. Only more questions. Why were his eyes open? How long had he been in the water? And why did her father think it wasn't an accident? As the body slid past silently, an answer crashed into her mind – the man wore no life jacket. But why would someone choose to die, especially in the cold sea? She watched the body slip away until she could barely distinguish it among the rolling swells and white caps. When it was gone, she turned back to her father, querulous again. He had lowered the notebook and was watching her tenderly.

"It happens," he said softly. "For some, the despair becomes too much."

Despair? She turned back to the sea, trying to imagine what he meant. Her mother was sad at times, but she had never given a sign that she despaired. The man in the water looked rich, she thought. Why would he despair? She returned to her seat in the boat, heavily. She searched the waves one more time for the body, without luck, before turning to her father again. He had closed his notebook and put the pen behind his ear, as he usually did when preparing to sail.

"There's nothing we can do," he said, using his science

teacher voice. "We'll alert the authorities when we get back. They'll come get the body." He pulled a rope, adjusting a sail. When he was done, he settled his gaze on her face, fatherly now. "Let's go home."

Her phone rang. Startled, Bryce picked it up from the car seat. Apparently she was close enough to town to get a good signal. It was a medical colleague. She tapped the phone with her thumb and lifted the device to her ear as she drove.

"Doctor Miller," she said in her office voice.

In town, she quickly climbed out of the car after carefully wedging it into a tight parking spot between a black F-something truck and a whale of a SUV sporting Texas plates. Both vehicles were too much steel and glass for her tastes. Back home, she owned a trim, generic hybrid which she drove every day from one garage to another without giving the car much thought. It had wheels. It played music and held her coffee cup as she navigated the commute. It was small, but did the job. Here in Alameda, however, the vehicles were monstrous. She researched the town before flying out, discovering to her surprise that it prospered. Although New Mexico had been settled by Spanish colonists only a few years before the Pilgrims landed at Plymouth Rock, she knew that state had never really boomed. It consistently ranked 49th or 50th in key economic and social indicators and most of its small towns, especially here in the traditionally Hispanic north, still grappled with a legacy of "honorable poverty" as her father once described being poor. Not Alameda. It had shed its humble clothes for finer things, aided by the new ski resort in the mountains. Digging a little deeper, she discovered a second reason. The town had been frog-marched to its current success by its business-savvy, take-no-prisoners Mayor, Geraldine Tate – the former COO of a disgraced global corporation.

Who she was about to meet.

The Mayor's office was on the second floor of the town hall, a nondescript brown building a block up from the lazy Alameda River in what appeared to be the historic center. Bryce wasn't sure because all the buildings surrounding her, even the old-looking ones, glistened under fresh coats of paint, looking like they were getting ready for a parade. An older male security guard inside the front door of the town hall greeted her warmly as she entered. She crossed the floor to a smartly-dressed young woman seated behind a lovely carved wooden desk who, at her inquiry, nodded efficiently at a nearby staircase. As Bryce dutifully headed for the stairs, she noticed the woman lift a phone receiver and punch a button on a console. She spoke a few words before returning the phone to its cradle, undoubtedly setting things in motion.

It didn't take long to find out what.

Emerging from the stairwell, Bryce saw Doreen rushing at her, wearing a yellow dress and black cowboy boots this time. The jewelry and the belt and the hair were all the same, however. As was the hungry look.

"Doctor Miller!" she exclaimed. "It's so good to see you again. Right on time too!"

"I think I was lucky to find a parking spot."

"I know! It's gotten so crazy," Doreen said, taking Bryce's hands and covering them with her own. "And to think it was a sleepy little place just a few years ago. It's been so exciting to watch all the changes!"

Before Bryce could reply, Doreen steered her through a tight U-turn in the hall.

"Do you live in Alameda?" Bryce asked when they were done.

"No. Santa Fe," she replied, sounding a bit defensive. "But I have a new office in town. That's because there's so much untapped potential here. It's very exciting!" She patted Bryce's arm. "Or as Mister Sampson likes to say, 'opportunity abounds!'"

"Does Mister Sampson have other investments in the area?"

"Not yet," the agent replied, her smile dimming the tiniest bit. "Actually, he hasn't even been here, but that's alright. That's why he hired me!"

"He's not in jail, is he?" Bryce asked before she could stop herself.

"No, dear," Doreen replied without missing a beat. "Don't listen to a thing that horrible Frank McBride tells you. He just likes to cast aspersions. Here we are!"

They had arrived at a closed door.

"Before we go in," Doreen said, lowering her voice, "I wanted you to know that the Mayor invited a few members of the community to the meeting. Is that alright? Everyone is excited by Mister Sampson's plan." She raised a finger before Bryce could respond. "And how it fits the bigger picture of prosperity for Alameda that will benefit everyone," she said, sounding rote. "When one does well, we all do well." She seemed to catch herself and patted Bryce's arm reassuringly. "A rising tide lifts all boats, right?"

"That's what I hear," Bryce replied flatly, knowing from first-hand experience this tired cliché just wasn't true. In fact, many of her patients were still waiting for the tide to come in. "Has there been any opposition to this plan?"

"Just the usual complaints," Doreen said with a shrug. She leaned in. "It's political. There's a small faction in town opposed to the Mayor's agenda. You know how it is. Some people just won't embrace progress."

She gripped the door handle and turned it before Bryce could reply.

The door opened, revealing a room packed with people. Bryce balked in surprise, but Doreen led her inside, firmly holding her arm. There were at least thirty individuals standing in a semi-circle, Bryce saw, all beaming at her. They were every shape and size: young, old, tall, short, bearded, bald, scruffy, natty, tan, pasty white, male, female. They wore a wide assortment of clothing, from blue jeans and casual dresses to suits-and-ties. Nearly all of them were Anglo, she noticed, though a few Hispanics were sprinkled around the room. There was one African-American in the back row, standing near a large wall map. No one appeared to be Native American, but she didn't want to presume. If the group had one commonality, they all seemed very fit. Some were definitely outdoorsy types, she thought, though she considered herself a poor judge since she rarely found time to venture outside except for her occasional surfing adventures. Still, it looked like a healthy group and apparently very happy to see her.

As Doreen directed Bryce toward the center of the semi-circle, a tall, thin, and especially fit-looking middle-aged woman turned around. She had a narrow, handsome face to go with her thin frame and a pile of sandy hair stylishly arranged on the top of her head. She wore a beige pant-suit outfit that had to be Italian in origin, Bryce knew, having seen similar ensembles on wealthy women at charity events for the hospital. This outfit, however, sat casually on the woman's slender frame as if she had thrown it on this morning. Except she hadn't. Bryce suspected it had been as carefully assembled as the individuals in the room. In fact, the woman reminded her of a type of senior administrator she knew well, including members of her own medical staff, who took it as a personal challenge to look as feminine as possible while not giving an inch on the power front. There was a quick way to double-check. Bryce dropped her gaze to the woman's feet. High heels, sure enough. How these women accomplished as much as they did in heels day-in-and-day-out was a complete mystery to her. She preferred running shoes.

As the woman came closer, Bryce noticed that her brown eyes were soft, suggesting a tenderness under the fancy clothes. She wore no jewelry and little makeup, likely another calculation, and her face suspiciously lacked the wrinkles that came with age and nonstop accomplishment. Altogether, she projected an aura of genuine self-assurance mixed with calculating femininity.

"Hello, Doctor Miller. Gerrie Tate." She extended a slender hand.

"Miss Tate," Bryce replied, shaking her hand. "Miss Mayor, I mean."

"Please, no formalities. It's not a town council meeting, thank god," she said with an easy laugh, causing a ripple of chuckles to spread through the crowd behind her. "Welcome to Alameda. Thank you for taking time to meet with us."

"Of course," Bryce replied, not sure what else to say.

"You know my good friend Doreen," the Mayor said, nodding at the smiling agent. "The three of us will talk together later, but first I wanted to make a few introductions." She extended a graceful hand toward the crowd. "I thought it would be nice for you to meet the community leaders who are helping Alameda grow and become a model for other towns in the region," she said, kicking easily into marketing mode, Bryce thought. "We're doing great things, thanks to a team effort. Please feel free to follow up with anyone later if you have any questions," she concluded with a warm smile.

"I will," Bryce said, marveling at the skill at which the trap had been set.

The Mayor stepped to one side and raised a finger.

"Tom is the chair of the Alameda Outdoor Bicycle Association," she said, pointing at the person nearest to her, who grinned at Bryce amiably. "Fred is president of the company that just built the new golf course, which we're very excited to have;

Mary is the CEO of the ski resort; Chalmers back there is head of the Trout Anglers Association; Sally is the new chair of the local hiking and mountaineering club; Jan is CEO of the music festival that we're planning, also very exciting; Ray is head of the Alameda Chamber of Commerce; Brian runs the new microbrewery pub in town; Kate is the head of the Dining and Restaurant Association; Max is the outgoing head of the Homebuilders Guild; our dear friend McKenzie behind him owns the historic Saint Sebastian hotel, which I fell in love with when I first came here; Philip Gorman is the long-time chair of the Trail Horseman's Association; Reynaldo Romero owns the company building the new conference center on the edge of town; Rhonda Pironelli is a tour guide and the runs one of the ski programs at the resort; Brigham next to her owns an Old West chuck wagon service...

Bryce recognized him as the African-American gentleman standing near the big map on the back wall. After giving him a nod, Bryce's eyes shifted to the map. It was slathered with little black squares that were grouped inside eight or nine blocks outlined with boldly colored boundaries – which looked a lot like property lines. The word *Alameda* sat resolutely above a particularly dense knot of black squares, which she assumed represented houses. Not far away was a block outlined in yellow filled with a large number of little squares. Above them were two words: *The Sun*. Her stomach dropped. During high school, she saw a similar map in a newspaper story about a housing subdivision planned for farmland on the edge of Boston. The front-page article was critical of the developers, hinting at kickbacks and other routine political corruptions. Shocked by the audacity of the businessmen, Bryce followed the story closely over the ensuing months, eagerly reading the numerous outraged letters-to-the-editor it provoked. In the end, however, no one was charged with a crime and the houses went up on schedule...

"...John is the head of the Four-Wheelers Club," the Mayor continued. "Stephanie represents the Retail and Gallery Owner's Association, which is growing by leaps and bounds, and Epifano Salazar over there is in charge of the veteran's lodge and makes the best red chile chicken empanadas I've ever tasted."

Bryce refocused, wondering what an empanada was and where she could get one. She was hungry. The room fell silent. She looked at the Mayor, who was counting heads as if she were a classroom teacher standing in front of her pupils.

"Did I miss anyone?" she asked cheerily. She didn't wait for an answer. "Good. Did everyone remember to bring a business card? Great. Any statements anyone wants to make? No. That's all then, unless Doctor Miller has any questions?" she said, turning to Bryce and arching her neat, thin eyebrows.

Bryce shook her head briskly. Not a single question came to her mind – except one. Did anyone here know who murdered The Sun's foreman?

"Alright," the Mayor said, clapping her hands. "Thanks everyone for coming and keep up the good work!"

Applause rippled through the crowd as it began filing toward Bryce, each person holding out a business card and grinning warmly. In the background, the room filled with eager voices conversing amiably. As she collected cards, nodding thanks and exchanging brief pleasantries with each bearer, her mind returned to the big wall map. Its incongruity gnawed at her. Individually, each person in line seemed sincerely nice and each activity they represented usefully economic or recreational, though she held a long-standing prejudice against golf as absurdly boring. Collectively, however, they all added up to the map on the wall. More houses. More roads. More murderous felines. *Death by a thousand cuts*. Where had she first heard that term? In one of her college classes, she guessed, though likely not one of her pre-med courses. One or two cuts usually sufficed in those cases. Here, however, the wall map charted the slow bleeding out of a community, a murder no less final, she suspected, than what happened to the foreman. The image of his body slipped into her mind. Were the issues linked? Not likely. Besides, she doubted any of the people in line would agree with her grim assessment. After all, everyone needed a job and a place to live. And a chance for outdoor fun – a sentiment she certainly shared!

Bryce realized that the pile of business cards had grown too large for her single hand, so she created a cup with her other one. Fortunately, the end of the line was near. She saw the warm, weathered face of the old veteran approaching. He wore a legionnaire cap over his gray hair. What was his last name, Salsetto? There was something about food too. Red chile chicken, right.

"*Buenos tardes*," he said with a nod as he deposited his card in her hands. "Come by the lodge for coffee some time. There's always a pot on."

"I will, Mister Salazar," she said warmly, peeking at his card. "I have to ask, what's an empanada? It sounds delicious."

A smile creased his face. "They're pretty good," he said in the lilting accent shared by the police chief. "They're little pastries. You fill them with meat or fruit and bake them in an oven. *Empanar*," he said in Spanish as his hands made a folding motion. "My wife used to make them. Fortunately, she didn't mind sharing recipes with this old goat."

They laughed. "Can I get them somewhere in town?" she asked.

"Maria's. But you'd better hurry," he replied, raising a cautionary finger. "I make them on Sundays and for some reason they don't last too long."

Bryce beamed. "As it happens, I'm going there later this afternoon."

"Good, good. But be careful *hija*, they're *picante*, especially if you're not used to red chiles," he said flashing an impish smile. "I grow them myself."

"I'll be careful," she promised, catching his drift and already sorting through her various defensive strategies for spicy food.

"Good, good," he said before pausing for a moment. "Did you serve?"

Bryce blinked. "Pardon? Oh, you mean the military! No, I never had the honor."

His smile was kindly. "Because you became a doctor?"

"Yes. Why do you ask?"

He shrugged. "I don't know. You just seem like someone who had. Your father?"

"No, sorry," she replied. "His brother served, however. Navy."

"Good, good," he said. He raised a cautionary finger again. "Picante, remember."

He moved off. Bryce glanced over at the Mayor and Doreen, who were both talking to a distinguished-looking older man who might have been the Chamber of Commerce fellow or maybe the one building the conference center, she couldn't remember. Taking advantage of their distraction, she crossed the floor quickly to the wall map. Many of the colored properties were filled with black squares, she saw. The map reminded her of a contagious pox outbreak she had studied in medical school. Housing Measles. Curiously, there were a few blank places on the map devoid of black squares, as if immune to the infection. There was a large nameless one snug up against Alameda on its south side, conspicuously empty. There was a smaller one near the Interstate highway to the east and a much larger one bordering The Sun on the north. This blank spot was so big it bled off the top of the map along its entire length. And there was a pox-free property adjacent to her ranch on its south boundary, rectangular in shape and also nameless.

"Any questions?" the Mayor said suddenly at Bryce's elbow.

Her voice was calm and friendly, but Bryce couldn't help taking a sharp step back as if she had been caught trying to steal a cookie.

"Sorry, I was just curious."

"Not to worry," the Mayor replied reassuringly. Although her expression was upbeat, Bryce saw that Doreen, standing next to her, appeared to be nervous. A quick glance around the room revealed it to be empty.

"Actually, I do have a few questions," Bryce said. She pointed at a cluster of black squares on the map. "Houses, right?" Doreen responded with a nervous nod. Bryce shifted her finger to the large blank spot adjacent to Alameda. "So, what's that?"

"The Tillman Boy Scout camp," Doreen volunteered. "It's been there since 1913. Every summer it hosts thousands of scouts from all over the nation."

"And it's blank because...?"

"Because it's a Boy Scout camp," the Mayor answered with a dismissive shrug.

"And that?" Bryce asked, shifting her finger to the smaller blank spot near the Interstate highway.

"The wildlife refuge," Doreen replied.

"It's owned by the federal government," the Mayor added in a disdainful tone.

Bryce swept her hand across the big blank spot north of Highway 70. "That?"

Doreen and the Mayor exchanged quick glances. "That's the Diamond Bar, as they're calling it now," Doreen said, lowering her voice slightly. "Represented by Mister Nibble, who you met yesterday."

Hearing his nickname, the Mayor couldn't hide a small smile.

"We have no idea what they're up to," Doreen continued.

"There's a rumor they're building a secret testing ground," she said, her eyes growing wide. She leaned closer. "Weapons research."

"Or a spaceport," the Mayor countered with a shake of her head, indicating her disdain for a plan so wildly impractical.

"A spaceport? Bryce asked, but the Mayor only shrugged. "Ok. What about that one?" Bryce asked, pointing at the rectangular blank spot below The Sun.

"That's Earl Holcombe's place," Doreen responded, her voice now neutral.

"Why isn't it filled in with houses like The Sun?"

When neither woman responded, Bryce turned sharply to them.

"He won't sell," Doreen said simply.

A small flood of anger rose in Bryce. She jabbed a finger at the heart of her ranch, filled with little black squares. "But I'm expected to?"

"Isn't that why you're here? To sell the ranch?" the Mayor said calmly. "In any case, the map is a planning document, not a presumption. The county requires maps for its Master Plan or nothing gets approved. We think of it as a kind of a wish list, that's all."

"That's all?" Bryce replied, not mollified. "Did my uncle ever see this wish list?"

The women exchanged looks again, this time each daring the other to go first.

"He saw an earlier version at a public meeting," the Mayor ventured, "without houses on The Sun."

"How did he react to the plan?"

When the Mayor hesitated, Doreen leaned forward conspiratorially, lowering her voice again. "He came to the meeting dressed as a chicken."

Bryce's eyebrows shot up. "A chicken?"

"I think he was supposed to be a wild turkey," the Mayor corrected.

"But he looked like a chicken," Doreen protested. She widened her eyes at Bryce. "He flapped his wings."

Both women were unable to suppress an amused smile at the memory. Bryce felt like she did when a surf board suddenly vanished from under feet while riding a wave.

"Why did he flap his wings?" She asked.

"Your uncle was trying to make a point," the Mayor replied, waving a hand dismissively. "It had something to do with the loss of wildlife habitat, I think."

Bryce glanced at the map. "Seems to me that's not an unreasonable objection."

"Perhaps, but showing up in a bird costume didn't help his cause," the Mayor said, lifting a neat eyebrow. "Neither did flapping his wings."

"It was funny," Doreen added. She leaned in again. "And kind of embarrassing."

"Maybe that sort of thing works better in California," the Mayor speculated to Doreen.

As Bryce felt her outrage drain away under their smiles, an idea popped into her head. It was the opportunity Dale asked her to watch for.

"Did the foreman see this?" Bryce nodded at the map.

The women exchanged another look, this time one of caution. Doreen cleared her throat. "He knows about Mister Sampson's plans, yes."

"What was his response?"

"He made threats," the Mayor said calmly.

Bryce couldn't disguise her shock. "Threats? Against who?"

"Against Mister Sampson, and us," the Mayor replied, nodding at the map. "Against the Town Council. To block our plans."

"Block? How?"

The Mayor made a face. "That wasn't clear exactly."

"Did he threaten violence?" Bryce asked, incredulous.

"Not specifically," the Mayor replied. "He yelled insults mostly. But you never know what people will do under the right circumstances," she added in an ominous tone.

"He was angry," Doreen cut in, sounding sympathetic. "I think your uncle's death upset him terribly."

Bryce tried to imagine the polite man she had spoken with on the phone last week shouting insults in public, but couldn't. "When did he make the threats?"

"Four weeks ago?" the Mayor said looking at Doreen, who nodded. "Unfortunately, he repeated them at another meeting about a week ago."

"A week ago? Did the police chief do anything?"

Something shifted inside the Mayor. "Dale escorted the foreman outside, where he belonged," she said with finality. She turned abruptly and began walking toward her large desk, which sat serenely under a bright window.

"Honey," Doreen said in a confidential tone, touching Bryce's arm again. "I'm sure the foreman didn't mean what he said. Have you spoken to him yet?"

Bryce's stomach turned over. "No."

She wanted to ask another question but the Mayor walked back carrying a white envelope which she handed to Doreen.

"Doctor Miller," the Mayor said in a tone Bryce instantly recognized as the start of a lecture. "Believe it or not, I respected your uncle's decision to wear a chicken suit. There are a number of people around here who have strong feelings about the economic development taking place and have let their feelings be known, including his foreman. What no one seems to realize or remember, however, is that not long ago this town was dying."

She let the words sink in before proceeding.

"Alameda's population had dropped by half since World War Two. Unemployment doubled during the same period as had the number of people on the public dole," she said, scornfully. "Stores were shuttered. High school graduates were leaving in droves, never to return. Why should they? They had no prospects here. Ranching, logging, mining? Please. Residents faced a choice: change or watch their town die. They chose change. We created a business plan together and put it to work. Your uncle didn't like it and he let us know. But your uncle arrived here with a bucket of money under his arm."

"As did you, right?" Bryce interjected.

"I did well in my career, that's true," the Mayor replied smoothly. "But when I came here I chose to help Alameda get back on its feet, not flap my wings." She paused again. "In the past twelve months, nearly one hundred new jobs have been created in the area, all by private enterprise, which is the only way it should be done in my opinion. I realize that's just a drop in the ocean where you're from, but around here it's huge."

Point made. "And what's the role of The Sun in all this?"

"The community needs a significant asset to attract people of means to live here, not just visit," the Mayor said matter-of-factly. "Your ranch is perfect."

"People of means?" Bryce repeated. "Rich people."

"The Sun is the missing piece of the puzzle," Doreen added quickly, trying to sound helpful. "It's exactly the boost the economy needs. We can't do it otherwise."

They fell silent. Bryce glanced between them. Apparently, the lecture was over. She turned back to the wall map trying to imagine the ranch covered with houses. Instead, the image of the dead foreman materialized in her mind. Was there a connection? How much were those black squares worth in dollars? She did a quick calculation. A *huge* amount. Was it enough to motivate a murder?

"Doreen?" the Mayor said, nodding at the envelope.

"Yes, sorry," the agent said, snapping to attention. "I spoke with Mister Sampson this morning and this is what I'm authorized to offer." She extended the envelope to Bryce. "I don't know what your uncle paid, of course," Doreen said, returning to her unctuous form, "but I suspect this is a wee bit more."

Bryce stuck the pile of business cards in her hand into a vest pocket and reluctantly accepted the envelope, still thinking about the foreman. Was the housing development what he wanted to speak to her about? Had he been silenced? Maybe she wouldn't open the envelope. Bryce tapped the envelope against her palm thoughtfully. Detecting a slight movement, she glanced at the Mayor, who had shifted her weight impatiently. A peek at Doreen revealed that her carnivorous look had returned.

Bryce decided to open the envelope. She had asked for bids after all and it remained her intention to sell the ranch to *someone*. She unsealed the back of the envelope and after a brief hesitation pulled out the solitary piece of paper inside. She unfolded it slowly, making a promise to herself that no matter how big the bid she would, under no circumstances, give the Mayor and the agent the satisfaction of hearing her gasp. She lifted the paper up to her face.

And gasped.

ALTHOUGH IT WAS ONLY a few blocks away, Bryce walked past her next appointment. She had been reviewing the tense conversation in the Mayor's office as she passed in front of a nondescript glass door sandwiched between a cheerful art gallery and an upscale fishing store. Her intuition said she had arrived at the right place, but all she saw when she looked around were two graceful mannequins in a window sporting stylish khaki outfits and holding fly fishing rods. Backtracking impatiently, she found the words *Alpine Services* neatly stenciled on the glass door. Behind it, a narrow staircase rose steeply upward. There was no other indication of the nature of the business that lay inside, which didn't surprise her at all. She stabbed a button below a small speaker on the door jamb.

"Doctor Miller?" said Bill Merrill's voice immediately.

"Yes," she said tersely.

There was a soft clicking sound near the handle. Bryce pushed the door open and began to climb the stairs quickly. She wanted the meeting to be as brief as possible. On the drive from the ranch that morning, she decided she wouldn't dishonor her uncle by sacrificing the ranch to oil-and-gas development no matter how much money they offered. The business with the chicken outfit and the flapping wings confirmed her decision, though it sounded a bit humiliating. Why had he done that? In any case, she couldn't abide the idea of oil wells herself. What about the foreman? Did he know about Bill Merrill's plans? Was that why he wanted to talk? To warn her? Or vent more anger? He hadn't sounded upset on the phone, just worried. Still, he had a temper, clearly. Could he have provoked the wrong person?

At the top of the stairs, she paused in front of a solitary wooden door. The amount of money that Mister Sampson offered for the ranch swam into her head. She had to admit she fantasized about what to do with so much cash. Pay off the balance of her medical school loans, of course. Make a substantial contribution to the cancer center at the hospital was another no-brainer. It was always short of the funds it needed, though never short of patients. She'd write checks to the anti-war organizations she was involved with too. Big checks. Maybe splurge for a surfing vacation someplace remote and expensive. What else? She didn't need a new car. Buy a house? She had owned one for a few years before selling it abruptly. She wasn't sure she wanted another one, at least not until she had a family, but she didn't want to think about that right now. Stocks? That would be difficult. She could already hear her father's voice in objection, disdainfully complaining about the greed of Wall Street. He wasn't wrong. Her father. She could take care of him in his retirement, though he insisted his needs were few, which was true. She sighed. What a problem to have! Still, it didn't make deciding between suitors for The Sun any easier.

She pushed the door open.

Bryce entered a large, handsome office bathed in warm light falling from four tall windows. Her attention was immediately caught by the beautiful glass table in the center of the room surrounded by fashionable black leather chairs and hovered over by a small cut-glass chandelier. Nearby, a large drafting table rested against a wall. Expensive office equipment, including a fancy espresso machine, filled two corners of the room. The art on the walls alternated between desert landscapes and pleasantly abstract shapes. She knew this room, having seen countless medical and corporate versions – everything quietly shouting power and money. Don't defy its occupants, it said. She noticed there were no maps visible or any other sign of the company's activities. In fact, the only evidence of the business conducted here was an old-timey photograph of an oil derrick blowing its top which hung on a wall that separated two doors leading to interior offices.

Bill Merrill suddenly emerged from the right-hand one, looking almost exactly as he did during his visit to The Sun yesterday though without the cowboy hat.

"Doctor Miller, good to see you again," he said, extending his hand and showing his teeth. "Thank you for stopping by."

"Of course," she replied, shaking his hand firmly.

An older man emerged from the other office. He wore a

conservative business suit, nicely tailored, had small, dark eyes, a head full of neatly groomed gray hair and a face that looked like it hadn't smiled in years. He didn't offer a greeting, not even a nod of his head, but moved stealthily instead to the far side of the glass table where he stood behind a chair.

"This is John Stansert. A colleague of mine here at the company," Bill said, nodding at the man. "Please, have a seat," he said to her, indicating a chair at the corner of the table.

As she pulled the chair out, she saw a white envelope sitting on the table.

"How did your meeting with the Mayor go?" Bill asked as he settled into a chair across from her, right in front of the envelope.

"You mean with the agent," Bryce countered. "Miss Wainwright."

He shrugged affably. "Same thing."

Bryce saw the older man lower himself into a chair at end of the table. "The meeting went well," she said casually.

"I read somewhere they plan to build two thousand houses in the area over the next ten years," Bill said. "That's about five times the current amount."

He let that fact sink in.

"The Mayor seems to have a lot of support," Bryce said.

"Not as much as you might think," he countered. "Especially outside town limits where she can't impose her will. And she's got opposition in Alameda too."

"What sort of opposition?"

"One of the Council members. Nathaniel Goldfarb. Moved here a couple of years ago. He's become a real thorn in her side."

"What doesn't he like?"

Bill shrugged. "Growth. He wants to close the gate behind him like everyone else," he said, wielding his smile again. "In any case, the county commissioners refuse to approve the Mayor's Master Plan, which is a problem for her."

Bryce recalled Earl's comment. "But they've approved your plans?"

Bill's smile waivered briefly. "Correct."

He reached out with a hand and carefully pushed the white envelope across the table toward her. "That's why we're prepared to make you a very generous offer."

"An offer to drill oil wells on The Sun."

"Natural gas," Bill corrected. "There's a difference. It's cleaner energy than oil. We like to think of it as a bridge fuel to renewables."

"Renewables?" she asked skeptically, glancing at Bill's colleague. "So how many wells would you put in during this...transition?"

"It depends," Bill replied smoothly. "There are a lot of variables. Geological layers. Infrastructure costs. The global marketplace, things like that." He smiled again.

"You won't tell me, in other words."

"It's proprietary information, I'm afraid. Competitors, you know."

"Proprietary information about something that I own?"

His smile didn't waiver this time. "Correct."

Bryce sighed. She tried to conjure an image of her uncle in a chicken suit, wondering what he would do, or wear, here in this room.

She pushed the envelope back. "No, thanks."

Bill seemed surprised to see the envelope in front of him. He leaned forward, resting his arms carefully on the table not far from the envelope and looked her steadily in the eye. "How many wells would be too many for you? I'm curious. A hundred? Ten? One?"

"One," Bryce shot back.

"But three hundred large houses are ok?" Bill countered. "With all the roads and shops and golf courses? Not to mention all those furry murderers?"

He pushed the envelope toward her slowly.

She pushed it right back. "But houses aren't oil wells."

"It's natural gas, like I said..."

"It's called fracking, right?" she interrupted. "People are protesting against it in upstate New York. I saw it on the news."

"People protest anything these days," Bill objected.

"Like war?" Bryce retorted, looking at him coolly.

To her surprise, he nodded. "Like war. But this is different," he continued. "It's new technology. And like any technology there are bumps in the road. We're working to fix them. I assure you we can recover the gas deposits under your ranch in a responsible manner."

He pushed the envelope back.

"Haven't we heard those assurances before?"

"Our industry has made mistakes in the past, I agree," Bill said. "But those days are behind us. It's not the Wild West anymore. We can be responsible stewards of the land."

Bryce studied him for a moment. "Let me know when that day arrives."

She pushed the envelope back.

"You won't even take a look?"

"My uncle would be outraged. He willed me the ranch for a reason," she said in a steady tone. "And it wasn't to see The Sun drilled for gas wells."

"Your uncle isn't here. You are. Just take a look."

He pushed the envelope back. "You mentioned the war," he added quickly. "You may think poorly of us, but we are doing our part for energy independence from hostile nations."

"Isn't that just an excuse for more drilling?"

"Have you seen energy prices lately?" Bill said, his eyebrows rising. "We need more domestic production, Doctor Miller. It's as simple as that."

He had a point. Even though she didn't drive very much, Bryce knew gasoline prices at the pump had soared recently to near record levels. It had become a flashpoint already in the presidential campaigns – as well as the subject of vociferous complaint among the parents of her patients.

Bryce stared at the envelope. "My uncle would roll over in his grave."

She pushed it back.

"Do you know that for sure?" Bill said, narrowing his eyes at Bryce. "Your uncle was a businessman, not an environmentalist despite the chicken wings."

He showed his teeth. Bryce glanced at Mister Stansert, who was watching her carefully. The slightest hint of a smile creased the corners of his eyes.

"How well did you know your uncle?" Bill asked, pushing the envelope back slowly, as if it were the last time. "I think he would have at least looked at our offer."

Bryce stared at the envelope again. "Matt Harris, his foreman, called last week to warn me about something…"

There was a sudden sound of disgust to her left. "A punk and a criminal," snarled Mister Stansert. Surprised, Bryce turned.

"What?"

"There's been some vandalism to company assets recently," Bill interjected quickly. "In one of our fields east of the freeway. Your foreman was a suspect."

"Was?" Bryce shot back. "Did something happen to him?"

"I don't think so," Bill said, glancing at his colleague.

"What sort of vandalism?" Bryce asked.

"Property damage. I'm not at liberty to discuss it. Talk to the police chief. Or maybe the FBI agent in charge of the investigation."

"FBI?" Bryce turned to Mister Stansert. "Why did you call him a criminal?"

"He had a record," Bill answered. "And a temper. He confronted us at a meeting. The police chief had to get involved."

Mister Stansert made a confirming snort of disgust.

"When was this meeting?" Bryce asked.

Bill shrugged. "I don't recall. Sometime after your uncle's death, which is about the time the vandalism began," he added.

Bryce looked away, digesting this news. Vandalism? She tried to imagined why Matt – and she had begun to think about him by his first name now – would jeopardize his job at the ranch by engaging in something like that, but couldn't. It didn't make sense. Of course, if he thought he was going to lose his job anyway...

Bill cleared his throat. Bryce looked back. He nodded at the envelope impatiently. "Please open it. You did ask us for a bid after all."

With an audible sigh, she lowered her eyes to the table and pulled the white envelope toward her. Had Matt been committing crimes? Did he learn something he wanted to tell her? Had he been prevented from doing so? She opened the envelope and slowly removed the sheet of paper, promising herself not to make eye contact with Bill Merrill again no matter what its contents said. She could deny him that much. She took one glance at the bid and dropped her hands into her lap in shock.

She looked up at Bill, who showed his teeth.

BRYCE DIDN'T HAVE any trouble finding her next appointment – there was a large sign hanging above the sidewalk. *Maria's* it said simply.

She was grateful. On the walk, she had focused on calming down after the tense meeting in the Alpine Services office. Normally, she wasn't easily provoked or unnerved, a condition she likely picked up from her Midwestern mother though her coaches in high school cultivated it too, but she didn't feel like she had won the match with Bill Merrill. He had skillfully thrown her off balance, especially with the business about high gasoline prices and the need for energy 'independence' whatever that meant. "Drill, drill, drill" had become a dreary chant among the Republican presidential candidates. Although the two Democratic hopefuls objected to its jingoism, she knew the argument resonated in the working-class community where she grew up. Even her father wasn't immune to its appeal. The issue put her in an uncomfortable position – how to refuse the oilman's offer without being perceived as 'un-American.' Maybe he was right about fracking technology? He had sounded reassuring. On the other hand, Earl warned her that he was a smooth-talking SOB.

She approached the front door to the restaurant. According to Frank McBride, it had the best food in town, though he didn't say anything about its red chile chicken empanadas. The thought made her stomach rumble. She was famished. His suggestion that they meet at the restaurant rather than the office of a lawyer he knew was eminently alright with Bryce, even though Mexican food was a bit of a stretch for her taste buds. Her parents had not been adventurous eaters, to put it mildly, the exception being the Jewish deli near their home. Her father had a weakness for smoked salmon, no doubt an extension of his love for the sea. When they could afford it, lox and bagels were a Sunday morning treat. Consequently, her mouth and stomach protested if she pushed her luck too far. Red chile might revive their complaints. Still, her stomach growled hungrily at the thought.

Opening the wooden door to the restaurant, Bryce spied a sign in one of its window panes. *For Sale*, it said.

The interior was more Spartan than she expected, though comfortable in a well-used sort of way. The tables and chairs were plain and plasticy as were the booths along the walls, most of which were filled with people. It certainly smelled good! New Mexican food wasn't Mexican food, Bryce knew, but she wasn't clear on the differences. The state grew its own chiles, red and green, but beyond that it was a mystery. Her tastes tilted toward fish and stew. Still, there was something deliciously pungent in the air making her stomach rumble as she edged toward the back of the restaurant. She found Frank alone in a corner booth, nursing a cup of coffee and looking melancholy. A white envelope sat quietly on the table near one of his elbows. His appearance was much like before – the Nature Unlimited golf-style shirt, a serious expression on his bearded face, and slicked-back hair, though it looked like he had used less gel this time. The tilt of his head was different, however – downward in glumness. His hands were frozen around the coffee cup and his eyes were fixed on the black liquid inside, his mind a mile away. She recognized the look immediately.

"Is someone sick?" she asked as she slipped into the booth opposite him.

"Doctor Miller!" Frank said, sharply raising his head. "No. Why?"

"You look like you could be sitting in a hospital waiting room," she said, "waiting for news from the surgeon."

He shrugged dejectedly. "It feels that way some days," he said. "I just heard we lost a big purchase in another state. It was a ranch on an important elk migration route at the edge of a national park. They'll subdivide it into thirty-five acre lots for houses instead."

"I'm sorry," Bryce said sincerely. Her stomach grumbled. "I

don't mean to change the subject, but I understand the chicken empanadas are good here," she said, looking around for a waitress.

Frank nodded. "They're the best."

"Why is the restaurant for sale?" she asked.

"Maria wants to retire. Too many Texans now. How did your meetings go?"

"They were interesting," Bryce said, turning back after failing to spot an employee. "The Mayor laid a trap for me."

"She's an evil bitch," Frank said. Then he shrugged lightly. "Not to put too fine a point on it. What did she do?"

Bryce smiled wryly. "Every business in town was there." She pulled out all the business cards from her vest pocket and placed the pile on the table. "And she lectured me about the need for economic growth after they all left the room."

"I've heard that lecture," Frank said, poking through the pile of cards in curiosity. "I call it her Stump Speech. Do you know her background?"

"No. Didn't her company go under?" Bryce said, turning her head. Something spicy smelled really good two tables away, where a couple sat happily eating their meal.

"Spectacularly so," Frank said. "It made national headlines for weeks. She was the former Chief Operating Officer for Mega-Comm. MC? Do you remember them?"

"No," Bryce said, now scanning the food at other tables.

"Global telecommunications. One of the early bastards and the most aggressive. They were infamous for throwing huge parties in the Moroccan desert every year that cost millions of dollars. Anyway, they got caught defrauding their investors, including some of the Big Boys on Wall Street. The feds were called in and now the former CEO is doing ten-to-twenty at a federal prison in Safford, Arizona."

"What about Miss Tate?"

"She got out before the company blew up. She's smart. And now she's working her corporate magic here in Alameda." He picked up one of the business cards. "I'll be damned. She pulled a friend of mine into her evil orbit. He used to be a government biologist."

He tossed the card tiredly onto the pile as Bryce searched vainly again for a waitress. Her stomach rumbled. "She didn't seem to think highly of the public sector," she said.

"She hates the government almost as much as she hates environmentalists."

"You must not be too popular," Bryce said, twisting to look in a different direction. "Does anyone work here?"

"We're not extreme," he replied, shaking his head. "Maybe for her, but certainly not compared to some of the militants around here."

"Militants? Here?" she asked, turning back. "What do they oppose?"

"Just about everything. But mostly cattle."

"Cattle? Are they all vegetarians?" she said before turning to search again.

Frank shrugged. "I don't know. We've got malcontents, anarchists, and outcasts here. Take your pick. Your foreman got into a fight with one of them."

Bryce turned sharply back to him. "Which one?"

"One of the leaders. Tall. Obnoxious."

"A fight over what?"

"They had a difference of opinion over cattle, I think," Frank said. "Dale broke it up. Both of them were drunk, he told me later. He also said the environmentalist came out on the short end of the fisticuffs and didn't take his defeat very graciously."

Bryce narrowed her eyes at him. "Do you think he's still angry?"

Frank swirled the coffee remains around in the cup. "Maybe.

I overheard him at a meeting telling his friends that the foreman was dodging him." He put his cup down. "Do you know about the landing strip?"

Bryce blinked. "No. What landing strip?"

"The Mayor's first plan for your ranch had an air strip on it, so the rich could fly their jets in and drive to their fancy homes without having to rub elbows with us commoners. The foreman yelled at the Mayor about it, who lost her cool and yelled back, which is unusual, the evil bitch. It was great."

He smiled at the memory as he picked up the coffee cup for a sip.

"I heard my uncle dressed up as a chicken and flapped his wings."

Frank made a face. "Yeah, that was unfortunate. Did Bill Merrill make you an offer?"

"He did."

"I thought so." He put down the cup and pushed the white envelope toward her. "That means we don't stand a snowball's chance in hell," he said gloomily.

"I don't want their money."

"Are you sure?" Frank countered. "A lot of other people don't mind taking it."

"I mind." Bryce drew the envelope toward her slowly. She paused. "Why didn't my uncle simply will your organization the ranch? Why did he give it to me?"

Frank shrugged. "Maybe he wanted you to get rich."

"Is there a reason why he didn't give it to you?"

Frank looked at his hands uneasily for a moment. "Yes. Cattle. Nature Unlimited doesn't keep the properties we buy. We look for land with high biological value to protect it from people like Bill Merrill and Mayor Tate then we sell it to the federal government. In this case, The Sun would be added to the federal wildlife refuge over near the Interstate."

"So, no cattle."

"No cattle."

"And the community doesn't like that idea?"

"They hate it. They hate the federal government. They hate us for selling private land to them. They want us to stop."

Bryce sighed and stared at the table top for a moment. It was all so complicated! She poked at the white envelope idly with a finger. Should she tell Frank about Matt's death, she wondered? He would find out soon enough.

A young waitress suddenly appeared at the end of the table. Holding two menus, she was dressed casually and looked very tired.

"Hello Frank. Sorry for the delay," the waitress said. "It's been hell."

"I can imagine. She's not very fond of Texans either," Frank said to Bryce. "Don't worry about us Abby. We'll behave."

"Thank you," she replied wearily, placing the menus on the table. "I'll be back."

As the waitress walked away, Bryce made a decision. She leaned over the table toward Frank. "Is any of this worth killing for?" she asked, lowering her voice.

"The food?" Frank asked, alarmed. "Or Texans?"

"Landing strips. Oil-and-gas. Houses. Rich people."

Frank looked at her warily. "Possibly. Why do you ask?"

She looked around surreptitiously. "Matt Harris is dead," she said in a whisper. "Murdered. Earl and I found him yesterday in a big water tank on the ranch."

Frank's eyes widened in shock. "You've got to be joking."

"No one's joking. Someone bashed in his head. I saw it."

"Christ. Are there any suspects?"

"The ranch hand is missing."

"Estevan?" Frank asked, frowning deeply.

She nodded. "He took off. Brunhilda the horse is missing

too." Bryce leaned forward. "But Earl doesn't think he did it. What about this environmentalist that Matt fought with? Would someone kill over cattle?"

"People have killed for less," Frank replied.

"Is it possible the environmentalist killed him?" Bryce said.

"I have no idea," Frank replied, still sounding shocked. "Murder?"

"Matt called last week wanting to tell me something urgent when I arrived," she said, lowering her voice even more. "Do you have any idea what he wanted to say?"

Frank shook his head. "No."

Bryce sighed. "No other rumors?"

He thought for a moment. "Actually, yes. About your uncle."

"My uncle?"

Frank lowered his eyes, thinking. "It was at his wake. Out on the ranch. The foreman pulled me aside and said he thought your uncle died under mysterious circumstances at that winery in France. But he seemed to be drunk, so I didn't pay any attention to it at the time."

Bryce leaned closer. "What mysterious circumstances?"

"I don't know," Frank said, lifting his eyes to meet hers. "But the foreman said he was going to look into it."

The waitress suddenly appeared at the table, ready to take their orders.

As Bryce pulled up to her uncle's house amidst the long shadows of early evening, Seymour appeared at the top of the porch stairs, wagging his tail. Earl had agreed to take the dog back to his ranch but called her a few hours ago to say a canine rumble occurred with his male dog, causing distress all around. Earl decided to deposit Seymour at the house, which he did unceremoniously as Bryce discovered when she reached the top of the stairs. A dog bed and blanket rested in a heap along the porch. Seymour's bowls and two cans of tuna sat casually nearby, as did the bag of kibble, which had fallen over, spilling partially, though it didn't look like Seymour had eaten any. The poor animal still seemed miserable, she thought as she scratched his ears fondly. And why not? His person had disappeared. Never to return.

"Come on, handsome," she said, giving Seymour a final scratch. "Let's go inside. We need to get some vitamins into you," she said, knowing what she sounded like. "I don't think an all-tuna diet is healthy, even for a dog."

Bryce gathered up his bowls and the cans of tuna. She'd come back for the bedding. She was eager to have a quiet evening and not fret about mysterious circumstances of any sort. After her conversation with Frank, she had taken a long walk around Alameda, thinking hard, but no final decision about the ranch's sale revealed itself. She would wait to see what Mister Nibble...Malcolm had to say. Or his boss, she supposed. Standing on the bridge over the Alameda River, she decided there was only one clear course of action: go back to her uncle's house and try some of his expensive wine! As she walked past the old mill, heading back to her car, Bryce sensed someone following her. Twice at street intersections, she checked behind her, but no one was there. Passing a fancy restaurant, she stopped to study the menu posted outside even though she wasn't hungry. She peeked over her shoulder. No one lurked nearby. It had been two long days and she was feeling jumpy, she told herself. Still, the feeling wouldn't go away.

"Let's open one of these cans of tuna for you," she said to Seymour, his tail wagging. As she reached for the handle, however, she hesitated.

The front door was partially open.

A jolt shot down her spine. She didn't leave doors open normally. Although the door had been locked when she arrived yesterday, she had left it unlocked this morning when she left for town, figuring that's what you did in the country. Had she forgotten to close it? She was pretty certain she had pulled it shut in the rush to make her appointment. If so, who had opened it? Earl? Dale? Someone else? She cupped her eyes with her hand and peered inside through a window. She hadn't left any lights on and the dying day made the house ominously dark. Seymour whined near her feet, eager to enter. Why? She glanced down. Did he know something she didn't? As she looked through the window again, her phone rang in the vest pocket, startling her. She pulled it out slowly, trying not to feel irrationally afraid. Fortunately, it was just another call from a doctor in Boston. She silenced the device and then hit the 'mute' button for good measure. She noticed Seymour was trembling.

"Everything alright?" she asked him, not certain she wanted an answer.

No, everything was not alright, of course. Someone had murdered the ranch foreman. She pushed the front door open slowly. As soon as it was wide enough, Seymour dashed inside and disappeared into the gloom. Bryce listened. The house was completely silent. No dog sounds anywhere. Where had he gone? She opened the door fully and then groped for the panel of light switches on the wall inside while keeping an eye out for the dog. Finding a switch, she clicked it and bright light suddenly cascaded across the porch behind her. A quick glance revealed nothing unusual. Another click of a switch and a light came on above her head, inside the house.

No Seymour.

Bryce stepped inside, closing the door behind her. Although she had spent the night in the house, she felt like she was seeing everything for the first time. In the gathering gloom of the two-story living room, she could see the leather furniture, the bronze men on horseback, and the dining table, lorded over by the antler chandelier. Nearby was a large stone fireplace, cold and dark. On the left side of the fireplace, a staircase went up. On the right side of the fireplace, around the corner, were stairs that went down, likely to the wine cellar though she hadn't explored it yet. Across the way was a breakfast nook with a small table and two chairs. In the morning it had an extraordinary view of the ranch. Next to it was the open, spacious kitchen, full of silver appliances, including a fancy European-made stove. A granite-topped island, with two steel sinks, sat in the middle of the kitchen. In the left corner of the house, near where she stood, was an office which she had inspected briefly the night before. It was connected by a bathroom to the guest bedroom in the right corner, where she had spent her restless night. She had no idea what was upstairs.

She heard a faint clicking sound from somewhere to her right. She jumped. Was it the dog? This was crazy. She crossed quickly to the granite island in the kitchen, dropped the bowls and cans on its top, and then punched switches on various walls, flooding the kitchen, breakfast nook, and living room with light. When she was done, she found herself standing next to the large fireplace. Who opened the front door? Had the house been burglarized? A brief survey from where she stood suggested that it had not. All the bronze horsemen were still in place, it looked like, and there were no obvious gaps among the paintings. Ditto with the appliances. She'd check the wine cellar, but it was likely locked tight. Besides, if someone had wanted to steal her uncle's art or alcohol they'd probably have done it by now. She heard more clicking.

"Seymour?" she called out, breaking the leaden silence.

He emerged from the shadows of a short hall in the corner of the kitchen, passing in front of a floor-to-ceiling cupboard before entering the living room near her, his nose to the floor. His toe nails clicked softly on the hardwood. He pursued the scent around the granite island into the breakfast nook. Was he searching for crumbs? Seymour kept circling, pausing once in the kitchen briefly before disappearing back into the darkness of the short hall. Bryce followed, trying to quell the fear that had begun to gnaw at her. Could the trespasser be the ranch hand, Estevan? Had he come back to the ranch? Unlikely, she told herself. Besides, everyone seemed to think highly of him, Earl especially. Not a killer. But you never knew. When she was in eighth grade, a quiet, unassuming neighbor of theirs stunned the community by striking another neighbor with his car, killing him. He claimed it was an unfortunate accident, but a police investigation proved otherwise. A jury agreed. Bryce's mother told her evasively that a "family indiscretion of a romantic nature was involved." Her father was blunter. In college, a boyfriend surprised Bryce with a well-concealed vein of anger that came out violently one day during a minor traffic dispute with another motorist. Shocked, she sat helplessly in the passenger seat as he lost control. The following week, he was no longer her boyfriend.

In the dark of the short hall, Seymour whined. Bryce flicked on a light. He sat in front of a closed door at the end of the hall. There was another door on the left, partially open, filled with darkness. Bryce walked toward the dog cautiously, peering briefly into the dark crack, seeing nothing. Seymour whined again, staring at the closed door. He trembled. She grabbed the handle and pushed the door inward, exposing more pitch blackness into which Seymour vanished. She jabbed a switch on the wall. Light exploded, banishing the darkness and revealing the gray insides of a large, two-door garage. It was completely empty except for a pile of wood strips stacked against a far wall – which is where Seymour paced back and forth, sniffing. Rodents, she guessed. Bryce exhaled slowly, not realizing she had been holding her breath. She pivoted suddenly and threw open the other door in the hall. She punched the light switch, revealing a washer and a dryer sitting innocently against a wall. There was a plastic table and an ironing board as well, looking lonely. Seymour whined again in the garage, still pacing.

Bryce returned to the living room, determined to dispel her anxiety. She flicked on the light in the guest bedroom, exposing the minor mess she had made that morning. It looked unchanged. Or did it? Her suitcase sat at the foot of the bed, its top open. Had she left it that way? It wasn't like her to be so untidy. She peered inside – and nearly jumped out of her skin when Seymour suddenly appeared from nowhere. He stuck his head into the suitcase boldly and gave its contents a snuffle.

"No, you don't," she said firmly. "Nothing in there for dogs."

A bathroom light went on next, revealing nothing unusual though she took a peek in the shower to make certain. She opened a door on the opposite side of the bathroom which she knew led to the office. There was a large table in the center of the room covered with a riot of magazines, books, and articles as well as a short stack of architectural drawings. There were piles of papers in two corners and a large white board on a wall covered with scribblings. She stepped closer to the board. The scribblings looked like a To Do list: call this person, review something, secure a permit. A permit? And what were the architectural drawings for? She'd figure it out later.

Turning, she was surprised to see two digital flat-screens set in the opposite wall, both blank. There was a control panel below them, equally inactive. They were linked to the surveillance camera at the gate, she assumed. Did two screens mean two different cameras? She didn't want to think about it. Right now, all she wanted to do was look under the big table.

No murderer.

She exited through the other door, entering the living room. The large fireplace loomed on her left. Around the corner was the staircase, going up. Time to investigate the second floor, she decided. Halfway up, the staircase turned – and a chill washed over her. There was a light on. Why hadn't she noticed it the night before? She climbed the steps carefully and then froze on the top step. The hall light shone brightly, exposing two doors, one on the right and one on the left. The door on the left was open, revealing a partial view of a fully lighted bedroom. This wasn't good. She listened for a moment, holding her breath, but everything was deathly quiet.

"Seymour!" Bryce called down the stairs. "Handsome! Come here for a moment."

Nothing happened. She listened for a whine or a skittering of toes on the wooden floor, but heard nothing.

Bryce decided to enter the bedroom. She eased the door open slowly with a finger, revealing a fancy four-poster bed against one wall, stripped of linen, and a variety of ornate western-style furniture against the other three walls. The metal table lamps looked imported, she thought. There was a big rug on the floor. Was it an animal skin? It looked like an animal skin. Hopefully, it was fake but she didn't want to think about it. What she did want to consider was the open bottom drawer in a wooden chest nearby. Everything else in the room was closed up tight. So why was it open? She crossed the floor and looked inside, but it was bare. She opened the drawer above it – also bare. She closed it slowly, fighting the chill again. Someone had been here. Were they still here?

She flung open the doors to the walk-in closet. Empty.

With a flick of another switch, Bryce saw that the lavishness of the master bedroom extended to the bathroom, where opulent faucets and a gilded sink glistened under a bank of soft lights. A mirror filled the wall above the sinks. The counter appeared to be made of marble. Italian, she guessed. The shower was as luxurious as everything else. Even the toilet looked foreign. For a man who didn't mind wearing a chicken suit and flapping his wings to protest the loss of wildlife habitat, her uncle apparently spared no expense in pursuit of his comfort. Was that a contradiction? She didn't want to think about that either right now.

She returned to the bedroom and crossed to the empty drawer. She peered inside. It wasn't empty after all. In the upper right-hand corner sat a key. She pulled it out and turned it over. It had a tag. *Garage*, it said. She unzipped her left-hand vest pocket and pulled out a small brass circle that held three keys. She compared them to the key from the drawer, but they didn't match. Had there been other keys? She squinted at the drawer. It had the feel of an interruption. She imagined someone opening it – or removing its contents – until the Mozart tune suddenly chimed downstairs. She imagined him or her freezing.

She needed to check the other room.

She reentered the hall, flicking the bedroom light off behind her. The other door opened into a small gym filled with top-line equipment that looked like it hadn't been used recently, or at least dusted. An interior door led to the Swedish sauna, which smelled faintly of sweat, or mould. No lurking murderers anywhere.

As she reached the bottom of the stairs, Bryce heard a whine and could see Seymour sitting at the front door, wanting to be let out. When she opened the door for the quivering animal, he shot down the stairs, disappearing into the night. Maybe that hadn't been such a good idea, she said to herself. Would he come back? She listened for a dog bark but heard only silence. Inky blackness surrounded the house. There was no moon. Or the clouds were too thick. She exhaled slowly.

There was one final room to check.

Bryce closed the door against the cooling air and crossed the living room to the stairs, intending to visit the cellar. She flicked the light on and headed down the steps, which turned once. Coming face-to-face with a vault-like metal door at the bottom, she pulled out the brass keychain again. At their last meeting, the probate lawyer gave her a black key to the wine cellar, smugly cautioning her against enjoying this part of her inheritance too much. Earlier, he had shared an official estimate of the wine collection's value, which had taken her breath away once more. Some day she really did need to find out what her uncle did to make so much money! She aimed the key at the lock and gripped the handle. She froze.

The door was unlocked.

The lawyer hadn't mentioned another key, but it seemed logical enough. One in her hand, the other key in the house, hidden safely. Except, not hidden any longer. Did Matt drink wine? Not likely, recalling the beer bottles along the edge of his kitchen sink. How about Earl? Did ranchers drink wine? Did murderers? Bryce pushed the door open. Blackness ebbed outward toward her. The door creaked once on its journey into the darkness and then was silent. It came to a rest somewhere in the gloom. There was a musty smell in the air, like old shoes or rotting grapes. She listened carefully to the cellar's silence, hearing only a faint hum. She needed light. She felt around for a switch, but without success.

She froze. A pair of tiny red eyes stared back at her from across the cellar.

Bryce widened her search on the wall until she found the switch. Light flooded the cellar. No intruder lurked anywhere. Instead, racks of wine bottles stood floor-to-ceiling against two walls, each bottle cubbied in an individual hole. About twenty cubbies were empty. There was a table inside the door and the floor was covered with saw dust. Straight across from her were two panel boxes, looking electrical. One displayed a sequence of flashing black numerals – humidity, she supposed – and the other glared back with two red lights. Bryce stepped into the room and surveyed the racks. There were two hundred bottles at least, she calculated. Were any missing? The probate lawyer had given her an inventory, she suddenly remembered. She'd come back to count.

Bryce headed back upstairs, leaving the cellar door unlocked. She opened the front door, where Seymour sat patiently outside.

"I'm glad to see you," she said sincerely. "Where have you been?"

Seymour came inside without answering and headed straight for the granite island in the kitchen. Once there, he sat on his haunches and looked at her meaningfully over his shoulder. He still looked sad, she thought, though maybe less so.

"Tuna, I got it," she said to him.

Before closing the door, Bryce peered into the silent night. Was she just being jumpy again or had someone actually entered the house? If so, when? Whoever it was now possibly possessed a key to the wine cellar and maybe the outside doors. Maybe it was Matt after all, or a neighbor, she said to herself, taking advantage of the situation to help themselves to expensive wine. She'd know more when she did the inventory. She'd deduct one for herself. Surely, her uncle had a wine opener – probably a fancy French one. The can opener! Had they found it during the search of Matt's house? Probably. Who would steal a can opener? No one. There had to be a logical explanation. Maybe it fell into a trash can or ended up in the foreman's messy bedroom.

Bryce leaned on the door jamb, still studying the gathering gloom outside. If there were logical explanations why did she feel so unsettled? It wasn't even her house really. Nor was it her ranch. Not for long. The bids slipped into her mind. So much money! Earl had mentioned her uncle's dream for The Sun. Was it right to cash out that dream and go on her merry way? But what choice did she have? None. What were the mysterious circumstances involving her uncle that Frank had alluded to? Did she even want to know? She shivered again in the cool air and closed the door.

She hated feeling unneighborly, but she decided to lock it as well.

WEDNESDAY

Bryce's phone buzzed insistently on the table.

Her hand drifted over it, wavered, and then dropped, missing the device. She groped, found the off button, and all was quiet again. Her hand returned to the mouse. With a deft movement of her wrist and a tap of her finger, the large, dark malignancy she had been studying on the computer screen shrank to its normal cancerous size. Another tap and a new view of the tumor slid onto the screen. Tap, and everything exploded into color. Tap, gray again. She squinted. The image condensed, revealing the lower tip of a bone in a leg. She zoomed in, back to the tumor. She clicked on the next slide, retreated three slides, and then clicked forward to the original image. Satisfied, she clicked on an icon, pulling up the report she had been working on and continued with her notes, typing quickly. A pause and another click brought up a table of data. Then it vanished. Typing continued. Click, and the image of the tumor returned. Click, it went away.

Bryce sat at the dining table in the darkened living room of her uncle's house. Outside, traces of dawn streaked the sky. A lamp excavated from her uncle's office sat next to the laptop, pooling the table with warm light. Seymour snoozed on his bed contentedly nearby. The only sound in the room was the clicking of computer keys. She typed swiftly, grateful for the opportunity to catch up on a case and for the distraction it provided. Bryce was part of a team of doctors in the Boston area that had formed shortly after her arrival at the hospital, each specializing in the diagnosis and treatment of rare cancers. The intra-hospital team approach had worked wonders, she thought. This particular patient, a young boy, had been referred to her from a clinic in rural Maine, where his doctor worried about the rapid progression of his tumor, a type of chondrosarcoma, lodged in a knee. It was only Grade Two, thankfully, but this type of tumor was resistant to chemotherapy. Worried, the doctor sent Bryce his files shortly before her trip. It was an increasingly common scenario as she and her team developed a reputation as 'go to' doctors for certain cancer scenarios. It meant a rising workload, but she didn't mind. It felt good to work, even on a remote ranch.

Her phone buzzed again. She silenced it this time without missing.

It wasn't her father calling. Everyone else could wait. They spoke an hour ago, part of a pattern of talking in the early hours of the morning they developed after her mother's death. Bryce picked up her habit of rising early from him. She recalled childhood memories of his quiet return through the back door of their home as she ate breakfast under her mother's watchful eye. For years, he conducted morning bird surveys in their neighborhood as part of a science project that he began in college. Migration routes, rare species, and first arrivals in the spring were his main interests. He loved birding, a passion, however, not shared by his wife or much appreciated by his daughter, who preferred to spend her outdoor time in cleats or dribbling a basketball. Years later, she asked him what he had learned during his walks.

To her surprise, he avoided a direct answer at first. Eventually, he admitted that the changes he detected in bird populations alarmed him. Things weren't normal any longer, he told her. Natural rhythms were out-of-order. Then he squeezed her hand affectionately.

Suddenly, the perky Mozart tune played in the air above her head.

Bryce froze. When the tune didn't repeat, she rose from her chair rapidly, grabbed a sweater that she had tossed into a leather chair and headed toward the glass door. Seymour rose from his bed, following close on her heels. After pulling the sweater over her head, she scooped up a pair of binoculars sitting on a small table near the door that she had noticed the previous evening. She pulled the handle, sliding the door open quickly. Outside, she crossed the observation deck to the railing near the BBQ grill and lifted the glasses to her face. On the entrance road, a solitary pair of headlights traveled toward her in the early light. Bryce studied the vehicle for a moment.

"It's Mister Holcombe," she said to Seymour, who stood at her feet. The dog tilted his head at her inquisitively. "Good," Bryce continued. "I have some questions for him. Like what to do with you, my friend, when I leave on Sunday."

She lowered the binoculars and looked fondly at Seymour, who tilted his head again. Then he alerted, his ears flashing forward as he stared into the shadows beyond the railing. Bryce followed his gaze, but saw nothing unusual, thankfully. Her nerves were still jangly from the evening, even though the night passed uneventfully. Seymour slept soundly on his bed in the guest room with her, not rising once. Fortunately, she found a box fan in the closet, which she pulled out and switched on, filling the room with white noise. She had one in her apartment back home and used it religiously to drown out the unceasing city sounds. She was a light sleeper, which she hated. If awakened, she would lie in bed and fret over the upcoming day's work, or her father, or the war, making it difficult to fall back asleep. The last thing she needed was to lie awake fretting about an intruder. Or murder. Within minutes of hearing the fan's comforting whirring, she fell fast asleep.

Seymour relaxed his ears.

"Where would you like to go?" she asked him. "Did Matt have a best friend?"

At the foreman's name, Seymour tilted his head up at her.

"I can't take you with me," she said sadly. "I would if I could. No wide open spaces, however. And no cattle. You'd go crazy. I do sometimes. Why am I talking to a dog?"

She raised the glasses again and scanned the grasslands, which had begun to glow softly under dawning skies. She loved searching for things with binoculars. As a kid, one of her favorite duties whenever she and her father stayed out on the water longer than planned was to hunt for a navigation buoy to help them find their way home. There were no helpful buoys on The Sun, however, or at least none that she recognized. It was new country to her. She lifted the glasses slightly to study the land on the other side of the river. She saw a set of car lights on the highway, looking lonely. Then a solitary, bright light caught her eye among the gloomy forested hills that rose above the flat-topped escarpment in the distance. This was the Diamond Bar, as she recalled, the big property owned by Mister Nibble's boss. She peered at it. The light was too strong to be a street lamp on an entrance road. As she stared at the light, it blinked once, as if a large object had passed in front of it briefly.

Seymour whined. Bryce lowered the binoculars sharply. He stood attentively, his tail wagging. Earl's truck had disappeared below the hill and she could hear its grumbling engine in the stillness. Bryce lifted the glasses to her face again and did a quick search for the light in the dark hills. It stood there as before, unwavering. What could be its purpose, she wondered? She searched the hills for another sign of civilization, but failed. Wait. There was part of a building, maybe. It was impossible tell through the dense mat of trees. What was going on over there? Suddenly, Earl's truck emerged noisily from the woods into the parking area. Bryce lowered the glasses and headed for the porch stairs, with Seymour on her heels. Pulling alongside her car, the truck shut down quickly, filling the air with silence. By the time she reached the bottom of the steps, Earl had opened his door and climbed out, not looking happy.

"You need to answer your phone, young lady!" he said sharply. "I called twice."

She pulled her phone from under her sweater. *Earl Holcombe* it said, twice. "Sorry. I was working," she said, chagrined. "I get a lot of calls and I was tired of the interruptions."

"Well, I'm your interruption now," he said gruffly as he walked toward her.

Bryce smiled. "What were you calling about?"

"To tell you I was on my way. We've got chores to do."

"Chores?" Bryce replied. "What chores?"

"Ranch chores. Get in," he instructed, nodding at the truck. He whistled once and Seymour leaped effortlessly into the truck bed. "They can't wait."

"I can't go, I'm sorry," Bryce stated. "I just don't have the time."

"You need to make the time."

"Why?" she protested.

He squinted at her. "Doctor Miller, until you sell this place you've got a responsibility to take care of it, starting with the thousand head of cattle out there that need attention."

"I thought cattle sort of took care of themselves," she said meekly.

"You thought wrong."

Realizing how harsh that sounded, Earl softened his tone. "That's not the way we do it here. Your uncle and I decided the herd needs to be moved every two or three days. It's better for the land. I'll explain it later. Right now, with Estevan gone and Matt dead, they'll be anxious to move to fresh feed. Come on. We can talk on the way," he said.

When Bryce hesitated, he added "I know who killed Matt."

Her eyes widened. "Let me get my hat and some sun screen!"

A few moments later, she shut the passenger door after slipping onto the seat. On her head sat a Boston Red Sox ball cap. Earl shifted the idling truck into gear and headed down the driveway.

"Red Sox?" he asked. "Did you go to the World Series last fall?"

Bryce nodded. "My parents have season tickets. My mother was a huge fan."

"They swept the Rockies," Earl stated, "which disappointed a lot folks around here, I can tell you. She must have been thrilled."

"I went with my father."

Earl grimaced. "My apologizes, I forgot. But she must have been excited when they won in '04. What had it been, ninety years?"

"Eighty-six. She about had a heart attack she was so happy," Bryce said with a smile. "It was all she talked about for a month afterward, much to my father's chagrin."

"He isn't a baseball fan?" Earl asked.

"Not anymore. He doesn't like all the hype. I think he kept going to games to be outdoors in the fresh air," she said. "And to spend time with my mother." Bryce looked out the window for a moment. "My mom and I were the sports nuts in the family. We followed all the teams, Bruins, Celtics. And she came to every one of my meets."

Reaching the bottom of the hill, Earl turned right onto the main road. Realizing she wasn't buckled in, Bryce pulled the shoulder strap across her body.

"What sort of meet?" Earl asked.

"Swim team, mostly. We went to the state finals during my sophomore year, though we didn't win. I did track-and-field too. And basketball. Soccer. Total sports nerd. It's how I thought I'd get to college."

"But you became a doctor instead," Earl said with a nod.

"That's right," Bryce replied but didn't say anything else for a moment. "How about you? Follow any teams? The Rockies?"

Earl snorted. "No. Just the Sooners," he replied. "University of Oklahoma. We're talking football, of course." He squinted at her again. "How come you don't have much an accent, if you don't mind me asking?"

Bryce laughed. "My mother. She thought it sounded provincial and would hold me back, so she basically forbid it. I think she was embarrassed by my father's accent. *South Boston*," she said, pronouncing it thickly.

Bryce expected Earl to say something else, but he had fallen silent and stared straight ahead. Looking around, she saw they were approaching the foreman's house. She could see strips of yellow *Do Not Enter* tape stretched across the front door. The silver pickup was gone from the driveway. The corral was still empty. She recalled the expression on Earl's face as he sat in his truck Monday evening after they found Matt's body. She kept quiet.

They passed through the oasis of the Headquarters in silence and then turned left at a fork in the road. After crossing a noisy cattle guard, Bryce cleared her throat.

"What was Matt like?"

"He was the best ranch foreman I ever met," Earl replied with a nod. "And I've met a lot in my time."

"What made him so good?"

"He had a natural, gentle way with animals. I've never seen anything like it. They were like his best friends, even the bulls." Earl nodded his head for emphasis.

"If he was so gentle with animals, why did he get into so many fights?" she asked. "That's what people were telling me yesterday."

"That's a good question," Earl replied. "I never could sort that out. Maybe it was just the alcohol, I don't know."

"Did Matt drink wine as well as beer?" she asked.

Earl frowned. "Not that I know of. Why?"

"The door to the wine cellar was unlocked," Bryce said. "I did a count this morning and there are fourteen bottles missing."

"Fourteen? How do you know?" Earl asked.

"I checked against the inventory the probate lawyer gave me. Someone took them."

"It's pretty good wine. I'm surprised they didn't take more," he said wryly. "Are you sure it wasn't your lawyer?"

Bryce laughed. "I'm pretty certain."

Earl squinted at her. "Do you know how to fire a gun?"

"Excuse me?" Bryce replied, taken aback.

"A gun. With bullets," he repeated, but in a friendly way.

"I've never shot a gun in my life. And I don't care to learn," Bryce said, running through various scenarios again in her mind involving an intruder in the house. "I don't need a gun to defend myself."

"Your uncle said the same thing. Then he bought a bunch of guns."

Bryce blinked. "He did? Why?"

"Because that's what you do," Earl replied, as if that were reason enough.

Bryce processed this information as Earl steered the truck to the left at another fork. Why would a man who dressed up in a chicken suit to protest the destruction of wildlife habitat buy a bunch of guns? Did he feel threatened?

"How many guns did he buy?"

"Five," Earl replied.

Bryce stared at him. "Where did keep them? I didn't see any in the house."

"They're in a gun safe. It's in a closet in the office."

She had missed the closet. What else had she overlooked? She made a quick survey of the house in her mind. Was there an attic, she wondered?

"Do you want the combination to the safe?" Earl asked, a bit impishly.

"No! I don't want to shoot anyone, thanks. Besides, the world has too many guns as it is." When Earl turned his head to her to object, she quickly changed the subject.

"Who do you think killed Matt?" she asked.

He nodded. "I'll tell you. He had a run in recently with Mister Nibble," Earl began. "Kevin, I mean. It was in town. Matt wouldn't say much about it, but I learned later from Dale that it was an argument of some sort. Apparently Kevin gave as good as he got. You wouldn't think it, would you? He's just a little squirt of a feller."

"Was it physical confrontation?"

"No. Dale said there was only shouting. They were in the street near the Saint Sebastian hotel. Someone heard them from a window in the old mill."

He braked as he guided the truck through an open gate in a fence onto a narrow, rough dirt track. Bryce gripped her armrest.

"You've got to understand, no one has ever heard Kevin raise his voice," Earl continued. "He's always quiet as a mouse. That's one reason he's called Mister Nibble. So something must have upset him."

"And you think the argument might have led to Matt's murder?"

"I do. Four years ago, Kevin's boss began buying all the land north of you, including Quintana Mesa and everything above it." He nodded at the tall escarpment that dominated the view to the north. We think Mister Nibble is some sort of scout for him. Trouble is in all that time no one has breathed a word about what's going on up there."

"What did Matt do exactly?"

"He rode onto the Diamond Bar not long after your uncle's death. I don't know where he went, or if he got up on the mesa, but when he got back he told me he didn't see anything. I think he did, however." Earl's tone was ominous again. "That's why he and Kevin argued."

Up ahead, Bryce could see a dense, black mass a short distance away. She noticed that Earl was aiming straight for it.

"What do you think they're doing up there?" she asked, thinking about the bright light she saw earlier in the hills.

Earl shook his head. "No one seems to know, not even Dale, which is saying a lot. But I have my suspicions. I think it's a secret training ground."

Bryce turned her head sharply. "For what?"

"That's what Matt went to find out. All I know is that main entrance on the north side, up near the state line, is heavily guarded. That's why Matt could sneak in, because they weren't looking this way." He gave her a look. "Quintana Mesa is a natural barrier, but I think that's why they want The Sun."

"To do what?" she asked skeptically.

"To create a buffer and keep people down here from learning what they're doing."

Bryce frowned. "Do you have any evidence for your theory?"

Earl shook his head. "I do not. But you'll know I'm right when they make you an offer you can't refuse."

Bryce thought about this for a moment. "And you think they killed Matt for finding out something?"

"Yes I do," Earl said, ominous again.

"You don't think Estevan killed him?"

Earl gave her another look. "I do not. He wasn't the type, in my opinion. I think he found Matt's body and took off."

"Why would he do that?" she asked, sounding skeptical again. "Dale said he wasn't here illegally. If he didn't kill Matt, why run?"

"Maybe Matt told him what he saw on the Diamond Bar. Maybe when he saw Matt dead he knew he was next."

"But you don't know that for certain," she protested.

"No ma'am, I do not. But I know I'm right," Earl said as he eased up on the accelerator. Looking through the windshield, Bryce realized that the black mass in front of them had resolved itself into a very large herd of cattle.

She turned back to Earl. "How does the missing horse fit into your theory?"

"That's a puzzle," he conceded. "Though I suppose Estevan might have taken the opportunity to steal her."

"How?" Bryce objected. "You said no trailers were missing."

"You can put a horse in the back of a pickup," he replied, "if you know what you're doing. And Estevan would have. Or maybe he didn't take her. Maybe someone else did."

"Who?"

Earl squinted at her. "Someone with a horse trailer."

"But wouldn't that be kind of obvious?" Bryce protested.

"Not at night," Earl replied, using his ominous voice again. "Here we are."

He nodded at the cattle herd through the windshield, which stood in a horizontal line facing them as if waiting for the start of a race.

"Is this all of them?"

"Yes ma'am. All one thousand."

He stepped on the brakes and guided the truck to a stop about twenty yards away. The animals stared at them eagerly while standing in a long line. Earl shut the engine off. Bryce could hear mooing sounds coming from the herd. They were magnificent-looking animals, she thought. Most were black, though a few were a rusty red color. They were surprisingly clean-looking too, though she had no idea what a dirty cow would actually look like.

Earl reached for the door handle. "You might get your camera ready. All your friends are going to want to see this."

"What are you going to do?"

"Just be ready."

He climbed out and whistled for Seymour who jumped over the edge of the truck and rushed toward the cattle. Earl strode after him. After pulling her phone out, Bryce climbed out of the truck and tried to catch up with Earl, but slowed when she realized that the only thing holding all the cattle back was a single strand of wire on widely-spaced white posts.

"That's a fence?" she said loudly.

"It's got electricity. It doesn't hurt them, but be careful. It can be quite a surprise. Hello girls!" Earl yelled enthusiastically at the cattle.

Bryce heard Seymour bark from the back of the herd and then saw him circle behind a solitary cow, urging the bovine back toward the pack. Mooing sounds filled the air as Earl walked toward the fence, aiming for an orange-colored handle set in the electric wire. The jostling among the cows visibly increased as he approached.

Bryce stopped walking when she realized what Earl was about to do.

"You're going to let them out?" she asked nervously.

"There aren't any bulls in there with them. You'll be fine," he yelled reassuringly. "They don't bite!"

Bryce heard another bark from somewhere behind the herd. She looked around, but there was no place to hide other than inside the truck and she wasn't about to give Earl the satisfaction of seeing the city girl run from a bunch of cows – even if there were a thousand of them only a few yards away!

"Stand right there," Earl shouted as he reached the fence. "Don't forget the camera." He reached for the orange handle. "Here they come!"

Bryce quickly pushed a button on her camera and held it out horizontally in front of her like a shield.

Earl dropped the wire.

The animals flowed toward her like a large black flood. A few stopped immediately to eat grass but the majority surged out of the gap in the fence, spreading out laterally on both sides. Bryce stared at the spectacle in front of her. The sheer mass of life was extraordinary. She tried to hold the camera steady as the edge of the great bovine flood reached her. At the last moment, a split appeared and cattle flowed smoothly around her as if she were a small rock. She breathed again. She peeked at the image in the camera. Animals filled the screen! Earl was right – her friends would be amazed. She looked up. Most of the cattle had their heads down, eagerly eating grass. She heard a bark. Earl stood thoughtfully at the gate, waiting for Seymour to round up the stragglers.

Two cows approached her, full of curiosity, their noses stretched out, and making sniffing sounds. Bryce couldn't resist. She brought the camera close to their noses, smiling in amusement at their distorted image in the lens. Eyes bulged as they inspected the phone. She could already hear the laughter it would generate among her friends back at the hospital. The two cows emitted short snorts before dropping their heads abruptly to the grass. "Enough of that," they seemed to say, "let's eat!"

Bryce lifted the phone and turned slowly in a full circle, trying to capture the scale of the image. No one would believe it – she barely could – but here she was standing in the middle of a giant herd of cattle! She lifted the camera higher. The ranch looked incredible in the morning light. Bryce had never seen anything like it in her life and expected to never see something like it again. Hearing Earl whistle for Seymour, she stopped her rotation when the camera reached the rancher. He had rehooked the orange handle to the fence and was now walking toward her, limping slightly in the grass. Looking up, he acknowledged her presence – and the camera – with a tip of his cowboy hat.

"Let's go," he instructed.

Reluctantly, she pushed the off button.

———————

BRYCE DID a tight U-turn on a side street in downtown Alameda, feeling frustrated. She hated being late as much as she hated making wrong turns and here she was doing both! She turned right at the next intersection. Where was the medical clinic? Here, somewhere. She should have studied the map on her laptop more closely, she grumbled. She could pull out her phone, she supposed, but there were only two dozen intersections in all of Alameda – who would have thought it would be so difficult to find one building! Part of the problem, she had to admit, was the confusing hodgepodge of architectural styles on display. The main street had a comfortable Midwestern feel dominated by a few two-story, glass-fronted brick buildings. However, turn onto any side street, as she was doing repeatedly, and most of the structures became unfamiliar, one-story, flat-roofed things. Adding to the confusion, other structures had pitched metal roofs supported by white columns. Then there were the two buildings covered with rusted corrugated metal sheets. They looked old, but had to be new. One appeared to be an art gallery and the other a brewery-restaurant combo. Was this rusty style hip? She had no idea. She just wanted to find the clinic.

Bryce crossed the main street, passing a hardware store nestled among a row of touristy shops, looking forlornly out-of-place. Next came the town hall followed by the old stone courthouse, which sat behind a grass lawn. Beyond it was the chaotic construction site for the convention center that she had glimpsed on a previous search of the block. A convention center! Alameda seemed like an unlikely destination for conference-goers, she thought. It was a three-hour drive from Denver and an equally long ride from Albuquerque. But never underestimate the power of marketing, she supposed – or the Mayor's sheer will. At the next intersection, she turned left, crossing another street. There it was at the end of the block! The town's clinic, hiding modestly in one of the flat-topped buildings. A steepled church occupied the next block and a little farther away she could see a shiny convenience store-gas station, looking generic. How bewildering! Maybe she needed to get out of the hospital more often, she thought to herself.

She parked the car in the small lot at the side of the clinic and climbed out quickly. In front of her, a young mother with three children, one in her arms, approached the facility. One of the children appeared to be crying softly. Bryce hurried ahead and opened the door for the family, nodding and smiling at the mother, who nodded in return. Bryce followed them inside. She stepped into a waiting room filled with soft light from four skylights in the ceiling. The chairs looked new, as did the reception desk. The smell of fresh paint lingered in the air. An attractive seascape filled three walls with leaping porpoises, grouchy crabs, and smiling octopuses. Or was it octopi? A large, pink one caught her eye.

"Are you Doctor Miller?" said a light voice.

She turned to face a pretty Asian-American woman, a few years younger than herself, who smiled warmly. She wore the requisite white coat over a blue blouse and dark slacks, a stethoscope around her neck. No high heels. She had a friendly face and kind eyes – always a good sign and probably quite helpful in a rural clinic where people were more polite, Bryce suspected. She tried to imagine what the most common medical complaint might be in a town like Alameda. Flu? Broken bones? Old age? The young doctor's hair was cut in a bob, adding to her cheery appearance. There was a single flower stuck in a lapel on her white coat. It was yellow-and-green and looked fresh, though Bryce had no idea what type of flower it might be. It was a nice touch, in any case.

Bryce smiled. "Sorry for being late."

"You're fine," the young woman said, extending her hand. "Doctor Thomas. Please call me Meili."

"Nice to meet you, Meili," Bryce replied, shaking her hand. "I'm embarrassed to say I took a wrong turn in town."

"I've done it too. The first time I arrived in Alameda, I kept looking for a stoplight. It took me a few days before I realized there aren't any."

"How long have you been here?"

"A little more than a year."

"I like your flower," Bryce said, nodding at Meili's lapel.

"Thanks. It started as a lark but it's become something of a tradition now. Patients like to bring me a flower when they come in."

"That's lovely! I wish we had flowers. Where are you from?"

"Chicago. Land of a million stoplights. Then Baltimore for medical school."

"Johns Hopkins? How did you get to Alameda?" Bryce asked.

"Mayor Tate upgraded the clinic and advertised for a new director. It's a nonprofit, which means I can pay off part of my loans with public service, which is helpful, as you know. And I thought it would be an interesting place to work," she said with a light shrug.

"Were you right?" Bryce asked.

"Oh yeah," she replied with a warm laugh. "It's quite the place."

As if on cue, the clinic door opened. Another mother entered, toting two children this time, and crossed to the reception desk where a young woman sat in front of a computer. Bryce's phone began vibrating in her vest pocket, as it had for much of the morning with the exception of the silent – and tranquil – drive between her uncle's house and town. She reached inside the pocket and gave the infernal device a practiced squeeze.

"You're here for the preliminary exam of the body?" Meili said to Bryce, indicating a door to their left, which they began to walk towards.

"Yes, if that's ok."

"Of course! But I should tell you Doctor Creider has already completed it."

"He has?"

"He came in early," she said in a warning tone. "Have you met him before?"

"No. I've only been here a few days. Why?"

"He's a wonderful pathologist. And very...opinionated," Meili said, picking her words carefully. "He's originally from New Hampshire. Retired to Dunraven a few years ago. Said he was weary of New England winters."

"Isn't Dunraven north of here?"

"Yes, it's on the Interstate up near the Colorado state line." Meili replied. "It's the largest town in the area. I think it had a big gold mine back in the frontier days. It's got lots of retirees today."

They had reached the door. "What about Doctor Creider?" Bryce asked.

"He unretired," Meili replied, gripping the door handle. "He decided the hospital in Dunraven needed his help." Meili paused and gave the room a glance. "He doesn't think the locals know what they're doing," she said in a low voice. "And I don't just mean medically. He has kind of an attitude."

She opened the door and they entered an artificially bright, clean all-purpose room that had been recently renovated, Bryce thought. It had steel cabinets and medical equipment on countertops and three hydraulic tables in the center of the room – one of which was occupied by a body under a white sheet. But there was no one else.

"Doctor Creider must have stepped out," Meili said as they crossed to the body. "Did you know the victim, Matt Harris?"

"No, unfortunately," Bryce replied quietly. "Had he been a patient of yours?"

"I only saw him two or three times. He had a broken ankle last summer. Then he cut himself on some rusty barbed wire and came in to get a tetanus boost. Last time I saw Mister Harris was about four weeks ago. He had a sore throat and was running a temperature. He thought it was the flu, but it turned out to be mononucleosis."

"Mono? Interesting. Did you notice any sign of physical damage? I understand he had quite a temper."

"Yes, actually. I saw that his knuckles had scabs on both hands, as if they had been bleeding recently. I asked, but he said it was just ranch work."

A door in the far wall flung itself open suddenly and a tall, broad-shouldered man entered, blocking the sunlight. He had a cell phone in one hand and with the other he shut the door hard behind him. He looked to be in his early sixties, Bryce judged, with longish, curly gray hair, a tight beard, and impatient blue eyes. His face was narrow, contrasting with his large frame. He walked easily and seemed fit for his age. She could easily imagine him riding a bicycle around town, upset at all the traffic. Instead of a white coat, he wore an oxford-style cream-colored shirt, a black belt, and nicely-tailored slacks that bespoke financial security. His shiny, black shoes looked foreign. It all added up to a self-assured attitude that Bryce recognized instantly: early Baby Boom. The high-achieving, barrier-crashing, half-generation that changed the world – and knew it. Trouble was some of them didn't know when to quit, in her experience, even when the world they had helped to create began behaving in ways they didn't like. It just made them work harder – and become grouchy.

He clipped his phone onto his belt as he approached.

"Wes Creider," he said in a growl to Bryce without offering his hand. "You must be Doctor Miller." He didn't wait for a response. "That was the police chief. He's going to be late, of course." His tone was disdainful.

"He's probably pretty busy," Bryce said on Dale's behalf. "I saw they made the announcement about Matt's...the victim's death. I imagine it's pretty big news around here."

Meili nodded silently from across the table.

"I've already examined the body," Creider said while pulling the sheet off, apparently uninterested in the topic. He pulled a pair of glasses from his shirt pocket and placed them on the end of his nose.

"Nothing particularly unusual to report. The body had been in the water between twenty-four and forty-eight hours. Cause of death almost certainly due to a single blow to the back of the head from behind." He leaned over the corpse, pointing. "Probably never saw it coming, the poor bastard. Crushed the occipital bone as well as the C1 and C2 and possibly the C3 vertebrae. The object was blunt or round and delivered with a great deal of force. Undoubtedly, death was instantaneous. Nothing else exceptional about the body. Residue of chewing tobacco in his mouth, naturally. Multiple scratch marks on both forearms, most of them old. A healed puncture wound on his right shoulder that's probably five years old; a misaligned toe on the left foot that was probably broken once; a four-inch scar on his left knee; genital herpes, no surprise there," he said, sounding disdainful again.

He picked up the foreman's right hand. "Contusions on the knuckles," he said, pointing to red spots, "with evidence of more in the past."

"What caused them, do you think?" Bryce interjected quickly.

"The boy was a brawler, I'd guess," he replied, making a disapproving face. He let the hand fall to the table unceremoniously.

"A drinker too, I understand," he continued. "I wonder what his liver looks like. Anyway, I've arranged for the autopsy to be done later today. I've ordered toxicology and hematology tests as well, but don't hold your breath."

"What do you mean?" said Bryce, looking up from the body.

"Clues to his death?" Creider said with a shrug dismissively. "What are they going to find? That he was drunk? Did drugs? He was young. He got into a fight. The end."

"But someone dumped his body in a cattle tank."

"Trying to hide the evidence. They were probably drunk too."

"You think it's that simple? Matt died in a drunken brawl?" Bryce asked, sounding skeptical.

"That's what the evidence suggests," he replied. "I'd go with simple around here."

"I'd still like to see the final reports," Bryce countered.

He shrugged. "Hopefully, they'll be understandable. I read one last month that looked like it was written by someone who barely graduated from high school."

Meili raised her eyebrows at Bryce surreptitiously.

"It's a rural part of a poor state," Bryce said.

"That's no reason for sub-literacy," he shot back. "At a minimum, the hospital could hire staff who can spell correctly. And don't get me started about the nurses."

"Do you think the person who hit him was right-handed or left-handed?" Bryce asked, changing the subject.

"Can't say yet. You own the ranch where he was found?"

"I do," Bryce said slowly, still looking at the body. "For the moment. Do you think he smoked? I found a pile of cigarette butts in his back yard."

"Not if he was a chewer. I mean, how stupid can one person be?"

Bryce looked up. "Is that a medical opinion?"

"No," he replied, sounding contrite for a moment. "Hold on."

He pulled a small notebook out of the pocket of his nice shirt. He unclipped a pen from the pocket and began to write quickly, frowning as if afraid he might forget whatever he was thinking about. Was this how pathologists normally worked, Bryce wondered? The scribbling went on and on. She shot Meili a quizzical look, who shrugged.

"There," Creider announced, stabbing the notebook page once with the tip of the pen. "I just remembered a few things I need to pick up at the grocery store."

Bryce's eyebrows shot up.

Creider replaced the pen and notebook in his pocket. "I understand you're an oncologist," he said to her. "Have you ever treated anyone with Ewing's Sarcoma?"

"Excuse me?" she replied in surprise.

"Ewing's Sarcoma," he repeated drily. "You're familiar with it?"

"Of course. It's extremely rare. Why?"

"There was a cluster of Ewing's cases in a small town east of Dunraven back in the seventies," Creider said. "I just learned about it last month."

"A cluster? How many cases?"

"Seven."

Bryce frowned at him sharply. "Seven! Statistically, that's insane."

He nodded. "That's what I thought. I did some digging, which was harder than I expected. Looks like the cases were squelched by the local authorities for some reason. Eventually, I discovered that a doctor from University Hospital in Denver conducted an investigation for the state medical examiner, but his report is missing."

"Missing? What do you mean?" Bryce asked. She glanced at Meili, who widened her eyes, saying "this is all news to me!"

"I mean, it's missing," Creider replied with a shrug. "No one can find it. I'd say it was lost deliberately but incompetence is more likely."

"But you just said the cases were squelched."

He shook his head. "But not by a conspiracy. They just wanted the story to go away and pretend it never happened. Prideful ignorance. It's kind of a badge-of-honor around here. Anyway, the town was called Hannigan. It doesn't exist anymore, as you can imagine. All but two of the victims have died. Apparently, they never found a cause."

"They don't know the cause," Bryce said quickly. "Ewing's is a genetic mutation that presents after birth. Some researchers think it's related to radiation exposure. Are there any sources of radioactivity in the Hannigan area?"

"Not that I'm aware of," Creider responded. "The geology here doesn't favor uranium deposits. I've looked into it. Gold, copper, coal, yes. I suspect the source was agricultural. Pesticides, probably."

"Pesticides?" Bryce said, knitting her eyebrows. "Isn't this ranch country?"

"Not near Hannigan. It's corn and wheat out there. Tons of chemicals. Pesticides, herbicides, fungicides, you name it. God bless our food system," Creider said sarcastically. "I'll keep looking for the report, but there were no more cases after that cluster, which makes the whole episode very strange."

"That is strange," Bryce said, thinking. "I'd like to see that report too."

"Don't hold your breath," he said, sounding disdainful again. "The bureaucracy around here is as bad as a Third World nation." He removed his glasses and checked his watch. "I'm going to go. Tell the chief I'll send him the results when they're ready."

"Shouldn't we wait?" Meili protested. "Dale will be here any moment, I'm sure."

"Mañana, right?" Creider said as he put his glasses back in his shirt pocket next to the notebook. "The unofficial state motto."

"It's Spanish," Meili said to Bryce's frown. "It means 'tomorrow.'"

"That's what it is supposed to mean," Creider corrected. "Except here what it really means is "not today.""

He began to walk toward the back door. "Take your car in for repairs, if you want to find out," he said over his shoulder to Bryce. "Ask them when it'll be ready." He picked up a black briefcase by the door that she had not noticed before. "They'll tell you "tomorrow" every day for a week."

Creider opened the door, revealing bright sunlight. "Mañana, ladies."

He disappeared into the light. The door slammed shut. Bryce shot a look at Meili, who rolled her eyes briefly.

"You were right," Bryce said, smiling.

Meili was about to say something when the door from the clinic opened suddenly. Dale entered, looking tired.

"You just missed him," Meili said.

"That's alright," he replied, shaking his head wearily. "I'm not in the mood for Doc Creider this morning."

"Rough?" asked Bryce.

"Rough. The Mayor's on a warpath. Murder's bad for business, apparently. Scares the tourists away. Who knew?" he said sarcastically. "Anything I need to know here?"

"He got into a fight, by the look of his hands," Meili replied.

"Nothing surprising about that, I'm sorry to say," he said, walking to the table. "What about the head wound?"

"Creider thinks it was a single blow from behind with force."

"That's what I suspected," Dale said. "How long had he been dead?"

"Twenty-four to forty-eight hours," Meili answered.

"Hmm, could have been Saturday night. I asked around town, but no one saw him at any of the bars." He studied the foreman's body thoughtfully for a moment. "I should tell you we found evidence of blood at the tank. It's on the ground, near the four-wheeler. I'm having it analyzed, but I'll bet its Matt's."

"So that's where he was killed," Bryce said.

"Maybe," Dale responded, still studying the body.

"You aren't sure?" Meili asked.

"I noticed it because the dirt was a slightly different color than the dried mud around the tank," Dale replied. "It may not mean anything important, but I'm having both types of dirt analyzed as well."

"Do you still suspect the ranch hand, Estevan?" Bryce asked.

"Yes, for now. Unfortunately, the tire tracks didn't tell us much. The quad was driven to the tank from the ranch head-quarters. There's another set of tracks over them which look like they belong to a truck, possibly Estevan's. We should know soon. The four-wheeler was clean of prints, by the way. Whoever killed Matt wore gloves, it looks like."

"Suggesting premeditation?" Bryce asked.

Dale frowned. "Maybe. Matt's work gloves are missing. We drained the tank to look for them, without any luck." He gave Bryce a wan smile. "Sorry about that. Earl says your cows will be fine," he said reassuringly. "We can't find his wallet either."

"Suggesting what?" Meili asked.

"It could mean anything," he said. "Maybe he dropped it. Maybe the killer stole it."

"Any news about Brunhilda?" Bryce asked.

"No, nothing yet." Dale checked his watch. "I hate to change the subject, but there are some people who would like to speak with you, if that's ok," he said to Bryce. "I've herded them into the town hall. Would now be a good time? It would help me a lot."

"Sure," she replied helpfully. "How many people?"

"Two individuals, each of whom wants to buy the ranch, I believe. And two groups, one of which wants to lecture you."

She frowned. "Lecture me? About what?"

"The sins of man. They're environmentalists." He shrugged. "It's about the Alameda chub, probably. The fish. The other group is there to lecture *them*. Isabella Ortiz is their leader. She lives in Peñasco and blames the greenies for the area's poverty. Don't worry, Deputy Sandoval is there to keep them apart."

Bryce's eyebrows shot up. "Keep them apart?"

"There's been bad blood," Dale said. "Greenies shut down the timber mill in Peñasco some years ago. It wasn't these guys, but that doesn't matter to Isabella. She's as hard-headed as the Mayor. Don't tell her I said that, by the way," he added quickly.

"Didn't Matt get into a fight with an environmentalist?" Bryce asked.

"Yeah, they were both drunk. I broke it up and made them shake hands, not that it did any good, I think."

"When was this?"

"Last fall. October, I think." He checked his watch again. "We need to scoot."

"I'll send over the report to you," Meili said quickly, "as soon as Doctor Creider decides we can have it."

Dale chuckled. "Mañana, right? Let's go this way," he said, nodding at the back door. "I was dropped off, so we'll walk. It's not far. Thanks, Doctor Thomas, you're a peach." He headed for the door.

"Nice to meet you," Meili said to Bryce. "Good luck!"

"SHE IS A PEACH," Bryce said to Dale as they quickly crossed the parking lot behind the clinic. The chief walked fast, she noted.

"She's a godsend. The best thing the Mayor has ever done for this town."

"Not the new golf course?" she asked, unable to resist.

Dale smiled coyly. "I wouldn't know, I prefer fishing." Reaching the street, he turned left sharply. "Unfortunately, there's a rumor going around that Doctor Thomas might be leaving. Her husband started a family practice in Houston and apparently it's taking off."

"That doesn't sound good for Alameda," Bryce said, hurrying to keep up.

"It'd be devastating," he continued. "Not only is she terrific, but she's also the third clinic director we've had in six years. The last one was more like Doc Creider."

"Why do they leave?" she asked.

"Money, mostly. But the last one was spooked by all the blue skies."

Dale plunged into the street suddenly, Bryce close behind. She could feel her phone begin to buzz in her pocket, but she ignored it.

"Seriously? I think the sky here is incredible."

"Me too," he said. "But the doctor told me she felt exposed."

Reaching the sidewalk on the other side of the street, Dale turned left. "There are some things you need to know about the investigation," he said, lowering his voice. "First off, we're pretty certain we found the murder weapon."

"You did! Where?"

"Behind Estevan's trailer. It's a metal pipe, about two feet in length. There's blood on one end. Looks like someone tossed it as far as possible into the grass."

"Someone?" Bryce asked, confused. "You mean Estevan."

Dale turned right at an intersection, maintaining his pace. "It certainly looks that way, but why would he leave it behind for us to find so easily? Why didn't he keep it in his truck and throw it into an arroyo later?"

"What's an arroyo?" Bryce asked, feeling sheepish once more.

Dale cocked an eyebrow at her. "I think you'd call it a wash where you're from. Anyway, we've got a million of them around here. Any one would be a perfect place to hide a murder weapon."

As he spoke, Bryce realized they were passing a real estate office. Colorful signs for fancy homes and empty land with attractive views filled the window. She slowed her pace to peer at the prices. Her eyebrows shot up.

"I also wanted to tell you we searched Estevan's trailer," Dale said. "It looks like he left in a hurry. Maybe too much of a hurry."

"What do you mean?" she asked, catching up.

"He left behind pictures of his family in the bedroom. He has a wife and three kids in a village near Oaxaca. He's completely devoted to them. So why leave the photos behind?"

"Maybe he fled in a panic."

"Possibly, but he also left behind a sleeping bag," Dale replied. "We found it stuffed into a duffel bag behind a chair."

"Why is that important?"

"Well, he's not checking into any hotels right now, I imagine," Dale said with a chuckle. "But he left something else more important. Money."

"How much?"

"Couple of thousand dollars. Squirreled away in a hidey hole behind the stove." He gave her a look. "Why did he leave *that*? If he had time to steal a horse and load it into his truck he had time to grab his sleeping bag and his money."

"Maybe someone else stole Brunhilda."

"Maybe. Or maybe someone else killed Matt."

"Then why would Estevan flee?"

"I don't know yet," Dale replied as a large SUV rumbled past followed by a white truck sporting an orange flag tethered to a tall flexible pole.

Bryce suddenly realized they were passing the upscale fishing store that she saw yesterday. A moment later, she saw the words *Alpine Services* stenciled on the glass door. She glanced up to the second floor in time to see someone standing at a bright window, staring at them through the glare, looking like the unsmiling Mister Stansert.

"What if Estevan was afraid?" she asked, hurrying again.

"I doubt it. He was a tough *vato*."

Bryce could guess what he meant. "Did you search Matt's house? Maybe Estevan stole something."

"We did but nothing stood out as missing."

"Maybe Matt had something hidden that Estevan wanted," she tried.

Approaching another intersection, Dale came to a stop. "I don't know," he said with a sigh. "Things aren't adding up yet. We need to find that animal."

"Don't they microchip horses these days?" Bryce asked.

"Yes and I suggested it to your uncle," he said, sounding exasperated, "but all I got in response was a lecture about Big Brother."

Bryce frowned. "Big Brother? I think we're a little late for that."

He gave her a funny look as they waited to cross the street.

"What about Doctor Creider's idea that Matt died in a fight?" she asked.

"Not likely," Dale replied as he stepped into the street. "Whoever struck him was aiming to kill. Matt had strong opinions, but none worth dying for."

"Earl said Matt rode his horse onto the Diamond Bar to find out what was going on up there," Bryce said, following.

"Yeah, I know," Dale said, watching the oncoming traffic as he walked. "I reminded Matt it's called *trespassing* and told him not to do it again."

"Earl thinks they have a secret training ground up there."

"I'm not surprised," Dale said with a weary chuckle. Reaching the curb, he turned to his left and paused, waiting to cross the next street.

"One thing you have to understand about Earl," he said, sounding as if this were an old story, "he loves a good conspiracy.

Ask him about black helicopters and the United Nations some-day, but only if you have an hour to spare."

Bryce frowned. Black helicopters? She started to say some-thing but she suddenly could smell coffee to her right. Good coffee. She needed some, badly. Turning her head, she saw a café just down the street with two tables outside, beckoning.

"As for what's actually happening on the Diamond Bar," Dale continued. "I don't think anyone has a clue. They run a tight ship up there."

He stepped into the street. "Do you have any more theories?"

Bryce squinted in the direction of the café but followed the police chief. "Yes. Frank McBride told me my uncle died under mysterious circumstances. At least Matt thought so."

"I hadn't heard that one," Dale said, sounding surprised. He looked over his shoulder at her. "Did anyone in your family think his death was suspicious?"

"Not that I knew. He had a history of heart trouble. And a fondness for donuts," Bryce said disapprovingly, feeling doctorly. "But Frank said Matt was going to look into it."

"Do you think he found something?" he asked as they reached the opposite curb.

"I have no idea. Maybe that's why he wanted to talk with me."

Dale turned right and began walking fast again. Bryce felt confused. She pointed a finger straight ahead. Wasn't the town hall that way?

"You think someone killed Matt to prevent him from talking to you?"

"You asked for theories."

Dale squinted. "Ok. But how does Estevan fit into that picture? Or the horse?"

Bryce held up her hands. "I don't know. But someone kept him from talking to me."

"True," he said, thinking.

"What I do know," Bryce said quickly, "is that someone stole fourteen bottles of wine from my uncle's cellar."

Dale stopped dead in his tracks. "Fourteen bottles?"

"Yes," she said, surprised at his reaction. "The cellar was supposed to be locked, but it wasn't. I counted the bottles this morning and checked the total against the inventory list the probate lawyer gave me. Fourteen are missing. Someone had been down there."

Dale knitted his eyebrows. "It could have been Matt. Or Estevan. Or anyone. Rumor is your uncle had some pretty good stuff."

"It wasn't cheap, I can tell you that," Bryce said wryly. "I think there's an extra key to the cellar missing. Did you find one at Matt's house?"

"No," Dale said, perplexed.

"Did you find the can opener?" she asked hopefully.

"No," Dale replied skeptically as he began walking down the street again. "Is that still bothering you?"

"Yes. I think someone stole it."

Dale gave her a doubtful look. "Why would someone steal a can opener? Why not take Matt's laptop instead?"

"It's just a feeling I have," Bryce said. "I think someone stole a key to the front door of my uncle's house as well. There was a light on upstairs and a drawer was open. It had a key to the garage in it."

Dale frowned thoughtfully. "Hmm. Do you feel safe out there?"

Bryce's phone began to buzz in her pocket. "I have Seymour," she said, silencing the phone. "I'm ok."

Approaching another intersection, Bryce saw a restaurant across the street covered with what looked like rusty corrugated siding. It had to be the trendy brewery she spotted earlier during her search for the clinic. She could smell food. Her stomach rumbled – she was hungry again. Dale turned left abruptly at the intersection. Hurrying to catch up, Bryce could see the town hall at the far end of the block.

"My cousin's a locksmith," he said. "Let's get those locks changed tomorrow. Any other theories?"

"Bill Merrill said Matt had a criminal record, is it true?" she asked in a low voice.

"Yes. He was arrested twice for petty larceny in Michigan where he grew up. Stole some electronic gear. But that was years ago."

"He said Matt was a suspect in some vandalism going on in an oil field. What was he talking about?"

"Yeah, I don't know what's going on out there," Dale said wearily. "Some sort of eco-sabotage. Sugar in diesel tanks, that sort of thing. Juvenile stuff, if you ask me. Matt wasn't a suspect, as far as I know. Anyway, the FBI's on it. They asked me to keep an eye on a group of anarchists who live in the woods near the Boy Scout camp."

"Anarchists?"

"That's what I call them. They claim to be fighting for the environment, but they're mostly hot air. Anyway, you'll be meeting some of them in a minute."

"I will?" she asked, alarmed.

"Don't worry, they're harmless. The big one is the guy Matt got into a fight with." Bryce's eyebrows shot up. "Deputy Sandoval is there, as I said."

"What about you?" she asked.

"I can't. The FBI is faxing me something, so I need to get back."

He came to a stop and nodded at the town hall a short distance away.

"About the people I mentioned. Mister Doom and Mister

Gloom are waiting for you inside," he said, lowering his voice. "That's what I call them. The tall one, Mister Doom, leads a religious cult that's pretty big out West. Apparently, they're looking for a place to build their Headquarters." He paused. "All their churches are underground."

Bryce's eyebrows jumped. "Underground? Why? Are they worried about nuclear war?"

Dale shrugged. "Maybe they don't like sunshine. They're millennials. End-of-the-world, and all that. As for Mister Gloom, all I know is that he's not from around here."

"And that's not good?" she asked, picking up on his tone.

"Not in this case," Dale replied without elaborating. "Don't worry about the other two groups. They're just here to huff-and-puff. Give Deputy Sandoval a sign when you've heard enough." He began to move off.

"Wait!" Bryce exclaimed, bewilderment overwhelming her. A murdered foreman? A missing rodeo horse? An end-of-the-world prophet? She searched for the right words.

"I don't know what to do," she said, almost stammering. "About the ranch. I thought this would be simple."

"It's not your fault," Dale said reassuringly. "The valley has become incredibly tense the last few years. Emotions are high, anger especially. I'm not sure where it all came from," he said, shaking his head. "I grew up here. We had our moments, but it's never been like this. *Zafado*. Insane. Out-of-control." He sighed. "It's like everyone has decided to take a crazy pill at once."

That sounded familiar. "And not just here," she said, thinking about a peace demonstration she attended last year on Boston Common and the heated argument she lost to a virulent Iraq War supporter – lost because he called her a vulgarity and spit in her face.

"I'll call my cousin about the locks," Dale said. "You'll like him. He's another character. He'll be out tomorrow." He began to walk away. "If you need anything before then, holler!"

She needed a lot of things, like someone normal to buy the ranch. A murderer apprehended. And a lot less anger in the world. Was there an antidote to crazy, she wondered? Maybe one of those giant pharmaceutical bastards would find one. She took a deep breath and turned to look at the town hall door, a few feet away.

Zafado indeed.

BRYCE SMILED at the friendly security guard as she entered the town hall. Behind him in the large room, she saw two men stand up from a row of chairs along the left wall and come forward. Farther away, in a ripple effect, two groups of individuals rose from chairs on opposite sides of the room and began to approach as well. The three people in the group on the left, one woman and two men, were young and Anglo and had an unkempt appearance, Bryce thought. The other group consisted of four people, one of whom was an elderly man, shuffling slowly. His arm was held by a striking woman whose dark hair was pulled back into a severe ponytail. Everyone in this group was dressed neatly and they all appeared to be Hispanic, but Bryce didn't want to make presumptions. What was quite clear, however, was the uneasy buffer the groups maintained between them as they walked toward her.

As if on cue, a police officer stepped into her vision from the right. It was Deputy Sandoval, who she recognized as the stone-faced young man that had interviewed her and Earl at the water tank on Monday. He was conspicuous in his police uniform, not to mention the firearm on his belt. He gave Bryce a tiny nod of recognition – and reassurance.

"I'm Reverend Pendergast," she heard someone say.

Turning, she confronted the tallest man she had ever seen in her life. Actually, she knew basketball players who were taller but none were as rail-thin as this man. He looked like a human exclamation point, Bryce thought. His large head was covered with a mat of unruly brown curls that hid his ears. He had a large nose, sallow cheeks, and worry-lines around his soft brown eyes. His clean-shaven face narrowed to a sharp point at his chin. He wore a stiff, white shirt and jet-black pants which were too short, exposing white socks and skinny ankles. For such a tall man, his body tapered to unusually small feet, she thought, housed in brown sandals, looking homemade. He was missing a belt, she noticed. His only adornment was a western-style tie, wrapped neatly around his throat. As he approached, she was surprised by his warm smile, perhaps because she assumed someone called "Mister Doom" would lack a smile altogether. On the contrary, he seemed to radiate a great deal of kindly charm, in a gaunt sort of way.

"I'm Bryce Miller," she said, extending her hand even though he hadn't.

"I'm so glad you could meet us," he said in a friendly tone, taking her hand and shaking it longer than necessary.

By "us" she assumed Pendergast meant the scowling, short, heavy-set man who stepped up next to him, obviously unhappy that the good Reverend had reached her first. He had a dark complexion and raven-colored hair, which extended down his back in two long, elegant braids. He wore heavy silver bracelets on both wrists and a thin, rounded, leather tie that held a huge turquoise rock at his throat. It was his black eyes, however, that caught her attention. They were as cold as stone. His expensive, tightly-tailored Italian-style suit, aggressive attitude, and unfriendly face made her think of a mafia don.

"Nicholas Rack. Nice to meet you," he said without warmth.

He didn't stick out his hand either, she noticed. They were an absurd pair, she couldn't help thinking, standing next to one another: tall, short, thin, stocky, fair, dark, happy, sour.

"How can I help you?" she said pleasantly to both of them.

"Congratulations on your inheritance," Pendergast said quickly, preempting the other man. "It must be such an honor to care for such a magnificent part of the Lord's creation. I took a drive out there yesterday. Oh my!" he exclaimed, beaming.

"And I suppose you want to buy it," Bryce said, hurrying him along.

"It would be our great honor to be the temporary steward of that sacred ground where we would enjoy the freedom..."

"And who are you exactly?" Bryce interrupted impatiently.

He nodded and handed her a business card with a flourish. *Church Empyrean and Jubilant (CEJu)* it said. The words were printed over soft clouds in a blue sky. There was a post office box, the name of a town in Montana she didn't recognize, and a solitary phone number but no email address or web site.

She frowned. "Empyrean? Isn't that a mythical island?"

"It's the highest part of Heaven," Pendergast replied, smiling. "Though you could think of it as an island, I suppose. Dante called it the dwelling place of God. '*Such was the living light encircling me,*'" he recited enthusiastically, "*leaving me so enveloped by its veil of radiance that I could see no thing.*'" He beamed at her again. "Think of it as an island filled with light and fire."

Rack grunted doubtfully.

Bryce sighed and exchanged glances with Deputy Sandoval, catching his subtly raised skeptical eyebrow. "Aren't there a lot of ranches in Montana?" she asked Pendergast. "Why do you want to buy one here?"

"A fresh start," he replied ambiguously. "And we love the idea of building our global Headquarters in the heart of the sun."

"Light and fire, right," Bryce said. "How many members do you have?"

"Almost one hundred thousand," Pendergast said proudly.

Bryce blinked. *All worshipping underground?* She tried to imagine what that meant, but couldn't. Did they pray in basements? Bomb shelters? Did they actually dig holes and put churches into them? She had never heard of such a thing. But then she wasn't a church-goer, preferring to spend her Sunday mornings working or relaxing, so who was she to say?

She turned to Rack. "And you?"

He was ready with his business card. He made a point of stepping in front of the Reverend deliberately, she noticed, as he handed it to her. He made eye contact and held it, challenging her to look away first. Bryce grimaced. She hated it when men did this sort of one-upmanship nonsense. It was disrespectful and rude, especially to female colleagues. There was one young doctor in her hospital with an intentionally bone-crushing handshake that made her cringe every time they crossed paths. Fortunately, Mister Rack didn't bother with that formality. In any case, she wasn't playing his game, so she dropped her eyes to the card. It was blank except for two words – *Wanamassiee Casinos* – and a phone number.

She looked up sharply. "Casinos?"

His cold eyes were still on her. "I represent the largest Native American gaming corporation in the nation," he said in a low, rough voice. "We're looking to expand."

"Into northern New Mexico?" she asked, genuinely surprised.

"Yes. It would be located on your ranch down by the freeway," he said. "Halfway between Denver and Albuquerque."

"A casino on The Sun?" Bryce wondered aloud. She looked at Deputy Sandoval again, this time catching the shadow of a grimace.

"A small casino," Rack corrected.

There was a noise of disgust from behind him. Bryce saw that it came from the woman with the ponytail, whose group had pulled up a few feet away. Her face was a combination of scorn and defiance.

"What would happen to the rest of the ranch?" Bryce asked Rack.

"They'd develop it," warned the pony-tailed woman, who Bryce assumed was the Isabella Ortiz that Dale had mentioned. "Look at what they've done in other places. They're casino Disneylands. Count the number of golf courses. They've lost respect for the land."

"Not true," said Rack coldly. "We respect the land."

Ortiz made another noise of disgust.

"I should mention, Doctor Miller," interjected Pendergast suddenly, "that our plan would have almost no impact on The Sun. You might not even know we were there."

"That's because you pray in rabbit holes," Rack said rudely.

Bryce wasn't in the mood for this. "Wanamassiee?" she asked Rack, reading the word on the card.

"Wanamassiee," he replied, correcting her pronunciation. "We've been a federally-recognized tribe since 1866."

Bryce squinted at him. "Headquartered where?"

Rack hesitated. "Florida. Our business is diversified, however, with many enterprises in different states," he said quickly. "Casinos are just one part of what we do."

"Aren't there casinos already in New Mexico?" Bryce asked, now feeling irritated at his manipulations.

"Yes. But there is room for more."

The Ortiz woman behind him made another derisive sound. "That's right. Plenty of poor people to go around."

"Gambling is a sin," Pendergast added darkly.

"Not anymore," Rack shot back.

"That's because it's ok now to prey on the vulnerable," Ortiz said. "As long as it makes somebody money."

Please! Bryce wanted to shout, her unhappiness rising. Why did people argue with each other so much?

"Gambling is a false idol for pagans," Pendergast continued.

"I'm Catholic," Rack spat defiantly. "What the hell are you?"

"We believe the Bible is the Word of God. Fire and jubilation."

Bryce blew out her cheeks again in exasperation and turned hopefully to the three young people standing behind the Reverend, but each of them looked totally bored.

"You're a bunch of loonies," Rack said to Pendergast.

"Alright!" Bryce said loudly, suddenly raising her hands. "I've heard enough. Thank you for your interest in the ranch. I'll be in touch if I want to hear more." She walked straight past the Reverend and up to the three young people.

"Yes?" she said impatiently.

Caught by surprise, two of them turned automatically toward the biggest of the group, a tall, strapping young man with blond hair, steely blue eyes, and a square face that looked like it hadn't smiled in years, Bryce thought. She assumed this was the man that Matt fought with while drunk. How had he won? The guy was huge. Bryce didn't want to think about it right now. Against her nature and only because she was worn out, she decided to just think of him as the Teuton.

"Do you want to buy the ranch?" she asked him, suspecting he didn't.

"No," the young man replied, his voice deep and lecturing. "We want you to turn the property into a sanctuary."

"A sanctuary for what, the fish?"

"For the wolf," the Teuton replied in a threatening tone.

The other two activists, who might have been brother and

sister for all Bryce knew, turned their faces to her and nodded emphatically.

Bryce frowned. "What wolf? Is there a wolf here?"

"Not yet," the Teuton said.

"The first one that shows up gets shot," announced a male voice. Turning her head, Bryce saw that the other group had come up close behind her. The man speaking, who looked to be the same age as Miss Ortiz, held his body in a defiant pose.

"Are there actually any wolves nearby?" Bryce asked quickly, trying to think of something to defuse the tension.

"No," said Ortiz. She had a kind face and eyes, Bryce realized. Sadly, they contrasted with her angry words. "There isn't one within five hundred miles of Alameda."

"They'll be here sooner or later," the young woman said hotly to Ortiz. "And there's nothing you can do about it."

"There's plenty we can do about it," said the first man menacingly.

"You already took away our jobs," the old man holding Ortiz's arm said suddenly.

The two groups moved closer together. In fact, Bryce realized that she was effectively surrounded. Pendergast and Rack were standing behind her and Deputy Sandoval had worked his way around Ortiz's group and now stood quietly opposite Bryce at the edge of the squabblers, ready to intervene. She felt like the center of a bulls-eye.

"We'll defend the wolves if we have to," declared the young woman.

"What wolves? I thought this was going to be about a fish!" Bryce objected loudly, fully exasperated now. "Isn't there some special fish on the ranch?" No one responded. "There's not a fish on The Sun?" she tried.

"The Alameda chub," the Teuton said. "It's on the Endangered Species list."

"That's a lie. It's not been listed," Ortiz corrected.

"It will be soon," the Teuton said darkly.

"They're trying to use the chub and the wolf to end all cattle ranching in the area," Miss Ortiz said to Bryce. "The way they used the Mexican owl to shut down the timber industry here."

"No more logging in our forests," the young woman activist declared. "We don't care who loses their job."

Bryce glanced at Deputy Sandoval, but he was watching the Teuton very carefully.

"And no more cattle," said the Teuton. "The waste of the West."

"See?" Ortiz said to Bryce. "They just want us all off the land."

Bryce noticed that the circle continued to compress around her. Deputy Sandoval had come closer too, looking uneasy.

"We have to be brave and walk away," the young woman said. "We have to leave these lands alone. Let them go back to wilderness. Say 'enough is enough.'"

"Our families have lived here for nearly three hundred years," Ortiz shot back.

"No more cattle," said the Teuton, his voice rising. "No more hunting. No more fishing. No more timber. No more roads. No more houses..."

He had balled his fists, Bryce saw. Looking behind, she saw that Pendergast and Rack had edged inward as well, their faces eagerly soaking up the raw emotions. She felt dizzy. She was back at the peace rally in Boston suddenly, the Iraq War supporter yelling in her face. She had tried to reason with him, calmly explaining why the war was such a terrible mistake. It had only inflamed his anger. Then he got too close, violating her personal space, his voice rising. When he made a rude, sexist comment about the female presidential candidate, Bryce lost her cool. Incensed at his blatant chauvinism, she argued with him nose-to-nose that it was time for a woman to take charge. Or an African-American. That was bait, she knew, and felt bad for doing it. He exploded, of course. He spat out a racist taunt and when she called him out he used the vulgarity...

"Take your fight to Wall Street," Isabella Ortiz said. "They're the enemy!"

"We'll start with cattle ranching," the Teuton said.

"That's discrimination!"

"Call it what you want," the young woman said, stabbing a finger at Ortiz's group. "We're winning and you're losing,"

Bryce spun on her heel. She didn't want to hear any more. She pushed between Pendergast and Rack, her eyes locked on her target: the front door. She was being rude, of course, but she didn't care what anyone thought right now. She wanted only one thing – to be outside and far away from all the squabbling and nastiness in the world, away from the finger-pointing and the verbal assaults. Crazy pills? It was more like a malady, she thought. A sickness without a cure.

Reaching the front door, Bryce flung it open. Light and fresh air flooded across her face and body like a warm embrace. She stepped outside, pulling the door closed behind her quickly. The angry voices disappeared, replaced by a blessed quietness that filled her heart. She closed her eyes and leaned against the door, holding the handle tightly with her hand to make sure it stayed shut for the moment. She exhaled slowly and then listened to the quiet. She could feel a breeze on her face, dry and soft. There was a flag flapping somewhere close, she could hear, reminding her of the small banner that flew for years above the main sail of the catamaran. She missed the sea.

No one dared take crazy pills out there.

A HAWK SCREECHED.

Bryce opened her eyes and lifted a hand to shade her face. Where was the bird? It screeched again. There, high in the bright sky, floating majestically alone. Was it an osprey? It didn't sound like one and she was pretty sure they didn't live in the desert. The bird banked and circled back on a current, beating its wings occasionally. She squinted, wishing she had brought the binoculars. The raptor was brown but it didn't have enough white underneath or on its head and it didn't have the dark band around its eyes that always made her think of a bandit. Not an osprey. What then? It cried again, long and plaintive, sounding lonely. Was it looking for a mate? Food? It banked again. More likely, it circled a nest, she thought, protecting its young. She took a big gulp of air, closed her eyes again, and lowered her hand. The sun felt good, dappling her through the leaves of the large tree that shaded the picnic table she sat upon at the Tillman Boy Scout camp, a short drive south from Alameda.

A breeze tickled her face. She loved osprey, having watched them dive for fish for many years. They were a favorite of her father's, who kept a record of sightings whenever they went sailing or searched in tide pools as part of his science projects. She loved the way the hawk would glide slowly over the water, hover, and then dive suddenly, disappearing in a splash, emerging seconds later with a fish, beating its wings heavily. As a child, she was shocked to learn they had almost died out. The chemical DDT, sprayed widely for decades in a futile attempt to control mosquitoes, decimated osprey and bald eagle populations on the East Coast, her father told her. As a young man, he joined the national campaign to ban the notorious insecticide. Their success in 1972, the year of her birth, played a big role in his decision to dedicate himself to chronicling the osprey's comeback, amassing piles of observational data over decades. Recently, he gave all of it to a famous ornithology department at one of the Ivy League schools at their request. It was a great honor but it caused more than a few tears in her family. A long chapter in their lives had ended...

Bryce opened her eyes. Not far away was the camp's lake, large, shiny, and empty, though the shore was crowded with canoes, lined up side-by-side, ready to go. There had to be at least a hundred of them, she calculated. She could hear hundreds of excited voices nearby. Young male voices. Boy Scout voices, sounding like a happy hive of boyness, buzzing and swarming the large staging area to her right. Upon her arrival at the camp, she had been amazed at the sheer quantity of boys out and about, each dressed in khakis with blue or red bandannas on their necks, running around, laughing, carrying duffel bags, throwing objects at one another. Her father had never been a Scout, though he went hiking with former schoolmates who had been. Uniforms weren't his thing. Although her parents never pressured her to join the Girl Scouts, knowing that she preferred team sports to hawking cookies, she regretted it a little bit now.

Glancing over at the noise, Bryce saw that a person had separated themselves from the squirming mob of boys and was walking toward her. He was a middle-aged man, dressed in a Boy Scout uniform, with a bushy head of hair and dark eyebrows. He wore shorts, exposing skinny legs in white socks. She jumped off the picnic table and walked toward him, raising a hand to give him a friendly wave. As he approached, she could see he had a round, sun-tanned face and an easy smile. He wasn't tall and had a solidness through the chest that stretched his khaki uniform a bit overmuch. It also gave him an imposing feel, like someone who was both avuncular and used to being obeyed. As he came close, she could see that nearly every square inch of his shirt was covered with colorful Scouting patches, which he wore comfortably. A red bandanna around his neck completed the outfit.

"Doctor Miller?" he said. "Tom Wilkins, camp Scoutmaster." He extended a hand, which she shook eagerly. "I received your message. Sorry it took so long to get away."

"No worries. It's a lovely day and I know you're swamped," she said brightly. "Thank you for agreeing to meet with me."

"My pleasure. Yes, it's the start of what promises to be a busy summer," he said with a straightforward smile.

"How many boys do you usually have here?"

"About eight thousand altogether over the entire season," he said, putting his hands on his hips. "We're one of the biggest Scout camps in the country. So it gets pretty crazy. I was sorry to hear about your uncle."

"Thank you."

"I only met him a few times, but he seemed like quite the character."

"He was," Bryce said, nodding. "Did you ever meet his foreman?"

"Matt? Yes, I did. He and our Head Wrangler worked our horses quite a lot together and I'd tag along occasionally to learn what I could." He leaned forward slightly. "I'm from Cleveland." He leaned back. "But mostly I got a kick out of the rope tricks Matt would do for the boys. He'd come out for a few of the big campfires. They loved it. He was a talented young man. I'm sorry to hear about his death. How can I help you?"

"You probably know I inherited the ranch from my uncle," she replied. "I intend to sell it, but...," she faltered. Wilkins raised his eyebrows at her, waiting. "But I'm having difficulty finding someone I want to sell it to."

"Really?" he said, frowning mildly. "I figured you'd have lots of interest."

"Interest isn't the issue," she said quickly. "It's the kind of interest that's the problem. I don't want it covered in gas wells, for example." She took the plunge. "I'll cut to the point, Mister Wilkins. Would the Boy Scouts like to buy the ranch?"

"The Sun?" he said, sounding surprised. He whistled long and low. He didn't say anything else, however.

"We share a boundary," she added hopefully.

"We do. And it would make a lot of sense to put the properties together."

But... Bryce knew he was about to say the word. "I'll sell it to you for a discount!" she said quickly.

They laughed together. "A discount for The Sun?" he said. *But...*was still on his lips.

"Please," she tried.

He inhaled deliberately and looked off thoughtfully toward the bright lake. He was trying to figure out how to let her down easily, she knew, and her heart sank.

"Not a chance?" she asked.

"I'm afraid not," he replied. When he returned his gaze to her, she could tell he had dropped the formal Scoutmaster thing. In fact, he looked a little sad. "We'd love to, but it's just not possible."

"Why not?" she asked anyway.

He surprised her by glancing over his shoulder, back toward the swarming mass of boys back among the buildings.

"Confidentially?" he asked in a quiet voice. "We can't afford to maintain this place," he said, nodding at the land surrounding them. "It's one hundred sixteen thousand acres. We have two thousand miles of trails, fifty-two backcountry camps, forty-one structures, some of them historic, hundreds miles of roads, a bunch of busted wells, ancient pipelines, a herd of horses... it's tough to maintain it all. Another property would be impossible."

"I see," she said, not hiding her disappointment.

He looked at the ground for a moment. There was more.

"You probably heard that Scout numbers are down," he said, looking up and sounding emotional, to her surprise. Bryce shook her head. "They're plummeting," he continued. "Nationwide, the organization has lost four hundred thousand members in the last five years. With no end in sight."

"I had no idea," Bryce said. "What's happening?"

He studied the lake again. "There are a lot of reasons. Changing times, changing values, competition from other activities, decreasing involvement by parents, less interest in the outdoors generally."

He paused again. She waited.

"It's going to get worse too, in my opinion," he said finally.

"Why?"

He didn't move for a moment, then he raised his hand to his face, mimicking a smart phone. He put his hand back on his hip with a sigh.

"It's that bad?" she asked.

"Do you have kids?"

"I don't," she replied. She immediately recalled a conversation she had with a visiting researcher over lunch at the hospital not long after her cell phone made its commercial debut last year. He was convinced – without proof yet – that they would prove to be as addictive as crack cocaine, especially for children. Bryce shook her head at him in disagreement. It couldn't be true, she insisted. They'd never allow something like that on the market, right? Besides, her Blackberry hadn't been addictive – a comment that drew a long, bemused look from the researcher. She remembered poking at her salad with her fork.

"You don't allow them here, do you?" she tried.

"No," Wilkins replied. "There aren't too many yet, and the kids adjust pretty well without them. But it's just a matter of time before..." He let the words drift off. "In any case, it adds up to not buying your ranch, I'm sorry. Truly."

Bryce nodded. It had been such a good idea.

"I've got to go back," he said, indicating the chaos behind him. He had slipped back into Scoutmaster mode. "I appreciate you thinking of us. Good luck." He gave a brief wave, turned and began walking away briskly.

She sighed and leaned heavily on the picnic table, turning her face to the sky.

BRYCE FINALLY PULLED into the parking area in front of her uncle's house. The day was late and she felt completely worn out. After her failure at the Boy Scout camp, she had gone for a long drive, south and east, following a paved road through lovely, open country that eventually carried her back to the Interstate highway. Shortly after leaving the camp, she passed a sign for Earl's Rafter T Ranch – the letter T looking like it had taken shelter under an upside down V. She didn't feel like visiting, however, so she drove on. Eventually, she reached her objective, the Ossabow Wildlife Refuge, after passing through two more ranches, one covered with widely-spaced houses. This was the Refuge that Nature Unlimited would enlarge if they purchased The Sun, she recalled Frank saying. Her disappointment was big. There were a only few shallow ponds, some marshy spots along a thin creek, a handful of wading birds, and a small, plain brown building with a long handicap ramp, suggesting that it was the Refuge Headquarters. There weren't any cars in the parking lot. She kept going.

A short while later she found herself on the Interstate, heading north and trying to ignore the large field of gas wells looming to the east. She kept driving to Dunraven, thirty miles away, curious about the town. It wasn't terribly impressive either, she thought, though the large gold mine behind the town looked historic. She had stopped at a rest area on the edge of town and spent a few minutes reading a sign that explained how Dunraven had been attacked in 1890 by an outlaw gang determined to rob the bank and was met with equally determined resistance. Bloodshed followed. More 'Guns and Guy' stuff, she thought with a sigh. There wasn't an information sign, she noticed, about Hannigan or the cancer cluster that Doctor Creider had mentioned though the town site was only a few miles away probably. She decided to head back to The Sun.

At the exit, she slipped off the freeway and headed west toward Alameda. As she drove, she contemplated her ranch suitor dilemma, without arriving at an answer. Rack and Pendergast hadn't helped make her choice any easier and she hadn't heard a word yet from Kevin Malcolm. This situation wasn't at all what she expected.

Could you sell a ranch over eBay, she wondered?

Pulling up to her uncle's house, Bryce killed the car's engine, opened the glove compartment, and pulled out her cell phone, where she had banished it for the duration of the drive. Her hiatus from the crazy nonstop world was officially over. Through the windshield, she could see Seymour standing on the porch wagging his tail vigorously. Bryce tapped the phone's security code as she climbed out of the car and then grimaced when the device vibrated in her hand continuously as messages and voice mails avalanched in. She refused to look. Instead, she plodded up the stairs and scratched Seymour's ears as soon as she could, thinking he looked none the worse for being left outside all day.

"Hey, handsome, I could have used your company today. Did you get a tan out here?"

She lifted the phone to her face. There were forty-two new messages and emails waiting for her attention. Not so bad. She began scrolling through them with a thumb while reaching for the door handle with her free hand. Suddenly, she hesitated.

Had she locked it? Yes. Definitely. She grabbed the handle. Locked. She let out a small sigh of relief as she fished for the house key in her vest (to her mother's consternation, Bryce had refused to buy a purse all her life, preferring many-zippered outdoor vests and deep-pocketed pants). Seymour stood nearby, wagging his tail at double speed.

"What do you think handsome, is it tuna-time?"

She unlocked the door and threw it open, stepping aside as Seymour rushed in. She watched him for a moment in case he alerted, but he ran into the kitchen instead and sat on his haunches, casting a look back impatiently at her.

Bryce embarked on a series of chores, one-handed, as she continued to scroll through her messages. She grabbed Seymour's bowls and bed and hauled them inside; she uncorked the wine bottle from the previous evening and filled a glass, offering some to Seymour in jest (he wrinkled his nose at the smell); she opened a can of tuna using her uncle's fancy electric opener while listening to a voice message; in the living room, she pushed the laptop's 'on' button; in the bathroom, she splashed water on her face and rubbed it dry with a towel – then picked the phone up again; back in the kitchen, she inspected the nearly empty cupboards for something to eat, feeling like Old Mother Hubbard but with a phone stuck to her ear; next, she opened the freezer where she saw five or six packages wrapped in white paper, looking meat-ish. Frozen hamburger? She wasn't much of a meat eater, but she wouldn't say no to an occasional steak. She dropped one package on the plate in the microwave with a *thunk*. She hit the 'defrost' button.

She was working the computer keyboard rapidly with both hands, phone trapped again under her ear, when the microwave timer beeped five times, indicating the cessation of its labors. Famished, Bryce stood up and began to cross to the kitchen.

The merry Mozart tune suddenly played in the air.

Without breaking stride, Bryce rerouted herself toward the glass door, feeling slightly annoyed. She threw it open and headed outside, Seymour close behind. She crossed quickly to the observation deck rail. Although the ranch was deep in the evening's shadows, she could tell there was no one on the entrance road. There was no dust plume in the air either. She squinted at the gate itself, but it was too far away to make anything out. Mostly, she saw the trees and shrubbery that crowded both sides of the tall structure. Had an animal set off the alarm? Bryce decided to double-check. She beelined to her uncle's office, stepped in front of the video monitors and pressed their 'on' buttons. The screens jumped to life. Two cameras were mounted on the gate, she saw, one pointing at Highway 70 a short distance away and the other pointing down the long entrance road toward the house. Both views were empty. No animals. Nothing at all, in fact. Something moved behind her suddenly, giving her a start. It was Seymour, appearing in the office doorway. He cocked his head slightly.

"Beats me," she said to him with a shrug.

Back in the kitchen, Bryce gave the white-wrapped meat package in the microwave a squeeze, turned it over, shut the door, and punched a button. The machine began to whirr again. She refilled the wine glass and crossed into the living room. As soon as her bottom touched the chair in front of her laptop, the Mozart tune jingled again in the air. She froze for a second in consternation, then popped up. Nearly tripping over Seymour, she made her way rapidly to the office and stepped smartly in front of the two video screens again. Nothing. She leaned forward carefully to make sure she wasn't missing something. The long road was empty as was the brief stretch to the highway. What had triggered the alarm?

She marched out of the office, across the living room and emerged a moment later onto the observation deck holding the pair of binoculars. She lifted them to her eyes as soon as she reached the railing. Still nothing. Bryce stared through the glasses for a long time, surveying the long road and the entrance gate carefully in the gathering gloom. Weird, she thought to herself, fighting off a small pang of anxiety.

Her phone suddenly rang in her pocket, causing her heart to leap. She pulled it out slowly. It was Earl.

"Mister Holcombe," she said into the phone, relieved to hear his voice. "Yes, I did hear the alarms...no, no one is on the road," she said. "It's empty. Yes, I turned the monitors on." She cast a glance at Seymour, who was watching her intently nearby. "Deer?"

She put the binoculars back to her face and scanned the gate.

"I don't see any," she said into the phone. "Could it be a smaller animal?" She listened, still scanning. "What about raccoons? Ok. Could it be wind? No. Dogs?" She asked, lowering the glasses and giving Seymour a playful frown.

He flattened his ears.

"What about birds?" she said into the phone. "Unlikely," she said to Seymour. "Has this happened before? Not that you're aware of. Malfunction? Alright. Bye." She hung up. "Maybe a malfunction," she said to the dog. "But unlikely. He sounded worried. Anybody come on the ranch today that I need to know about?"

When Seymour didn't answer, Bryce lifted the binoculars and surveyed the grasslands surrounding the house, which were now mostly in shadow. Scanning to her right, she could barely make out the ranch Headquarters through the trees that formed the little oasis around the buildings. Every structure was dark. For a moment, she thought she detected a quick movement near the rambling office – like the flash of an animal or the flap of a banner. But it wasn't repeated. She swung the glasses around and lifted them to survey the Diamond Bar, looming darkly on the horizon. She found the solitary light in its usual place. It refused to blink this time.

She lowered the binoculars and sighed at Seymour. "Let's go with malfunction," she said, giving him a smile. She headed back to the house. As soon as she stepped inside, the Mozart alarm chimed again.

This time she ran to the office. As she arrived at the monitors, she caught a glimpse of something brown as it flicked off one of the screens. It was the camera facing the highway. As she watched, a truck zoomed by on the road suddenly, traveling fast. On the other screen, the camera facing the ranch – there was nothing. Bryce studied the two opposite views. It was possible, she calculated, to trip the gate sensor without being seen. There appeared to be a gap in the camera angles along the horizontal line of gate. She couldn't see the ranch's boundary fence that she knew existed, stretching away in both directions. Watching the fence wasn't the purpose of the surveillance cameras, of course. They were supposed to catch visitors, or trespassers. Maybe an animal had sneaked around the fence, or was stuck on the other side somehow where she couldn't see it. She liked it better than a malfunction.

Her phone rang in her vest pocket. She pulled it out. Earl again.

"I'm looking at the monitor screens," she said as soon as she put the phone to her ear. "I thought I saw a flash of something as I got here, but the road on both sides is empty...."

She listened. Then she grimaced. She turned to look around the room. "No, I haven't searched the house," she said, trying to decide if she should be worried or irritated. "Yes, Seymour's here. He follows me everywhere," she said looking at the dog, who sat in the doorway again. He cocked his head at her. "No, he hasn't alerted."

She listened, frowning.

"No, Mister Holcombe, I don't want the combination to the gun safe," she said into the phone, sounding exasperated. "Alright." She walked to the closet in the corner that she had missed the other night and pulled open the door. A black gun safe sat there quietly. "It doesn't appear to be open," she said. "Check it?"

Her stomach tightened. Was the safe open? She reached slowly for the handle, gripped it, and turned it slowly. The handle didn't move.

"It's locked," she said into the phone, not disguising her relief. She listened.

"Mister Holcombe...Earl, I don't want the combination, as I said. I don't want a gun, thank you!" She heaved a sigh at Seymour as she listened. "You've made your opinion on the matter very clear, yes, but I refuse to arm myself. You have your principles, I have mine."

She listened again.

"I know my uncle changed his mind...I don't know why...I don't know what his principles were, to be honest..."

Seymour turned his head suddenly, looking into the living room. A moment later, he disappeared. Bryce froze.

"I need to go. Seymour's disappeared," she said to Earl. "I'll call you back."

She hung up. She peered out the office door, looking both directions. Nothing. She stepped into the hall and walked cautiously toward the living room, noting that the house had become much darker with the dying day. Where was Seymour? She was just about to call his name when the dog appeared in the kitchen, his nose on the floor. He circled around the island before following the scent into the hall that led to the garage. Mice again. Bryce exhaled.

She decided to check the wine cellar. She flicked on a light and headed down the steps quickly. At the bottom, she grabbed the handle to the cellar door and pushed. Locked. After a moment of hesitation, she pulled her keys out, unlocked the door, and heaved it open, revealing pitch blackness. She listened, but heard only silence. She hit the light switch inside the door and entered the room. Nothing had changed. The wine racks looked the same. She'd have to count all the bottles again to determine if another one had been pilfered, which she didn't feel like doing right now.

She locked the door and headed back up the stairs. She kept going to the second floor, flicking on lights as she went. She poked her head into the gym first, followed by the master bedroom – but all seemed normal. No open drawers or shadowy figures lurking in corners.

As she returned to the ground floor, she realized the glass door to the observation deck was still open. Through it, she saw Seymour standing near a railing, his ears forward. Suddenly, he turned and trotted toward the porch, disappearing out-of-sight. Was someone approaching the house, she wondered? She stepped onto the deck and glanced at the entrance road. No vehicles. No dust. Moving to her right so she could see down the porch, Bryce noticed Seymour standing tensely at the top of the stairs, his gaze aimed at the trees beyond the edge of the house. As Bryce watched, something moved in the woods. A deer. Three. Heads came up. Then the deer shied, heading deeper into the darkness.

"Come on handsome, let's go inside," Bryce said, breathing again.

The moment she turned toward the glass door, the Mozart tuned played again inside the house. Bryce froze. The timing was too coincidental. Was someone watching her? It certainly felt like it. She turned sharply to look at the entrance gate, but saw nothing new in the gloom. What was going on? She stepped to the deck railing and peered down into the main parking area, seeing only her car. A soft clicking to her right indicated Seymour's arrival. He looked up at her curiously.

Turning back toward the house with a frown, Bryce suddenly spied a white piece of paper attached to the big BBQ grill. Had the paper been there this morning? No. It had not. A small shot of fear ran through her body. Her heart beat faster. The phone suddenly buzzed in her vest pocket. She silenced it.

She slowly advanced toward the grill. A slight breeze lifted the bottom half of the sheet, which was taped to the BBQ by its upper corners. The sheet of paper had two large words printed on it.

GO HOME it said.

Bryce stopped and bunched her fists. Turning toward the grasslands, she took a deep breath, feeling all the frustration of the past few days rise up.

"I'm trying to!" she yelled into the shadows.

She looked down at Seymour, who had flattened his ears. "It's not your fault," she said, reassuringly. He wagged. With a sigh, she walked to the BBQ, pulled the sheet off aggressively, ripping its corners, and began to walk back to glass door.

The phone buzzed in her pocket. She pulled it out. Earl again. Lifting the device, her arm froze and she stopped walking abruptly. There were words on the other side of the sheet. She turned it over slowly. A shot of fear ran through her body.

VAYA CON DIOS it said.

THURSDAY

Bryce casually shut off her buzzing phone, content to continue staring at the tumor on the computer screen, her chin cupped tiredly in her left hand.

Immediately, the phone buzzed again and Bryce once more turned it off. She doubted it was Earl calling and she didn't want to talk to anyone else. She sat in semi-darkness of early morning, the pooled light of the lamp falling on a pile of papers on the table that flowed outward from her like a tide. She had intended to spend this time reading another medical report but couldn't concentrate for lack of sleep. After the fourth Mozart alarm last night, Earl insisted on inspecting the sensors on the gate, but he found nothing amiss. Animals, he concluded. She decided against showing him the message stuck on the BBQ. Instead, she locked herself inside the house with Seymour after Earl left and went to work, spreading medical reports across the table and shutting out anything to do with ranches, cows, rapacious suitors, angry activists, or murder victims. A bottle of wine helped – her second. Fortunately, the alarm remained silent. On the far side of midnight, she finally threw herself into bed, her head swimming with images of tumors, lists of data, and a perky, bewigged Mozart beating time in a Vienna opera house.

The phone buzzed a third time. Maybe it was Dale, she thought with a jolt. She uncupped her chin from her hand and picked up the phone. *Unknown Caller* it said. After a brief hesitation, she accepted the call, putting the phone to her ear.

"Yes?" she said tentatively and then listened. She stood straight up.

"Mister Malcolm! Thank you for calling...This is a fine time...No, not too early. I've been working...peace and quiet... Yes, I am enjoying my stay. It's a very beautiful place."

She drifted toward the glass door as she spoke, relieved that he had finally called. Maybe she would get this ranch sold after all! Outside, the morning was coming on quickly, spreading soft light across the ranch.

"He'd like to meet? Of course! *Here?* In twenty minutes!" Bryce stopped dead in her tracks. "Ok," she said into the phone. "Is there anything I should know about or do in advance?" She listened. "No. Ok. See you shortly."

He was gone before she could remove the phone from her ear. Bryce exhaled loudly, causing Seymour to look up from the rug where he had been quietly lying.

"The Big Kahuna is coming here," she said to him, prompting a bout of tail wagging. "No, I said Kahuna, not tuna. I really need to stop feeding you that stuff."

She thought for a moment. "I don't even remember his real name," she confided to Seymour. "Isn't that terrible? It's Dan something. Edwards? Andrews? Jones?" She tapped an inquiry into her phone. "Richards. Stanley Richards." She kept reading. "Founder of...oh my!" She turned to the dog, who cocked his head at her. "It says he's now the fourth richest man in the world. And he'll be here in twenty minutes."

Bryce surveyed the room. The pile of papers on the table was an irredeemable mess, but the chairs could be straightened up, the wine bottle put away, stray trash collected, dishes done, the coffee pot cleaned... She strode into the kitchen and stared at the dishes and the general mess. She had cooked the hamburger the night before, which was delicious, but she skipped the dish-washing in her stress and fatigue. She glanced at the wall clock as she pushed up the faucet handle, creating a jet of water. Moving fast, she tossed the dishes into the sink, squirted liquid cleaner on them, grabbed a frying pan from the stovetop and dropped it in, followed by her coffee mug and every bit of silver-ware she could find. Next, she plucked a dishcloth from a hook on the side of the island, wetted it and began vigorously rubbing the countertop. She noticed Seymour nearby sniffing for the stray bits of food she was sending flying.

"Good boy!" she said encouragingly. Should she put him in the bedroom? No, if Mister Gazillionaire didn't like dogs, he'd have to deal with it.

She wanted Seymour's company.

A moment later, she turned off the water, judging the foam in the sink to be high enough. What to do with the dishcloth? She opened a cabinet door underneath the sink and tossed it inside. She lifted the lid to the garbage can, noting that Seymour watched her with interest. Did it smell? Not much, she thought, but what did a gazillionaire consider to be too smelly? Did her uncle keep air freshener someplace? She decided not to bother with a search and shut the lid. She glanced at the wall clock. Twelve minutes to go. She crossed quickly to the guest bedroom and pulled the door shut. She did the same with the office door. Would he need to use the bathroom? Hopefully not. She straightened the chairs in the living room and removed her sweater from the sofa. Should she move Seymour's bowls? Yes? No? This was crazy! What was the protocol for hosting one of the most powerful human beings on the planet? Should she primp? No. She hated primping – another lifestyle decision that had driven her mother to distraction. Stanley Richards would have to accept the way she looked right now. Besides, it was her ranch. Bryce headed back into the kitchen. She sighed. She had missed a dish. She tossed it into the foamy water with a splash. Seymour sniffed at a bit of the suds that landed on the floor.

"No, you don't," Bryce said, opening the sink door and wiping up the spill rapidly with the wet dishcloth.

She stood up, putting her hands on the counter. Should she make coffee for him? All she had was instant. No. He owned the largest coffee company in the world.

Bryce stepped into the breakfast nook. The table and two chairs sat tidily in place. If he wanted to chat this would be a good location, she thought. Chat? She read somewhere that nearly one-fifth of all Americans interacted with at least one of his companies *daily*. She knew that one of his businesses was a major medical supplier to her hospital. She also knew he had recently purchased a large entertainment conglomerate to go along with the rest of his mammoth business empire. She remembered being surprised at the ease with which his purchases kept winning approval from federal anti-trust regulators. But she needed to stop feeling shocked at things like that with this Administration. Was Richards a Republican? Would he like Earl? What was she *doing*? Bryce scanned the living room quickly. Her uncle's western art collection would probably distract him anyway. Was he an art collector? She had no idea. She glanced down at Seymour, who sat on the rug nearby.

He flattened his ears under her stern gaze.

"You're a good boy," she said reassuringly. "You can stay out here just don't bite him, ok? Not unless I say," she added ruefully.

She checked the wall clock. Twenty minutes had vanished somehow. She cocked an ear, waiting for the Mozart alarm to chime overhead, welcome this time. She was beginning to feel nervous, she realized. If he wanted to meet with her, he probably wanted to buy the ranch. Should she try to negotiate with him? But how did one negotiate with a gazillionaire? One didn't, she suspected. She decided to push these questions away and wait for the alarm to go off, but it remained stubbornly silent.

Bryce crossed to the glass door and looked through it. The morning had brightened enough to see the ranch road all the way to the gate at Highway 70. It was empty. Seymour appeared at her feet. She slid the door open with a vigorous tug, allowing him to charge outside. She grabbed the binoculars from the side table and followed, leaving the door open so she could listen for the Mozart ditty. She walked to her usual spot at the deck railing and lifted the glasses to her eyes. She studied the entrance gate. Nothing. She scanned the road. Nothing. She slowly surveyed the ranch, seeing plenty: grass, river, mountains, sky. It all looked exceptionally beautiful this morning...

She heard a noise.

She lowered the binoculars, listening. Distant thumping. She continued to listen and then raised the glasses, redirecting them into the sky. It took a bit of searching, but eventually she saw it – a helicopter.

Coming straight at her.

Of course a helicopter. Wait! Where was he going to land? On the entrance road below the hill? It had to be five hundred yards away, she calculated, all uphill. She doubted Stanley Richards had the patience to walk that far. She crossed to the east side of the observation deck and leaned over the railing. Would it try to land in the main parking area? It looked to be big enough, barely, though her car occupied part of the space. The car! She ran inside the house, tossed the binoculars on the table and entered the short hallway that led to the garage. She flicked on the garage light, punched the door opener and scooted outside as soon as the large door had risen high enough. The thumping sound was loud now and a glance into the sky revealed the helicopter to be closing fast. She rushed through the second parking area, turned at the corner of the deck and then ran to the vehicle. The tops of the trees had begun to sway, she could see. She jumped into the car, backed up smartly and sped to the garage. She hopped out and hurried to close the door, but hesitated before pressing the button. She could see dust begin to swirl on the ground outside.

This was going to be interesting.

Bryce rushed into the living room. Fortunately, Seymour had the good sense to retreat to the rug, so all she had to do was slam the glass door shut. She could see a sleek, black helicopter positioning itself above the main parking area, kicking up a ton of dust. The roar of the blades was incredibly loud and she could feel the machine's vibrations through her feet. She moved to one of the windows near the front door, where she could see the pilot as he calmly turned the helicopter parallel to the porch in preparation for landing. Dust became dirt. She heard patio furniture begin to scoot along the deck. Soon, grit began pelting the glass. Bryce took a step back. You had to give Richards credit for dramatic entrances, she thought. Great swirls of dirt now flew up as the helicopter approached the ground. Bryce heard pings as small rocks hit the windows. Shortly, the whole scene became a roaring tempest of dirt and wind. Involuntarily, she took another step back as rocks pinged constantly now and the view was completely lost to the maelstrom.

She glanced at Seymour. "You men," she said in mock anger.

He flattened his ears.

Finally, the roar and the flying dirt ebbed slightly, indicating that the helicopter had touched down successfully in the tight space. Not that she had any doubt. Richards could afford the best pilot in the world. The roar fell another degree in pitch and she could hear the whine of the engine begin to diminish as well. Bryce grabbed the handle to the front door and held on until it seemed reasonably safe to go outside. Finally, she pulled the door open and walked to the top of the stairs, shielding her eyes against the wind and dust. The blades were spinning down quickly and would stop soon, as she knew from her experience with medical helicopters. But nothing she had ever seen in her life was as fancy as this machine. It had a stylish sleekness that shouted a high price tag. It was entirely black with tinted windows that made it impossible to see inside. She wondered what it had cost – many millions, surely.

The front passenger door in the machine opened suddenly and a very large man dressed in black stepped out heavily. He had the build of a world-wrestling champion, she thought, not that she was familiar with the sport, looking like he had been shoehorned into his suit-and-tie. His eyes were hidden behind dark sunglasses. He slid open the back door. A moment later, Kevin Malcolm appeared, looking much as he did on Monday right down to the skinny red tie, which danced around his neck comically in the swirling air. Climbing down, he flattened the tie against his chest with a hand and came forward, bending much farther over than necessary to avoid the slowly turning blades. Straightening up, he gave Bryce a perfunctory nod before moving to the side to wait for the guest-of-honor. Bryce glanced back at Seymour. He sat in the open doorway, a curious expression on his face. She fought a small surge of panic. Should she go down to greet Richards? She had met many rich people during her work at the hospital, but she suspected the stratospherically wealthy were something else altogether. She decided to hold her ground.

A moment later, the bodyguard began trudging up the stairs, his sunglasses-covered eyes fixed straight ahead. Bryce backed up a bit to give him room. Reaching the porch, he took a step to his left, stopped, turned around, and became rock-like, his hands casually crossed in front of him. Not once did he acknowledge her existence.

A man emerged from the depths of the helicopter. He was smallish, lean, and hatless, with extremely close-cropped silver hair, thinning on top. She noticed his very shiny black shoes as he stepped to the ground. The rest of his body was wrapped in a long, beautiful, black overcoat that looked like a cross between something one would wear to opening night at the Met and a coat from one of those Matrix movies. It was incredibly stylish in a severe, imposing, and utterly impregnable way. Stanley Richards. As soon as possible, she saw, he stuck his hands into its pockets, sealing himself neatly off from the world. The only part still exposed was his head, which he kept tilted down as he came forward. He appeared to be pale, clean-shaven, and regular-featured, improbably reminding her of a basketball coach she knew in high school. As he crossed to the stairs, she noticed he was a bit jowly in the cheeks, which surprised her. Maybe it was middle-age, not lifestyle. She suspected it was the only thing about him that was soft.

Richards kept his eyes lowered as he began to climb the steps. Kevin stayed near the helicopter, staring politely into the distance. The whine of the black machine had finally fallen to a conversational level. She wondered what she was about to hear.

At the top of the stairs, Richards turned to his right without lifting his gaze and walked directly past Bryce. He headed down the porch, his hands still tucked into his coat, and stepped onto the observation deck where he crossed to the far railing. He no more acknowledged her existence than had the bodyguard. Trying not to feel insulted, she turned to Seymour, noting that he had moved closer. He wagged his tail. With a nod to the dog to stay, Bryce walked to the deck where Richards stood motionless, his back to her, silently surveying the grasslands. She stopped near the head of the narrow stairs that led down to the other parking area, positioning herself within his line-of-view. He didn't look like her basketball coach after all, she decided. His profile was sharper, less forgiving. She waited. Was he going to say anything? Was she expected to go first? Confused, Bryce looked over her shoulder at Kevin back at the helicopter, but he seemed lost in thought, one hand casually stuck in a pant pocket. She glanced at the bodyguard, who still stood rock-like at the top of the porch stairs.

She turned back to Richards. The silence stretched out uncomfortably. Bryce decided to speak.

"Malignant astrocytoma," he said suddenly, his voice clear and strong.

She blinked at him in surprise. "Pardon?" There was no response. He continued to stare across the ranch.

Bryce frowned. "Astrocytoma? The brain tumor?"

Richards didn't move, staring at something she couldn't see.

"What do you know about it?" he said.

She knitted her brow. "It's not my specialty," she managed to say finally. "Besides, it depends on which type of tumor you…"

"Juvenile pilocytic astrocytoma," he interrupted.

"Oh." Bryce dug through her memory. "Those are usually benign."

"Not this one." His voice sounded harsh. He continued to stare across the ranch.

"Is it a high-grade astrocytoma?" Bryce asked, narrowing her eyes in concern. He didn't respond. "Anaplastic or glioblastoma?" she tried next.

"My niece, Natalie," he finally said, "is dying."

He said it so matter-of-factly that it sent shivers through Bryce. She waited, but he didn't say anything else. Why was he telling her this? She thought again. Astrocytoma…star-shaped tumors…early detection essential…teams of doctors…difficult to remove by surgery at higher grades...long odds...better the younger you are...

"How old is she?"

"Fourteen. She's at Albert Schweitzer in New York," he added, correctly predicting her next question.

"That's great!" Bryce said. "It's one of the best research institutions in..."

"It's her fifth hospital," he said, cutting her off. He continued to stare out over the grasslands.

Bryce exhaled quietly. "What's been done so far, besides surgery?"

"Radio therapy, chemotherapy, TTG, Mozapine, Gallium-24, IDP3, RDGP, subC..." his voice trailed off.

Bryce nodded. That list made sense. "Isn't there a promising genomic therapy being developed in the Netherlands..." she began.

"I bought the company," he interrupted. "And their French rival."

"I thought there was another competitor in Japan as well."

"I hired their lead researcher."

Bryce searched her memory of recent medical conferences. "Wasn't there something promising in Australia?"

"No," he said to the ranch.

The silence stretched on. Was she supposed to say something else, she wondered?

"I secured a blessing from the Pope for Natalie personally," he said suddenly.

Bryce's eyebrows shot up. *The Pope?* Did it work? She started to ask, but stopped. No, the tumor is malignant, he had said. Bryce shot another look at Kevin over her shoulder and was surprised to see him watching her. This is all super weird, she thought. A dying niece. A black helicopter. A gazillionaire who wouldn't look her in the eye.

"My sister is distraught," Richards said quietly, as if reading her thoughts. "Natalie is her only child." He paused. "I promised her I'd find a cure."

"What's the median survival rate for advanced...?" Bryce began.

"Fourteen months," he said, finishing for her. "It's been forty-two months since diagnosis," he continued. Then he fell silent again.

"That's really good..." Bryce began again.

"She's not cured," he corrected harshly.

Bryce decided to wait.

"Never in my adult life have I broken a promise," he said slowly, still looking away. "And never..." He hesitated. Suddenly, he turned his head, fixing her with blue eyes so intense and unblinking that she felt rooted to the deck, unable almost to breathe.

"How do I keep my promise?" he asked.

Bryce felt like a ton of bricks had suddenly fallen on her. How could he ask her a question like that? This wasn't her specialty! They'd been to five hospitals. He bought the Dutch company! How could he put her on the spot like this? She dug into her memory.

"I heard there's a clinical trial for high-grade astrocytomas starting at UC San Bernardino near Los Angeles, I think..."

"Too early," he said, his eyes boring into her.

Bryce closed her eyes, trying to concentrate. Cancer treatment had fractured long ago into subsets of subsets and it was nearly impossible to keep pace in fields related to her own work much less another type of tumor altogether.

"Pittsburgh..." she said, her eyes still closed.

"Inconclusive."

"What about Doctor Johnson's lab at Stimson..."

"The placebo did better in trials."

She scrunched her eyes together harder. "Doctor Nuprez..."

"A fraud."

"South Korea?"

"No."

That was it. She was empty. Bryce opened her eyes. She held up her hands defensively against whatever he was going to say to her, but his eyes had changed. They had softened around the edges and she realized he wasn't simply being a jerk – he was truly at a loss. He had tried everything. Her heart ached suddenly for his niece and her mother.

"I'm sorry," she said softly. "I know how you feel. I do. You pull out all the stops. You beg and you plead, you make calls, you search and then search again. You call doctors you never knew existed, then you call their colleagues. You pray and then you pray again. And despite doing everything humanly possible, despite every prayer..." she hesitated. "Some still leave us."

He dropped his eyes, looking thoughtful and sad. He was thinking. She opened her mouth to say something supportive when he raised his eyes. They were hard and cold again.

"Not acceptable," he said.

He turned his head and nodded at Kevin, who immediately circled his finger at the pilot, Bryce saw. There was a click and the blades began to turn slowly. Bryce couldn't believe her eyes. *He was leaving?* After grilling her like that? Because *she* couldn't come up with a cure? Twisting her head, she saw that the body-guard had taken a step forward. She turned to confront Richards, but he was staring coldly at the ranch again.

"Jeffrey Bayer," he said to the horizon. "Your lawyer."

She frowned. "What about Jeffrey?"

"Tell him the purchase agreement for The Sun will arrive in his office this afternoon," Richards said. Bryce opened her mouth to object. "We'll draw the papers up," he continued. "Whatever Bill Merrill offered you, add twenty percent."

Bryce was stunned into silence.

"I'm here until Sunday," he said. "I expect to sign the purchase agreement and all other documentation before I leave."

Richards turned sharply and crossed in front of her again without making eye contact. He headed toward the porch. Bryce followed him, frowning. She saw the bodyguard shuffle down the stairs as the whine of the helicopter engine rose steadily in pitch. Seymour watched Richards walk by. She sped up.

"Trouble is," she said to his back. "I'm selling The Sun to the Boy Scouts."

Richards froze on the top step of the stairs.

"No," he said dispassionately. Then he turned his face toward her, his eyes cold. "You're not."

He headed down the steps. Bryce squinted at Seymour.

"I have other offers!" she said loudly.

He continued on his way to the helicopter without responding. Bryce threw up her hands in exasperation. Wind from the blades began to spread dust around.

"What will you do with The Sun?" she yelled down at Richards.

He hesitated at the helicopter's door.

"Tell me and I'll consider your offer," she said.

Richards climbed in. Bryce shot a look at Kevin nearby and was surprised to see a sympathetic grimace on his face.

Sorry it said.

———

BRYCE YANKED THE DOOR OPEN.

Holding the GO HOME sheet of paper rolled up in one hand, she waved politely at the friendly security guard with the other hand as she entered the town hall, to which she had been summoned by the Mayor. In the sudden dimness, two figures walked toward her from across the large room. She recognized the smaller, broader one as Dale, dressed as before in a neat blue shirt, slacks, and hiking shoes, but the other man was a stranger. It was his cousin, she assumed, the locksmith. Dale had called her shortly after the Mayor's office did – and both had called while the helicopter ferrying Richards back to the Diamond Bar was in still the air, which was unnerving. How many eyes in Alameda had been watching the helicopter's transit back and forth, dying to know what was happening on The Sun? The Mayor certainly wanted to know, undoubtedly worried about the future of her Master Plan – and for good reason. Dale at least was discreet in his curiosity, talking first about setting up a meeting with his cousin before asking about Richards. Bryce wasn't sure how to describe the bizarre encounter - or how to explain that Richards had made her an offer that she couldn't refuse.

"Doctor Miller," Dale said with a friendly nod as he approached her. "I want you to meet my cousin, Isaac."

The taller man stuck his hand out, smiling energetically. He was broad across the chest, sinewy in his arms and exuded a healthy, weathered look as if he had spent most of his life working outdoors. His dark eyes sparkled, reminding her of Dale though they were even more mischievous perhaps than the police chief's. Bryce liked him immediately. He wore boots, jeans, and a plaid shirt, all of which had a comfortable, well-used feel. He held a gray, stained cowboy hat that looked like it didn't spend much time absent from his head. His handshake was both strong and sincere (she shook a lot of hands as part of her job). His wide smile – augmented by two missing teeth – was framed by a large, droopy, graying moustache, which made him look like a retired revolutionary, she thought.

"Isaac Vigil," he said in the same lilting accent as Dale. "It's very nice to meet you. I have to ask, what was Stanley Richards like?"

Bryce glanced at Dale. "Intense," was all she could think to say at first. "And not much for conversation. I think he's used to being obeyed."

"They say he's building a spaceship up there," Isaac said eagerly.

"You don't know that," Dale interjected.

"They're not making Tiddlywinks," Isaac retorted.

"No one knows what they're doing. Is he interested in The Sun?" Dale asked Bryce.

"Yes," she replied simply. The melancholy conversation with Richards ebbed back into her. "You're cousins?" she asked.

Isaac smiled toothily, nodding at Dale. "His father and my mother are *cuates* – twins. The Archuletas are from Peñasco on the Rio Chiquito," he continued. "The Vigils live in Quemado, farther up the river. It was a brave marriage. His great-grandfather shot a mule that belonged to my great-grandmother and both families have been sore about it ever since."

"She doesn't want to hear that stuff," said Dale. "Ike ran the timber mill in Peñasco for years until it was shut down by the greenies."

"Nah, I don't blame them," Isaac said, waving a hand. "They're like coyotes, just part of God's natural world. *La floresta*, on the other hand..."

He whistled low, shaking his head.

"The Forest Service," Dale said to Bryce helpfully. "They own most of the timber land around here and haven't been very good neighbors. It's a long story."

"The local office was shot up," Isaac said, also trying to be helpful.

"Shot up?" Bryce asked, surprised.

"It was back in the seventies," Dale said, preemptively. "It's a long story, like I said." He put his hand on his cousin's shoulder. "Let's stick to locks. Ike's your man."

"Right," Bryce said, pulling three keys out of her vest pocket. "Outside, garage, and that one's for the wine cellar," she said pointing at the black key. "Thanks for doing this. Help yourself to a bottle while you're down there. I've got plenty."

"*Gracias*, I will," he replied, grinning warmly.

"Don't be picky," Dale cautioned, causing both of them to chuckle.

"Do you know your wines?" Bryce asked.

"I know the two basic types," Isaac said, grinning and nodding at her question. "Alcoholic and non-alcoholic."

"Guess which one he prefers?" said Dale.

All three of them laughed. "I doubt my uncle bought any of the second variety," Bryce said. "Look what I found last evening on the grill."

She handed Dale the GO HOME sheet in her hand. He unrolled it and did a slight double-take when the read the message.

"Not very subtle, is it?" she said. "Turn it over."

Dale flipped the sheet. This time, he raised his eyebrows sharply. He held it up for his cousin to see – who shook his head in disapproval at the words.

"What?" Bryce asked.

"That's not how that phrase should be used," Dale replied. "Not as a threat. It's hard to explain. No one we know would do that." He exchanged glances with his cousin, who nodded in agreement. He held up the sheet. "Can I keep this?"

Bryce nodded, feeling last night's fear creep back into her body.

"Ike will keep an eye out while he's working at your place today," Dale continued. "But I don't like this. It means someone's been trespassing."

"Thank you," she said to Isaac. "The dog doesn't bite. His name is Seymour."

Dale smiled. "Let's go see the Mayor."

He nodded at his cousin, who responded with an affectionate salute. Their bond was obvious, Bryce thought enviously as she followed Dale across the floor. She had cousins on her father's side, but they weren't tight. She saw them at Fourth-of-July BBQs, weddings and funerals. She had never met any of her Nebraska relatives and none attended her mother's funeral. Maybe someone's ancestor shot a mule. More likely, it was simply a matter of numbers – both of her maternal grandparents had been single children. As had she. Bryce caught up to Dale, who was inspecting the GO HOME sheet of paper again as he walked. What was he worried about, she wondered? Was it just trespassing – or something else? He lowered the sheet abruptly as he approached the young female receptionist seated behind the attractive wooden desk that guarded the stairwell.

"Is she ready for us?" Dale asked.

"Oh yeah," the receptionist replied, her tone a mixture of permission and warning.

"Thanks." As soon as they began climbing the steps together, he leaned toward Bryce and dropped his voice. "There's something I need to tell you."

"Have Matt's test results come back?" she asked eagerly.

"Not yet. No news about Estevan or the horse either. It's something else. I received the police and medical reports from France this morning about your uncle's death." His tone was ominous. "They said copies were sent to your lawyer, but you never saw them?"

Bryce shook her head. "No. Why?"

"They listed your uncle's death as a Probable Suicide."

Bryce stopped abruptly on the landing. "What? No one said anything to me! Why would they think that?"

"He was loaded with Phenobarbital," Dale replied quietly. "And alcohol, though that might be because he was staying at a winery." He shrugged slightly. "Do you know any reason he'd be taking Pheno?"

"No. I know it's often prescribed to treat seizures."

"No family rumors of epilepsy?"

"Not that I heard. I think he struggled with depression. He seemed pretty subdued at my mother's funeral. How much Pheno was in his system?"

"I don't remember. Enough, apparently."

"It might have been accidental," Bryce countered. "Can I see those reports? And I'll find out who his personal physician was and get his file."

"Doctor Tadesh," Dale said. "I've already ordered it. There's a third option."

Bryce frowned. "Not accidental? And not a suicide?"

Dale raised his eyebrows. "Did he have any enemies?"

She exhaled. "I wouldn't know, though I suppose you don't become wealthy like that without making a few enemies." She wagged a finger at the police chief. "You know, the probate lawyer said something that didn't really sink in at the time. I was the only person at the hearing, which surprised me and when I asked him who was inheriting the rest of my uncle's estate he said there was no other estate. The ranch was it."

"He was supposed to have more?"

"A lot more. I know he was heavily invested in the stock market and real estate, at least according to my mother."

"Maybe he put it all into the ranch," Dale suggested.

"Maybe. Or maybe something happened to it?"

"You think someone stole it?" Dale asked.

"Or his investments took a hit in all those Wall Street shenanigans going on. What was that bank that just failed? Wolf Something"

Dale shook his head and frowned thoughtfully. "Can you look into it?" He tilted a chin up the stairs. "We shouldn't keep her Honor waiting."

He headed up the stairs quickly with Bryce close behind. "Do you think Matt found out something?" she asked.

"If he did," Dale replied, "then it might be a motive for murder."

THE MAYOR STOOD at one of the large windows facing the street, her hands clasped behind her back. She didn't turn as they entered the office but continued to stare into the light, looking unusually contemplative, Bryce thought. What was up?

"Good morning Mayor Tate," Dale said. "Doctor Miller is here too."

As the Mayor turned, Bryce could see that she looked much as she had on Tuesday. Though the clothes were different, the same arrogant charm was fully in effect.

"Good morning," the Mayor said, sounding official. "Thank you for coming in."

"Always happy to help," Dale replied, not sounding the least bit sarcastic.

Crossing to the Mayor's desk, he placed the GO HOME sign on the corner and pushed it forward, making sure she noticed.

The Mayor read the words and then cocked an eyebrow at Dale. "You could have just sent me an email."

They laughed, surprising Bryce. Apparently, this was a familiar repartee.

"Someone put it on the grill at her house yesterday," Dale said to the Mayor. He turned to Bryce. "This sentiment isn't terribly uncommon in Alameda, though sometimes it's accompanied by a wave of the middle finger."

"Those are the polite ones, I can assure you," the Mayor said.

She walked around the desk. Whatever she wanted, Bryce thought, here it came.

"I understand you had a visitor this morning." She folded her arms and leaned against the desk. "What's he like? Not many people have had the privilege of speaking with Mister Richards in person. Lord knows, I never did."

Bryce searched for the right words. The medical stuff they discussed was no one's business. "You don't really 'speak' with him, I think. He speaks and you listen."

"What did he speak to you about?"

"He demanded The Sun."

"What did you tell him?"

Bryce couldn't resist. "I told him I'm selling it to the Boy Scouts."

The Mayor's eyebrows shot straight up. "You are?" She looked at Dale, whose expression mirrored the Mayor's, Bryce thought, though perhaps more hopefully.

"Maybe," Bryce replied evasively.

"Did the Scouts contact you?" the Mayor asked. She didn't wait for an answer. "I thought the camp is falling down around their ears. It certainly looks like it!"

"They're just having a little trouble with membership, that's all," Bryce tried.

"That's all? That's everything," the Mayor said. She unfolded her arms and waved a hand dismissively. "Actually, I'm not surprised. That Scouting stuff is so, you know, Dwight Eisenhower." She gave Bryce a calculating look. "Whatever Stan Richards offered you, Bill Merrill will match, you know."

"I don't care," Bryce replied, shaking her head. "I won't let The Sun be covered with gas wells."

"Good," said the Mayor, standing up straight and putting her hands on her hips.

"I'm not excited by a country club either," Bryce added

quickly. "Or a jazz festival." She kept going. "Or boutique shops, or fancy restaurants, or feline murderers, for that matter. Am I forgetting anything?" She snapped her fingers. "Yes! Or an air strip."

The Mayor shot a suspicious look at Dale, who was grinning slyly at Bryce's tirade.

"You forgot your chicken suit," the Mayor said tartly to Bryce. "And you've been talking to Frank. It doesn't matter. They don't have the money. Besides, how many of those chubby fish things are there left in the river anyway, twelve? Please."

"I've met other buyers," Bryce tried.

"Who? The Mole and the Shark?" the Mayor shot back. "One's praying for the world to end and the other one just smells blood. As for the purported wolf sanctuary, those three malcontents probably have sixty-four dollars between them. Anyone else?"

The Mayor tilted her face downward a bit and stared at her.

"Not yet," Bryce said. "Where's a Hollywood movie star when you need one?"

"They're all on drugs," the Mayor said with a disdainful shake of her head. She stepped around the desk. "Forget Mark Sampson, or whatever his name actually is. I have investors. Let us buy the ranch. We'll match Richards. No air strip, no country club, no jazz festival, no shops. I can't do much about the feline murderers," she said with a shrug.

"Just a bunch of great big houses?"

"Investors want returns," the Mayor said matter-of-factly. "That's the way it works."

"No golf courses," Bryce countered.

The Mayor's eyes grew big in shock. "Where were you born? In America, you have golf courses."

Bryce cast a glance at Dale, but his expression was carefully neutral.

"If you want, we can donate a portion of the ranch to the wildlife refuge," the Mayor said with a shrug. "Maybe those chub fishy things will swim down there," she said, raising a hand and wriggling her fingers in the air. "Would you consider our offer?"

"Do you want The Sun bad enough to antagonize Stanley Richards?" Bryce asked.

The Mayor made a small face, indicating she had contemplated this question. "Possibly not. But I'm always open to negotiation. I can talk to Mister Nibble..." She caught herself. "I mean Mister Malcolm. But are you open to our offer?"

"I can give it some thought," Bryce said noncommittally.

The Mayor drummed her fingers on the table top. "Alright." She turned to Dale. "Now, Chief Archuleta. About this murder. Have you caught that immigrant yet? Steven what's-his-name?"

Dale inhaled wearily. "Estevan. Gutierrez. No. He's still missing. As is the horse."

"Annabelle."

"Brunhilda," Dale corrected.

"Whatever. He wanted to steal her so he killed the foreman. Simple."

"Not simple," he shot back. "We have circumstantial evidence that someone else might be involved."

"Who?"

Dale cleared his throat. "We don't know yet."

"Then find out!" the Mayor instructed. "How complicated could this be?"

Dale frowned at the insinuation. "That's not how a murder investigation goes, I'm afraid," he said, controlling his voice.

"And how many murder investigations have you directed?"

"None. Alameda didn't used to be that kind of place until recently."

They squared off in silence. Bryce's phone suddenly buzzed in her pocket. She pulled it out discreetly and took a peek.

"It's Earl," she said, lifting the phone to her ear.

"Just arrest somebody," the Mayor said airily to Dale. "You can let them out later if it's the wrong person."

Bryce snapped her finger, trying to catch their attention. "What?" she said into the phone. "Someone found Brunhilda? Where?" She looked at Dale. "Up in the forest?"

"Ask him who it was," Dale said sharply.

"Who found her?" Bryce said into the phone. "Abelard?"

The Mayor made a dismissive sound.

"He's one of the Sasquatch-hunters," Dale said.

"Sasquatch hunters?" Bryce said, not sure she heard him correctly.

"He's a crazy person," the Mayor added.

Bryce listened to Earl again. "Well, apparently, he's a crazy person with GPS coordinates for a horse."

Dale shot a smile at the Mayor, who petulantly replaced her hand on her hip.

EARL CLOSED the trailer door with a loud clang.

"It still doesn't make any sense to me," he said as he latched the door by dropping a bar in place. "I can't think of a good reason she'd be this far up in the mountains unless someone rode her here deliberately."

As Earl walked around the corner of his horse trailer, Bryce looked up from the GPS unit that Dale had lent her.

"You said she was still wearing a saddle?"

"That's what Abe told me," Earl replied.

Bryce frowned. "Abe? You mean Abelard, the Sasquatch guy?"

"The same." He squinted at the dense forest surrounding them. "Are you sure we're in the right place?"

Bryce checked the GPS unit again. "Yes. Brunhilda should be about six thousand meters south of here."

"How many miles is that?" Earl asked as he approached two fully-saddled horses tethered to his trailer, one brown and one gray.

"About four," Bryce replied, "as the crow flies."

"It's going to feel a lot longer than that in this country," Earl warned. He began to untie the reins of the gray horse from the trailer.

"You think the rider abandoned her?" Bryce asked.

"It looks that way. Maybe he was spooked."

"By Sasquatch?"

Earl grunted when he realized she was joking. "What I want to know is why she hasn't worked her way back to the ranch yet?" Earl said, pushing the gray mare back. "Horses have sense. They want to go home. But Brunhilda is still here."

That sounded familiar, Bryce thought with a sigh.

"There must be something preventing her," Earl continued, now untying the other horse. "That worries me. Come on."

He tugged on the reins of both horses, pulling them gently away from the trailer. They had parked at a locked metal gate that barred their way from going any farther down a narrow dirt road through the forest. Earl had brought his trailer to town to fetch Bryce and then surprised her by following the river up Alameda Canyon instead of driving back toward the ranch. Earl said Brunhilda had been spotted by Abelard in rugged country on Forest Service land high above the Boy Scout camp. He was skeptical at first, saying there was no reason for the horse to be up there, but Bryce confirmed the coordinates, drawing on her GPS knowledge from sailing. Her dad kept a unit on the cata-maran but rarely consulted it except to mark the location of unusual bird sightings and ecological features, preferring to find his way around the islands the old-fashioned way. On the drive up the canyon road, Earl asked about Stanley Richards, as she expected. His demand for The Sun confirmed Earl's suspicions that Matt had transgressed onto Diamond Bar property and witnessed something that he should have not have seen – and paid the price.

"What would prevent Brunhilda from leaving?" Bryce asked, following Earl.

"She might be tied to a tree or hobbled," he said as they approached the metal gate. "Or injured," he added.

"How did the guy know she was alive?"

"He saw her shake her head."

"Why didn't he go get her?"

"Abe?" Earl replied, sounding surprised. "All he cares about is finding Bigfoot. Can you open the gate?" He nodded at a barbed-wire gate adjacent to the metal one that blocked the road. "Just lift the loop," he said helpfully.

Bryce slung a plastic line attached to the GPS unit around her head and shoulders. "Who's Abe again?" she said, squinting at the gate.

"Abelard deLonge," Earl said somewhat dramatically. "Professional Sasquatch Hunter. He has a card."

Bryce chuckled as she inspected the wire loop that bound the thin wooden post of the barbed-wire gate tightly to a larger wooden post stuck firmly in the ground.

"Are you sure he isn't looking for the buried Spanish gold you talked about?"

"No. That's someone else," Earl said. Bryce looked up at him in surprise. "Squeeze the posts together and lift the loop," he instructed, pointing. "Watch out, those barbs can draw blood. Do you want gloves?"

"I'm alright," Bryce said. She pushed on the thin post with

one hand, but it hardly moved. "How long has Abelard been searching for Sasquatch?"

Earl shrugged. "Ten years, I think."

Bryce gave him a look of astonishment as she gave the thin post a big push. The metal loop popped off, freeing it. "Has he found anything?" she asked.

"Not that I heard," Earl replied. He pointed at the bottom part of the thin post. Bryce saw that it sat in a wire loop near the ground. She lifted it free and quickly peeled the gate back, creating a gap for Earl and the horses.

"But he keeps looking?" Bryce said, struggling to keep the floppy wire fence from collapsing to the ground.

"Yes ma'am," Earl said, leading the horses through the gap. "Apparently, the longer he can't find the Big Guy the more convinced he is that he's here somewhere."

Bryce frowned. Earl's words recalled a troubled colleague she knew in medical school who became convinced one winter that a ghost haunted his apartment building. She and others repeatedly helped him search for the elusive apparition, but the only evidence they ever uncovered was the mysterious disappearance of her friend's pizza orders, though the ghost apparently had an appetite for Chinese food as well.

"That doesn't make sense," Bryce said as she dragged the fence back into its original position now that Earl and the horses were through. "Why does he persist?"

"I think he's Canadian. You might want to step on this side of the fence," Earl warned as he grabbed the pommel of the saddle of the gray horse.

"Oh!" Bryce exclaimed, realizing her mistake. She stepped through the gap and placed the bottom part of the post back in its loop. "Should I even close it?" she asked.

"Yes," Earl ordered. With a practiced motion he stuck his left foot into the stirrup and swung himself up and into the saddle.

"First Law of the West. Always leave a gate exactly how you found it."

She pushed the top of the post toward the upper wire loop. It didn't even come close. "What's the Second Law?"

"There is no Second Law. Are you sure you don't want gloves?"

"No, thanks," Bryce grunted, trying again with the post. "I thought Sasquatch lived in Oregon or California."

"So did I," Earl said, organizing the reins as he waited for her to finish.

"Why does Abelard think Sasquatch lives in New Mexico?" Bryce said in tight voice as she strained to close the fence. The top of the post now touched the wire loop.

"Because he thinks Bigfoot speaks Spanish."

What? Bryce shot a look over her shoulder at Earl, but saw that he was teasing her. She returned her attention to the post and redoubled her effort, trying desperately to not look like the newbie she felt like.

"I don't know why Abe thinks Sasquatch lives up here," Earl said, watching her work, his hands folded across the pommel of the saddle. "He must have some reason. He's a funny little guy."

Bryce pushed on the fence post with all her might, her arms starting to shake, but wasn't making much more progress.

"That's the problem with you liberals," Earl said. "No upper body strength."

Bryce grimaced and pushed harder, ignoring the pain in her arm as something pricked it. The head of the post was near the loop now. Just another inch! She gritted her teeth and gave a mighty push – either it was going to make it or she would fail.

She made it.

She stepped back quickly, wiping her hands on her pants and trying to look as nonchalant as possible. She checked her arm – a few bloody scratches. No problem!

"We have upper body strength," she said to Earl, sounding triumphant. "We just choose to conserve it."

"That's good to hear," he said, smiling. He handed her the reins to the brown mare. "Next time, pull the bottom loop up higher. It'll be easier. To answer your question, I think Abe first came out here when he heard about the latest round of cattle mutilations."

Bryce shot him a look of shock. "Cattle mutilations? Are you serious?"

"Yes ma'am," Earl replied. "Ask Dale. The cattle belonged to relatives of his. It started way back in the seventies, though not here, and went on for quite a while, off and on. The first mutilation in these mountains was in 1991, up near Milton. Caused quite a ruckus."

Bryce grabbed the pommel, preparing to climb up. "What are you talking about? Why would anyone mutilate cattle?" she asked, managing to get her foot into the stirrup.

"Nobody knows. Some people think it was religious. By that I mean a cult. The animals were all mutilated in the same way. Hoo boy," he said at the memory.

Bryce hopped three times on her right foot and then launched herself successfully into the saddle. "Mutilated how?"

"I'd rather not say," Earl replied tersely. "You can ask Dale."

Bryce frowned. "Did they stop?"

"There were a few more in the late nineties, same deal, but none recently, thank god. They never found a culprit."

"Did Dale investigate?" Bryce asked, testing her reins and shifting in the saddle.

"He did. He called in all kinds of experts, but no one could figure it out," Earl replied, watching her carefully. "You said you could ride a horse?"

She stopped fidgeting. "Yes," she replied. She felt a little guilty that she hadn't told him the whole story – the only horses she had ever actually ridden were bareback ones on the beach during her surfing breaks. She figured it was like riding a bicycle or a surfboard. You were fine as long as you didn't fall off.

"Do people think Sasquatch did it?" she asked.

"I don't," Earl replied.

"But Abelard does?"

"I don't know what Abe thinks. You can ask him, if you can find him." He gave his horse a gentle kick. "Let's go."

Earl began to ride down the dirt road, but Bryce lingered for a moment, feeling bewildered. Cattle mutilations? Sasquatch hunters? Buried gold? An abandoned rodeo horse in the wilderness? She leaned on the pommel of the saddle wearily. The Sun. What was she going to do with it? The easy way would be to give in to Richards. Twenty percent more than Bill Merrill's offer! She swooned in the saddle and then realized she needed a drink of water. She grabbed a battered plastic bottle that Earl had placed in a saddle bag and opened its top. Bryce lifted it to her mouth, thinking about her lawyer. She hadn't called Jeffrey yet as Richards had instructed her to do. She hated being bullied. She could accept the Mayor's proposal, she supposed. How would Richards respond? Not well. Let the two of them duke it out – except the collateral damage to the community might be significant. Bryce recalled one of her father's favorite proverbs: "When the water buffalo fight in the marsh, it's the frogs that pay." She'd talk to Frank McBride, she decided. Save the Alameda Chub, or whatever it was called, cattle or no cattle.

She kicked her horse gently forward.

As they rode through a meadow, Earl drifted his horse back to ride alongside Bryce, who was studying the GPS unit again.

"Why do you think the War in Iraq is a good fight," she asked, looking up.

The question seemed to catch Earl by surprise. "I take it you think it's not?"

Bryce shook her head. "I don't. I believe we were lied to from the start."

"I know it looks that way now," Earl responded patiently, "but I still think Saddam was up to something."

"Except nobody can produce any evidence what it was, even five years later."

"I understand that. But I trust the President," Earl said confidently.

"I'm glad somebody still does," she retorted.

They were approaching a small creek. Earl gave the ground a quick look and then steered his horse to the left in order to cross at a less muddy spot.

"Do you really trust this Administration?" Bryce asked after catching up.

"I believe in obeying the law. That means trusting the government, or else things fall apart. That's just plain history."

"Fortunately, Thomas Jefferson and John Adams didn't feel that way."

"John Adams defended British soldiers involved in the Boston Massacre in court, right there in your hometown," Earl countered. "He got six acquitted. Adams called it one of the best pieces of Service he ever did for America."

"And three years later a bunch of liberals threw British tea into Boston Harbor," she countered in turn. "Using their upper body strength, by the way."

"A bunch of radicals, you mean. Dressed as Indians," Earl said, giving her a look.

"Would you have been a Tory or a Rebel?"

"A Rebel, of course," he said firmly. "When a government becomes tyrannical, you have to take corrective action, like Jefferson said."

"And our government isn't tyrannical?"

"No ma'am."

"You obviously haven't been to a protest rally recently."

Earl chuckled. "No ma'am. And I never intend to."

"Well, if you did you'd see an incredible amount of police in riot gear pushing us around. What did the first President Bush call them? Jack-booted thugs?"

"They're just keeping the peace," Earl said casually.

"At a peace rally," she retorted, not hiding the sarcasm. She frowned. "I'm confused, I thought conservatives wanted less government."

"We do."

"And you think that's what you're getting with this Administration?"

"It's better than what either one of the Democrats running for President is proposing," Earl countered. "You think either of them wants less government control?"

"I think they want what's right for anyone who earns a paycheck," she pushed back. "Did you actually vote for the President?"

"Twice," he replied.

"Why? Because he's from Texas?" She smiled at him, shaking her head. "He's an oil-and-gas guy! His party is in bed with Wall Street. They only care about millionaires like themselves. They don't give a damn about ranchers like you."

"I know that."

That surprised her. "Then why did you vote for him?

"Because he wasn't a Democrat," Earl replied. "They care about us even less."

Bryce fell silent, unable to come up with a rejoinder. His point made sense, she had to admit. Democrats had abandoned the rural vote long ago.

"There's something you need to know about Dale," Earl said.

"He served in the First Gulf War and both of his children are serving right now in Iraq. His son is a translator serving a second tour with the Army and his daughter is in the Air Force. Dale doesn't wear his feelings on his sleeve, but he's patriotic."

"I'm patriotic."

"I'm not saying you aren't," Earl said, giving her a look. "But your uncle said things about the war that ruffled a few feathers around here. I think he regretted it."

"Why?"

"Making the ranch work properly was always going to be difficult for him, but he made it harder by sharing his opinions. He needed to be neighborly. I told him that but he didn't listen. A lot of folks around here have served in the military or have kids serving."

"Every protestor I know is supportive of the troops," Bryce said.

"Are they?" Earl asked skeptically. "It doesn't look that way sometimes. Let's just keep in mind we're all Americans. That's the only thing I want to say." He nodded at the dirt road ahead which was narrowing to a trail. "Are we heading in the right direction?"

Bryce raised the GPS unit to her face. She pointed. "No. We need to go that way, uphill and to the west."

Earl headed away from the road. "Let's find that horse."

THEY RODE across a rocky gap in the forest, angling upward, the warm sunlight filling their faces. Bryce pulled alongside Earl.

"Did my uncle seem depressed to you?"

Earl made a face. "Not that I noticed. Why?"

"The French police listed his death as a possible suicide."

"That's the French for you. They think everyone is depressed."

Bryce smiled. She shifted her weight in the saddle. "Did my uncle ever say anything about having epilepsy?"

"Epilepsy? No. Why would he tell me that?"

"He wouldn't, you're right," Bryce said. "It's just that he apparently died from an overdose of epilepsy medication."

Earl squinted at her. "I thought he had a heart attack."

"I did too. We all did. Ironically, if I had known about his epilepsy I might have been able to help him."

"But you're a cancer doctor," Earl protested.

"My husband was a neurologist," Bryce said. She looked away for a moment. "Epilepsy was one of his specialties."

Earl squinted at her. "The other day you said you weren't married. Did he die?"

Bryce smiled wanly. "Not exactly. We divorced. We married in medical school and moved to Boston together, though he took a job at another hospital. That was a mistake. With our hours, doctors probably shouldn't marry each other. We told friends that we had a long-distance relationship across town. Eventually, he met a fundraiser at a charity event."

"A fundraiser?" Earl asked. "Why would he be interested in someone like that?"

"She's nice. And she isn't a protestor."

Earl squinted at her. "You married a conservative, in other words."

"No, he was liberal," she replied. "And a coward. He refused to stand on any principle if it interfered with his career."

"Well, you're wrong about the war," Earl said, "but I'm glad you stood on principle. Not many people do these days."

Bryce nodded. "My uncle didn't seem depressed?"

Earl shook his head. "No ma'am. As I said before, we talked about his plans for the ranch quite a lot. He was going to build a hotel on The Sun."

Bryce blinked at him. "A hotel? Where?" she said, shocked.

"The part near Alameda," Earl replied matter-of-factly. "He said he wanted to tap into all the tourists coming through."

"But what about the chicken wings he flapped?" Bryce protested.

Earl shrugged. "Don't ask me. I think he needed the income. In any case, he showed me the drawings for the whole deal. They're in his office."

"Oh!" Bryce said, suddenly thinking of the pile of architectural drawings. "A *hotel?*" she asked again, not hiding her incredulity.

Earl smiled. "He was excited."

"He was?" Bryce exhaled audibly.

"Ideals have a way of getting a reality check out here, Miss Miller," he said. "As they should. Come on."

THEY STOOD next to their horses on the crest of a ridge with an amazing view of the mountains above and below. Bryce had a pair of binoculars glued to her face.

"She should be close," Bryce said.

Earl pointed down the slope. "Look down there. Abe said he saw her in the bottom of the canyon."

"What is she even doing here?" Bryce asked as she tilted the glasses downward, scanning the canyon below. All she could see were dense trees.

"I think whoever rode Brunhilda was trying to hide her."

"Why would they do that?"

"To frame the Mexican," Earl replied. "Estevan, I mean."

Bryce gave him a sideways look from behind the binoculars. "Frame him for killing Matt? So, you think whoever killed him tried to make it look like Estevan drove off with Brunhilda in his truck?"

"Yes I do. Keep looking," he said, nodding at the canyon.

Bryce resumed her search. "But who would do something like that?"

"You know what I think," Earl said matter-of-factly.

Bryce turned her face to him again. "Stanley Richards? You think he'd do something like that?"

"Yes, I do," Earl said, using his ominous voice.

"To keep Matt from talking to me or to get his hands on The Sun?"

"Both maybe. Keep searching." He nodded again.

Bryce turned her face back to the glasses, but paused to think. She turned to Earl sharply. "If your theory is correct, what does this mean for Estevan?"

Earl shifted slightly in the saddle, as if uncomfortable. "Not good, I think."

"Maybe he just ran away," Bryce said, "and someone took the opportunity to frame him."

"I hope so. But I doubt it." Earl said somberly. He nodded at the canyon. "Let's find that horse."

Bryce returned the binoculars to her face. She now focused on a small opening in the woods she saw earlier. "I see something!" Bryce announced. "It's a part of a horse."

Earl frowned. "Which part?"

"The rear part. There's a tree blocking the view. She's alive! It just swished its tail! She's lying on the ground."

Earl turned to her sharply. "Lying on the ground?"

"She's on her right side."

"That's not good! Let's go!"

As they reached the small opening in the forest, they jumped off their horses. A short distance away, Bryce saw a horse lying on her side, a saddle on her back, not moving. Earl hurried forward.

"Tie their reins to a tree," he ordered. "Dear God."

She did as she was told and ran after Earl. Brunhilda was a beautiful shade of light brown with a small white blaze on her face, Bryce could see as she approached. Then she saw the blood. Brunhilda was on the ground because she had been hobbled and fell down at some point. A leather strap formed a figure-eight around her front feet before stretching back to her left rear foot. Attached to the strap were three black loops, each enclosing one of her feet. They had rubbed horribly and blood covered her hooves. The contraption looked ghastly and medieval, raising a deep anger in Bryce. There was more blood on Brunhilda's head too. Whoever had abandoned her didn't bother to remove her bridle and blood flowed from the front and sides of her muzzle, looking like the bit tore up her mouth from inside.

"What's happened to her?" she cried.

"Someone left her to die," Earl replied angrily.

At the sound of their approaching voices, the horse lifted her head and suddenly tried to rise to her feet, kicking out with her one free leg, while emitting a high, distressful whine that broke Bryce's heart. She began to rock violently, thrashing in the pine duff and dirt.

"Try to hold her down!" Earl ordered as he moved behind her to the left. "One of her legs might be broken and we don't want her getting up. I'm going to get the bridle off her!"

Bryce rushed to the right, aiming to get around Brunhilda's bucking rump and wildly kicking free leg. Earl fell to his knees behind her head, placing one hand firmly on the saddle and the other on the side of her head, pressing down gently as she thrashed.

"Whoa, girl," he said in a calming voice. "Whoa there."

Bryce could see bloody welts up and down the back of Brunhilda's immobilized leg. "What are those?" she cried, pointing.

"Coyotes tried to get her," he replied. "She's been down for a while."

Bryce fell to her knees behind Brunhilda's back, next to Earl, and immediately put her hands on the animal's rump, which kept bucking as she tried desperately to get up. The horse continued to make a horrid, high-pitched cry.

"Hold the saddle!" Earl ordered. "Don't let her get up!"

Bryce threw her weight sideways on the saddle, trying to keep Brunhilda down. She spread her arms across the horse's belly and flank while turning her head to watch Earl. "Sssh! Sssh!" she kept chanting. He unbuckled a thin leather strap under Brunhilda's neck and then deftly pushed the top strap of the bridle over her ears. A moment later, the bridle landed on the ground, covered in blood. The horse grunted and surged upward.

"Hold on!" Earl yelled as he grabbed her head.

Bryce closed her eyes, concentrating on maintaining contact with the saddle, whose side was digging into her ribs. "Sssh! Sssh!" Brunhilda collapsed onto her side again and for a moment Bryce feared her momentum would cause the horse to roll onto her back. She pressed down. A squeal filled the air and Bryce was aware of legs thrashing on either side of her head as Brunhilda sank into full panic.

"We need to cover her eyes!" she heard Earl yell from somewhere to her right.

Without thinking, Bryce slipped off her vest as fast as possible and tossed it to Earl. He caught it with one hand and a moment later draped it over the horse's face. He continued to press gently on her neck and head with his hands.

The horse convulsed and squealed, but a moment later Bryce could feel the fight begin to drain from her body. "Sssh! Sssh!" Bryce repeated, still sensing the animal's fear and pain. She tried to will calmness into the horse through her hands and arms. It seemed to work. Gradually, Brunhilda calmed down, though her sides continued to heave.

Earl released her head and stood up.

"I'm going to remove the back hobble," she heard Earl say. "Keep holding her. When it's free, she's going to try to stand again."

Brunhilda's sides continued to rise and fall heavily, reminding Bryce of the regular rhythm of ocean swells. Bryce lifted her head to watch Earl as he carefully bent over Brunhilda's lower back leg. He worked quickly and before she knew it, he stood up stiffly and stepped back.

"It's free," he said simply.

Brunhilda didn't react, other than to stretch her hobbled leg out awkwardly and lift her head off the ground, the vest still sitting placidly over her face. Bryce decided to shift her body slightly toward Brunhilda's head, moving her knees one step and stretching her right hand out along the horse's neck, smoothing it reassuringly. "Sssh! Sssh!" she said over and over until the horse lowered its head slowly back to the ground.

"Good. Stay there, I'm going to go get something," Earl instructed.

He turned his back and began walking toward their horses, which remained tethered to the tree. Brunhilda seemed to relax a bit, so Bryce decided to study her wounds, lifting her torso slightly while keeping her hands in place. The horse's mouth didn't appear to be actively bleeding but her ankles and lower forelegs were raw and bloody. She had been out here for days. Who would do such a cruel thing to a horse? Bryce lifted her body slightly higher to peer at the coyote bites on the back of her flanks. They were actively bleeding as well. It must have been terrifying for Brunhilda, lying on the ground, immobilized, pain shooting through her mouth and legs, trying to stop stealthy predators from tearing her up.

Bryce lowered herself back down. "Sssh. Sssh," she said soothingly to the miserable animal. Matt's killer brought her here to die in misery. Who could be so soulless? A cold-blooded murderer could, she supposed – but one that knew how to saddle and ride a horse. Hobble one too, she thought, though it was almost impossible to imagine anyone who grew up with horses doing something this cruel. Could it have been a city person instead? She saw Earl returning, limping slightly. He carried a leather halter attached to a green rope. As he approached Brunhilda's head, she became restless again, apparently hearing his footsteps. She began to strain against Bryce's attempts to keep her calm. "Sssh! Sssh!"

"Put these on," Earl instructed.

He handed her a pair of yellow leather work gloves as he knelt down in front of the horse. She released contact with Brunhilda as she put the gloves on quickly, feeling a little bit like she was back in the hospital. Earl pushed the vest away from the horse's face and slipped the halter around her head with practiced ease before she could react. He quickly buckled a thin black strap under her chin although she kicked her head up once in a feeble protest.

"What do you want me to do?" Bryce asked.

"Hold this," he replied, thrusting the end of the green rope toward her. "Hold it tight with both hands. When I remove the hobbles, she'll probably try to run. Whatever you do," he warned, "do not let her get away. Stay there until I say so. I'm going to check her legs."

Bryce nodded and took hold of the rope firmly with a hand. Earl replaced the vest over Brunhilda's eye before standing up. He came around behind Bryce. He studied the coyote bites on her back legs briefly. He circled around her back legs, frowning like an appraiser at an auction who didn't approve of what he saw, it seemed to Bryce. He stopped at her front legs, scowling now.

"I don't think anything's broken," he announced. "Which means she might try to run. Go ahead and get up."

Bryce rose to a standing position. As Earl bent over the hobbles, Bryce stepped quietly in front of the horse, holding the rope with both hands

"Get ready!" he warned.

Earl did something to the hobbles and suddenly the horse was lunging onto its front feet with a deep grunting sound. Then it squealed in pain. She threw her head up.

"Hold on!" Earl yelled. "If she gets away she'll die on the mountain!"

Bryce held on. Brunhilda tried to charge toward the small clearing in the forest to her left, but shrieked in pain as her front legs suddenly buckled. She tipped toward the ground, but didn't fall. Bryce tracked her actions, trying to keep slack in the rope by staying in front of Brunhilda's head. The horse stumbled forward. Bryce seized the opportunity to take up the extra slack in the rope by wrapping its end around her lower hand, creating a much stronger grip. Just in case.

"Easy girl!" she said. "Easy."

Brunhilda recovered from her initial shock and suddenly made a determined attempt to get away. She backed up this time, leaning heavily on her one good leg. She jerked her head violently, but Bryce held on, hopping once across the ground.

"Hold her!" Earl yelled.

"Easy girl," Bryce repeated. "Stay here."

Brunhilda tried again. She turned sideways and tried to pull Bryce off balance, but she was able to absorb the horse's tug. Almost. She was forced to hop forward again. Brunhilda shifted her weight, still making a terrible sound.

"She's going to give you a big pull," Earl warned.

Bryce was ready. Or so she thought. Brunhilda reared up partially, pitching Bryce forward suddenly. She lost her balance. Her athletic instincts kicked in. As she began to fall, she pushed with her forward foot and twisted slightly, which caused her to turn in the air and land on her butt, exactly as she hoped. Her arms were pulled over her head by the horse, but she held the rope. Now she was being dragged forward on her back. She closed her eyes and dug her heels into the dirt, making as much dead weight friction as possible. Her grip held. She knew about ropes from sailing, how they felt in her hands, what they could do, even if this was attached to a terrified two-thousand pound animal. She was pulled across the ground, foot by foot. Something struck her head. She twisted her body slightly to avoid it. And she held on.

An eternity later, she stopped moving.

She could hear Brunhilda's heavy breathing – but not the whine of pain and fear anymore. She opened her eyes and turned her head. The horse had given up the fight. Her head drooped nearly to the ground. She looked exhausted, starved and in pain.

"Good job!" Earl said admiringly somewhere to her right.

A moment later, he walked into view and grabbed the halter. He looked at Bryce on the ground. "I take back what I said about liberals and upper body strength."

Bryce wanted to laugh. "Is she alright?" she asked instead.

"No. But she won't run now."

Bryce rolled over and sat up, still clutching the rope. Her arms were sore, her butt hurt and she was probably bleeding from wherever the rock or stick had hit her on the head. She felt great. Brunhilda looked awful, however. Earl bent over to inspect the bloody gashes on her forelegs, which had been rubbed raw by the hobbles.

Bryce struggled to her feet. "Did they really mean for her to die up here?"

"Absolutely," Earl replied. He attempted to stroke Brunhilda's cheek gently, but she pulled away. Bryce came forward, holding the end of the rope out for him.

"How could someone be so cruel?" Bryce said, extending her hand toward the horse. To her surprise, Brunhilda let her stroke her cheek.

"You'll have to ask Dale," Earl replied, taking the rope from her. "He's the expert in these things. But don't underestimate what people will do to get what they want."

"Stanley Richards?" Bryce asked quietly.

Earl didn't reply. Instead he reached out and patted the horse's neck reassuringly. "Come on, let's get her back to where she belongs."

———

THERE WAS a small crowd waiting for them behind Alameda's medical clinic. Apparently, word of their discovery had spread.

Pulling into the parking lot, she spied Dale, hands on his hips, standing next to Deputy Sandoval near the clinic door. There was a second Deputy with them that she didn't recognize. He wore the same gray uniform and stony expression, but he was taller than Sandoval and apparently Anglo, though she didn't want to presume. Doctor Thomas stood nearby with a young woman that she supposed was one of the clinic's nurses. Meili's arms were filled with the medical supplies that Bryce had requested, including bandages and anti-infection agents. After unsaddling Brunhilda at the trailhead and loading her into the horse trailer, Earl asked Bryce to dial Doctor Franklin, a veterinarian and old friend of his, as soon as they reached cell range. Franklin was the last large animal vet in the valley, he told her, and had planned to retire five years ago but couldn't because there was no one to replace him. When he didn't answer his phone, however, Bryce called Meili and together they devised an emergency plan of treatment for Brunhilda, who had limped and bled all the way back to the trailer. Every stumble broke Bryce's heart.

She scanned the rest of the small crowd as they came to a stop. Many were strangers though Bryce recognized Isaac Vigil standing near Dale, his arms folded across his chest. She also saw Isabella Ortiz, the woman who had confronted the environmentalists in the town hall the other day. She was talking to a heavy-set man with a smooth face who gave Bryce the impression of being a politician. She also recognized a few faces from the big meeting in the Mayor's office on Tuesday, including the friendly old guy from the veteran's lodge. Three people stood behind the main group, back toward the street. One was a stranger in sunglasses, the second was Reverend Pendergast, a head taller than anyone else, and the third was Frank McBride, looking glum. As their eyes met briefly, Frank raised his hand and gave Bryce a little wave. What was up with him, she thought? Conspicuously missing was the Mayor, Bryce noticed, though her young receptionist stood in the crowd. Next to her was a bearded, roundish man wearing a blue T-shirt emblazoned with the grinning mug of Homer Simpson. To her surprise, she glimpsed the casino guy, Rack, in the back of the crowd, looking as chilly as before. No Doreen. No Bill Merrill. No Mister Nibble.

As soon as Earl shut off the engine, he climbed out of the truck. "Did you reach Doctor Franklin?" he said loudly to Dale, who had come forward.

"I did," he replied. "He was out at the Catanach place tending a sick bull. He's on his way in."

"Good," Earl replied tersely. "Let's get her out."

He moved swiftly toward the back of the trailer, Bryce climbed out and paralleled him on the other side. She peered into the trailer at Brunhilda, wondering how horses could tolerate such cramped quarters. Her head was up. She wanted out. As Bryce reached the corner, she practically bumped into Earl, who was lifting the drop bar. A second later, the large door swung open with a loud creak having been given a big push by an impatient Earl. The door was caught by Isaac Vigil before it could crash into the trailer's side. Dale appeared next to him, looking agitated. For good reason, Bryce thought.

Earl stepped smartly into the trailer. "Watch her rear end as she steps out, Doctor Miller," he instructed.

He untied the horse quickly. As she began to back up, Bryce studied the deep welts on her back legs, which were still bleeding. Earl said the coyotes had attacked that morning, likely after Brunhilda had fallen. She wouldn't have lasted the day, he told her, if Abelard hadn't found her.

"Whoa girl," she heard him say.

Brunhilda tensed as the edge of the trailer approached, favoring the formerly hobbled leg by lifting it, causing her to hop. She sensed the edge and refused to go any further.

"Come on girl," Earl said soothingly.

Meili appeared, her face filled with concern. Bryce pointed at the welts, which sent a shot of shock through the young doctor.

Brunhilda stepped backwards into the air. She landed awkwardly, squealing briefly as pain coursed through her legs. She paused, half-in and half-out of the trailer. Earl was silent, apparently waiting for her to recover. The small crowd had come closer. Brunhilda took a sudden backwards hop and was free of the trailer. Earl followed closely, tightly holding the green rope up near the halter. The horse didn't make any more sounds, though she limped badly on her front legs and was breathing heavily. Bryce heard a few gasps from the crowd, followed by scattered clapping as Earl turned Brunhilda around. She really was a magnificent animal – and now she was safe.

"Ok," Earl said simply to them.

Bryce and Meili went to work. For the next twenty minutes, they cleaned and bandaged the horse's many wounds, working diligently and efficiently even though Bryce hadn't tended to injuries like these in years. She followed Meili's lead, holding the bandages for her and applying the anti-infection agents where directed, wound by wound. Some would need stitches, Bryce thought. Brunhilda's legs would need x-rays. Nothing appeared to be broken, but she was no expert by a long shot. The closest she ever came to a vet class was a lecture she attended by a medical researcher specializing in equine cancers. Nobody in twelve years of schooling had taught her how to treat a coyote bite. Brunhilda lifted a right front leg as they worked, obviously in distress. The damage to her tendons and muscles was unknown but possibly extensive. Would she ever gallop in a rodeo again, Bryce wondered?

As they neared the end of their work, Bryce became aware of the murmur of men's voices. Earl and Dale were conferring and behind them Isaac was speaking with animation to the heavy-set man. Was he possibly Abelard? No, Earl had called him a "funny little guy." The rest of the crowd appeared to be listening to Earl, who had raised his voice, sounding agitated. She returned her attention to the bandage she had been inspecting, but she could clearly hear snippets of Earl's diatribe, including the words *Matt, canyon*, *Diamond Bar, Richards*, and *investigate*. He was sharing his theory, she realized. The crowd could hear it too, she was certain. Peeking over her shoulder, Bryce saw Dale nod patiently and then say something in a low voice that she couldn't hear. Suddenly, she realized the men were all looking at her. Earl pointed.

Apparently, he was explaining her role in preventing Brunhilda's attempted escape. Heads nodded. Upper body strength, right.

Bryce returned her attention to the horse. Meili was deftly wrapping a final bandage around the rear leg that had been bound by the hobble. The bleeding had stopped, which was a relief. Brunhilda had accepted the sting of the medications and the fuss of the bandages well, only lifting a foot twice in objection. The resilience of animals was remarkable. She went once with her mother to an animal hospital for a fat cat emergency (a false alarm as it turned out) where she witnessed a vet crew in the parking lot unloading a golden retriever strapped to a medical stretcher. The animal had suffered a terrible accident, possibly a collision with a car. As the dog was carried up the stairs of the hospital, it spied its owner, who was in tears, and wagged its tail.

Bryce stood up. The murmuring of men ceased.

"What's the prognosis?" Earl asked.

"The bleeding's stopped," Meili responded, standing up as well. "A few of the wounds might be infected, but not terribly. I'm worried about her tendons, though. They appear to be damaged. When will Doctor Franklin arrive?"

"In about twenty minutes," Earl replied. "He's got a portable x-ray scanner with him. That means we'll know pretty quick if she needs to go to the hospital."

"Where would that be?" Bryce asked.

"Dunraven," Earl replied. "I assume that's what you want? Brunhilda belongs to you, don't forget."

She had forgotten. "Of course," Bryce answered. "She's being incredibly brave."

"Yes, she is," Earl said, patting the horse on the neck.

Bryce caught a nod from Dale. He wanted to talk privately.

"Are we good?" Bryce asked Meili.

"Yes, thank you for your help," she replied. "I don't think there's anything else we can do right now."

Bryce gave her a hug, needing one herself. "Thank you."

She and Dale stepped out of earshot of the crowd. The heavy-set man and Isaac Vigil maintained their energetic conversation, Bryce noticed, looking now like an argument.

"Do you know who did this?" Bryce asked, getting right to the point.

"Not yet," Dale replied. "I've got a tracker coming in from Taos who'll go to where you found the horse to look around for evidence."

"Where do you think Estevan is?"

Dale grimaced. "Earl thinks he's dead. Killed by whoever rode Brunhilda into the mountains, but I'm going to hope for the best. Let's keep our fingers crossed."

"Someone tried to frame him?" she asked.

"It looks that way," Dale conceded. "But until we find him, we can't say for certain. Otherwise, we're taking guesses."

"And Stanley Richards?" she asked, still focused. "Are you going to question him?"

"About what?" he retorted. "Earl's conspiracy theory? I don't think so. I'll need a lot more evidence before I can even think about approaching him."

"He leaves on Sunday."

"I know that."

Bryce sighed. "What about this Abelard character?"

"Abe?" Dale shook his head. "I've asked him to come in, but he's not a suspect. He didn't have to call Earl about the horse, after all." He put hands on his hips. "You know, it might not be Richards," he said simply.

"Who then?" she said impatiently.

Dale glanced around quickly and then lowered his voice. "I spoke this morning with the French detective who investigated your uncle's death at the winery. His English wasn't great, but it made it clear he has doubts it was suicide despite what the official report said."

"Why does he think that?"

"There wasn't a note or any indication that your uncle planned to kill himself," Dale said. "And his hosts at the winery insisted he was happy right up to the time of his death, though maybe "happy" is a relative term with the French." He shrugged. "Anyway, there were no obvious signs that he was depressed. I left another message for your uncle's doctor, Tadesh, but he hasn't called me back. Is that something you can look into?"

Bryce thought for a moment. "I might be able to pull strings. What?" She could read anxiety on his face. There was more.

Dale took a deep breath. "I asked the FBI to run a search on your uncle and his name came up in connection with an ongoing securities fraud investigation they're conducting in New York."

"New York? What sort of investigation?"

"They wouldn't tell me any details, but I got the sense it has something to do with an investment bank on Wall Street. A real estate company too. Probably part of this nonsense going in the market. Does any of this ring a bell?"

Bryce shook her head. "No. Was he involved in something shady?"

"They wouldn't tell me," Dale replied, "even though I asked five different people. I've got another lead I can try."

It was Bryce's turn to glance around. "Are you suggesting my uncle was murdered?"

"It's a possibility, don't you think?" he said quietly. "If your uncle didn't commit suicide, then why did he have so much Phenobarbital in his stomach? It wasn't an accident, I'll bet. Just think about it. I've got to get back to this." He nodded at the scene behind them and then signaled to the two deputies, requesting their presence. "If I find out something more I'll let you know. But keep this under your hat for the time being."

"Wait!" Bryce raised her hand to catch his attention. "You think Matt found out something about this investigation? Is that why he wanted to talk to me?"

He nodded thoughtfully. "Possibly."

"That would link his murder to my uncle's death," she said.

Dale nodded again but before he could say anything else the two deputies arrived, looking stone-faced. "You know Deputy Sandoval," Dale said to Bryce. He nodded to her once. "This is Deputy Midas. Kurt Midas."

Bryce smiled at the young man, but to her surprise he didn't smile or nod back. In fact, he seemed to glower at her. Maybe she was just overreacting, she thought.

Dale handed her a business card. "I realized this morning that you didn't have all our contact info. If you feel threatened in any way by anybody, call us. We'll be right out."

"Thanks," Bryce said, taking it.

Dale waved to Isaac, who had come forward. He carried a set of keys in his hand.

"*Buenos tardes*," he said. "I'm very sorry about your horse. She's a beautiful animal. Here are your keys."

"Thank you," she said, taking them from his hand.

"No, thank you for letting me work at the house. It's a lovely place. And I didn't take any wine," Isaac said with a smile.

"If you don't drink it, I will," she said wearily, causing them to chuckle. "How much do I owe you?"

He waved a hand dismissively. "*Nada*. It's the least we can do."

"Thank you," Bryce replied. "I appreciate everyone's help."

They nodded and began to move away, but Dale only made it a few steps before he turned around sharply and came back to her, snapping a finger.

"I forgot. Mister Nibble called me," he said, then corrected himself. "I meant Mister Malcolm, of course. He wanted me to give you a message. Call your lawyer?" Dale frowned. "Mean anything? He said it was urgent."

Bryce sighed.

"They've probably sent Jeffrey the paperwork for the sale of the ranch," she said. "I'm supposed to call him and authorize it."

"Have you decided then?" When Bryce didn't respond, Dale nodded at the card in her hand. "Call us if you need to."

He moved off. Bryce sighed. Jeffrey. Maybe he was on vacation, she hoped, though she doubted it. He never went on vacation. She plucked her phone from the vest pocket, tapped in the code and began scrolling through her messages. There were two voicemails from Jeffrey Bayer, New York City. She studied the words "Call Back" for a moment. Someone cleared their throat. Bryce looked up in alarm.

It was Frank McBride.

"I don't mean to interrupt," he said. "I know you're busy. I'm sorry about Brunhilda. Is she going to be ok?"

"Yes, I think so," Bryce replied, glancing over at the horse. "I'm glad you're here. I wanted to talk to you about The Sun," she said eagerly.

"Yes, about that." He came closer, looking doubly glum, she thought. A small knot of dread formed in her stomach. "I've been ordered to pass along a message," he said with a grimace. "From my boss. Actually, it came from his boss."

"What message?"

"About our offer for The Sun." Frank paused. "It's been pulled."

"Pulled? Why?" she said, not disguising her disappointment.

"Because they're cowards," he spat out. "Our Board learned about your visit from Richards this morning. Two of them essentially work for the bastard and three others are mortified that he'll buy their companies or crush them under the heel of his leather loafers, which is probably true." He shrugged wearily. "It's what we get for putting Wall Street CEOs on our Board. I bet Teddy Roosevelt is spinning in his grave. Aldo Leopold too."

"Who?"

"It doesn't matter. There's no more offer, I'm sorry."

"I'm sorry too," Bryce said. "Richards is demanding the ranch. I was hoping you might still be an option."

Frank began to say something, but stopped.

"What about the Alameda chub?' she tried.

"I guess it will have to figure out a way to survive on its own," he replied with a sigh. "Pretty much like everything these days."

"Do you have any idea what Richards wants the ranch for?"

He shook his head. "No."

"So, what should I do?" she asked plaintively.

"I don't know. I'm sorry." He spun on his heel suddenly and walked away, sticking his hands into his pockets. Bryce thought about calling after him, but her phone started buzzing in her hand. *Now what?* Looking down, she saw it was Jeffrey! She scrunched her eyes closed for a moment in exasperation before lifting the phone up. She stared at his name. The sale agreement was waiting. All she had to do was give him the green light and this craziness would go away. Just a tap and she could go home.

She tapped.

"Jeffrey?" she said into the phone. "It's Bryce. Sorry I've been scarce. You wouldn't believe what's been happening out here. Well, you might actually. You've received a fax from Stanley Richards' office, right? About The Sun? Yes, but we can talk about that later. Right now, I need your help with a file. A medical file. About my uncle."

She began walking back toward Earl and Brunhilda.

Bryce beeped her car open.

It was late in the afternoon and she was relieved to be going back to the ranch at last. Earl had offered her a ride to the town hall, where she had parked the rental, but she declined, preferring to walk despite the soreness she felt everywhere. It also gave her a chance to clear her mind of the day's events and calm her nerves, though a warm shower would help most of all. Bryce opened the car's door and plopped heavily into the driver's seat. The rest of the afternoon had gone well. Doctor Franklin, a gruff older man with wire-rim glasses, examined Brunhilda for nearly an hour, finding nothing broken or badly torn. The horse just needed a lot of healing. Earl volunteered to take her back to his ranch. He'd put her in with his mares which would help psychologically since horses prefer to be together, he said.

Bryce pulled the car's door closed, trying to recall the quickest path back to The Sun. She was pretty sure that if she headed east she'd intercept the main road through town. A left turn would place her on Highway 70 and take her back to the ranch. She could be in the shower at her uncle's house in twenty minutes. The house. Uneasiness crept back into her suddenly. She felt in her vest pocket for the new keys that Isaac had made, reassured by their steely edges that no one had entered since he finished. Seymour! She couldn't wait to see his happy face.

Bryce inserted the keys into the ignition – and froze.

There was a white sheet of paper tucked under a windshield wiper. Bryce could read the three handwritten words plainly – because they had been placed face down on the glass for her to see. GO HOME NOW it said in the same style as before. Bryce opened the door quickly, stepped out, and grabbed the sheet. There were no other words. She balled it up in anger and exhaustion. She plopped back down in the car seat and tossed the ball into the passenger well, where it rolled around for a moment before coming to rest on the floor. She stared straight ahead until a truck passed by her door noisily, causing her to jump. Her heart was beating fast. This was crazy. She reached for the key again, turning it smartly and relieved to hear the engine purr to life. She checked the side-view mirror to make sure the traffic was clear before glancing into the rear-view mirror. She froze again.

She opened the door quickly and climbed out. It took three long strides to reach the end of the car. She turned, her heart pounding now, though whether more with anger or fear she wasn't sure. A single word had been etched into the ranch dust that covered the back window of the car by someone's finger, like a high school prank. Except his was no prank.

BITCH, it said.

Bryce pulled a sleeve down over her hand and angrily wiped the word away forever. She turned sharply to survey the street around her – was someone watching? The sidewalks were empty. A car passed through the intersection behind her and a large truck ground its gears a block away, but that was all. She scanned the buildings, but no one was peering back at her. In fact, the whole scene was disquietingly peaceful. Bryce exhaled, unable to shake the feeling that someone was watching. Should she call Dale? What would she tell him? That a grumpy local wanted her to go home? *She wanted to go home!* No, she wasn't in the mood for another fuss. She had new keys and new locks, she'd hurry back to the ranch. She walked back to the driver's side, opened the door and plopped into the seat again. The engine still purred. She pulled the seatbelt across her body while carefully surveying the terrain surrounding her.

All clear.

She pulled away from the curb, turned left at the intersection and then right at the next one, even though it took her away from the road that led to The Sun. She did a couple of figure eights around downtown, in fact, each larger than the last, keeping an eye out all the while for any suspicious vehicle following her. Nothing happened – except she ran a stop sign accidently. A ticket would be fine. She'd be happy to see a policeman. But none appeared, so she turned onto the main road that led north out of town and stepped on the accelerator, determined to get as far away from prying eyes in town as possible. A large SUV blasted past her going in the opposite direction, surprising her. She needed to pay attention to the road. As he approached the Alameda High School on her right, Bryce eased up on the gas pedal. A short while later, she saw the attractive little yellow signs with a black sun that her uncle had placed on the fence to indicate the boundary for the ranch. Ever the marketer, he was. Where had he planned to put the hotel, she wondered? On the property near here or on the south side of town someplace? *A hotel?* What was he thinking?

She heard a whine behind her.

In the rear-view mirror, she saw a man on a motorcycle – she assumed it was a man – riding her bumper. He was dressed in black with an impenetrably black visor in his helmet. Where had he come from? He revved the motorcycle's engine, wanting to pass apparently. Bryce scanned the road ahead. It was straight for a short stretch before dipping out-of-sight, probably to cross a creek. The rider revved the engine again, sounding impatient. Bryce slowed the car as the dip approached. It looked wide enough to accommodate a speedy motorcycle, she thought, as long as there was no oncoming traffic. Pretty straightforward. Still, something about the rider and the revving unnerved her, so she silently prayed for a clear road. As the dip approached, the rider began to sashay back-and-forth behind her, ready to go. Finally, the road tipped downward – revealing a semi-truck coming down the other side perfectly timed to prevent the obnoxious motorcyclist from blasting past her and disappearing into the haze. He revved his engine again. Bryce considered pulling over, but there wasn't an obvious spot to do so. She decided to wait.

She reached a narrow bridge over a creek at the same time as the semi-truck did. No room for error, she thought to herself as the big vehicle blasted past, going faster than she expected, rocking the car. She caught a glimpse of water under the bridge, reflecting the sky. When she looked up, she saw enough empty road ahead to tempt a motorcyclist, if he wanted to try. He didn't. He sat on her tail, revving and sashaying, though less impatiently, it seemed to her. It felt more like goading now. Fear seeped into her bones. She eased up on the accelerator, slowing the car and sending the rider behind her a clear message: go around now! He didn't go. Now it was too late. The top of the drainage beckoned. Once on top, there wouldn't be an excuse. She was pretty sure the road stretched out flatly for a decent distance. Fine. She stepped on the gas, determined to reach the crest as quickly as possible. The motorcycle faded for a moment – then came roaring back, hard on her bumper, the black visor menacing in the mirror.

The fear spread.

She reached the crest in time to see another car approaching. Honestly! It was another SUV and it seemed to take forever to arrive. Bryce fixed her attention on the road, which was clear and straight to the horizon – once the abominable SUV passed. The motorcycle's engine revved loudly behind her. Finally, the SUV swooshed by. More tourists, it looked like. Bryce concentrated on the road, trying to ignore the fear that had snuck into her bones. *Come on, come on* she said to herself. *Go.*

He went. In a blaze of noise and speed, the motorcycle rider swept around her and gunned down the highway as if it were a racetrack. Bryce couldn't help marveling at his speed, recalling an absolutely crazy motorcyclist she met years ago in Costa Rica who had been sent to fetch her at the beach for a short ride into the village so she could purchase more beer. It was the most harrowing ride she had ever taken. He went eighty, at least, down potholed dirt roads and across the remnants of cracked asphalt like he did it every day – which he no doubt did. Bryce liked speed and considered herself to be no slouch in the thrill-seeking department, but this time she had to close her eyes and pray that by some miracle they would survive.

The black-visored motorcyclist had disappeared. She exhaled. Yellow ranch signs still flicked past on the fence to her right. Beyond them, boundless grasslands. A moment later, the road bent lazily to the left and began to rise. Bryce frowned. She didn't recall this turn. She thought the road was a straight shot to the ranch entrance. Of course, she had a lot of things on her mind on the various drives back-and-forth to town. She hadn't even noticed the high school the first time she approached Alameda! Another semi-truck appeared on the road and then roared past, hitting the rental with a small concussive blast of air and rattling her nerves. Bryce eased up on the accelerator again, trying to calm down. Somewhere up ahead on the left was the entrance road to the Diamond Bar, she recalled, looking freshly paved and flanked by two large 'Private Property – No Entry Allowed' signs. How had Matt found the courage to trespass? Why did he do it? Had he seen the solitary white light as well?

Bryce froze in mid-thought.

She saw the motorcyclist. He had pulled into a road turnout and climbed off the bike. He stood near a barbed-wire fence with his back turned, urinating. As Bryce passed him, fear flooded back in. She recognized him! He had the same body shape as the man in the crowd behind the medical clinic, the one wearing sunglasses and standing off to the side. Was that a coincidence? Bryce decided she didn't need to find out.

She stepped hard on the gas.

The car made a whining sound, objecting to the extra exertion. It reluctantly kicked into passing gear. Bryce kept pressing, scanning the rear-view mirror as she did. How many miles was it to the ranch entrance? Too many. Another semi-truck appeared on the road, this time in her lane. Could she make it around him in time? She pressed the accelerator to the floor while edging into the other lane in order to see around the truck. The road disappeared, bending to the right. No! She swiftly came up behind the semi-truck, braking hard at the last moment, cursing silently. A yellow 'No Passing' sign flicked by on her right suddenly. She studied the road behind her, waiting.

He came.

He shot up behind her like a torpedo, pulling up only inches from her bumper. Her first instinct was to hit the brakes hard and see what happened. Instead, she decided to stay behind the semi-truck for the moment. Maybe the cyclist would blast by her when the road straightened out again. The entrance to the Diamond Bar suddenly flashed past on her left. How far was it to The Sun's gate from here? The motorcyclist pulled even closer to her bumper and revved the engine angrily, scaring her. Keeping her eyes on the truck, she reached into her vest pocket and pulled out the phone. A quick glance told her what she suspected – there was no signal at all. Maybe he didn't know that, however. She lifted the phone to her ear, turned her head slightly to create a profile and moved her jaw, pretending to talk. It didn't work. The black visor just glared back at her in the mirror. He revved his engine again. Bryce saw a *Pass With Care* sign go by on the right shoulder of the road. She dropped the phone into the passenger seat and gripped the wheel with both hands. If he didn't pass her, she'd pass the truck.

He didn't move from her bumper. Bryce counted to ten. Nothing. She drifted into the left lane, peering around the truck. Clear. She slammed the gas pedal to the floor. The car lurched into its passing gear. It inched its way forward, finally clearing the truck. She quickly drifted back into her lane just ahead of the semi-truck, deliberately matching its speed, leaving no room for a motorcycle to squeeze in between them. The road ahead was still clear. She waited. The motorcyclist suddenly pulled around the truck and charged forward. He slowed as he approached her bumper, as if gauging the risk of trying to get in behind her. She eased up on the accelerator a bit, praying the driver of the semi-truck wouldn't blast her with his horn in irritation. The rider pulled even with her. Maybe it was all just a huge misunderstanding, she thought to herself.

He turned his head toward her – and gave her the finger.

Fear spread all through her body. She stared straight ahead, pressing the gas pedal just enough to stay ahead of the semi-truck. The motorcyclist zoomed off suddenly in a blaze of speed. What was going on? Why was she being harassed like this? What had she done wrong? She stayed safely in front of the truck until the ranch entrance gate appeared. At the last moment, she braked and turned sharply to her right, surveying the highway ahead. No motorcyclist. Passing through the gate, she looked around quickly on both sides of the fence. Nothing. She caught a glimpse of the sensor on the gate and the two surveillance cameras up above, pointing in opposite directions. She looked down the road toward her uncle's house, sitting quietly on its hill. No dust plume was visible, even a small one.

She breathed again.

AT THE HOUSE, Bryce climbed out of the car and waved to Seymour, who wagged vigorously at the top of the porch stairs. Was she relieved to see him! She climbed the steps quickly and scratched his ears. She pulled out the new keys, unlocked and opened the door, embracing the stuffy air inside the house, which smelled like new furniture and old art. Inside, Seymour did a quick snuffle through the kitchen, caught a scent and followed it to the guest bedroom. Rodents again, Bryce thought balefully. She didn't want to think about it. She had just one thing on her mind now. Wine. After locking the front door behind her, she strode across the living room. As she slipped into the stairwell leading to the cellar, she pulled out the keys again. At the bottom, she tested the door – locked. Good. She inserted the new key, turned it, and pushed the door open. She flicked the light on, crossed directly to the nearest wine rack, grabbed a bottle randomly by the neck, turned, and headed back upstairs without bothering to close the cellar door.

She'd do it later, she promised herself.

She slapped a clean wine glass onto the top of the kitchen island and lifted up a fancy cork removal contraption that she found in a drawer the other day. A moment later she pulled the cork free, creating a small 'pop' that caught Seymour's attention as he came back into the kitchen.

"Cheers!" she said to him before draining the glass in one gulp.

She took a deep breath when she was done. "That wasn't bad," she said to the dog, which had drifted over to the glass door to look outside. She lifted the bottle up to her face and peered at its label. "*Chateau Volpone*. Never heard of it." She shrugged.

Seymour whined at the door, wanting to go out. Clutching the empty wine glass, Bryce crossed the floor and opened the sliding door for the animal. He slipped out and rushed to the corner of the deck where he stood attentively. What was he looking at? Usually, he wanted tuna this time of the day. She, on the other hand, wanted another glass of wine. She gave the door a tug to close it and headed back toward the kitchen. Halfway there she heard Seymour bark suddenly. Bryce stopped and turned. She hadn't heard him bark except out in the pasture with the cattle. He now stood at the top of the narrow stairs, staring at something down in the small parking area. What did he see? He barked again. It was an alarm. Fear returned. He disappeared down the steps.

"Seymour!" she called.

The glass door exploded.

Bits of glass pelted her face as she raised her arms. She twisted and crouched down as the glass continued to pepper her body, feeling like tiny, angry pinpricks. She dropped the wine glass and slumped over, covering her head with her arms. She lay still. Nothing else happened. Silence returned. After a moment, Bryce looked at her hands. They were bleeding, but not badly. She peered at the floor around her – not as much of the door's glass had hit her as she thought. Nevertheless, the splintering sound still reverberated in her ears. She glanced over her shoulder. There was a neat, largish hole in the upper third of the glass door. Cracks radiated outward in every direction, but the door had held, shatter-proof, apparently. She quickly inspected her arms and legs, but she wasn't too much worse for the wear. The bleeding on her hands could easily be stopped. Where was the dog? Bryce snapped her head around to look at the door again.

"Seymour!" she cried again.

No dog. She thrust her hands into her vest pockets. No phone. She had left it in the car, on the passenger seat, where she had dropped it earlier!

She rose heavily to her feet, took a step toward the glass door, and then quickly stepped to one side. The shot could have easily come from the entrance gate, she realized. The shooter could still be there. *That was one helluva shot*, she thought. Was he trying to kill her or just scare her? The image of the man in sunglasses at the clinic rushed back into her mind. He knew about Brunhilda! And he had heard Earl's rant about Richards and the Diamond Bar. *Richards*. Was he behind this after all? Was he trying to intimidate her with a professional killer? Or was it someone else? Wall Street? Her mind raced. If her uncle had double-crossed someone and then willed the ranch to her to protect his investment...

Suddenly, the window in the breakfast nook blew out, spraying glass throughout the kitchen. Instinctively, Bryce turned away and covered her face with her hands. When nothing else happened, she peeked through her fingers.

What was she doing? She needed to reach the police! Bryce looked around desperately. She spied her uncle's wall phone in the kitchen. Dead. What else? Her laptop! She reached into her pants pocket and pulled out Dale's business card. Without hesitating, she crossed the living room floor to the big table, grabbed her computer, and retreated quickly to the guest room. She slammed the door behind her and dropped to the floor, flipping the laptop open as she did so. After punching the 'on' button, she studied Dale's card. There were four email addresses. She would use them all. Bryce drummed the carpeting impatiently with her other hand. *Come on, come!* She glanced back at the door, listening. No Seymour. Wait! She rose to her feet and rushed through the bathroom to the office, peeking around the corner of the door before entering. It only took a step or two to see both of the video monitor screens, which she had left burning. They were empty. Where was the shooter?

She struck the wall with her fist.

She went back to the bedroom. The computer was ready. She typed furiously, reading from Dale's business card. *Help!* her message said. *Phone in car...bullet...attack...* She hit Send button as soon as she was done, closing her eyes in frustration and something like a prayer. Wait! She might be able to reach her phone in the car through the garage. It was worth a try. She opened the bedroom door carefully. All clear. She bolted around the corner, entering the short hall that led to the garage at full speed, duck-ing, just in case. Inside the garage, she slapped the button and the outside door began to rise slowly – and noisily. She stared at the growing gap, half-expecting to see human legs on the other side and a gun cradled in someone's arms.

But no one was there.

Bryce crossed the empty garage and peeked carefully outside. She could see the small parking area to her right, below the observation deck. She'd have to run across it and turn the corner to reach the front of the house where the car was parked. No. She couldn't make it without being exposed to the shooter if he was still at the entrance gate. It was too far. Wait. What if he wasn't there any longer? What if he had left? Mission accom-plished. She took a deep breath and closed her eyes, trying to calm her nerves. Bryce heard a plaintive bark. Seymour! Her eyes popped open. It sounded like he stood on the observation deck, probably at the glass door, wanting his tuna. He barked again. What to do? She could run back into the house and try to save Seymour by opening the front door or she could try for the phone. Maybe the shooter was distracted by the dog's barking or maybe he *expected* her to help the animal. Maybe she could make it to the car after all...

She put a foot on the gravel.

He wasn't distracted. She heard the crack of a gun in the distance and a second later the wall above her head exploded, raining bits of plaster and wood down on her. She covered her head with her arms and zig-zagged as fast as she could back through the garage. At the door, she smacked the wall button hard, her fear and frustration getting the better of her now. The garage door began to close squeakily. She opened the hallway door, mostly with her shoulder, and staggered inside, but not before watching the garage door shut.

There was no Seymour standing at the glass door, Bryce

could see when she reached the end of the hallway. Where had he gone? She turned left into the kitchen and ducked, covering her head again. She beelined for the shelter of the granite island, where she hid, crouched. Taking a deep breath, she peeked over its top – but saw nothing. No dog. No shooter either. The house was dead silent. The sun had fallen since the start of her ordeal, casting gloomy shadows into corners. She peered around the base of the island at the shattered glass door, but still no Seymour. What should she do? She needed eyes. Where were the binoculars? There, on the little table near the door. She could make a dash directly across the living room for them, or detour through the guest room, the bathroom, and the office. Undoubtedly, the shooter had binoculars too, or a scope on the gun, and was watching the house carefully for her next move. She exhaled loudly. Why hadn't he killed her? Why torment her like this? She didn't want to think about it.

She ran for the glasses.

Nothing happened. Grabbing the binoculars, she flung herself to the right, aiming for the office door, which was closed. She crossed in front of a window, then the front door, ducking as she ran. But nothing happened. She opened the office door, stepped inside, and slammed it behind her. Leaning against the wall for a moment, she tried to catch her breath. She closed her eyes. No! She opened them – she needed to see outside. Wasn't there a window in this room? There was, on the wall to her left. The venetian blinds were up and she could see tree branches not far away. It was the back of the house, essentially, so she should be safe from the shooter's line-of-fire – if he still stood at the gate. She could search for Seymour through the window. Maybe he had chased a deer into the woods.

The gun safe popped into her mind. Is this why her uncle had bought guns? He wasn't trying to be culturally correct among his new neighbors – he wanted to protect himself! From whom? Stanley Richards? The Mob? Wall Street bankers? The FBI? She took another deep breath. Would she actually use a gun in this situation if she had one? No. She would not. The world was going crazy as it was, it didn't need her contributing to it by firing guns. She'd figure out how to protect herself some other way. First, however, she wanted to find Seymour. She pushed off from the wall, heading for the window. Before she could reach it, however, the merry Mozart tune played in the living room, faintly but unmistakably.

Bryce froze.

He was coming! Her heart beat heavily. She turned and slowly approached the video monitors. He would be on his motorcycle, his head hidden in the black helmet, riding fast down the entrance road. Bryce looked at the screens.

Where she saw a police car, its lights flashing, driving rapidly toward the house.

FRIDAY

Bryce quietly turned on the table lamp.

She glanced over at Deputy Sandoval, asleep on the leather sofa near the fireplace, his uniformed back turned toward her, but he didn't stir. She carefully placed her laptop in its usual place on the living room table and pulled the chair out slowly, wincing at the scraping sound it made on the wooden floor. The deputy didn't stir. She caught the eye of Seymour, who stood nearby in the pre-dawn darkness, and pressed a finger to her lips as she sat down. He cocked his head at her. Bryce lifted the top of the computer, pressed the 'on' button, and cupped her chin in her hands, waiting.

She was tired. A sound had awoken her not long ago, causing her to lie very still in the bed, listening to the house over the comforting noise of the box fan. She heard the sound again – a gust of wind that rocked the walls, creating a deep creak in the timbers. She sat up and flicked on the bedside light. Sleep was now impossible. She might as well open the electronic file that Dale had sent her the previous evening, the one containing the French autopsy report about her uncle. She had glanced at the two-page English summary, but she was too exhausted and upset to tackle the French, a language she didn't know at all, especially its unfamiliar medical terminology. Then there was the email from Jeffrey that arrived shortly before she shut the laptop down for the night. It had a file attached to it as well – her uncle's medical records from Doctor Tadesh! Good for Jeffrey. But she didn't feel like opening it then, despite her deep curiosity. She'd open both files now.

Bryce rubbed her face as the computer completed its start-up cycle. It had been a chaotic evening. Between Deputy Sandoval's timely arrival in the police car, followed closely by Dale, the subsequent police work, Earl's worried visit, and Isaac's noisy repairs to the glass door and window, the mayhem didn't subside until nearly midnight. Already bone-weary from the long day, Bryce could barely think straight much less speculate with Dale about what had happened. Her description of the motorcyclist didn't fit anyone they knew. Her speculation that she might have seen him at the clinic when they brought in Brunhilda wasn't very helpful. As for the gun shots...Isaac gave a long whistle of admiration when he arrived, matching everyone's opinion of the shooter's skill. It didn't take long for them to find the slugs deep inside the walls. Military-grade, Dale told her, fired from a high-powered rifle – easily purchased by almost anyone. No surprise there, she thought. Eventually, he sent everyone home except for Deputy Sandoval. Dale patted her on the arm reassuringly as he left, which she appreciated. He had already commented on how calm she seemed to be. "Doctor's nerves" she explained, combined with years of sailing on the sea with her father. No room for panic out there.

She didn't tell him just how frightened she actually felt. Nor did she tell him her determination to take charge of her destiny from here on out.

The computer was ready. She opened the autopsy file first and began by reviewing the two-page English summary. There was the Phenobarbital overdose, of course, but her uncle had cardiovascular issues as well, it said, and had suffered a mild heart attack ten years ago. His cholesterol levels were elevated and there were signs of deterioration in his kidneys. Kidneys? What was that about? Next, she clicked through the autopsy report itself, squinting at the French words in a mostly futile attempt to comprehend their meaning. She'd have to call up a translation service on the Internet that specialized in medical terminology to make any headway. Instead, she decided to read the medical file that Jeffrey had procured somehow from Doctor Tadesh. Maybe she'd toggle back and forth with the autopsy so she could get a clearer picture of her uncle's health and why he had died. Bryce already knew the quick answer – the overdose of Phenobarbital – but the quantity of medication wasn't terribly high or at least not in amounts usually associated with a deliberate attempt to end one's life. Curious.

She realized that she needed to refresh her memory with a quick review of the drug. As she typed the query, Bryce glanced over at the deputy on the sofa, but he hadn't moved. Outside, she could see the pale dawn beginning to spread across the sky. She dropped her gaze to Seymour, who had settled comfortably on the rug a short distance away. His eyes were closed. She turned to the screen. *Phenobarbital...* $C_{12}H_{12}N_2O_3$....hepatic... discovered in 1912...the oldest and most frequently prescribed anti-epilepsy medication...cheap...highly controlled...First-Line recommendation from the World Health Organization... bioavailability greater than 95 percent...onset within five to ten minutes of ingestion...decreasing levels of consciousness... biological half-life: fifty to one hundred hours...duration: four hours to two days...body develops a tolerance to the drug requiring ever larger doses to accomplish the same effects... detox required...forbidden to be used with alcohol...the combination is a popular method for suicide...

She stopped reading and toggled up Tadesh's medical records. Did her uncle in fact have epilepsy? She read the file quickly. He did! *Abnormal synchronous neuronal activity in the brain...recurrent unprovoked seizures... heterogeneous condition (like cancer or heart disease)...*The treatments stretched back at least twelve years to about the time he began to see Tadesh, she saw from the dates in the file. Twelve years! Could it have been longer? Who had been his previous doctor? She'd ask Jeffrey. Bryce searched her memory. Had her mother mentioned anything about her brother having epilepsy? She hadn't communicated with him very much, she knew, but this was a pretty big secret to keep from the family. No. Her mother hadn't said anything. Maybe she didn't know. Bryce returned her attention to the medical file. Had Tadesh prescribed Phenobarbital? Yes. What doses? The correct range. Bryce clicked forward a few pages, scanning. She froze suddenly.

She stared at three words: *Phenobarbital overdose treatment...* Her uncle had gone over the edge once before. Where?... Treated at a private hospital in San Francisco... 2005... *Coma*, it said. She exhaled carefully and then clicked forward again, slowly...2007... another overdose... *two week stay in the hospital required...gastric intervention performed...* Surgery! What was the specific date? Bryce squinted as she searched...April 25th – two weeks after her mother's death. Only two weeks! Was that a coincidence?

Bryce leaned back in the chair heavily, causing Seymour to lift his head. She glanced at the back of the deputy again, but he was as rock-like as before. Wait! She leaned forward and toggled up the two-page English summary of the autopsy. What day did her uncle die? *10.4.08* – April 10th, 2008. Almost exactly the anniversary date of her mother's death! Another coincidence? But they hadn't been close, Bryce thought to herself, so why would he choose that date to die? If that's what he did, in fact. After all, no suicide note had been found in his room at the winery and his French hosts had been adamant about his good spirits in the preceding days. Bryce cast her memory back to her mother's wake, two weeks prior to his hospitalization in 2007. Did he seem sick? Not that she could recall, though they had only one exchange. He asked questions about her life, her job, her father, her former husband. Her uncle seemed very tired, she remembered, and yes – not well. His complexion was mottled, he walked with a slight limp, and she thought he looked too heavy for his frame-size and age (ever the doctor, even in grief). One more thing: he had grown a beard!

She toggled up Tadesh's file and kept reading...*elevated blood pressure.... increased urination...occasional blood in his urine...signs of kidney deterioration...swelling in ankles, feet and fingers...photosensitivity... all possible early signs of age-related Lupus nephritis,* Tadesh had noted. Lupus! That's what her mother had! Antiphospholipid Syndrome, to be exact. If her uncle had early signs of the same disease it suggested... Bryce clasped her hands to her face suddenly. It suggested a DNA link, of course, meaning it was inheritable. Bryce dropped a hand to the table top and tapped it thoughtfully with her fingers. There were tests for genetic predispositions for lupus, she knew, but she hadn't considered taking one since it seemed to be an isolated case in their family.

She glanced down at Seymour. He had closed his eyes again and appeared to be sleeping. So did the deputy, who hadn't moved a muscle. Bryce looked out the window again, seeing that the dawn was making steady progress.

Her uncle seemed changed after the funeral, Earl had said. She dropped her hands to the laptop's keyboard, typing *Phenobarbital and depression* quickly. She read...not everyone affected in the same way....the drug can cause changes in behavior...side effects...very good data collected over many years...doctors no longer prescribing it as much due to concern that its potential side effects outweigh its benefits...more of a crisis drug now...

can be addictive in certain cases...main side effects are sleepiness and fatigue...others include: depression, dizziness, anemia, slurred speech, memory loss, fevers, rashes, loss of sexual drive, stomach upset, low levels of calcium and folic acid, trouble paying attention and increased risk of suicidal thoughts...

Suicide. Maybe after all. Bryce followed a hyperlink. At a university medical site, she read a research paper on the association between antiepileptic drugs and the idea or desire to commit suicide, called *suicidality* in medicalese. People taking drugs like Phenobarbital were more than three times more likely to shows signs of suicidality than people taking a placebo, she read, which the researchers said was significant. No kidding. They called for a review by the Food and Drug Administration – a call that apparently had been heeded. An advisory panel would meet this July, she read on another site, to consider changes to federal guidelines on antiepileptic medications. In the meantime, specialists are warning doctors to pay close attention to the mood and behavior of their patients, especially any sudden changes. The site provided a list of warning signs that might signal an increased risk of self-harm:

- Talking about suicide.
- Withdrawing from family and friends.
- Struggling with depression.
- Preoccupation with death and dying.

Bryce froze as she read the next bullet:

- Giving away prized possessions.

She clasped her hands to her face again. Is that why he had willed her The Sun? Was it a sign of suicidality? But he had been happy, according to his French hosts! And there was no proof, as far as she knew, of him ever talking about ending his life. Of course, she hardly knew him. She'd ask Jeffrey to investigate. Wait! When had her uncle changed his will? Bryce's hand flew to the mouse. She clicked quickly through a number of folders on her laptop until she found the one she wanted. Why hadn't she thought about looking at this before? She double-clicked on the folder and then icon inside. The legal document filled the screen. She saw the date immediately: June 11th, 2007 – not long after her uncle's release from the hospital. Would he have been in the right state of mind? She scrolled down the document, reading the words that shocked her so profoundly the first time. Nothing. She kept going. At the bottom, something caught her eye. There had been an adjustment to the will, though it wasn't clear what it was. He had signed it. The date: March 31st, 2008.

Less than two weeks before his death.

Bryce leaned back in the chair heavily again, causing Seymour to look up. What had he changed in the will and why? Did her uncle actually kill himself? The dates suggested it but the lack of supporting evidence did not. Had he taken too much Phenobarbital by accident? She knew the drug was less effective over time, requiring higher and higher doses. But on the day he died, he took *a lot* of it. Of course, there was a third alternative: Dale's theory. Murder. Somebody could have spiked his wine with his own medication. What could have been the motivation, however? Was it linked to the FBI's Wall Street investigation? That seemed far-fetched to her. She could easily imagine a banking industry rife with fraud, greed, and moral turpitude (one of her father's favorite words), but murder? She doubted it. Besides, what did all of this have to do with Matt's death – or Brunhilda's horrific treatment? Nothing, she suspected, except the moral turpitude part. Still, one of the most important lessons she learned in medical school applied here: above all, be thorough.

Bryce leaned forward, grabbed the mouse and started click-ing. She was going to start over and read every page of each document carefully, taking notes as if this were one of her medical cases – which, in fact, it was.

THE MOZART ALARM suddenly split the air.

Bryce looked up. The house was no longer dark! Bright sunlight filled it from stem to stern. Hours had passed. The dog was gone. Where was he? There – standing at the damaged glass door, looking out. Bryce heard a grunt. It came from Deputy Sandoval, who had fallen off the sofa but caught himself with one arm before hitting the wooden floor. He rolled onto his feet, looking groggy. Mozart! Bryce rose to her feet, grabbed her phone, and headed quickly to the office. On one of the monitors, a large SUV barreled down the entrance road toward the house, raising dust. *Could it be that late?* Bryce thought, frowning. She poked at her phone. *9:30am*, it said. Yes, that late.

The suitors were coming.

As she crossed the living room on the way to the front door, the Mozart alarm sounded a second time. Deputy Sandoval was on his feet now, blinking. He nodded at her silently, his face a combination of sleepiness and chagrin. She nodded back. He checked his watch and headed toward the bathroom as she continued toward the door, Seymour hard on her heels. Outside, she turned left while the dog shot down the stairs. She walked quickly onto the observation deck, shading her eyes against the bright sun. The day looked cloudless. She had neglected to grab the binoculars, she realized, but it didn't matter. She could plainly see the red SUV driving rapidly and behind it a big, white truck, also raising a cloud of dirt.

There should be a third, she thought to her herself.

As the two vehicles approached the hill, Bryce whistled for

Seymour, doing a poor imitation of Earl's call. To her surprise, he appeared at the top of the porch steps, wagging his tail. A moment later, Deputy Sandoval emerged from the house, still looking chagrined, his phone stuck to his ear. Listening, he nodded to her once before turning to concentrate on his conversation. The perky Mozart alarm rang a third time (she doubted she would ever attend a classical concert again in her life). She could hear it leaking through the hole in the glass door, which Isaac had covered with cardboard and duct tape. Suddenly, the events of the previous evening came rushing back at her: the sound of the shattering glass. Fear.

She pushed it away. She had a ranch to sell.

She turned to the entrance road, shading her eyes again. A third vehicle had turned onto the ranch road from the highway. What would he drive, she wondered? A VW bus? A Mercedes? She squinted. It looked like a large, black SUV, the kind that VIPs drove around Boston. Hmm. The red SUV and the white truck had disappeared. Soon, everyone would arrive and the sales pitches would begin. Bryce turned to look at the grasslands, so lovely in the morning light. What an extraordinarily beautiful place. Why couldn't it stay as it was? Why couldn't her uncle's dream, whatever that was exactly, be fulfilled? Why did The Sun have to be ruined? She sighed deeply. The only choices these days seem to be between the lesser of contrasting evils, she thought. Oppression or war. Religious fanatics or secular despots. Half-truths or lies. Oil-and-gas wells or golf courses. Endangered fish or murderous felines. How did her father put it? *The sea doesn't care if you are right or wrong, it only cares if you lose your way.* It reminded her of a quote by a professor of medicine and founder of a Zen center in Boston that had literally inspired her to change her outlook on life:

"You can't stop the waves, but you can learn to surf."

The red SUV suddenly appeared in the parking area. It

braked hard. A second after its engine died, a door flew open and Doreen popped out, wearing a turquoise dress this time. Everything else was the same. In her hand, she carried a white envelope. She gave Bryce a cheery little wave before slamming the door and heading for the porch stairs. Off to the right in the woods, Bryce could hear the white truck approaching, its engine roaring loudly. Back down on the road, the slick, black SUV-limo thing continued its leisurely pace toward them. Bryce turned to Deputy Sandoval, who had finished his conversation and was clipping his phone to his belt below his rumpled gray shirt. He returned her look with a nod. "Good luck," he said silently.

A moment later, a slightly winded Doreen crossed the deck from the porch to Bryce, extending her hand and smiling warmly. "It's so good to see you again! I'm so sorry about what happened yesterday!"

She nodded at the shattered glass door as Bryce shook her hand.

"How did you know?" Bryce asked, surprised.

"I heard about it from Jason," Doreen replied, "who works at the gas station, who heard it from Charlotte, who read about it on something called Tweeter?"

"Twitter," Bryce corrected. "It's new."

"So I hear. It's just another fad, if you ask me," she said dismissively. "Anyway, I think Nate is behind it, the information, I mean. You'll have to ask him where he got it."

"Who's Nate?"

"Oh!" Doreen exclaimed. "I thought everyone knew Nate. He's on the Town Council. He runs a software company from his house, I think. I'm not sure what he does. It's not my cup of tea, if you know what I mean." She leaned closer. "He and the Mayor don't exactly see eye-to-eye." She resumed her previous posture. "How are you doing?"

Bryce shrugged. "Well enough."

"What a shocking thing. First that poor, dear horse, and then this." Doreen looked at the glass door, studying it with interest.

The white truck had arrived in the parking area. Its door opened and Bill Merrill climbed out, dressed almost exactly the same as before. In his hand was a white envelope as well. He showed his teeth from thirty feet away as he headed for the porch stairs.

"Who do you think the shooter was?" Doreen asked, snoopily.

"Someone who wants me to go home pretty badly," Bryce replied, turning back to her. "No idle gossip in town?"

"I wouldn't know," Doreen said unconvincingly. She cast a quick look at Deputy Sandoval, who was peering at the entrance road. She leaned forward again. "I think it's Stanley Richards," she said conspiratorially, dropping her voice to a whisper. "Didn't he make you an offer?"

She was fishing, Bryce could tell. "You could call it that."

Doreen raised the envelope. "Is that why you asked us to raise the bid?"

Behind her, Bryce could see Bill Merrill walking rapidly toward them. His white teeth had disappeared.

"Yes," Bryce said, nodding at the envelope. "Is that from Mister Sampson?"

"No," Doreen said quickly. "He's in jail."

Bryce's eyebrows shot up. "He is?"

"He's being extradited to Greece," she said quietly, sounding chagrined. "For fraud." She perked up suddenly, touching Bryce on the arm. "Anyway, I have a new client who you'll just love. Jonathan Cooper."

"That nut job?" Bill said loudly, arriving.

"You sound like that horrid Frank McBride," Doreen chided.

"He's what they call a 'radio personality,'" she said to Bryce, "quite well known nationally."

Bryce frowned. "I know him. Isn't he the jerk who wants the government to search people's homes and businesses for illegal immigrants?"

"The same," Bill replied. "He also likes to shoot lions and giraffes."

"He does?"

"Only in Africa!" Doreen said defensively.

"Mister Cooper is looking for a place to shoot wildlife here in America," Bill said to Bryce helpfully. "He wants to bring in exotic species and then set them free on a ranch for his buddies to hunt. They'll also shoot up the elk herd that comes to The Sun every fall. And anything that flies. They're dangerous too. One of his political friends got so drunk he shot his hunting partner with a shotgun. He lived, fortunately."

The women stared at Bill, who showed his teeth. "I did a little research."

Doreen grimaced and was about to say something when the black SUV-limo pulled into the parking area. Everyone turned their heads to look down at the impressive vehicle, which garnered a slightly raised eyebrow from Deputy Sandoval, Bryce noticed. The front door opened as soon as it came to a stop and a young woman stepped out. She wore a plain dress of some dark material with black shoes and a white collar fastened at the neck with a pin or narrow brooch. Her brown hair had been cut straight across above her ears, exposing a thin, pale neck. She looked fourteen, Bryce thought with a sinking feeling. She opened the back door and then ran swiftly around the back end of the SUV and opened the other back door. Two girls emerged on either side, looking like carbon copies of the first young girl. Nobody smiled. Bryce's sinking feeling deepened. The first girl opened the driver's door, bowing partially. After a moment, a young man stepped out and stood aside without acknowledging her presence. He looked like a male version of the girl, though older by five or six years, Bryce thought. He stretched his arms above his head lazily.

"Who is this?" Doreen asked.

"Another bidder for the ranch," Bryce replied.

"Where is Frank, by the way?" Bill said, looking around.

"Frank withdrew their offer for The Sun. Orders from above."

"I bet," Bill said, nodding. "No sense kicking the Big Dog."

The three girls had lined up, shoulder-to-shoulder, along the side of the SUV facing them, their hands straight down at their sides, their eyes cast downward. The young man stood by his door, looking bored.

"You're not afraid of him?" Bryce asked.

"Stanley Richards?" Bill replied. He chuckled. "No."

"You don't think he'll be upset if you match his bid?"

"The company that owns us is bigger than his," Bill replied. Then he shrugged. "For a while longer, anyway."

Bryce turned to Doreen. "What about your client?"

She saw the agent swallow once nervously when their eyes met, but Doreen regained her composure. "I haven't told Mister Cooper, yet. I'm sure he'll be fine with it."

There was movement within the SUV. A hand emerged, followed by the pale form of Reverend Pendergast, who unfolded himself awkwardly as he climbed out. He was dressed exactly as before, though his black pants were shorter this time, Bryce thought, exposing skinny calves. As he stood, he gave them a wave and a friendly grin, looking as happy-go-lucky as before, in contrast to the downcast faces of the young girls lined up against the vehicle. Pendergast held a white envelope in his hand.

"Who is this guy?" Bill asked doubtfully.

"I know who he is. He's a prophet," Doreen said skeptically. "Or so he thinks. Pender something. They pray underground."

She gave Bill a look. They turned to look at Pendergast, who had reached the bottom of the porch stairs and began to climb slowly. The young girls remained in place, Bryce noticed, their eyes cast downward, and the young man still looked bored.

"Fire and jubilation," the Reverend said in a friendly tone to the policeman as he reached the porch. Deputy Sandoval appeared to be suppressing a smile and avoiding a peek at the Reverend's high-water pants.

"His name is Reverend Pendergast," Bryce said in low voice to Bill and Doreen. "Church Empyrean and Jubilant. They think the world is going to end in an epic hail storm." She gave them a look. "Remember Noah's Ark? It's like that except they believe all the oceans will rise up into the air one day as a result of God's fiery wrath, freeze in the clouds and fall back to earth as fist-sized hail, destroying everything on the planet that isn't a mountain followed by a scorching fire that will cleanse all remaining sin after which the righteous emerge from underground and dance joyfully in praise of their new world."

They stared at her.

"I did a little research too," she added.

"Doctor Miller!" Pendergast said as he approached. "Good morning. Thank you for your call. It is an honor to be here on this fine day." He nodded at Bill and Doreen. "I understand it's going to be nearly seventy degrees."

"That's right," Bryce replied. "Not a cloud in the sky."

Both Bill and Doreen arched their eyebrows at her.

"Better to hear his Word," the Reverend said, raising a hand high. He lowered it. "Though for everything else, it's good to have a cell phone, don't you agree?"

He smiled at Bill and Doreen.

"Reverend Pendergast," Bryce said, pointing with her hand.

"Doreen Wainwright, real estate agent, and Bill Merrill, Alpine Services."

"Fire and Jubilation."

"They're making offers on The Sun as well." Bryce turned to them. "The Reverend is looking for land for his church's new underground Headquarters," she said, keeping a straight face. She turned back to him. "You have almost one hundred thousand members, is that right?"

"Correct," Pendergast said. "Praise the Fire."

"They all pray underground?" Doreen asked, incredulous.

"They do in their hearts," he said, spreading his hands. Then he shrugged. "But no. That's why we want to buy the ranch."

Doreen shot a look at Bryce. Behind the Reverend's back, Deputy Sandoval had come forward. He gave Bryce a 'thumbs up' sign. It was a question. She nodded and he moved away, back toward the porch. Glancing in the parking area, Bryce noticed that the young girls hadn't moved a muscle. The young man, however, had lit a cigarette.

"If you don't mind me asking," Bill said to the Reverend, "why would you build your underground Headquarters here specifically?"

"Right," Bryce said, unable to resist, "apparently there's a lot of natural gas here."

"Because it's the Heart of the Sun, as I told the good doctor," Pendergast replied solemnly. "The Heart of the Fire." He raised his hand again into the air. He suddenly jerked a thumb over his shoulder. "And it's close to Denver. I'm a Broncos fan."

"How did you even know it was for sale?" Doreen asked.

"It was ordained. When the time comes, the Word spreads quickly among the Brethren," he replied and then shrugged. "And I saw it on the Internet."

"The Internet? I didn't post anything!" Bryce objected.

"I may have," Doreen said sheepishly. "Just a few words. And a photo. Or two."

Bryce sighed audibly. There was a puff of blue smoke from the parking area, she noticed. She thought about yelling down to the young man to put the cigarette out.

"Bids," she said instead.

She stuck out her hand. One by one, they gave their envelopes to her.

"I don't know how much you need," Doreen said, returning to her unctuous form, "but I'm certain my client can match any other bid."

"Us too, Doctor Miller," said Bill. "We did some recalculations."

"The Sun Be Praised," Pendergast said as he leaned forward to hand over his envelope. "We threw in a bit more, just to be safe."

She stared at the white envelopes for a moment, thinking about everything she had learned this morning about her uncle. What would he have thought about this?

"Ok, thanks," Bryce said, tapping the three envelopes against her palm.

"Congratulations," Bill said cheerfully. "How does it feel to be rich?"

"I didn't feel unrich before," Bryce countered. She dropped her eyes to Seymour, who had wandered onto the deck and sat patiently nearby.

The Mozart alarm went off inside the house suddenly. Bill and Doreen looked around in confusion while the Reverend tilted his head heavenward in wonder. Deputy Sandoval appeared from inside the house. He nodded at the entrance road, where Bryce could see a car speeding toward them.

"Is there someone else coming?" Doreen asked, squinting.

"Not that I know," Bryce replied.

"Is that the short fellow?" Pendergast asked, following her gaze. "The one with all those casinos?"

Bryce shook her head. "I didn't invite him. I'm not interested in gambling."

"That looks like Mister Nibble's car," Doreen said, sounding alarmed.

"Kevin Malcolm," Bryce said to Pendergast, who nodded pleasantly. "He works for Stanley Richards."

Pendergast's eyes opened wide. He turned and headed for porch. "Thank you for the lovely time," he said over his shoulder. "See you later."

Doreen was right on his heels. "Take care dear."

Bill followed her. "You know where we're at if you have any questions."

Bryce raised her hands. "I thought you weren't afraid of Richards!"

"I'm not," he said loudly. "But better safe than sorry!"

Deputy Sandoval judiciously stepped inside the front door as each of them hustled down the stairs as fast as possible. Hitting the ground, they fanned out to their vehicles. The young girls came to life. One held the door of the fancy SUV for Pendergast while the others headed to their respective places inside. The young man threw the remains of his cigarette to the ground and stomped on it. Doors slammed, engines growled. Shortly, everyone was backing up in the parking area chaotically.

Bryce watched the show, leaning on the observation deck rail. As the vehicles departed, she looked down at Seymour, who had come close to her.

"Whoever gets the ranch," she said to the dog, "I'm going to find someone with a Save the Tuna Fund and write them a big check."

Seymour cocked his head at her, causing her to smile.

Bryce closed her eyes wearily. She could hear birds singing. There was a gentle creak of a tree someplace, swaying in the breeze. She soaked up the soft air and the stillness – until she heard a slamming door. When she opened her eyes, she surprised to see an empty parking area. Where did he go? She heard footsteps. Kevin was coming up the narrow staircase behind her, having apparently parked in the small lot. Why was he here? Bryce felt a sinking feeling. She considered for a moment hiding the envelopes in her hand, but decided against it. She didn't care what Kevin Malcolm, or his boss, thought.

Reaching the top of the stairs, he turned to look at the ranch over the railing without making eye contact with her, behaving just like Richards.

"Mister Malcolm," she said, folding her arms.

"Doctor Miller," he said, turning and making eye contact briefly. "How are you?"

"I'm fine. How can I help you?"

Kevin squinted at the damage to the glass door, appraising it, she thought. Was he proud of the shooter's work?

"Your boss is behind this, isn't he?" she asked.

He turned to her sharply, looking surprised. "Absolutely not."

She didn't believe him. "You're saying he's not trying to bully me?"

"No."

"A lot of other people think otherwise."

He narrowed his eyes at her. "Who?"

Instead of answering, Bryce exhaled loudly in exasperation. "So, if I choose to sell The Sun to someone else, Mister Richards would be fine with that?"

"No, he would not be fine with that." His tone was menacing.

"Why are you here?"

"To tell you to call your lawyer," he said coldly.

"I've talked to Jeffrey," Bryce said with a small shrug.

"About the sale of the ranch," Kevin shot back. His laser eyes bored into her. "You haven't talked him about that."

For a little guy in a skinny tie, he was remarkably intimidating, she thought. "What if I decline to sell Mister Richards the ranch?"

"That's not an option."

"I have options," she countered, holding up the envelopes.

"Not in this case. I thought he made his intentions clear," Kevin said, looking at her coldly again.

"He did." She nodded at the shattered glass door. "And keeps doing it."

"We're not responsible for that," Kevin replied without looking at the door.

"I don't believe you!" Bryce said loudly.

He turned to leave. "Believe what you want. He departs on Sunday."

"Answer one question," she said with energy. He stopped and turned his head toward her. Bryce held up the envelopes again. "I know what everybody wants to do here, except him. Tell me what Stanley Richards plans to do to with The Sun or no deal."

To her surprise, he nodded sympathetically. "I understand your frustration," he said. "But I'm not at liberty to say anything about his plans. I'm sorry."

He stepped down the first stair.

"So, he does have plans!" she declared.

He paused on the step. "As I said, I'm not at liberty..."

"Tell me what's going on at the Diamond Bar," she interrupted, nodding at the mesa escarpment and the dark hills to the north. "I understand that Matt rode up there to find out."

That got his attention. He turned to her. "I'm not at liberty to discuss that either."

"So he was up there!" Bryce exclaimed.

Kevin looked at her steadily. "You mean did the foreman trespass illegally onto private property? Yes, he did."

"Did Matt see something up there that he shouldn't have?"

"I don't know what he saw."

"Come on. Do you deny having an argument with him near the hotel in town?" Bryce asked, feeling frustrated. "Dale told me about it."

"I do not deny it," Kevin replied after a pause.

"What was the argument about?"

"I'm not at liberty to discuss it." Kevin turned away and took another step down the staircase, giving Bryce the impression the conversation was officially at an end.

"Earl thinks your boss ordered Matt's murder," Bryce said, strongly. "For what Matt saw on the Diamond Bar."

Kevin froze on the next step.

"Was it a coincidence Matt was killed before he could speak to me?"

"We don't know anything about that," Kevin said coolly.

"I don't believe you. And now I'm being harassed by a professional killer until I sell The Sun to Mister Richards," she said, now angry.

Kevin looked up at her sharply. "That's not true."

"Then who's shooting at me!" Bryce shouted. "It has to be your boss."

"It's not," Kevin replied emphatically.

She took a step down the staircase, coming close to Kevin. "Does Mister Richards know that Matt trespassed on the Diamond Bar?"

Kevin hesitated. "He does," he said finally.

Bryce came down another step. "And he was alright with that?" Kevin looked her in the eye but didn't respond. She came closer. "He ordered you to threaten Matt into silence, didn't he?" she said.

Kevin shook his head. "No."

"Then what did you and Matt argue about?"

He turned his head toward the sprawling grasslands. He was debating with himself, Bryce could tell. She waited. When he didn't say anything, she decided to try again. "What did you argue about that night?" she said steadily.

"It was about a girl," he said quietly to the grass.

That surprised her. "What girl?" Bryce said.

Kevin turned back to her, looking sad. "My girl."

He suddenly headed down the stairs to the parking area. Bryce put a hand on the rail to steady herself, feeling the surfboard vanish under her.

"DECIDE YET? Or are you still waiting?"

Bryce stared at the menu. "I'm starving," she said, "but I'm still waiting. Sorry."

The waitress nodded patiently and walked away. Bryce continued to stare at the menu uncertain what to order. The last time she ate at Maria's she had tried the chicken empanadas which were delicious but too fiery for her taste. She needed four glasses of water to finish them off. She put the menu down and began to rub her face, feeling worn out. What was she doing? She should just call Jeffrey, pick an absurd price, and instruct him to fill out the papers selling The Sun to Stanley Richards. It would be all over and she'd avoid a potentially career-damaging confrontation with one of the world's wealthiest men. What did she care what happened to the ranch? Sure, she liked the cows and the open space and she worried about the endangered chub in the river, but there wasn't a way out of that thicket that she could see. Earl couldn't buy the ranch and Frank withdrew his offer. Apparently, her uncle had a plan for the property but now his life and death were a mystery too. She could give the ranch away, she supposed, to a charity or nonprofit organization. But there were tax implications, she was certain, and that sort of process was never simple as it seemed, she knew. Bryce cupped her face in her hands.

"There you are," said a voice.

Bryce looked up in time to see the Mayor slip into the opposite side of the booth, looking unhappy. She was dressed mostly the same as before, though this time she wore a burgundy-colored suit and had a thin string of pearls around her neck. And her hair wasn't as carefully prepared, perhaps. In fact, she looked a bit frayed around the edges, Bryce thought. She carried a white envelope in her hand, which she deposited on the table before casting an uncomfortable glance around the restaurant, looking like a fish out-of-water.

"Thank you for agreeing to meet me here," Bryce said.

"It's fine. Good to circulate, I guess," the Mayor said. "I'm sorry to be late. There was a problem at the convention center construction site I needed to straighten out."

"I hope it wasn't serious."

"They're all serious around here," the Mayor replied tiredly. "And unending. I don't know what it is, but things seem to take forever to get done. It's certainly not what I'm used to. Whoever said "All calculations based on experience elsewhere fail in New Mexico" didn't know the half of it."

"Before I flew out," Bryce said with a smile, "a colleague at the hospital warned me that the water might not be safe to drink here."

The Mayor chuckled. "On our first visit to Santa Fe, my ex-husband thought he needed to bring his passport."

"Why did you come to New Mexico?"

"Vacation, that first time. Well, the first four times. Santa Fe, Taos, skiing, the opera, you know." She smiled at the memories.

Bryce saw the waitress serving food to a couple at a nearby table and tried to catch her attention. "After that?"

"Business, once," she replied.

"What brought you to Alameda?"

"Divorce," the Mayor said quickly. Bryce expected her to say something more, but the Mayor fell silent, looking at her hands.

"Who did you work for?" Bryce asked.

The Mayor gave her a look. "You don't know?"

Bryce tried to remember what Frank had told her. Right! That company that went bankrupt so spectacularly. She was one of the founders.

"Telecommunications?"

"Correct," the Mayor replied, looking at her hands again. "The day after I graduated from business school, way back in the 1980s, a guy I knew called me out-of-the-blue and said he had an idea for a company he wanted to start. His plan was to provide a bundled discount service for long distance phone calls, back in the day when there were such things. I thought it was a brilliant idea."

"I remember," Bryce said. "Didn't we use calling cards?"

The Mayor slapped the table lightly. "Yes! Can you imagine! Anyway, he and I, Hugo was his name, started the company in a three-room office in the back of his father's insurance building and we built it into an international business with twenty-five million users. Hugo was CEO and the public face of the company while I was in charge of mergers, which is where the real action was. I was good. We bought thirty different companies, including one of the pioneers of the Internet. We acquired almost every competitor, whether they wanted to sell to us or not, the fools. It was lovely."

She smiled at the memory.

"Was Hugo your husband?"

The Mayor laughed. "No, thank God."

"Then what happened?" Bryce asked as she kept a surreptitious eye out for a waitress.

The Mayor smiled wanly. "Eventually, we became the largest telecommunications company in the world. And then the largest bankruptcy filing in U.S. history."

Bryce returned her attention to the Mayor. "What happened?"

"Hugo happened," she replied, sighing. "While I was focused on mergers, he got greedy behind my back and began using fraudulent accounting practices to inflate our stock value. As if he weren't wealthy enough! He did it in cahoots with two old buddies of his that ran the accounting firm who did our books. It was an Old Boys network. They liked to go deer hunting together, can you imagine?" She waved a hand. "Anyway, it turns out they were propping up the company's value with fraud."

The waitress appeared, as if by magic. "Are you ready to order?" she asked.

"I'm not," said the Mayor abruptly. "What do you serve?"

The waitress handed her a menu. "I'll be back."

Bryce raised a finger to object, but the waitress was gone. She dropped her hand to the table. "Then what?"

The Mayor half-smiled again. "When the tech bubble burst in 2000, our stock began to fall, panicking Hugo and a lot of our investors. Meanwhile, the telecommunications world was changing rapidly, as you know. I was trying to stay ahead of the curve by buying start-up tech companies and Internet providers, but then I made a big mistake."

She paused, looking sad.

"I tried to buy one of the Big Boys," she continued. "They fought back. It was a complete disaster. The feds blocked the acquisition and our stock plummeted. Hugo freaked out. He said some things to me he shouldn't have, so I walked out."

"And came here."

"Eventually," the Mayor said with a shrug. "Actually, I discovered Alameda by accident. I was searching for Milton. It's a ghost town at the far end of Union Valley, up in the mountains. I love ghost towns. Have since I was a kid. Anyway, I took a wrong turn and ended up in Alameda instead. I thought it was cute. Lots of possibility. And here I am, trying to get a plumbing contractor to do his job."

"And Hugo? Isn't he in prison?" Bryce asked.

"Yes!" the Mayor replied, slapping the table again. "Guilty on all charges. Fraud, conspiracy, falsifying documents, lying to federal regulators. But he got off with a light sentence, the bastard," she said, shaking her head. "Never underestimate good lawyers."

"I don't," Bryce said, meaning it.

"And now they're trying to get him out of prison on a technicality," she said in an exasperated tone.

"But you didn't get prosecuted?" Bryce ventured.

"No." She fell silent, looking pensive, Bryce thought. She waited. The Mayor clasped her hands tightly together on the table.

"Why not?" Bryce asked.

The Mayor looked up. "Because I'm the one who turned Hugo in."

Bryce let that soak in for a moment. The Mayor lost her career, in other words, as a penalty for what she did. That's how she got to Alameda, Bryce realized suddenly – a kind of corporate Witness Protection Program. Exiled to rural New Mexico.

"Is Hugo mad at you?" Bryce asked quietly.

The Mayor met her eyes. "Furious. I think he wants to kill me."

"I'm sure he doesn't," Bryce said sympathetically.

"You don't know Hugo." She picked up the menu with a frown and unfolded it. "What do you recommend?"

"Are you worried?" Bryce asked.

The Mayor looked at her. "About the food?"

"About Hugo."

"No." She returned her gaze the menu. "I'm sorry about what happened last night," the Mayor said, changing the subject abruptly. "It sounds terrible. You must be upset. I spoke with the Chief this morning. He said it was a professional job."

Bryce drummed her fingers on the table top. "He told me the same thing. Do you have any theories who might be behind the shooting?"

The Mayor continued to scan the menu. "I don't."

"Earl thinks it has something to do with the Diamond Bar," Bryce said, lowering her voice. "He thinks they're trying to force me to sell The Sun to Stanley Richards and leave as quickly as possible."

"By terrorizing you?"

"Does that sound like his style?" Bryce asked.

The Mayor made a face. "Actually, that's subtle for Stan Richards."

"It is?" Bryce said, not hiding her incredulity.

"He's done worse," the Mayor said casually. "We tangled once over a company I tried to buy. The poor woman caught in the middle, the one who started the company, someone killed her pets. All eight of them, one by one," the Mayor said, shuddering.

Bryce gaped. "You're kidding! Richards did that?"

The Mayor shrugged. "They never found out who did it."

"How could anyone do something that horrible?" Bryce said, shocked.

The Mayor raised her eyebrows and looked at her over the

menu. "What line of business are you in? That's right, you're a doctor. You heal people." She lowered her gaze and squinted at a menu item. "Just remember what was done to that poor horse."

"Do you have any idea who did that?" Bryce asked, frowning deeply.

The Mayor leaned forward slowly, giving Bryce a steady look. "Yes. It was a man," she said quietly, and then leaned back. "That whittles it down by half the population." She peered at the menu. "I think I'll try an enchilada."

Now it was Bryce's turn to lean forward. "Do you have any idea what going on up on the Diamond Bar?"

"No. But I can tell you the latest rumor. They're breeding Sasquatches."

Bryce blinked at her. "You mean, like a Sasquatch army?"

The Mayor lowered the menu abruptly. "Now, there's an interesting idea!" she said with a laugh. "I wouldn't put it past Stan Richards to try. Maybe he'll invade Texas. He could do us all a favor."

Grudgingly, Bryce laughed. She pointed at the white envelope near the Mayor's elbow. "Despite the Sasquatches, you're going to make a bid anyway?"

"I think I'll have the quesadilla instead," the Mayor said, scrutinizing the menu again. "Yes, I am." She lowered the menu and pushed the envelope toward Bryce.

"You're not afraid of Richards?"

"No," she said simply. "I don't have much left to lose anymore. Besides, it's been a long time since I got into a decent scrape."

"What about your investors?"

The Mayor shrugged. "They're grown ups. Mostly women, by the way." She nodded at the envelope. "This is the best we can do. We can't outbid him, but if you want an alternative to

Richards' bullying you can consider this offer instead. Plus, it'll make you fabulously wealthy."

Bryce pulled the envelope toward her slowly with a sigh. "Do there still have to be golf courses?"

The Mayor stared at her.

"Doctor Miller!" said a cheery voice suddenly. Bryce turned to see a hairy, heavy-set young man with twinkling brown eyes and a very full beard approaching. She recognized him from the small crowd in front of the clinic yesterday. This time he wore a green T-shirt and blue jeans, both of which looked somewhat stressed by his rotundity. The T-shirt carried a political message, Bryce thought, but she couldn't be sure because he stuck a large hand in her direction.

"Nathaniel Goldfarb," he announced. "But everyone calls me Nate. Nice to meet you. I recognized you from the photo on your hospital's web site."

Bryce shook his hand firmly. "I have a photo?"

"It's flattering! Hello Mayor Tate," he said with a nod.

"Hello Nathaniel," she replied, not sounding happy to see him. "Mister Goldfarb is a member of the Town Council."

"A token member of the opposition," he said, smiling.

"There's nothing token about you," the Mayor said pointedly, leaning back in the booth, half-smiling.

"I appreciate that. Sometimes we don't agree," he said to Bryce.

"We never agree," the Mayor corrected.

"True, but that's the great thing about democracy, right? The little guy gets a voice."

"I suppose," the Mayor said, sounding exasperated.

Nate turned to Bryce, "I stopped by to remind you about the meeting on Saturday afternoon. Can you join us?"

Bryce frowned. "What meeting?"

"I posted it on your Facebook page," he said merrily.

"I have a Facebook page? Oh that. I never have time to look at it." She turned quizzically to the Mayor. "There's a meeting tomorrow?"

"Apparently," she replied, sounding bored. "He likes to organize community meetings so people can tell us what's on their minds." She shrugged.

"Call me old-fashioned," Nate said cheerfully. "Anyway, I called this one so Dale could talk about the murder investigation and other things going on. Particularly what happened last night, if that's ok with you? People are pretty concerned, as you can imagine."

Bryce could imagine. "It's fine with me. What time is the meeting?"

"Two. In the community center. It's a Saturday, so I think a lot of people will be there. I hope you'll join us." He beamed at her again. "It'll be a simple agenda, I promise."

"Your agendas are never simple, Nathaniel," the Mayor warned.

"I think it's important to do things in the open," Nate said cheerfully to Bryce. "Democracy works better that way. Can you attend?"

"Yes," she replied.

"Great!" Nate replied warmly. He turned to the Mayor. "Hopefully, her Honor can join us too?"

"Did you post it to my Facebook page?" she said, still leaning against the booth wall.

"You don't have a Facebook page."

"Oh that's right, I forgot," the Mayor said, half-smiling. "I'll be there, I guess."

Nate beamed mischievously. "Great! It's always a good thing when elected officials come to public meetings, I say."

"Goodbye Nathaniel," the Mayor said.

"Wait!" Bryce interjected. "I'd like to say something at the meeting."

"Of course!" Nate replied.

Bryce put her elbows on the table and clasped her hands in front of her face. Was this a mistake? No. It had to be done. "They wouldn't be my thoughts, so much," she said to both of them. "It'll be an announcement instead."

The Mayor lifted her eyebrows. "An announcement about what?"

Bryce lowered her hands to the table. "Who gets The Sun."

BRYCE PUT her hands on her hips in exasperation.

She watched a line of men – and one woman – swing clubs at little white balls on a flat, slightly elevated grassy area under a hot sun. She squinted at them from under the shade of her Red Sox cap, trying to understand the appeal of their activity. White balls flew through the air, she watched, landing harmlessly in a green field a short distance away, where they sat there doing nothing. The process was repeated again and again. They aren't even aiming at anything, she thought to herself. Not far away, three people stood casually on a putting green. Two leaned on their clubs while the third took an interminable amount of practice swings before actually making contact with a white ball, only to watch it roll right past the hole. Then the three of them laughed. They were having a good time! Bryce didn't understand. She tried to recall Mark Twain's quip about golf – something about a nice walk being ruined?

She stood near the driving range of the Alameda Municipal Golf Course and Grill on the western edge of town, having driven straight here as soon as she hung up with Dale. He had called toward the end of her lunch with the Mayor wanting to speak privately about the investigation, though she wasn't sure exactly which one he meant. Matt's murder? The near murder of Brunhilda? The person who chased her on the motorcycle and shot out the glass door? The mysterious death of her uncle? All of the above? She suggested they meet at the first tee. She'd explain it when he arrived, she told him. On the drive, her heart skipped a beat when a man on a motorcycle zoomed past. He had a long gray beard, sunglasses and wore a red bandana wrapped around his head. No black helmet. No helmet at all, in fact. Was that legal? Massachusetts law required all riders to wear helmets. A few years ago, there had been a rally of bikers at the state capitol building in support of a bill to eliminate the helmet mandate. They created a fuss, roaring through town, waving American flags and denouncing the liberal "nanny state." As an individual, she could understand their argument – after all who didn't like feeling the wind blowing through their hair – but as a doctor, their position was ludicrous. It made as much sense as sailing without a life jacket!

Bryce detected a movement to her right and was grateful to see Dale appear on the paved path that led from the nearby clubhouse, walking fast toward her. He carried a manila folder in one hand and waved briefly with the other. She waved and turned her attention back to the golfers on the driving range, squinting at them. One man shanked a shot, sending the ball spinning into the desert scrub that bordered the fairway. The tidy, green grass ended abruptly, she noticed, replaced by thirsty-looking yellow and gray plants. How much water did they use daily to keep the grass happy, she wondered? Another swing. This time a young man drove his golf ball deep down the range, the club in his hands poised high in the air as he watched the long flight of the ball. That looked satisfying, Bryce grudgingly thought, except it didn't compensate for all the rest of it. But at least they were all outside!

Dale arrived.

"Why is this considered to be fun?" she asked him, nodding at the golfers. "They're just standing there! The ones over there walk around a little bit, fortunately," she said, pointing at the people on the putting green.

He chuckled. "I guess there's a reason they're called duffers."

"What does that word mean? I've always wondered."

He shrugged. "In Australia, it means cattle rustler."

"Really? Are there any of those type of duffers around here?"

"Not lately, thankfully," he replied. "But you never know. Cows and thieves. Pretty classic combination. Why did you want to meet here?"

"The Mayor wants to buy The Sun and she's insisting on golf courses. I've never been on one in my life, so I thought I'd come see what the fuss is all about. Did you know there are fifteen thousand golf courses in America? I looked it up."

"I didn't know that," Dale said. "All I can tell you is this one's very popular. People come long distances to play. It's been a big feather in the Mayor's cap."

Bryce squinted at him. "But does Alameda really need two more?"

"On The Sun? Won't those be private? This one's public at least."

She sighed. "Maybe golf is more fun in Scotland."

"Maybe." Dale held up the manila folder. "This is for you. It's Matt's autopsy report, plus his medical file from the clinic. It pretty much confirms everything Doc Creider and Meili told you, I think. Blow to the back of the head, old injuries to his arms and legs, contusions on his knuckles, a bunion in his left foot, a STD, a recent case of mono, tobacco-chew stains on his teeth, gum disease, liver issues. He was a heavy drinker too, as Creider suspected. And a smoker."

Bryce's eyebrows shot up. "Cigarettes?"

"Apparently. They're still running tests to see if there's a match with the tobacco in the butts we found at his house, but I'd say it was a safe bet. We're also waiting for the results of a chemical test, but Creider thinks there may be traces of wine residue in his stomach."

"Wine? I thought he was just a beer drinker."

"So did I."

Bryce considered this for a moment before taking the manila folder from him. "Looks like Matt had a few secrets," she said. "It makes you wonder what else he was hiding. Will there be a funeral?"

A golf cart carrying a couple suddenly zoomed past them. Dale waited until it had moved out of earshot.

"I haven't been able to reach Matt's next-of-kin yet, including his brother in Iraq," he said. "So, no." He nodded down the path that paralleled the first hole. "Let's walk." He took off. "I've been doing some digging on your uncle's Wall Street connections," he said.

"What have you found?" Bryce asked, following.

"Have you ever heard of a bank called Wolff Schmidt?"

"Of course, aren't they the ones who went bankrupt in March? Weren't they one of the biggest banks in the nation?"

Dale glanced over his shoulder to make sure they were alone. "They were, but they didn't go bankrupt, well, not exactly anyway. They were bought out by another bank that paid only a fraction of what the stock was worth. According to a financial report I saw this morning, your uncle owned a great deal of Wolff Schmidt stock."

Bryce considered this for a few steps. "How much stock?"

"I don't know exactly, but I think it was in the many millions."

"Did he lose it all?"

Dale began to speak, but they could hear a golf cart

approaching, so he waited again. "Apparently, he had a great deal of money still in the bank's stock when it collapsed."

"Do you think that made him suicidal?"

He gave her a look. "Wouldn't it make you suicidal?"

Bryce walked a few more steps in silence. "He changed his will a few weeks later, though it wasn't clear to me what he did."

"Can you ask your lawyer?"

Bryce nodded.

"Did the Mayor make you a serious offer? Is she willing to take on Richards?" Dale asked. "If you don't mind me asking?"

"She did. But I haven't made up my mind. How's Brunhilda?"

"I spoke with Earl on the way over here. She's better. She's a tough girl."

"Have you spoken to Abelard?"

Dale frowned. "No. He hasn't come in. I've called three times. I'm not worried. He disappears for a week or two sometimes."

"Doing what?"

He shrugged. "Whatever Sasquatch hunters do. Wander around, I guess."

"What's the latest about the shooter?"

Dale stopped walking. "He shot from the entrance gate. We found tire marks consistent with a motorcycle, but we can't confirm the make of them yet. I've got Sandoval and Midas scouting around the area, asking people if they've seen anything unusual."

"Was the GO HOME stuff a ruse, do you think?"

"No. I think it was part of the shooter's plan to scare you."

"Is he working for Richards, do you think?"

"I don't know." He looked at the fairway. "There's something funny going on. Could your uncle have known Richards somehow?" he asked in a low voice. "Could he have been indebted to him through this bank business or insulted him or something?"

"I have no idea. Do you have a theory?"

"It's just that something feels personal about all this," he confided. "I mean, why are they giving you a hard time? It doesn't make sense."

"Maybe there's something we're overlooking."

Dale made a face. "I don't know. It could just be about money, I suppose."

"What about Estevan Gutierrez?"

Dale shook his head. "No news. We're still looking."

"Kevin Malcolm came out to the ranch this morning," Bryce said, "to demand my capitulation. I asked him about the argument he had with Matt, the one you broke up. Did you know it was about a girl?"

Dale's eyebrows shot up. "I didn't. But I'm not surprised. Matt had a reputation as a ladies' man. He got into a fight with a guy over girl not long after he started working for your uncle. Mister Nibble, really? Interesting."

"Maybe he's trying to throw us off the trail," Bryce said with a frown. "Did you hear what they were arguing about?"

"No. They stopped yelling at each other as soon as they saw me. Abelard overheard them, though. He lives in the old mill nearby. He's the one who called me."

"Could it have been about the Diamond Bar?"

"I don't know. We'll have to ask Abe when we see him."

A golf cart zoomed past them suddenly carrying two young men, apparently heading to the first tee.

Dale looked at his watch. "I've got to go. You alright for the time being? The deputies will be back soon."

"I'm ok." Bryce said. "I just can't get my mind around the idea my uncle might have committed suicide. I think someone in the family would have suspected it."

"Wasn't he depressed?" Dale asked.

"I think so, but Earl said my uncle was planning to build a hotel on The Sun. Do you know anything about that?"

Dale shook his head. "I don't. Wasn't he the guy who dressed up in a chicken suit? I gotta run. See you later," he said, as he began walking away.

Bryce gave him a wave. She turned to watch the golf cart that had passed them pull up to the tee. The two young men hopped out energetically, golf visors on their heads. They laughed loudly and one punched the other in the shoulder before each of them pulled a club from bags in the back of the cart. They sauntered to the tee, their golf shirts flapping slightly in the warm breeze that had picked up, bringing with it a smell of dirt and dryness. The day was going to be warm, Bryce could feel. Very warm. One of the young men teed up.

Wait! She snapped her fingers. *The hotel.* There were architectural drawings on the office table in her uncle's house. Of course!

She turned her back on the golfers and hurried to her car.

BRYCE FLICKED on the overhead light in her uncle's office.

She glanced at the two video monitors on the wall, which burned brightly, but nothing was happening on the roads, which was fine. Upon leaving the golf course, she didn't tell anyone where she was going or what she planned to do. Maybe that was a mistake, she didn't know. Right now, she didn't care. She started by examining the large computer desk that occupied most of the wall to her left, but other than various electronic items, including a screen and computer tower, it was conspicuously uncluttered. However, judging from the huge mess on the big table in the center of the room, she determined that someone had transported everything that sat on the desk at the time of her uncle's death to the table. Sure enough, a closer inspection of the mess revealed piles of haphazardly placed business papers, files, and reports, not to mention a riot of Post-its and paper clips, three coffee mugs, two staplers and one calculator. Curiously, there were no photos of loved ones anywhere in the room, Bryce realized. Maybe his personal effects had been stowed someplace.

Or maybe he didn't have anybody to love.

Bryce circled the big table slowly. On the far wall was the large white board covered with the 'To Do' instructions and lists she had seen earlier in the week. There were dates attached to a few of the items, most of them in the future – not what she expected a suicidal person to write. What was on his mind? Two dates on the board had recently passed, she noticed. The first said "TG application due" and the other said "SL1 delivery," followed by the date. The rest of the items on the white board looked like reminders. "Call Luke" said one. "Go solar!" said another. In the upper right-hand corner of the board was a quote *"The landscape of any farm is a portrait of the owner himself"* – *Aldo Leopold*. Someday, she would have to figure out who this Aldo character was.

Below the quote were parallel black lines forming two columns, the first topped by the words "Projected Income" and the second one by "Known Expenses." The latter contained words but no numbers, including Fences, Diesel, Insurance, Salaries, and Well Repairs, among others. The first column, however, was blank. To be filled in later, it appeared. Was that a sign of a man feeling suicidal about a lack of money or a happy man getting ready to make plans?

There was a clicking noise. Bryce turned in time to see Seymour come around the end of the table, his nose close to the wooden floor.

"Hey you, want to help?" she asked. "Tell me what was on his mind."

Seymour disappeared under the table, following his nose.

Bryce turned to the mess on the table, looking for the architectural drawings that she had glimpsed the first night. She found them sitting in a relatively neat pile, partially hidden by the pile of desk debris. She cleared away the layer of papers and was immediately confronted with a highly detailed drawing of the exterior of her uncle's house – the one she was currently occupying. It looked like the north-facing side. She saw the narrow stairs leading to the observation deck, the glass door, the breakfast nook windows, and the gym window in the upper story. She turned the page noisily. The next view was the west side, with the garage. Then the south side, with three windows. The east side, with the stairs leading to the front door. A word caught her eye in the lower left corner of the drawing. *Freestone* it said. Was that the name of the house? Yes, it existed on all the sheets, she saw. She kept going. There were drawings of the wine cellar, the sauna, the big fireplace, a schematic of the living room filled with furniture, and the master bedroom. She kept turning the sheets – there were so many!

Then she froze.

She faced the exterior of an entirely different structure. It was huge – three stories tall with a main entrance in the center on the ground level. It had lots of windows and balconies on all three floors, shrubbery, lanterns on posts, and a chandelier inside the main entrance. She turned a page. There was a pool with deck chairs and a firepit. An awning stretched out from the back door. It all looked exactly like...a hotel. She glanced at the name in the corner.

Hearthstone it said.

Bryce flipped more pages quickly. Dining room, kitchen, guest rooms, laundry, reception desk, a suite, a massive stone fireplace, a western-style bar, a big gym...all so lovely! Everything had the feel of luxury and taste. She flipped more pages. Suddenly, she was looking at a drawing of a square cabin with round logs and a slanted roof, looking like a miniature version of her uncle's home. Bryce glanced in the corner. *Elfstone* it said. She turned a page, seeing an exact replica. *Dragonstone* it said in the corner. Turn. *Riverstone. Meadowstone. Dreamstone...* There were eight cabins total. And one large, fancy hotel. There was more, she could tell from the remaining drawings underneath, but she decided to search for a date instead. She found it below the architect's name and company, located in Bozeman, Montana.

January 12th, 2008, it said.

Her uncle had plans. Big plans. Why would he kill himself? He had things to do. She glanced up at the empty *Projected Income* column on the white board. The *Expenses* list was long. Was he in trouble? Did he need a big, bold plan to stay solvent? Had he counted on the Wolff Schmidt investment to pay the bills for the new buildings – money that vanished on him overnight? She recalled the bank account he had left her as part of his will. Operating funds, the probate lawyer had called it, for the ranch. It was a tidy sum, she thought, but probably not enough to keep the ranch going for long. Of course, she had no clue what it cost to run a place like The Sun. A chill suddenly struck her. Was this what Matt wanted to talk to her about, a money crisis? No. It was too pedestrian. Besides, Earl said he expected her to sell the property. Why would the foreman worry about money?

It had to be something else.

She began replacing the drawings in their original stack, turning the pages over in clumps with both hands. Finished, she was about to turn away when she noticed a sheet sticking out from a separate pile of debris. It looked like a map. With some effort, she pulled it out and held it up. It *was* a map – a bird's-eye view of the entire ranch. **THE SUN** it said at the top in bold letters. She spread it out flat as best she could on the pile. She immediately recognized Alameda on the left-hand side of the map. She could trace Highway 70 from town to the ranch gate. She kept going, following the entrance road with her finger until it reached her uncle's home on the hill, depicted on the map as a black square. *Freestone* it said. She quickly traced her path back to Alameda. Nearby was a hollow rectangle surrounded by eight little hollow squares. *Hearthstone*, it said below the rectangle.

She surveyed the whole ranch. Not far from the house, she saw a cluster of little black squares labeled *Headquarters*. Not far away was *South Well*, also a black square. She ran her finger upwards along a road until it found another black square. *East Well*, it said. There was a *West Well* towards Alameda, but it was hollow. To be built later, she assumed. Was there a *North Well*? She scanned the northern half of the ranch. No, apparently not, either actual or planned. She followed the Alameda River as it flowed across the map from left to right, meandering peacefully. There seemed to be fences and pastures, though not as many as she expected. There were also clumps of trees on the ranch, including a thick one near the southeastern boundary. She traced a thin line representing a road from the South Well to the clump of trees.

She froze. Hidden in the trees was a building. *The Shack* it said simply. Bryce stared at it. The symbol was black.

She peeled the map from the table.

THE CAR ROLLED GENTLY to a stop. Bryce lifted the binoculars from the dashboard and put them to her eyes. In the distance, she saw a single-story wooden cabin nestled carefully in a large grove of pine trees. There were no vehicles out front nor any other sign of life, much like the eerily empty cluster of buildings at the Headquarters that she had passed on the drive. Bryce widened the survey to include the surrounding forest, but nothing unusual leapt out at her. Why was there a hidden building on the ranch? Seymour grew restless in the back seat, anxious to get out. Did he know this place, she wondered? Bryce debated bringing him along, but decided in the end she wanted his company.

She was glad she did.

She replaced the binoculars and picked up the map of the ranch from the passenger seat to double-check her location. There had been no signs on the road from the Headquarters indicating a cabin or shack ahead or any suggestion this was a regular route. In fact, the road was in pretty poor shape, she thought. The car had scraped its bottom twice on high spots. Still, there were no other roads leading to *The Shack* on the map, suggesting this was the only way to get there – and that the cabin was deliberately hidden. Why? Perhaps the structure dated back to the early days of the ranch and wasn't occupied any longer. Maybe not.

Ten minutes later, she eased the car to a stop in front of the cabin. To her surprise, it looked both old and new, as if it had originally been built many years ago but rehabbed recently. The roof looked completely new, as did the electrical wire strung from its right-hand corner to a pole at the edge of the trees nearby. The wire disappeared into the forest, she saw. The cabin had a single door set in the middle with large windows on either side, both of which were obscured by closed curtains, and a porch under an overhanging roof. There was a bench swing filled with cushions at one end of the porch, attached to the roof by two chains. There were two wicker chairs on the other side, separated by a large wooden stump that doubled as a small table. On the stump sat two empty wine glasses and an uncorked bottle of wine – looking exactly like the bottles in her cellar.

Bryce reached for her phone.

There was no signal, of course. In the excitement of finding the map, she neglected to call Dale before leaving the house, which she now regretted. The prudent thing to do would be to go back to the house, call Dale and wait for one of the deputies. It's what you did on a ranch, be sensible, right? But she was here! And no one else knew, so she should be safe. It was alright, she decided, to look around a little bit. Besides, she had Seymour, who was eagerly waiting to be released from the back seat. Still, prudence suggested that she review the route back in her mind. She had followed the map carefully, turning right at the fork past the Headquarters, left at another fork. She drove past the South Well tank, keeping an eye on Seymour, just in case he picked up a vibe. Twenty minutes of rough road later, she bore left again at another fork, heading for the large clump of trees on the horizon hiding The Shack.

No wrong turns, she promised herself. Just in case.

When Bryce shut off the engine, the air filled with a foreboding silence. Seymour whined in the back. Did he smell something? Bryce climbed out of the car, followed closely by the dog. He hit the ground and began energetically sniffing it in widening circles. He was after something already, she thought. A deer or coyote scent, hopefully. Were there bears in these woods she wondered? Someone had mentioned an elk herd on the ranch. Where were they now? Bryce turned around to take in the sweeping view. No wonder her uncle had rehabbed the cabin – the vista was stunning! She could see the South Well not far away and in the distance the looming dark mass of Diamond Bar country. Had Matt sat here staring at it, wondering what was going on up there? Had he made a fateful decision, under the influence of another bottle of expensive wine, to find out?

Bryce closed the car door, jumping slightly at its *thud* in the stillness.

She studied the area surrounding the cabin for a moment.

To its left were a tree stump and a small woodpile under an open-sided lean-to structure looking like it had been a much larger pile six months ago, judging from the large amount of wood chips and other debris on the ground. The Shack had been well-used, she surmised. Beyond the lean-to, she saw an outhouse, with an actual half-moon cut into its door, looking ancient and unused among the weeds. A victim of the cabin's upgrade, she suspected. Near the old outhouse was a pile of wooden planks, looking like they had been stripped from the cabin during the rehab. Beneath her feet was a thin layer of gravel, looking fresh. She walked toward the porch, studying the ground. What few tufts of grass dared to grow up through the gravel looked crushed. Tires, she assumed. A few feet away to her right she saw a large divot in the soil with fresh edges, looking like an animal had recently dug down in search of prey. What animals dug holes like that here, she wondered? Were there badgers out West?

Bryce stepped onto the small porch. It creaked softly. There was something on the wooden floor behind the left wicker chair, hiding behind a leg. Bryce came closer and stooped to look. It was a cigarette butt. She lifted her gaze to the stump separating the chairs. Behind the wine bottle, sat an ashtray filled with more butts. Bryce heard a bark in the distance. She straightened up quickly, looking for Seymour, but he had disappeared into the woods. Had he followed a smell? Matt? Badger? Coyote? She considered calling to him, but decided she didn't want to disturb the silence. He could take care of himself, she was certain. Besides, she wanted to know what was inside the cabin.

She stepped carefully to the wooden door and listened, but everything was as silent as a tomb. She knocked twice. Nothing. She gripped the door handle carefully and turned it a fraction – it was unlocked. She pushed the door open.

And gasped.

Directly in front of her was a large, unmade bed. There were three pillows at its head, sitting on what looked like expensive satin sheets. Bunched up at the foot of the bed was a coverlet, also satin or something very similar. She took a step into the room. The sheets had nearly come off the corners of the bed, she saw, and the pillows had the feel of having been tossed there by someone in a hurry. Bryce took another step. There was a simple chest of drawers to the left, against a wall, and a closed door next to it. In the corner was a floor lamp. There was a night stand next to the bed and on it another uncorked bottle of wine.

Bryce peered behind the door. She saw a wood stove in the right corner, looking well-used. A teapot sat on its surface. Against the far wall stood a fancy-looking, two-burner kitchenette with a microwave. Next to it was small refrigerator. Neither of the appliances showed any sign of having been used recently, she thought. Completing the picture was a small table and a chair under the window. But what stood out the most in the room was the huge size of the bed.

As intended, Bryce suspected.

She crossed to the night stand. She opened a drawer near the top. She peeked inside, reached in and pulled out a single condom in its square wrapper. She reached into the drawer with her other hand and pulled out a handful of condoms. She smiled.

"Matt," she said out loud. "You devil."

Now she knew who stole her uncle's wine! She replaced the condoms and closed the drawer. Curious, she opened the door to her left, revealing a small bathroom. There was a sink with a medicine cabinet above it, a tub with a shower, two towels on a rack, and a weight scale on the floor. A pink bar of soap sat conspicuously on the edge of the sink. She opened the cabinet. It had a First Aid kit, shaving cream, toothpaste, and lipstick.

She opened a door below the sink. A plunger. Toilet chemicals. A box of sanitary pads.

She pushed the shower curtain aside. Three different kinds of shampoo and two kinds of conditioner. She sniffed the soap. Sandalwood. Not what she would expect a ranch foreman to use.

He didn't, of course.

She stepped back into the main room. There was a box of tea on the top of the kitchenette she had not noticed before. What about a can opener? None was visible. She thought about searching for it, but decided she didn't want to do any further damage to the cabin's criminal integrity, from a police perspective. Besides, it was clear what was going on.

Shack indeed. Lover's nest was more like it.

Bryce stepped outside. The view was truly inspiring. The perfect hideaway. A twig snapped. Seymour suddenly materialized from the forest to her left, his nose down. For a moment, she thought he might follow the scent into the cabin but instead he circled around the grounds, stopping briefly at the badger hole, before heading back into the woods. Where was he going? Then a thought struck her like a bullet: Seymour hasn't been here before! Matt left him behind at the house during his trysts. But why would he do that? The dog wouldn't care about Matt's dating life of course...unless Matt was worried the dog might recognize the girl later...in town...with someone else...creating an awkward situation...

Bryce turned around to study the cabin once more. Seymour would only be trouble if the get-togethers here were frequent or had lasted a long period of time. And the girl belonged to someone who Matt really, really didn't want to find out about the affair.

Like Kevin Malcolm. Was he the culprit? It didn't seem likely. Kevin wasn't the rider on the motorcycle, she could tell from his physique, but maybe Kevin knew people who did that sort of thing for a living? Of course, his boss certainly would. But why would he tell Stanley Richards about his love life? Why would Richards even care? Bryce considered the bodyguard who stood on her observation deck during Richards' visit. No. Wrong body type as well. Still, something was going on here that led to Matt's death, she was certain.

Seymour suddenly appeared again, trotting toward her, his tail wagging. She realized that he had emerged from a gap in the forest. A car-sized gap. She looked at the ground. Sure enough, a two-track was barely visible among the grass and weeds. She bent over for a closer look. The plants had been flattened recently – by tires. Bryce gave the cabin another study from where she stood, this time with fresh eyes, but nothing leaped out at her except a pile of construction debris a short distance behind the structure. Turning, she squinted at the South Well in the distance, looking black and forlorn. Beyond it somewhere was the Headquarters and Matt's place. Roads went in three directions from there, including the one toward her uncle's house – and the Mozart alarm. If the trysts were secret....wait, what lay at the other end of this track – the highway?

Seymour had circled around again, sniffing once more. He headed back down the track. The sensible thing to do, Bryce told herself, would be to go call Dale pronto, but she found her feet walking along the faint track instead. She just wanted to see. It was an old habit. She recalled the curiosity she always felt on the sea whenever she and her father approached a new island on their coastal explorations. What lay on the other side? She needed to know. They had maps, so they knew intellectually what was there, but it never satisfied. Much to her father's prideful bemusement, she had to see for herself.

Bryce followed the flat track through the thick woods. It wasn't rough. A passenger car would have no trouble managing it. Where was the highway? Suddenly, she heard a sound. *Swoosh* went a large vehicle, traveling fast. Three minutes later she arrived at a gate. Beyond it, Bryce could see the paved highway that led to Alameda to her right. Seymour was there too, sniffing the ground in front of the gate, the hair on his back standing up a bit, she thought. Why? No, she was wrong. He seemed fine, she decided. She walked up to the gate and peered over its top, careful not to touch anything. As she expected, she saw a new-looking lock. It was attached to a chain that bound the gate shut. Despite all the dark issues it represented, she couldn't resist another smile. He was clever, that foreman. She could almost imagine the wheels turning in his head as he drove up to the old, run-down cabin for the first time...

Bryce could hear another vehicle approaching at a high rate of speed. She turned to look for Seymour, finding him sniffing a gate post carefully. She could also imagine the anxiety of the young woman, Matt's squeeze, driving out from town or perhaps another ranch as she parked at the secret gate, fiddling with the lock, looking over her shoulder at the highway nervously. The sound of the approaching vehicle grew rapidly. Did people always drive so fast in the country, Bryce wondered? Did the young woman hide behind her car or a nearby tree at a similar sound? In a small community, was it worth the anxiety? Apparently. Bryce was about to call Seymour when she froze.

It was a motorcycle.

It blasted past her. The rider turned his head at last moment – it was him! The black-helmeted son-of-a-bitch! Shock and fear coursed through Bryce's body – he recognized her! Brakes suddenly squealed loudly. She saw smoke appear among the tires and then the rear part of the motorcycle swung outward, leaving a dark smear on the road. His right foot flew out to steady himself. He was turning around!

Bryce ran.

"Seymour!" she yelled, even though he stood nearby.

She bolted down the track as fast as she could, cursing her decision to not call Dale. What was she going to do? She looked back over her shoulder, but the track had already twisted enough that she couldn't get a clear view of the gate. Where was Seymour? Ahead of her, she saw, loping along, enjoying the run. Her heart beat hard. How far was her car? Hundreds of yards. Did the rider have a key to the gate? Probably, if he was associated with Richards. If not, it didn't matter. He'd get through somehow, with or without the bike. She looked over her shoulder again. Nothing. If he came after her on foot, she might have enough of a head start to reach the car, but it would be close. She kicked her pace up a notch, telling herself she was in the home stretch of a high school track race again, except propelled this time not by a desire to win but by mortal fear.

The woods thinned. She could see the opening that led to the cabin. She hazarded another look over her shoulder, but the track was dark behind her. Seymour ran ahead, still enjoying the exercise, bouncing on his feet. The opening loomed. She pushed herself harder. Seymour stopped briefly to sniff at the badger hole again. Except it wasn't a badger hole, Bryce knew now, ice shooting through her veins. Someone had removed evidence.

She had found the murder site.

Bryce crossed the open area in front of the cabin without pausing to look at anything, including the track behind her. He was either there, or he wasn't. She reached the car and threw open the driver's door. "Seymour!" she cried. To her relief he jumped in and made his way to the back quickly, happy to take another ride in the car. She threw herself inside after him, slammed the door and jammed the key in the ignition. It didn't fit! What was wrong! She tried again. No! Wait. She had the wrong key. She searched frantically in the pockets of her vest.

She found it! As she pushed it into the ignition, she stared at the gap in the trees where the track started. It was empty.

She fired the car up and threw it into reverse, spinning the wheels. She jammed on the brakes and threw the gear shift into Drive. She could hear Seymour flop against the back seat and she pressed the gas to the floor.

"Hold on!" she yelled.

She zoomed down the narrow road, checking the rear-view mirror as she went. No one had emerged from the forest yet. She hit a bump in the road, hard. She concentrated on the way ahead, hoping not to damage the car fatally. A few moments later, she sailed over a cattle guard, its *rackty-rackty* sound startling her. Had it made that sound before? A small panic rose. Was she on the right road? Yes. She could see the black shape of the South Well up ahead. She glanced into the rear-view mirror. The cabin was fading into the distance. No rider, on foot or bike. Where was he? The car hit another bump hard. When she had recovered, Bryce gripped the wheel firmly with one hand and extracted her phone from the vest with the other. There was no signal at all. Shoot! She stuck the infernal device back in her pocket while checking the side-view mirror. Nothing. She grabbed the map from the passenger seat and held it up awkwardly as she drove. *South Well*, she saw on it, straight ahead. Turn left at the fork, she remembered correctly. Keep going to the next fork. She pushed the map away.

As she approached the South Well, Bryce imagined the quad, carrying Matt's body, leaving the road near here, its driver aiming for the leeward side of the big tank. The motorcycle rider wouldn't have any trouble climbing the ladder to the top of the tank, or jogging back to cabin to fetch his car or bike, deed done. Bryce exhaled loudly as she drove. It made sense – except for Brunhilda. The poor thing! But why try to frame Estevan? Unless, he knew about the affair! Or witnessed the

murder. Was that why he was missing? Were there *two* victims?
A fork in the road loomed. Bryce turned left and then twisted
her head to look behind. There was no one on the road yet. Was
she missing something? Surely, the rider would chase her. A
mile past the well, the road rose up a small hill. Bryce stopped
the car on the crest and threw open the door, leaving the engine
running. She hopped out, binoculars in hand. She lifted them
to her face, aiming them back toward the cabin, barely visible
now among the trees. The road was completely empty. No one
could be seen at The Shack either. She lowered the glasses,
frowning. What had happened? She repeated the search, just in
case. Nothing. Seymour whined from back seat, eager to
get out.

"No, you don't," she said to him, blocking his exit with
her body.

Turning, she could see her uncle's house on its hill in the
distance and beyond it the outline of the entrance gate at the
highway. Was that a dust plume? She lifted the binoculars
quickly to her eyes.

The motorcycle and rider were coming down the entrance
road!

Fear shot all through her. He was coming for her! Where
could she run? Bryce threw herself back into the car and
grabbed the ranch map from the other seat. With her finger and
thumb, she measured the distance from the entrance gate to her
uncle's house. Then she walked the same interval along the road
with her fingers to where she was now, and then to the cabin.
Too far. He'd reach her first! And precious seconds were
draining away. Where could she run? There was a road that led
east before turning north, eventually exiting the property. Could
she make it? She lifted the glasses to her face. The motorcyclist
had reached the base of her uncle's hill, moving fast, she saw.
Bryce swung the binoculars to the right, searching. Where did

the north road cross the river? Was there a bridge? It wasn't clear from the map. She kept scanning.

A second later, she dropped the binoculars and pushed the map away. Wheels spun as she hit the accelerator, spraying dirt. She had to get ahead of the rider at all costs. She flew down the road, bottoming once in a low spot. She grimaced. She looked to the west, but the entrance road had dipped, obscuring the motorcyclist. Soon, the Headquarters complex would block her view. She could make it – maybe. Seymour was on his feet in the back seat, wagging his tail as he stared out the window, enjoying the fun. Maybe Matt drove like this, she thought to herself. She pushed the foreman out of her mind.

At the intersection with the main ranch road, she turned right, heading east. She could see the Headquarters in the mirror – no rider, yet. She flew down the road, praying that she wouldn't blow a tire. How far could she push the car? Far enough, she hoped.

At a fork in the road, she turned left and clattered across another cattle guard noisily, causing her to wince. Bryce glanced over her shoulder to the west road. She saw him! He had emerged from the Headquarters and was leaning over the bike's handlebars, as if urging it to go even faster than it already was, which was pretty damn fast. He'd be on her in minutes! The car bottomed on the road suddenly, making a sickening scraping sound. But it kept going. She steered it right at the next fork even though the road had deteriorated. Glancing back, she saw him closing fast, his black visor glaring at her.

The car thudded and she felt a shiver as it hit something hard. No more. She had gone far enough. She hit the brakes hard and threw a hand across Seymour in the back, preventing him from falling. As soon as the car stopped, she threw open the door.

"Seymour, follow me!" she ordered as she climbed out.

He leapt to the ground right behind her. Bryce could hear the angry whine of the motorcycle as it approached. She ran. Seymour quickly disappeared, but she couldn't worry about him right now. She heard a thunking sound as the bike navigated the rough spots in the road, coming closer. He'd make it a lot farther than she did in the car, she knew.

She kept running.

Suddenly, there was silence. Looking back, she saw that the rider had dropped the bike, laying it down sideways. He stepped around it smoothly, professionally, and pulled out a gun from his jacket. He began running after her, steadily, patiently. After all, where could she hide? She bent over, trying to make herself as small as possible, even though she knew it was ridiculous. A killer like him wouldn't have any problem hitting her. All she could do was keep running, even though the track had disappeared into grass. She'd do the best she could. A moment later, Bryce could hear his feet pounding. He'd be on her in seconds.

Just as she planned.

A few yards later, Bryce reached out and grabbed the orange handle. She made it! Bryce stopped running and pulled up sharply on the handle, releasing it.

"Get him girls!" she said to the cattle standing there.

She dropped the handle and one thousand hungry animals surged forward.

Bryce stepped to the side of the gap and turned to watch the spectacle. The cows rushed at the rider, only a few yards away. He stumbled almost comically in his attempt to avoid being trampled to death. He looked terrified, Bryce thought. He waved his arms at the animals, but without effect. They continued to surge forward, a black and brown flood of beasts. In seconds, the rider would be engulfed. Panicking, he turned and ran back toward his bike, stumbling twice. The air filled with cow noise –

moos and grunts and the soft rip of grass being consumed – some of the happiest sounds Bryce had ever heard in her life.

The rider made it back to the motorcycle, still acting terrified. He leaped over the machine athletically and dropped behind its frame. A moment later, he came up gripping the gun in both hands, aiming at the nearest attacking cow – who ignored him, head down, eating. He aimed at another approaching animal, then another. They all ignored him. Soon, he was surrounded by grazing cattle, looking ridiculous as he waved the gun around. Bryce couldn't suppress another smile...

He suddenly pointed the gun at her!

Bryce dropped. She heard a sharp crack – he had shot at her! She regretted the smile. Now what? The herd coming through the gate had thinned considerably, which gave her an idea. Two, actually. Keeping below the backs of the cattle, she duckwalked across the gap in the fence, heading away from where the rider had last seen her. She moved as quickly as she could, weaving through the animals, her hands up to protect her body in case they didn't see her. But the cattle did see her – and they were very polite, she thought, making room as she worked her way across the ground steadily. What was the rider doing, she wondered? It was unlikely that he could work his way upstream against the flood to find her, though at some point the herd would thin out enough for him to try.

But she'd worry about that later.

Having crossed the gap and worked her way to the side of the herd, she decided it was time to try her second idea. She pulled out her camera punched the code and then the 'video' button. It began taping. She zoomed it to maximum with her fingers. Ready. She raised herself high enough to see over the cattle. The rider was still hiding behind his bike, looking like something out of a bad western movie, pointing his gun where she used to be standing. She caught him in the video lens. She taped.

Spying her, he turned sharply.

She dropped. She heard another crack of the gun.

After taking a deep breath to calm her nerves, she duck-walked farther to her right, trying to stay within the protective cover of the animals. Soft ripping sounds filled the air. There was an occasional moo, comforting her. She kept the video going on her phone, just in case. Right now, it recorded grass and cow hooves. Where was the rider? Would he come after her, knowing that she had him on video? Probably. She could stay hidden safely among the cattle for a while, she supposed, as long as she stayed down and kept moving – an idea that her knees didn't appreciate very much. Maybe she should pick out one of the girls up ahead and duckwalk by her side as she ate, become one with the cow...

Suddenly, she heard the motorcycle come to life. It coughed once and then revved loudly. Shortly, it began to fade.

Bryce peeked over the back of a cow, and then stood up. He was riding away. She lifted her phone up quickly, centering the image on his retreating back, keeping an eye out for his gun, but both of his hands gripped the bike's handles firmly. He sped up alarmingly, without looking back. A few moments later, he reached the main road – and turned left, to the east. He gunned the bike, flying down the road. Where was he going? Bryce kept filming. He looked over his shoulder, but not at her. Then the road dipped and he was gone.

Why did he flee? What was he looking at? Bryce peeked over her shoulder to the west. There was dust in the air near her uncle's house way off in the distance. She swung the camera around, needing its zoom to see what was coming. She lifted the phone up close to her face and peered through the lens, following the main road past the Headquarters until he found what the rider had seen: Earl's old truck, speeding down the entrance road, raising a cloud of dirt. Farther back were Dale's Bronco and a police cruiser. Its lights were swirling. Earl must have heard the gate alarm buzz at his house when the motorcyclist passed through! He had called Dale and hustled out to The Sun.

She let the video run for a moment longer, savoring the image as she listened to a sea of animal life graze contentedly behind her. She punched the off button.

Bryce lifted her head from the camera. All was calm. A breeze tickled her face. It was such a beautiful day in such a lovely place. The cattle had fanned out like a black-and-brown pool, filling the pasture. She heard a distant buzzing in the stillness, like an angry insect. It had to be the motorcyclist but he didn't appear on the horizon, no doubt lost among the folds of the land. Bryce took a deep breath and closed her eyes, feeling less shook up than she had a right to be. Maybe the nerves would come later. What would Earl say to her? Dale? What had just happened? Had the motorcyclist been aiming to kill? It felt that way. Or was it another attempt to provoke her into leaving early? A cruel one. Could Richards be that cold-blooded? Possibly. Probably. But why? To protect his employee? To intimidate her into selling the ranch to him before she became the next victim? To shield the Diamond Bar from prying eyes? Was Earl right after all? Was the business at the love nest a coincidence or a ruse? Had she walked straight into a set-up?

Bryce took another deep breath. Quietness rushed at her. She could still hear the gentle sounds of cows eating grass, soft ripping sounds that were oddly comforting. Farther away she heard the approach of vehicles, drowning the last vestige of the buzzing in the distance. The shooter would get away. There were plenty places to hide, she guessed with a sigh, even in open country. Maybe he wouldn't be back. Maybe he had made his point. Somehow, she doubted it. The job wasn't done - whatever the job actually was. She shuddered. Maybe she would call Jeffrey after all and put an end to this madness. She should just give in. Why not? Let it go. Get back to her crazy life in the hospital and forget about New Mexico. See her patients. And her father.

Go home.

The breeze touched her face again. No, she wouldn't give Richards the satisfaction.

She opened her eyes.

SATURDAY

The Mozart alarm went off for the tenth time that morning.

Bryce lifted a hand to shade her face as she peered up the entrance road. Who was it now? Another police car. Where was it going to fit? She leaned over the corner of the deck and studied both parking areas below, filled with vehicles from every law enforcement agency possible, it seemed: Alameda police, Dunraven police, county sheriff, state police, ATF, FBI (unmarked), Department of Homeland Security, the US Forest Service, NM Game and Fish, as well as a special agent from the New Mexico Department of Forestry, though she had no idea why he was here. To inspect the trees around the Shack, she supposed. Some arrived last night, but most trickled in this morning. Deputy Midas had the unenviable task of choreographing the parking circus in front of the house, while Deputy Sandoval was up at the Shack, guarding it. Earl was inside the house attending a meeting that Dale called to plan strategy with the twenty or so officers on hand. Her job, she decided, had been to shake hands, accept admiring congratulations, and stay out of the way. Fortunately, Seymour kept her company. He lay on the observation deck near the BBQ, watching her alertly.

An hour ago, Dale shared with her the results of an early investigation of the Shack and its grounds by the state police crime scene unit. It confirmed her suspicion that she had found the murder site. There were traces of human blood at the edge of the hole in the driveway, suggesting that Matt had been struck while standing there (watching the girl drive away?). Someone had removed the bloodstained soil with a shovel and moved it to the South Well where it had been deposited on the ground near the four-wheeler, apparently in an attempt to make it look like Matt had been struck there instead, Dale said. Results from the soil tests hadn't come back yet from the lab, but to his eye the stained soil at the tank looked exactly like the soil at the Shack. Furthermore, tire tracks suggested the quad had traveled back-and-forth on the dirt track between the well and the Shack a number of times and had been parked in front of the cabin. As for the murder weapon itself, Dale said the pipe they found behind Estevan's trailer did indeed carry traces of Matt's blood type and likely originated in the pile of construction debris behind the Shack, where a number of other steel pipes of varying lengths were found.

Apparently, the murderer had his pick of weapons.

The crime scenario thus far looked pretty straightforward, Dale continued. The love nest had apparently been discovered by a jealous spouse/boyfriend/girlfriend/lover who then killed the foreman with the pipe and tried to cover up their crime by framing Estevan, who was still missing. Whether the crime was premeditated or not wasn't clear at this point, he told her, however its cover-up was carefully planned. Matt's body had been moved from the Shack to the tank, the ground at the well "salted" with his blood, the murder weapon tossed behind Este-van's trailer, which had been intentionally cleaned out, and

Brunhilda ridden to the mountains to make it appear like the ranch hand had abducted the horse. Who had done all this remained a mystery, of course, but Dale said the priorities now were to identify the girl, find Estevan's truck, and locate Estevan. To this end, a crack FBI fingerprinting team was on its way from Albuquerque. If Matt's girl was in the database, she'll be known quickly. If not, police would begin questioning people in the area, women in particular (Bryce raised her eyebrows – *that* task won't be popular). Dale concluded by saying the main goal of their effort this morning was catching the motorcyclist.

Halfway through the meeting, as officers energetically discussed how best to go about finding the rider, Bryce decided she needed to step outside and collect her thoughts. Crossing the observation deck to the rail, she breathed deeply the sweet, cool air, which did more to calm her nerves than any talk of evidence or motives or plans to catch a killer. She closed her eyes and leaned on the rail. She couldn't get distracted, she told herself. Despite all that had happened in the past few days, she still had a ranch to sell – and a plane to catch tomorrow.

The Mozart alarm went off again.

Opening her eyes, Bryce could see another vehicle coming down the entrance road. More police, she assumed. She was glad. A widespread search the previous evening by the authorities to find the motorcycle rider had failed completely. He had vanished into thin air. Dale led the pursuit of the rider from the ranch, following Bryce's directions, leaving Earl and Deputy Sandoval to guard her though she insisted she was fine. After their arrival in the cattle pasture earlier, she had quickly narrated the discovery of the Shack to them, what she found inside, the secret track to the highway, and the subsequent chase, earning surprised looks and a long whistle of admiration from Earl when he realized how she had used the cattle herd to save herself. At the news of the shots fired at her, Dale jumped

into the Bronco and sped after the motorcyclist, his anger plain
to see.

Bryce squinted at the car on the entrance road. It was a
passenger car, not a police vehicle, though it could be another
unmarked one, she supposed. By habit now, her thoughts
turned to the binoculars, but she had left them inside and she
didn't want to interrupt the meeting. Where *had* the rider gone?
Dale suspected he slipped into the protective cover of the
Diamond Bar. Its property line paralleled Highway 70 for miles
in both directions from the point where the rider had likely
exited The Sun. There were locked gates along the boundary, as
well as two entrances to Stanley Richards' property. The first was
the paved road near Alameda, and the second was a dirt road
near the Interstate exit to Dunraven that headed north to the
ghost town of Montenegro, a 1920s-era coal-mining community
entirely owned by Richards. Both roads were blocked by heavy
gates – and no one was returning his calls, Dale said, raising his
suspicion even higher.

Before stepping outside, she overheard three other options
involving the rider's escape: he rode east to hide among the gas
wells on the other side of the Interstate; he had turned west,
slipped through town, followed the Alameda River upwards and
was now hiding among the dense trees on Forest Service land;
or he might have zoomed away altogether, never to return. This
last option fell into immediate disfavor, however, among the
assembled officers. The rider was a pro with a job to do, they
agreed – a job that wasn't finished yet. Bryce grimaced. Dale
gave her a reassuring nod from across the room, but it didn't lift
her mood much. Her spirits had sunk last night during the official interview with the state police. She had to interrupt it twice
to compose herself. The closest she had ever come to death was
an accident in eighth grade during a high school trip to Rhode
Island for a basketball tournament. A drunk in a car collided

with the bus as it crossed an intersection in Providence, sending eight girls to the hospital, including herself. Her jaw and her shoulder were both dislocated. It was the first time Bryce had seen Emergency Room doctors at work and they deeply impressed her with their skill and kindness – ultimately setting her on the road to medical school.

Dale and the policemen were also very considerate last evening, offering multiple times to suspend the interview if she wanted, though she refused. Bryce led them through her discoveries, starting with her uncle's plans for the hotel on the ranch. At the news of the unmade bed and the condoms in the Shack, the men chuckled (there were no female officers, she noticed). Dale didn't laugh, however, which she appreciated. Concerning a suspect, she told them about Kevin Malcolm's comment that he and Matt had fought over a girl, but Dale surprised her by expressing skepticism. He couldn't hear what they were arguing about that night, he told the other officers, and there was no other evidence that a girl had come between them. Besides, Matt's reputation wasn't a secret – now confirmed by the love nest. Certainly, he'd ask Kevin about his fight with Matt, Dale said, but he doubted it was the source of the foreman's death. Besides, the yelling match had taken place months ago.

Bryce tried to feel mollified by this, but something gnawed at her.

Unfortunately, after the interview she lost her temper briefly at the agent from the Department of Homeland Security. It began when Dale told her there was an old saying in police work: people kill for two reasons – sex and money. Every other apparent motivation for murder can be traced back to one or the other, and often both, he said. The Homeland Security officer, a meaty, sour-faced, red-headed fellow who had contradicted Dale a few times already that evening, shook his head aggressively. Ideology and religious extremism were motivators for violence too, he said, which Bryce recognized as the Administration's code for the followers of Islam. Dale tried to object, saying extremism wasn't at play in this case as far as he could tell, but the arrogant Homeland guy lectured him about maintaining perpetual vigilance for terrorists and defending national security – even on a remote ranch in northern New Mexico! He was being ridiculous as well as obnoxious, Bryce thought wearily.

"What, you think only a foreign terrorist could do something like that to Brunhilda?" she said suddenly, interrupting the agent. "And not an American?"

It was a shameless reference to the torture of prisoners by American soldiers in Iraq during the War, but she didn't care. The red-headed agent fell silent, glowering. No one else said a word. Dale tapped a pen against his cheek thoughtfully.

She excused herself from the room.

The passenger car disappeared below the hill. It would arrive in the main parking area soon, Bryce saw, causing Deputy Midas another headache. Suddenly, she felt exposed on the observation deck. She wasn't sure why. A glance at the entrance gate reassured her that it was still being guarded by a Highway Patrol car. A scan of the ranch and the land beyond revealed nothing. She looked over her shoulder at the living room through the broken glass door, but all the people inside at the meeting still had their backs turned. She glanced around and then tilted her head to scrutinize the window to the gym on the second floor. Nothing. She looked down at Seymour, but his eyes were closed. Why did she feel like she was being watched? She turned to the parking lot – and caught Deputy Midas staring at her. He dropped his gaze, but a beat too slowly, she thought. A chill crept in. He had given her a cool look the other day, she remembered. And he hadn't said a word to her this morning. Why did he seem unfriendly? Or was she just feeling jumpy again?

The passenger car appeared at the edge of the main parking area. As it edged carefully into a spot behind the police vehicles, Deputy Midas pointed to another place farther up, but a hand inside the car waved him off. The engine died. A moment later, the door opened and Doctor Thomas stepped out – to Bryce's happy surprise! She wasn't wearing her white doctor's coat, she noticed. Meili raised a finger at Deputy Midas, who had come forward to object, signaling to him "I'll only be a second." She looked up at Bryce, smiled and waved. Bryce came forward, preparing to hurry down the porch stairs, but Doctor Thomas held up a hand, saying "let me come up there instead." Bryce got the message – a private conversation was needed. Something was up. Seymour lifted his head, looking like he was about to rise to his feet, but Bryce pointed a palm at him and he relaxed.

A moment later, Meili stepped onto the observation deck. They embraced each other.

"I couldn't believe the news when I heard it," Meili said, her voice strained with emotion. "Are you ok?"

"I'm fine," Bryce replied. "A bit rattled. But I managed to survive."

"He shot at you! I can't even imagine! What was going through your mind?"

"Panic, mostly," Bryce said, frowning.

"I bet! But you kept your cool. Great idea about the cows."

Bryce kept frowning. "Thank you." She squinted at Meili. "How did you know I'd been shot at? I thought the police were trying to keep that a secret."

"I saw the video. The one you made," she replied, sounding surprised.

Bryce's eyebrows shot up. "Where?"

"YouTube. Nate linked to it on his Facebook page."

Bryce stared at her. How was that possible? She looked at the backs of the officers in the room again. She had given her phone to Dale, who had handed it to a young officer from Dunraven who then uploaded the video to a police laptop so it could be viewed, but Dale would never have allowed it to be shared with the outside world.

"Is something wrong?" Meili asked.

"It wasn't supposed to be broadcast. Does it say who posted it?"

"I don't remember," Meili said, shaking her head.

Bryce cast a glance down at Deputy Midas and saw that he was watching them. He looked away again. Meili suddenly took Bryce's arm and gently steered her toward the deck railing.

"There's something I need to tell you," she said in a low voice. "Doctor Creider wants to see you. He says it's urgent. He wouldn't tell me what it was over the phone. In fact, he instructed me to drive out here and tell you in person. No phones and no email, he said. Nothing that can be intercepted or overheard."

She let her words linger. Bryce remembered Frank and Earl's dark comments about the electronic reach of Mister Nibble and his boss.

"Just me, not Dale?" Bryce asked. Meili nodded. "What do you think he wants to tell me?" Bryce said in a whisper.

"I think he found something," Meili whispered back. "Big."

"Something to do with Matt's death?"

"No, or he would have included Dale, I'm sure," Meili replied. "It's something else, I think. He sounded...worried. He's usually so...self-assured, if you know what I mean. That's why I came right out here."

Men's voices could be heard in the distance. The meeting had broken up and the officers were spilling onto the porch near the front door.

"I've got to go," Meili said quickly. "I'm blocking traffic. Are you still going to the community meeting this afternoon?"

"Yes."

"Come to the clinic an hour earlier, if you can. Creider will meet us there."

"I will."

Meili gave her another hug. "Have you decided yet what to do with The Sun?" she asked as she let go of Bryce.

"No. You have any ideas?"

"I don't, I'm sorry."

Police officers had begun spilling onto the observation deck, conversing with each other and blocking a quick exit. Bryce pointed at the narrow staircase nearby and watched Meili disappear down it quickly. What did Creider want? If it wasn't directly about Matt's murder, maybe he had discovered something incriminating separately? But why had he sounded worried? Why the secrecy? Did his discovery link Matt's death to Richards? Or was it something else altogether?

Bryce suddenly realized that Earl was walking toward her. He was limping again and his face was filled with concern. Seymour rose to his feet and trotted toward him.

"How do you feel, young lady?" he said as he drew near.

"I'm alright. Thank you. How did it go in there?"

Earl shook his head. "Too much police business for my tastes," he replied, surprising her. "I'm with you liberals on this one. Feels like the government is watching our every move these days. Hello Seymour!"

The dog sat down at Earl's feet, looking happy to see him. The sounds of slamming car doors and car engines began filling the air.

"I wanted to compliment you again on your quick thinking yesterday," Earl said in an admiring tone. "I've seen cattle do a lot of things in my life, but never used to scare off someone. That was a good idea."

"Thanks. Did they come up with a plan to catch the guy?"

"They have a plan," Earl replied, sounding skeptical. "Whether they can find him is another question. They seem to think he's hiding on the Diamond Bar, everyone except that Homeland Security feller. Hoo boy. He's a piece of work." Earl shook his head.

"Why is he being so difficult?" Bryce asked.

"I guess there's been more sabotage in the oil field than they've been saying publicly. It's got the Department all riled up. But I sure don't see the link."

"You don't think Matt was murdered by Muslim extremists?" Bryce said, not hiding her sarcasm.

"I do not. I still think it has something to do with what Matt saw up there," he said, nodding to the north. "I know everyone thinks it's all about his love life now, but I know he saw something that upset him."

Bryce nodded as she studied the entrance road, noticing that Meili's car was halfway to the gate already. Three police cars weren't far behind. "How's Brunhilda?"

"Better," Earl replied. "She's one tough gal. But it got me thinking. The police keep talking about this guy being a professional killer and all, but why would he go to all that trouble and not simply shoot her? Why leave her like that to die?"

"Maybe he's just mean. Or don't you think the motorcyclist's a hired gun?"

"No, I do. Something just doesn't feel right, that's all."

"I agree," Bryce said. Behind Earl, she could see Dale working his way across the observation deck toward them.

"Either way, I think Stanley Richards is behind it," Earl said in a low voice. "And I think you should be very careful."

"I'm trying. Are you going to the community meeting?"

"Nate's deal?" Earl said, his voice rising suddenly. "I didn't even know about it until this morning!"

Dale stepped up beside the rancher. "Know about what?"

"The meeting this afternoon," Earl said grouchily.

"You didn't know? It's all over social media, Earl," Dale said teasingly as he patted Earl's shoulder.

"That stuff's a waste of time, if you ask me," Earl growled.

Dale shrugged. "Nate disagrees. He thinks it's going to change the world."

"Good for him," Earl said, sounding tired, Bryce thought. "The world could certainly use a change, though I doubt this is it."

"We'll see. Are you going to go to the meeting?" Dale asked.

"I am," Earl replied, perking up, "but the next time you see Nate remind him that some of us still work for a living."

"I will," Dale replied. "I need to speak to Doctor Miller."

"Ok. I'll see you there," Earl said to Bryce. He touched his hat.

"Come with me," Dale said, nodding her in the direction of the hot tub in the far corner of the observation deck. "There have been a few developments that you need to know about."

"Did you know the video has been posted on the Internet?"

"I do," Dale replied. "The Mayor saw it too and called me a while ago. She's on the warpath again."

"Who posted it?"

"I don't know. I'm trying to figure that out." He shook his head. "This is the downside to this Internet stuff. Nothing stays under wraps anymore." He stopped walking as they reached the corner of the deck. "Kevin Malcolm just called me back."

"What did he say?"

Dale glanced around. "He denies that he and Matt argued about a girl. He even denies ever having a girlfriend."

"That's not what he told me! What did he say it was about?

"Sports."

Bryce's eyebrows shot straight up. "Sports! Do you believe him?"

"I don't know," Dale replied. "That's why I need to talk to Abelard."

"He hasn't appeared?"

"No, he's still missing."

Behind Dale, Bryce noticed Deputy Midas entering the observation deck from the porch. He caught her eye briefly.

"One more thing," Dale said, lowering his voice. "I got a call from a friend of mine who works in the Attorney General's Office in New York. He and I were in the service together and I called him a few days ago because I knew he was investigating some of this Wall Street madness going on. Anyway, he said they were doing background work on Stanley Richards and your uncle's name came up. He said they had a business connection, though he wasn't allowed to tell me any details."

"Was it through that bank, Wolff Schmidt?" she asked.

"I have no idea." He lowered his voice further. "My friend also said, off the record, that this mess on Wall Street is going to blow up big time in the next few months. He told me to get all my stock out of the market, now." He gave her a look and then shrugged. "I told him the only stock I owned had four legs and a tail."

For the first time in a day or two, it felt like, Bryce laughed.

"What else?" she asked.

"We need to find Estevan's truck," Dale said, more to himself than to her. "It's the missing piece of the puzzle."

"Do you think it's on the Diamond Bar someplace?" she asked.

He shrugged. "Possibly."

Bryce realized that Deputy Midas stood not far away, looking like he needed to speak to his boss – or was he trying to eavesdrop? She nodded with her chin. Dale looked around.

"Ok," Dale said to the deputy. "I've got to go," he said to her.

An image suddenly flowed into her mind. Bryce snapped her fingers.

"Wait!" she called loudly, surprising both Dale and Deputy Midas. "There's something on the map you should see."

She walked quickly past them, heading for the front door to the house. Inside, she weaved around two officers still talking to one another in the middle of the living room, one of whom was the sour Homeland Security agent. He eyed her a bit suspiciously, she thought as she strode right past him. She didn't care. Reaching the big table, Bryce pulled her uncle's map of the ranch to her. Dale appeared at her side, his face creased with a frown, followed shortly by Deputy Midas. She stabbed a finger at the house symbol on the map then traced the main road to the ranch Headquarters. She kept tracing – but not to the Shack. The road forked and then forked again. Her finger kept moving to the east paralleling the Alameda River, following a thinner road symbol. She became aware that other officers in the room had crowded on either side of them, watching. Where was it? She had noticed an odd feature on the map yesterday. She backed up at a fork and took another road, still tracing eastward. Her finger left the road and began searching the far side of The Sun, close to the Interstate highway. The symbol was round with hatched lines along its edges. There! Her finger froze on the map. Everyone leaned forward. There were two words below the circular symbol.

Borrow Pit, it said.

"Did you see this?" Bryce asked Dale, who shook his head. "What is it?"

Dale caught the eye of Deputy Midas as he looked up, who nodded. "It's a big hole in the ground," he replied. "Perfect for hiding a truck."

THREE PAIRS of binoculars stared into the distance.

Bryce lowered hers first. She had no idea what to make of the mammoth hole in front of them. It was roughly circular, possibly a half-mile across, and at least thirty feet deep, though she could see spots where the bottom dropped another ten feet or so looking like a giant rat had taken bites out of the ground. The pit had steep sides all around its edge except for the long entry ramp near where they stood and a few slumped walls on the north side. Dale explained on the drive that borrow pits often produced raw material for road construction. He suspected this one opened in the early 1960s when the federal government began to build the Interstate nearby. It was so big, he told her, probably because the river sediment here is full of sand and tiny rocks – perfect for building a road's base layer. It had likely been mined for years, he suspected. Dale also said this type of high-grade sediment was very profitable to a land owner. Did her uncle excavate any of it, she wondered? Her impression was 'no' – an opinion shared by Dale who said there were no fresh signs of digging that he could see in the pit.

There was also no sign of Estevan's truck.

The second person to lower their binoculars was a tall, broad-shouldered older man with short, salt-and-pepper hair under his black police hat who was introduced to Bryce as a Captain in the State Police. She regretted not remembering his name even though he had been in charge of the group of police officers who had hunted for the motorcyclist during the previous evening. He seemed just as upset as Dale by their failure – and just as perplexed. He squinted into the distance. The third set of binoculars rested against Dale's face. There were four other policemen standing nearby, including Deputy Midas and the young policeman from Dunraven who had downloaded the video from her phone. Bryce had intentionally avoided making eye contact with the deputy after their arrival in order to concentrate on the puzzle in front of them, but she could feel his lurking presence. It was weird – he hadn't said or done anything malevolent, but she couldn't shake the creepy feeling he gave her!

"I don't see anything," said the Captain in a deep voice.

"There!" Dale said suddenly. He pointed to the far end of the pit. "I can see part of the pit edge where the dirt is slightly discolored."

The Captain and Bryce immediately lifted their binoculars to their eyes, following the line indicated by Dale's finger. Bryce stared hard but could only see the uniform gray of the pit walls topped by green grass that stretched to the horizon.

"The rest of it is obscured by that part of the side wall sticking out," Dale said, peering through his glasses. "But the top looks disturbed."

"You're right!" said the Captain.

"Let's go!" Dale ordered.

He turned and walked quickly to the Bronco, signaling to the other officers to get into their vehicles. Two of them had been inspecting the long, sloping ramp that led into the pit from where they stood. One of the men signaled to Dale and pointed at the ground. He walked over, followed by the State Police Captain, and they talked for a moment with the officers, nodding at the ground and at the pit. Shortly, they headed back.

"There appears to be a faint tire track in the dirt," Dale told Bryce as they climbed into the Bronco. "Either someone drove down here a while ago and the wind has been blowing the tracks away or someone tried to eliminate them by sweeping it with something. In any case, we'll swing around the tracks at the bottom to be safe."

Bryce nodded as Dale stuck his hand out the window, signaling to the other vehicles. At the bottom of the ramp, he made a looping turn to the left before heading across the pit, bouncing over its rough surface, driving a bit faster than Bryce expected. The pit felt oddly familiar, she thought. The long ramp, the sheer walls on all sides, and the uneven surface gave the place an unworldly feel, reminding her of the scene in the movie *2001: a Space Odyssey* where the astronauts approach the black monolith in the bottom of a pit on the moon. What would they find here? Nothing so exotic, she hoped.

Dale lifted his binoculars to his eyes, double-checking their destination. Halfway across the pit, he pointed.

"See that slump over there? The one slightly more brown than the others?"

Bryce followed his line-of-sight, but shook her head. She didn't see it.

"Part of the wall has collapsed," he continued. "It's not very big, but it definitely looks fresh."

Bryce tried again, but it all looked pretty much the same to her. "Could it have collapsed on its own?"

"Possibly, but we didn't have much of a monsoon season last summer," Dale replied. "That's when the big storms come," he added quickly, anticipating her question.

"What if the truck is here?" she asked instead. "What does it tell you?"

"Fingerprints would be really helpful, for starters," Dale replied as he briefly lifted the binoculars again. "But he's been very careful so far, so I'm not terribly hopeful. If there's dirt from the Shack in it that would be useful too, of course."

"No, that's not what I meant," Bryce said. "What does the truck tell you about Matt's murder? And what does it tell you about Stanley Richards?"

Dale drove on for a moment. "If the truck is here, it suggests Estevan was killed on the ranch, if that's what actually happened. It could also mean his death wasn't premeditated. Like I said before, maybe he doubled-back to the ranch and surprised the killer, who then got the idea to use Brunhilda to make it seem like Estevan came back to steal her."

"So, you're certain that Estevan is dead?"

"You're never certain until you are, right?" Dale said thoughtfully. "We can hope he's ok, but..."

They hit a bad bump in the road suddenly, though it didn't slow Dale down much, she noticed. A glance into the side-view mirror revealed a long trail of dust behind them.

Bryce turned back to Dale. "So, why were they trying to scare me into going home early, do you think?"

"To keep you from finding the Shack, I'd bet."

They hit another bump. Up ahead, Bryce could see that they were fast approaching the end of the pit. It was deeper here than where they had entered, she thought, and the walls were more sheer, except for a slumped section straight ahead.

"There it is," Dale said pointing at the slump.

Bryce nodded absently, thinking about Stanley Richards again. The dots just weren't connecting for her somehow. But what did she know? She was an over-educated cancer specialist living in a suburb of Boston who grew up sailing and liked to go surfing when she could find a few moments of spare time. What was she doing in the bottom of a big hole on a remote ranch looking for a body?

"Do you think he deliberately missed me?" she asked suddenly.

"The guy on the motorcycle?" Dale replied, confused.

"People seem to think he's a professional. Shouldn't I be dead?"

Dale stepped lightly on the brakes as the Bronco approached the slump of dirt against the pit wall. "Not necessarily. Your reactions were fast."

"Hmm," she said skeptically. "Has anyone found the can opener yet?"

Dale gave her a look. "Are you still on that?"

"I am. It bothers me. And one of the reasons it bothers me is because if it's a clue, it's one of the few that doesn't lead back to Stanley Richards. I mean, if there's one person in the world who doesn't need a can opener, it's him."

"Maybe it's in the Shack," Dale speculated. "It hasn't been completely searched yet."

They had reached the slump of dirt. Dale pulled up at a short distance away while the dust settled around them.

"By the way, if you can't match the girl's fingerprints in the Shack with someone," Bryce said, turning to him, "will you actually interrogate the women in the area?"

"I hope not," Dale said sincerely. "But that's up to the FBI."

"That's what worries me."

A moment later, doors slammed as everyone emptied out of the police cars. Bryce took a few steps forward then stopped, not wanting to get in their way. In front of her was a fresh-looking pile of dirt wedged up against a curve in the pit wall. Portions of the wall higher up on both sides had an overhanging feel. She looked down. The ground began to dip sharply as it approached the wall, looking it might have been one of those giant rat bites she saw earlier. Except it was full of dirt. She lifted her head again. A large portion of the wall above the pile looked as if it had collapsed. Its light-brown color contrasted subtly but clearly with the grayness of the adjacent walls.

"This looks good!" Dale said loudly. He pointed at the pile. "It's deep enough to hide a truck and all he had to do was dig out the overhang until it fell and then covered the rest."

The State Police Captain pointed silently at the ground.

"Tracks," Dale said, nodding. "Truck tires. Leading into the hole. Come on!"

Three officers came forward carrying shovels, one of them being Deputy Midas. Another officer stood nearby with a digital camera taking pictures. The State Police Captain and Dale conferred nearby while the young Dunraven officer held up his cell phone as if documenting the activity.

"No video," Dale instructed the young man. "I don't want to see this thing on the Internet later today. Find the truck's license plate instead."

The young officer nodded and lowered his phone.

Bryce studied the wall again. Dale was right, this was a clever place to hide a truck. Park it close to the wall, dig below the overhang carefully, then run.

"You guys ready?" Dale said. The three officers nodded. He took the phone from the young officer and peered into it. "We're looking for New Mexico BDT 439. The first one to find the plate gets a milkshake courtesy of the chief of the Alameda Police Department."

The men chuckled.

"Doctor Miller," he said, turning to her. "You own The Sun. This is your pile of dirt. Do we have your permission to remove it?"

"You do," she replied.

At Dale's nod, the three officers thrust their shovels into the center of the dirt with vigor. Ten minutes later, one of them hit metal. Dale and the Captain stepped closer. A few more shovel strokes revealed the top part of a bumper. From its angle, it appeared that the concealed vehicle was tilted downward, nose-first. Dale indicated to the officers to dig lower and as they removed dirt below the bumper, the rest fell away quickly, revealing the entire length of the bumper as well as a portion of the rear gate of a pickup truck. A long, narrow pile of dirt still remained on the bumper, however, obscuring the place where the license plate should be.

At a signal from Dale, the digging stopped.

With a nod, Dale deferred to the Captain who walked to the

back of the pickup truck, leaned over and carefully pushed away the obscuring dirt from the bumper with gloved hands. Bryce came forward, filled with curiosity. Was the license plate even there? Had it been removed? Is that something professional killers did normally? No, a plate became visible as the Captain lightly brushed away the remaining soil. It was yellow, she saw, with red letters. The Captain suddenly hit the plate with a big puff of breath.

BDT 439 it said.

He reached up and grabbed the latch to the truck's tailgate. He gave it a tug. It didn't move. He tried again, harder. The heavy tailgate fell with a crash, spilling a large quantity of dirt onto the ground like a dry, brown river. As it kept spilling, Bryce gasped.

Exposed in the dirt of the truck's bed were the hand, arm, and shoulder of a man.

———

BRYCE PACED BACK and forth in front of the pink octopi.

The medical clinic was surprisingly full, she thought. Most of the chairs in the waiting area were occupied, mainly with mothers and kids though there were two elderly couples waiting as well. No wonder Meili hadn't appeared yet. Bryce had alerted the receptionist on arriving, who promised to pass the word to Doctor Thomas. But no Meili. It was alright. It gave her time to think about the ranch sale. Upon their return from the borrow pit, Bryce had escaped into her uncle's office, closed the door, and cleared a space on the messy table. She carried a pad of paper and a pen and as soon as she sat down, she wrote the words 'Pro' and 'Con' across the top of the pad. She had faltered at that point, however. What were her best choices? Richards? Pendergast? The Mayor? That obnoxious radio talk show host who shot lions and giraffes? What about Bill Merrill, though she knew his gas wells would lodge themselves permanently on her Con list. She briefly considered again the casino fellow, Rack, but she still couldn't abide the idea that gambling was an acceptable type of economy. It didn't make anything, it just pushed money around – and usually in just one direction. Besides, it was clear the local community didn't want a casino. But did it want a millennial religious sect as neighbors instead? And what about those young girls? Or the insolent young man smoking the cigarette? Or Pendergast himself?

Why was this so difficult?

Bryce glanced at Deputy Midas, who had followed her into the clinic. Dale had assigned him to protect her, though Bryce wasn't sure exactly how safe she felt. The deputy stood against the far wall, both of his hands resting on his heavily weaponized belt. He gave her a cold look. With a sigh, Bryce returned her gaze to the lovely wall mural. Where was Meili? The door to the clinic opened suddenly, flooding the waiting area with sunlight. A young woman wearing a red blouse stepped inside. She scanned the room, decided it was too busy, apparently, and departed abruptly.

Bryce studied the octopi again, whose beaming smile filled the room with happiness. Against her will, her thoughts drifted to her former husband, David. Why did a person click emotionally with some people but not with others? She recalled a research paper she read on the chemistry of human relationships, which argued that it all came down to pheromones and proteins and other dull biochemical stuff. She loved science, but this was nuts. She imagined a man and a woman sitting at a noisy bar having their fingers scanned to see if they had the right protein match before flirting with each other. This was exactly the sort of reductionist nonsense that drove her father crazy. Science wasn't supposed to drain life of its inherent mystery! Thank god for pink octopi.

The door to the back area opened and Meili emerged.

"Doctor Miller!" she said with a smile. "Thanks so much for waiting. I'm sorry it took so long. Come in the back."

Bryce noticed that Meili wore a fresh flower in her coat's lapel.

As she began to follow Meili through the door, Deputy Midas came forward, apparently intending to follow them. Bryce held up a hand and shook her head. No. He pinched his face at her unpleasantly and seemed on the verge of speaking, probably about his boss's orders to stick close to her, but she held up her hand again. He reluctantly stopped walking and she let the door close between them.

"Is Doctor Creider here?" Bryce asked as they stepped into the clean room that they had been in before, noting that it was empty.

"Not yet," Meili replied.

"Isn't that a bit ironic, given his attitude last time?" Bryce said, unable to resist.

"I know. It's not like him to be late."

As they walked into the center of the room, Bryce noticed one corner was filled with what looked like carefully stacked medical supplies.

"Is the clinic always this busy?"

"Usually," Meili replied brightly. "Alameda's population has been growing quickly, thanks to the Mayor's efforts, which means some days it's nonstop around here."

"Do you have enough help? Does Creider help?"

"GP isn't his thing," Meili said, shaking her head politely. "And that's ok with me, if you know what I mean. I have two great nurses. We manage."

Bryce nodded. "Do you have any idea what he wants to tell me?

"I have a guess, actually."

"Does it involve Stanley Richards?" Bryce pressed.

Meili thought for a moment. "No, I don't think so."

She was about to say more when the back door opened. Doctor Creider entered, looking much as he had before, though the slacks and shirt were a different color and his shoes might have been different Italian brand. However, his impatient scowl was the same, Bryce noticed, as was the black briefcase he carried in one hand.

"There you are," he said even though he was the late one.

He paused to make sure the door was securely shut behind him. How big was this secret, she wondered? She shot a frown at Meili, who shrugged ever so slightly.

"Over here," he ordered, pointing to a counter against the far wall. "I don't have much time. But this won't take long."

No chit chat. Bryce smiled to herself. It felt familiar. She had been raised in a household that didn't like idle conversation very much, her mother preferring to get right to the point and her father preferring to focus on the weighty issues of the day.

Creider worked the combination locks on both sides of the briefcase simultaneously. He punched the buttons noisily and lifted up the top.

"I want to start by taking back what I said before," he announced as he reached into the briefcase. "Well, part of it anyway."

Bryce frowned. "What part?"

"The part about incompetence," he replied, not sounding very contrite. "Around here, I mean. In this case, I was wrong."

He lifted a large accordion-style folder out of the briefcase, which Bryce recognized immediately as a type used to hold medical files. This one was secured by a flap over the top and a simple latch. Creider closed the briefcase lid with an elbow and placed the folder on its top. Judging by its size and his need to use both hands, Bryce estimated the report inside, or whatever it was exactly, to be hefty.

"I thought the authorities had misplaced this, remember?" he asked.

Bryce shot Meili a frown.

She thought furiously. "You mean the missing report on the cancer cluster," Bryce said, snapping a finger. "Seven cases of Ewing's sarcoma, is that right?"

"Correct. Though it's a little more complicated than that, as I found out," Creider said. "Anyway, the State Medical Examiner hired a doctor from Colorado to investigate. His report wasn't misplaced, however, like I thought. Turns out, it had deliberately been lost. Destroyed, in a sense. But on whose orders? That's the sixty-four thousand-dollar question."

"Why would someone do that?"

He lifted the report up. "The answer is in here, I suspect."

"How did you find it?"

"I asked my son to look for it. He's a software engineer, or so he says. I wrote him and didn't think about it again because I assumed the report was lost for good, and because my son didn't respond to my email, as usual." He shrugged. "Anyway, this arrived yesterday by express delivery, out-of-the-blue."

He thrust the report at her. "He sent me two copies. This one's for you."

Bryce took it from him a bit grudgingly. "How did he find it?"

"That's a good question. I asked my son the same thing. All I got back was a two word text message." Creider paused. "Deep Net."

Bryce had heard the phrase before, but wasn't sure what it meant exactly. She turned to Meili, but she made a "don't ask me" face.

"Apparently, it's a part of the Internet where they store stuff that people want to keep hidden," Creider said. "Such as certain medical files. State secrets. And investigative reports that no one is supposed to see."

"How did your son find it?" Meili asked.

"I don't know. I'm not sure what my son actually does for a living. I suspect it's high security cyber stuff, probably for a corporation. Not a world I'm interested in, to be honest. It's important, however, because of the other two-word text he sent me later."

Creider paused again for effect, looking pensively at her.

"What did the text say?" Bryce asked.

"It said "Be Careful." Although I don't know what my son does exactly, I take his warning seriously. As should you."

Bryce opened the folder, glancing once at Meili. She pulled out a thick document, seeing almost immediately four large words stamped across the top: NOT FOR PUBLIC DISSEMINA-TION. Meili came close to see for herself and Bryce could sense her frown as she peered at the words.

"Have you looked at this?" Bryce asked Creider.

"Briefly. It's written by one Doctor Steven McGrath, formerly chief epidemiologist at University Hospital in Denver, Colorado."

Bryce looked up. "Formerly?"

"He's missing." Creider said matter-of-factly. "He disappeared shortly after this report was submitted to the New Mexico Medical Examiner's office in 1985. Was it a coincidence? I don't know. The police investigated it as a Missing Person case since there was no note, but they never found him. His wife didn't think there was foul play and believed that he would walk in the door of their house any day. But it's been twenty-three years. She's in a nursing home now." Creider shrugged. "I did some research."

He turned to close the lid of his briefcase.

Bryce narrowed her eyes and tried to recall quickly what she knew about cancer clusters. She knew that a lot of alarms were raised every year to medical authorities about suspected clusters, particularly by family members or coworkers who think they've spotted a trend. But nearly all of them turn out to be coincidences or were statistically unsupported. To trigger a medical investigation, the disease rate being reported as a possible cluster had to be verified as higher than the background rate in the population as a whole, she knew, though unusual groupings of cancer by geography or by age sometimes provoked a closer examination. Even if a review was merited, often the clinical history of a patient was enough to dispel a link with another patient, even if they were related or lived nearby. Red flags went up, however, if the cancer type was rare, tightly concentrated geographically, or highly unusual for a certain age range – all of which might be at work here with the patients that Creider mentioned previously.

They weren't all false alarms. There had been high profile cases of cancer clusters over the years, she recalled, including the infamous early 20th century "radium girls" who worked in factories painting the faces of watches with a substance that contained significant amounts of radium which they ingested when they licked their brushes to keep them wet. It was notorious for another reason: not only did the company lie to the women about the danger posed by the radioactive paint, it later tried to smear their reputations by claiming their symptoms were caused by syphilis contracted by their promiscuous sexual activity! It was enough to make one's blood boil, Bryce remembered feeling when she read the case study. Another awful example involved Marines stationed at Camp Lejeune in North Carolina who drank tap water contaminated by harmful chemicals and developed liver and kidney cancers, among other diseases. Then there was tobacco, of course, the largest and most deadly cancer cluster of them all!

"Did Doctor McGrath identify the probable source of the cancer cluster?" Bryce asked as Creider turned to leave, his briefcase back in his hand.

"Yes, but he was careful in his language," he replied as he checked his watch. "He thought it might be connected to agricultural chemicals. Apparently, they were running field trials on a new herbicide out near Hannigan in the early-1970s. The trials were part of the approval process for the herbicide required by the government."

"Was it approved?"

"It was. No surprise there, as I'm sure you know," he said cynically.

"But the cancer showed up later," Bryce guessed.

"Correct. And Doctor McGrath found a link. Then his report disappeared, probably because the corporation that made the chemicals didn't want word to get out about possible harmful effects."

Bryce let his words sink in.

"And then McGrath disappeared," he added. "And today the corporation is now one of the biggest chemical companies in the world with a well-deserved reputation for attacking its critics relentlessly. Thus my son's warning to be careful, I think."

Bryce weighed the report's heft in her hands. "Do you think Stanley Richards owns the company?" she asked.

Creider shook his head. "I don't know. He can't own everything."

The door to the waiting area opened suddenly, revealing Deputy Midas. He stuck his head into the room. Rather than his usual chilly disposition, however, his face carried a worried expression, Bryce thought. *Was everything ok?* it seemed to say.

"I'll be out in a minute," Bryce said to him, politely.

He nodded and retreated, closing the door.

"I've got to go," Bryce said, placing the report back into its accordion folder.

"So do I," Creider said. He began moving toward the back door. "The report is yours. Do with it what you will."

Meili spoke up. "Didn't you say that two of the cancer patients were still alive?"

"As far as I know, yes," Creider replied as he reached the door.

"Who has the original report?" Bryce asked.

Creider stopped and turned. "Another good question," he said in a worried tone. "My son sent me copies for a reason, I suppose. Maybe he wasn't supposed to have access to the original, I don't know, or was afraid of something." He nodded at the accordion folder. "In any case, I wouldn't let that copy out of your sight."

He pushed the door open and was gone.

"Holy smokes," Bryce said after exhaling at length. "A dangerous report and a missing doctor," she said to Meili. "Just what I need right now."

Doctor Thomas smiled. "I bet! I have to go too. I have some patients to see, but I'll be at the community meeting. You ok?"

Bryce nodded. She wasn't ok, of course, but she didn't know what she could do about it at this point other than go to the meeting and see what else the Fates had in store for her.

"Do you know who you're selling The Sun to yet?" Meili asked as she began walking toward the waiting room door.

"No, but I've made a list," Bryce replied, leaning on the counter.

"Well, that's a start!" Meili said brightly.

Then she was gone.

BRYCE KEPT her head down as she entered the noisy community center.

It was a smaller building than she expected, but perhaps that's why a new convention complex was being built two blocks away, she guessed. The center was a solitary one-story structure separated from the street by a well-watered grass lawn and ringed by parking spaces, each one occupied by a car or truck, she saw with a sinking feeling. The small lot behind the building was full too, as she drove past. She ended up parking two blocks away, which was fine except for the odd experience of having Deputy Midas follow her to the center in his patrol vehicle. To her surprise, he had offered her a ride from the clinic, but she declined, planning to use the short drive to sort out her thoughts about the ranch sale. Instead, she kept turning over Doctor Creider's information in her mind, stoked by another look at McGrath's report after climbing into her car. Seven cases of Ewing's sarcoma over a ten square-mile area of farm country! No wonder the state Medical Examiner ordered an investigation. As for McGrath himself, a quick search on the Internet via her phone as she sat in the car revealed more questions than answers. One newspaper story about his disappearance noted that he and his wife were estranged at the time, apparently due to her unstable behavior. Another story speculated he fled overseas to escape their marriage. A different account hinted that he entered a Witness Protection Program, though it didn't say for what reason. None, however, mentioned the McGrath report or the cancer cluster.

Yet more mysteries, Bryce thought as she walked rapidly to the center.

Deputy Sandoval stood at the front door. She was happy to see him again and he gave her a slight smile and nod of recognition as she arrived. She wanted to apologize for being late, but decided she needed to keep quiet and think again. She carried the pad of paper with the Pro and Con lists she had ended up making for each suitor, intending to review them before it was her turn to speak at the meeting. She had also brought along the copy of McGrath's report, not wanting to let it out of her sight. As she followed an older couple to the door, she noticed Deputy Midas park his patrol car directly in front of the building quite conspicuously, she thought. Was it meant as a warning for someone inside? If so, for whom? But she didn't want to think about it right now. She lowered her head to avoid any eye contact, thinking hard. She had a decision to make! She tried to review the Pro and Con lists in her mind but she couldn't concentrate. She had a suitor in mind, but couldn't bring herself to decide conclusively. Like the rest of them, there were too many Cons!

As she followed the older couple inside, she became instantly aware of the noisy chatter of many voices. She looked up briefly. She had entered a narrow lobby speckled with knots of people. Ahead of her were open double doors that led into a large room from which the intense buzz of human voices spilled. She lowered her head again. Was this a good idea? She could postpone her decision until tomorrow, she supposed, or call the winning suitor when she returned to Boston. It would give her more time to weigh her choices. That hadn't been her original plan, of course, but nothing on this trip had gone as planned, the least of which was getting shot at! On the other hand, she had never been a very good procrastinator. *Get it done* was her motto. Besides, the community had a right to know the fate of The Sun, which was probably one reason so many people were here. Who would the crowd choose if they could, she wondered? Maybe she should ask for a show of hands! That would be an interesting discussion, she contemplated, though it would likely set off more fireworks...

"Doctor Miller!" said a cheery voice.

Bryce looked up in time to see Nate coming at her, his hand extended and a big smile on his hairy face. He wore a red T-shirt bearing the logo of a popular movie franchise.

"It's great to see you again," he said. "Thanks so much for coming."

He was an unlikely politician, Bryce thought as she gripped his hand. He looked like a tech geek she knew at the hospital who had limited social skills, but obviously Nate was a different sort of fish.

"Looks like a big crowd," she said.

"Huge!" he said heartily. "The hall is nearly full. People are anxious to hear from Dale about the investigations. And I know they're all anticipating your decision. It could have a huge impact on Alameda."

She caught his point: don't pick the Mayor's alternative.

"How's this going to work?" Bryce asked, nodding at the room as they worked their way toward the double doors.

"The agenda is straightforward," Nate said. "I'm the moderator and crowd control guy. I'll say a few words and then turn it over to Dale. There'll probably be a lot of questions for him. When Dale's done, you can get up and talk about your decision. Any hints?"

"Yes," Bryce replied, leaning close. "I'm selling The Sun to you."

They laughed. "Funny," he said as they approached the double doors.

The volume of human voices had risen substantially and Bryce could glimpse the heads of many people seated in many chairs within the room.

"Crowd control?" Bryce asked him, remembering his comment.

"Yeah, there are some grumpies in the hall," Nate replied casually. "Grumpy with each other, not with you," he quickly added. "I'll handle them and if I can't, that's what these guys are for." He nodded his head at something behind them.

Bryce turned and saw Deputies Sandoval and Midas following a short distance away. They nodded at her in unison. For the first time that day, Bryce felt butterflies form in her stomach. She had been too preoccupied to feel anxious about the meeting. Normally, nerves were not a problem. The confidence she gained over the years sailing at sea, especially on solo excursions as she grew older, combined with the countless sports competitions she had participated in during high school and college (as well as dealing with arrogant fellow doctors) had largely banished the butterflies. There were exceptions, of course. Surfing in front of experts, was one. Selling a historic ranch was bound to be another.

"Doctor Miller!" a voice cut through the hubbub. It was Dale. He had emerged from inside the room, followed by the stoic State Police Captain, who nodded at her. Dale signaled her to follow him.

"I'm going to head up front," Nate said to her. "See you in a second."

He shook another hand as he walked through the doors. Bryce followed Dale into the noisy room. In front of her were at least twenty rows of folding chairs stretching to the front, split by an aisle, with eight or nine chairs on either side. Most of them were full of people. Her heart sank again.

"How are you doing?" Dale asked, his voice full of concern.

"I'm alright," she lied.

He steered her to the right. Bryce saw a knot of police officers standing just inside the double doors, many of whom she recognized from this morning's meeting at her uncle's house. She could also see people standing close together all along the back wall. The chatter in the air became deafening. She tried to focus, but she felt dizzy suddenly. Dale was saying something to her, but she needed to lower her head again, this time to scatter the butterflies in her stomach. Nate mentioned grumpies. Did that mean the environmentalists were here? Why? Did they think she would actually declare the ranch to be a wolf sanctuary? Dale called them anarchists. Were they here to disrupt the meeting? Would they be that disrespectful? They could – it was another sign of the times. Three years ago, she traveled to New York City with friends to attend a First Amendment rally in support of free speech and the right to gather in peaceful protest only to see the rally disrupted by a gang of right-wingers and angry counter-protestors chanting about how much they loved the Constitution.

Bryce suddenly realized Dale was talking to her about Estevan Gutierrez.

"What?" she said to him, interrupting. "Sorry."

"Estevan had been shot," he repeated, slowing his pace. "In the forehead. Either he knew who the killer was or the person fooled him enough to get close."

Bryce blinked, trying to focus. "Did you find anything else?"

"Not yet. I'll get Doc Creider to look at the body."

She came to a stop and put a hand on his arm. "What about Abelard? Has he come back yet?"

Dale frowned. "No. He's still missing."

She grimaced. "So we don't know what Kevin actually said to Matt?"

"Not yet."

"Isn't that a problem?" she said, lowering her voice. "No rumors about who might be Kevin's girlfriend? Or Matt's?"

"Not yet. Everyone seems to have covered their tracks really well."

"Young lady!" said a voice behind them.

Turning, she saw Earl a few feet away, his cowboy hat in his hand, coming toward her, looking worried.

"I don't mean to interrupt. I just wanted to wish you good luck," he said kindly.

"Thanks. I need it."

"I imagine you've just about had enough of us."

"No, I'm going to miss everybody when I go back," she protested.

"We're going to miss you too," Earl said sincerely, "though we certainly have more than enough liberals around here these days." It was a joke. "Have you made a decision about the ranch?"

Bryce looked at both men. "No," she said quietly.

"Well, you'd better decide quick," Earl warned. "This crowd's expecting to find out."

Bryce nodded and dropped her gaze to the pad of paper in her hand. Where was the Mayor's list? There. Not many Pros. Lots of Cons. Golf courses. She suddenly felt Dale take her by the elbow and gently guide her to the right, following the back wall. He might have been saying something to her but the decibel level in the room had jumped, she could swear, drowning out everything. She saw over-shined leather shoes. She looked up – into the face of the beady, sour-faced Homeland Security officer whose name she couldn't remember. He squinted at her as she passed by. Muslim extremists in Alameda, New Mexico, right.

Fortunately, the next face she saw along the wall was friendly – Frank McBride. He smiled warmly at her. "Good luck," she heard him say over the din.

Thanks, she nodded in reply.

Next to Frank stood a knot of men in black cowboy hats, jeans, boots, and button-down shirts, looking like younger versions of Earl. She didn't recognize a single person. They were ranchers, she assumed, but from where? Neighbors? They nodded their heads at her and touched their hats politely as she walked by, but none smiled. Beyond them, Bryce saw a group of men and women standing in the corner of the room dressed in drab olive and green uniforms. Among them was a tall man she recognized from this morning's law enforcement meeting. He nodded politely to her as well. She peered at the patches on their shoulders. Forest Service. The line of people standing along the wall petered out. As she and Dale reached the corner of the last row of chairs to their left, two or three people turned their heads to look at them, including a man she remembered as one of the golfers from the driving range. He beamed at her.

The butterflies returned.

Dale released her elbow as they turned the corner. They began to walk up the side of the room. The general hubbub had begun to die down, she noticed, no doubt in anticipation of the show about to begin. At the front of the room, Bryce could see a table and two chairs for them and a podium for Nate, who was working his way up the opposite side of the room, still shaking hands. She surveyed the crowd – there had to be at least two hundred people. She turned her head to look at the people standing against the other walls. There was a large group of young people in the far corner, some carrying hand-made signs which prominently contained the word WOLF in big, black letters. She didn't read the rest of the messages because her eye caught the large frame of the Teuton standing in the center of the group, glowering at the room. Standing near them was the lanky, slightly stooped shape of Reverend Pendergast, leaning casually against the back wall. He was alone, his face tilted upward, though she couldn't tell if he was praying or just bored. Next to him stood a man and a woman dressed in khaki uniforms. Wildlife officials? Where was the Mayor? There, across the room, standing near the podium, power-dressed like before, her hands on her hips as she glared at Nate's slow progress up the rows.

"Follow me," Dale said suddenly.

They had reached the corner of the front row. Bryce followed him to the lonely table, dropping her eyes to study the worn beige carpeting on the floor as they walked. The buzz of conversation in the room had dropped by half, she calculated. Nate wouldn't have any trouble getting it to cease altogether when he started the show. Her heart sank again. She had no idea what she was going to do. She had endured what felt like the longest week of her life and she was no closer to a decision about The Sun than she was when she arrived on Monday. Even the lists she had started in her uncle's office earlier this afternoon hadn't helped yet. Her uncle! Why had he done this to her? Dear Niece, I'm sorry to have died without warning and left you a 140,000-acre chunk of prime real estate that everyone covets and maybe is willing to kill for! Good luck!

She heard a dull scraping sound on the carpet. Dale had pulled a chair out for her. She nodded her thanks as she sat. She placed the pad of paper, sitting on top of the accordion folder with the McGrath report, on the table in front of her. Dale sat in the other chair. Nate had reached the podium finally. Beyond him, Bryce could see the Mayor frowning at the crowd as the hubbub continued to fade, her hands still on her hips. Someone coughed.

Nate pulled the microphone from its cradle on the podium and tested it by tapping it against his palm loudly. Someone had closed the double doors in the back, Bryce noticed. Deputies Sandoval and Midas flanked the doors stoically, their hands resting on their belts. With a jolt, she realized Bill Merrill stood against the back wall to the right, his arms folded resolutely across his chest and his cowboy hat hanging from one hand. A deep frown creased his face. Doreen too! She stood against the same wall, just over from the oilman, dressed in deep green and looking anxious. They were separated by a distinguished man that Bryce recognized from the meeting at the Mayor's office. He was the Chamber of Commerce fellow, she was pretty sure. On the other side of Doreen stood the bearded young man who owned the brewery, as she recalled, and between him and the environmentalists stood Nicholas Rack!

Just as Nate was about to speak into the microphone, one of the double doors opened and Meili slipped into the room. Spotting her, Nate pointed to some of the empty seats in the first row, but she waved him off politely and headed toward a blank spot along the left wall, giving Bryce a small wave of encouragement. Nate cleared his throat into the microphone. The crowd grew quiet. Bryce's mind raced again. What if she surprised everyone and picked the wolf sanctuary? That would be a shock! She glanced at the Teuton. No. Whatever the merits of a sanctuary, she couldn't give The Sun to someone dark like that. There were too many self-righteous types in the world as it was. Nate was speaking, she realized, but she wasn't listening. Someone coughed again.

One of the double doors opened again and an unsmiling Kevin Malcolm stepped into the room. Deputy Midas immediately moved two steps over, creating room along the wall. Kevin stepped into the space, put his hands behind his back, and gave Bryce a hostile look from across the room. She lowered her head and stared at the table top. All the suitors were here, which meant they all expected to have a shot at the ranch, which meant all but one would leave very unhappy...

"You ok?" Dale asked her quietly.

She nodded and pulled the pad of paper toward her, revealing the thick accordion folder underneath. It earned a cocked eyebrow from Dale.

"A medical file," she said.

"Someone must be pretty sick."

She half-smiled, appreciating his attempt to lighten the

mood. She picked up a pen resting on the table and turned her attention to the Pro/Con lists for each suitor. After a moment of deliberation, she struck through two items on the same line. Dale peeked over her shoulder, curious.

"What are you doing?" he asked quietly.

She crossed off two more items. "Trying to decide who gets the ranch."

"Interesting. Is that something you learned from your parents?"

"No. Benjamin Franklin," she said tersely. She looked up apologetically, realizing she was being rude. "I learned it from a professor in college. This is how Franklin made decisions. He'd make lists for and against something. If they were equal in weight, he'd cross them out. Whatever's left, wins. It works pretty well. The trouble is you're supposed to do it over a couple of days, not at the last minute."

Bryce could tell that Nate was reaching the end of his opening comments. Dale would be next. The room was nearly silent. Dale seemed remarkably calm, she thought. She just had to pick among multi-million dollar offers – he had to deal with a dead ranch foreman, a dead ranch hand, a tortured horse, a professional killer on the loose, a boss on the warpath...

Nate cleared his throat.

"Who should I sell The Sun to?" she whispered suddenly to Dale.

He was listening to Nate and seemed surprised at the question. "I don't know," he whispered back. He glanced at her lists. "Eenie, meenie, miney, moe?"

She smiled. It wasn't a bad idea, though Franklin would disapprove...

Someone coughed again in the audience.

"As you know," Nate was saying, "there have been some disturbing events over the past few days."

Dale turned to listen. Bryce dropped her gaze to the lists again. She struck two more items off. She wasn't making much progress. The Cons lists were too long. There weren't enough Pros. She sighed. Nate was still talking, saying something now about the search for the man on a motorcycle. Bryce felt Dale shift restlessly in his seat. Someone coughed again.

Bryce froze as an electric jolt ran through her.

She knew that cough.

She looked up sharply. She saw a sea of attentive faces, all watching Nate at the podium. The cough had come from somewhere near the back of the room, toward the left. She scanned the faces, waiting. The cough came again, sounding wet. Bryce caught a glimpse of a hand rising to a face. She leaned to her right. It was a young woman in a red blouse – the same one who had briefly stepped into the clinic that afternoon!

Bryce turned to Dale. "Who's that coughing?" she asked in a whisper.

He had been preparing to rise to his feet. He gave her a serious frown.

"Wait," Bryce said. "Listen."

A moment later, the cough was repeated. Dale leaned to his left, still frowning. He scanned the back of the room. "It's Charlotte," he said, turning back. "Charlotte Scott. She works the front desk at the electric co-op. Why?"

Bryce stared at him. "That's a mono cough. She has mono."

"And?"

She gripped his arm. "Matt had mono. Meili said he came into the clinic four weeks ago for treatment. Mono has a three to four week incubation period. The timing works."

Dale's frown deepened. "Charlotte and Matt?" He shook his head. "It's impossible."

"Why?"

"I would have heard about it, for one thing," he declared, still whispering. Bryce's eyebrows went up. "Ok. She's married for another."

Bryce's eyebrows went up even more.

"That's not what I meant." He leaned close, nearly whispering. "She's married to a guy who is a sniper with the Army..."

Bryce's eyes opened wide.

"No, he's been stationed in Iraq for the last six months. There's no way he could..."

Dale's voice drifted off and he dropped his gaze to the table.

Charlotte coughed. Nate was still talking, thankfully.

"Excuse me," Dale said.

He stood up quickly and pulled out his cell phone. He walked to the far corner. After punching in a number, he lifted the phone to his ear and turned his back.

Bryce turned to Nate, who had paused, and made a rolling motion with her finger. He nodded and cleared his throat again into the microphone. The cough in the back of the room came again, quieter this time. Was Charlotte worried, Bryce wondered? She should be. Nate was talking again, but many of the people in the crowd were watching the police chief. Bryce detected a motion to her left. Turning, she saw Dale motion to Deputies Sandoval and Midas to come forward, which they did quickly. He still had the phone stuck to his ear. Nate had faltered momentarily at the podium. Bryce gave him another rolling sign and he resumed speaking again. Behind him, the Mayor had come forward, her face full of alarm.

Bryce turned back to Dale, who was conferring with the deputies now.

"Well, since Dale is busy for the moment," Nate was saying, "perhaps Doctor Miller would like to speak to us about the future of The Sun."

Bryce whipped her head around. *What?* She wasn't ready! Nate was giving her a friendly smile. He nodded his head at her.

No! She scanned the room in desperation. She saw the two deputies walking quickly toward the back. Where were they going? She glanced at Nate and shook her head at him. *No!* She looked at the lists again on her pad and then raised her head to watch the deputies exit smartly through the double doors. All the eyes in the room, however, were looking at her.

Suddenly, Dale was whispering into her ear.

"Her husband asked for emergency leave from his unit nine days ago," he whispered. "To come home to Alameda. Family crisis, he told his commanding officer."

Bryce shot him a look of shock.

"I'm going to try to talk to Charlotte," Dale whispered again. "I don't know what she'll do, but if she runs, then your theory is probably correct."

He stood up quickly and walked to the left. All eyes were on him now, including her own. Dale turned the corner of the first row of chairs and began striding down the side.

Nate must have assumed the police chief was going to follow his deputies outside because he cleared his throat again. "It seems we have a small delay," he said. "Does the Mayor want to make any announcements?"

The Mayor came forward wearing a deeply puzzled frown. She took the microphone from Nate but looked like she was searching for something useful to say. Bryce turned back to Dale. He had stopped three rows from the end and was now making a subtle "come with me" hand gesture to Charlotte. Bryce leaned to the right. The young woman had a finger pointed at her chest. *Me?* Dale nodded, but Charlotte turned her head abruptly toward the front of the room and neutralized her expression. The Mayor had stepped to the podium, apparently oblivious to the drama unfolding in the third row. She and Nate exchanged a quiet word as many of the faces in the room turned their attention to them. Not Bryce. She watched Dale try again with Charlotte, his hand gesture more emphatic this time, but her eyes remained fixed straight ahead. She seemed to be struggling to repress a cough, Bryce thought. She looked scared too.

Dale took a step to his right, putting a friendly hand on the shoulder of an elderly man who occupied the seat in front of him. Dale gestured with his other hand again, not hiding the message at all now. Bryce saw Charlotte swallow. She was very pretty, Bryce thought, probably Matt's age, with dark, curly hair, high cheekbones, and a smooth complexion. It wasn't hard to imagine what had happened. Bryce wasn't entirely sure what an electric co-op was, but she could easily visualize Matt chatting up the attractive young woman at the front desk during visits to the office to pay a bill or order some sort of repair. She might have been flattered by the attention of the charismatic, good-looking cowboy...with a husband away for months at a time...

Charlotte stood up suddenly. Her face was trying hard to maintain a neutral mask, but underneath it was cracking, Bryce could tell. Fear was breaking through. Her secret was no longer a secret. Charlotte moved. Rather than turn toward Dale, however, she faced the other way and worked her way past the people in her row until she reached the main aisle. Then she sped toward the back of the hall, apparently heading for the double doors. Bryce watched Dale track her along the side of the hall, walking quickly. She held her breath. Her husband was a sniper! Could it be true? Could all their theories have been so wrong?

Dale turned the corner at the last row, but it was clear Charlotte would reach the doors before him. Except, she didn't. She turned abruptly to her right, aiming for the exit door in the far wall that led outside. She quickened her pace to a half-trot. Soon, she was running. She ran past the environmentalists, who had lowered their signs and were now gawking at the spectacle unfolding in front of them. To Bryce's surprise, Dale maintained his steady pace across the room even though Charlotte would easily beat him to the exit. She extended both arms and hit the release bar in the middle of the door at full speed. It made a 'clank' sound and opened smoothly, revealing bright light outside.

Charlotte left the hall and the door closed slowly behind her.

Bryce looked at Dale, who had turned his head and was trying to catch her eye. He nodded emphatically at her before pushing the door open himself and stepping outside.

The room was silent.

Bryce dropped her eyes to the table, her mind racing. A secret love affair. A jealous husband. A cold-blooded crime of passion. A cover–up. A tortured animal. Missing people. So much sickness in the world. Division and anger. Not enough tenderness, love or kindness.

She stood up at the table.

"I'm keeping it!" she announced to the crowd.

Heads swiveled toward her as one. She could feel the eyes of Bill Merrill, Doreen, Rack, Pendergast, and Mister Nibble boring into her from the back of the room.

She didn't care.

"I'm keeping it," she repeated. "The ranch. The Sun. I've decided not to sell it. I'm keeping the cattle too. It will stay a ranch!"

The room stared at her.

"My uncle had a vision for The Sun," she said, "as a working ranch that could help the community. He willed it to me, I believe, to keep that vision alive. Not to sell it and get rich. I have all the money I need…"

She paused as the stunned silence persisted.

"But I need your help. I can't do this alone. I want this to be a community effort. I want us to work together…"

She fell silent. No one had moved a muscle. She had made a huge mistake. What was she thinking!

She sat down miserably.

Someone moved in the back of the room. It was Frank McBride. He stepped forward, raised his hands and clapped. The sound was lonely, Bryce thought, in the silence. Still, she appreciated his effort.

Then there was another clapping sound, from her right, loud. It was Nate, near the podium. He clapped vigorously and gave her a nod when their eyes met. Meili stepped forward from her wall, also clapping. Someone in a cowboy hat stood in the crowd. It was Earl! A woman stood. It was Isabella Ortiz, the community activist, followed by all the people in her row. They clapped. Others stood too and clapped. Not all. In the back, Bryce saw some of the environmentalists cross their arms unhappily, including the Teuton. She looked across the room at the knot of ranchers. They weren't applauding either. More people stood – the golfer guy, Mister Salazar from the veteran's lodge, the woman who owned the Saint Sebastian hotel, and the Boy Scout leader she had spoken to earlier in the week – they all stood and clapped!

Bryce breathed again.

Doreen left abruptly. As she passed in front of Bill Merrill, he put on his hat, gave Bryce a cold look and headed for the double doors as well. Reverend Pendergast followed, his normally cheery face transformed into a dark scowl. Rack was next. He didn't even bother to make eye contact. A moment later, Kevin Malcolm turned to leave, but not before giving Bryce a dark look. How would Stanley Richards take her decision? Not well, she suspected. She'd worry about it later. Bryce had avoided looking at the Mayor. She looked now. To her surprise, she didn't seem upset. She wasn't applauding, but she wasn't scowling either. She stood at the podium, her hands folded in front of her, looking thoughtful. Maybe she was planning her counterattack. Maybe not.

As the clapping began to fade, Bryce noticed movement in the back of the room. The environmentalists had decided to leave, pushing their way out the side exit, taking their signs with them. The double doors suddenly opened in the back and Dale entered, followed closely by Deputy Sandoval. What had happened to Charlotte? Did Deputy Midas catch her? Dale raised an arm into the air and signaled the Mayor that he wanted to speak.

"Everyone!" the Mayor said into the microphone. "Everyone! Listen! Give Dale your attention!" She pointed. "In the back of the room!"

Heads turned and the low murmur of voices that had begun to build died quickly. Dale dropped his arm. Bryce noticed a flash of sunlight to her right as the exit door in the front of the room opened briefly behind the podium.

Bryce dropped her gaze to the lists of Pros and Cons. What had she done! Was she crazy? She could think of a dozen Cons off the top of her head! She had a job. She wasn't moving to New Mexico. She had no one to run the ranch. She didn't know the first thing about cattle. She liked to sail and surf and be a doctor! She couldn't think of a single Pro, other than preventing The Sun from being developed by the others.

Dale was talking but he was too far away to be heard clearly. The Mayor had stepped away from the podium to listen, as had Nate. Bryce was aware that someone was approaching, but she continued to stare at her lists. Had she really decided to keep the ranch? Was she *nuts*? No. The decision felt right, in an odd way. Her uncle was making plans for the property when he died. Maybe she could talk with Frank and Earl...

Something poked her in the ribs.

"Don't move," a voice growled in her right ear. "Don't even look up."

Involuntarily, she turned toward him. She saw a young man hidden behind sunglasses wearing a woolen cap pulled down over his ears.

The object poked her ribs again. "I said don't!" he growled again.

She looked down, fear spreading all over her body. It was him, of course, the man on the motorcycle. She recognized his frame-size. He was wearing sunglasses no doubt to reduce the chance someone in the room would recognize him as Charlotte's husband, the professional Army sniper. It had to be him. Her spirits sank. Dale was still talking. Bryce lifted her head a tiny bit in an attempt to make eye contact with Deputy Sandoval at the back of the room, but the gunman poked her in the ribs again.

"Get up," he hissed. "And keep your eyes down!"

She stood. He put his hand on the small of her back and pressed her to the right, toward the exit. Her mind raced as she walked. What could she do? She raised her eyes, searching for anyone's shoes nearby, but there was no one. The gunman was hiding behind her too, so it was doubtful anyone would notice what he was doing. She slowed her pace, but he pressed harder on her back, almost pushing her. She could feel her heart beating heavily.

"Don't!" he threatened. "I told you!"

Wait! Before she could think twice, she twisted her head to look at the table top behind her. He poked her again.

"What part of *don't* don't you understand?" he hissed.

"I need that," she whispered, nodding at the accordion folder. "It's a medical file."

"Too bad for your patient," he said. "Let's go."

He pushed her forward firmly. The McGrath report! She couldn't leave it behind! Why hadn't she grabbed it right away?

Who would find it first? Dale? One of the deputies? Dale was saying something about the FBI to the crowd. Should she shout? Would he actually shoot her? Of course, he would.

That's what he did for a living.

As they approached the exit, he removed his hand from her back, but he kept the gun firmly pressed against her right side. She had no doubt she would be shot if he needed to get away. He had already killed twice and now had been exposed. What did he have to lose? She, on the other hand, had everything to lose.

They were at the door.

"Push it open," he ordered.

She pushed the bar and squinted as bright light struck straight her square in the face. She could smell the fresh air as they stepped outside. She heard the door click behind her.

"Go right and keep your eyes on the sidewalk," he ordered harshly. "I know where your car is."

He sounded scared, she realized. Her mind raced. "Where are we going once we get there?" she tried.

"No talking either!" he barked into her ear. "Just walk."

She could hear a vehicle approaching on the street and was tempted for a second to look up, but he anticipated her thought and poked her ribs with the gun. She kept her head bowed submissively. Her mind raced again. He was desperate. He needed a hostage. There was no other escape for him now that his secret was out. What did criminals do with hostages? Bargain. But bargain for what? She felt his hand on her back again, giving her the shivers. He pressed her to walk faster. They had reached the end of the building and were going to turn the corner. In a second, they would be hidden from sight. Her mind kept racing. Was there something she could do?

"Don't try anything!" he hissed, correctly anticipating her thoughts again.

He was definitely scared, she thought, beneath the tough guy image.

"Head down!" he ordered as they stepped off the curb. He pushed her forward, directing them across the street.

"What are you doing to do to me?"

"Shut up!" he barked.

She took a deep breath to calm herself. His plan had fallen apart. He had asked the Army for Emergency Leave to come home to deal with a family crisis, Dale said. In other words, he found out about the affair between Matt and his wife somehow. He came home in a rage. Perhaps it wasn't her first infidelity. Maybe it was the straw that broke his back. Maybe he came home to kill. Did he watch them drink wine on the cabin's porch? Waited while they made love? Seethed. Struck. Panicked. If Charlotte learned later about her husband's plan to come home, she would know he killed Matt. She would talk.

He needed a plan.

They reached the opposite curb. He pushed Bryce hard to the right again, almost causing her to stumble. She studied her feet. She knew where they were – almost at her car.

"Keys," he demanded suddenly.

She unzipped the pockets on her vest and dutifully complied. As he accepted the keys with his free hand, she lifted her head slightly if see if she could recognize anyone in the street, but he quickly poked her again with the gun, harder this time.

"Down!" he ordered, making her feel like a dog.

They reached the car. She heard the familiar single 'beep' as he unlocked the doors with the remote unit.

"You get to drive," he hissed. "Keep your head down," he added unnecessarily as they walked around the front of the car.

She opened the door and climbed in. He slammed it, hard. A moment later, she could hear the door behind her open. The car shifted as he sank into the back seat, causing her to wish that she had opted for the less expensive two-door model instead. She waited, head bowed. She heard a jangle of keys then something touched her roughly on the right shoulder. The keys jangled next to her ear. She took them and inserted the key into the ignition. A moment later, the engine came to life.

"I'll need to lift my head to see where I'm going," she said.

"No kidding," he said sarcastically. "Let's go."

As she raised her head, she felt it touch the barrel of the gun behind her right ear. She closed her eyes and tried to calm her nerves. He needed her alive. It was his only hope.

"Which way?"

"Left," he ordered. "Go three blocks then turn left again."

She tried to see Alameda in her head, but failed. "Where are we going after that?" she asked, opening her eyes.

"The Sun," he growled. "No wrong turns," he warned.

No wrong turns, she promised herself.

BRYCE COULD STILL SEE a trace of dust lingering in the air.

She sat in a chair facing the broken glass door inside her uncle's house, her hands bound tightly behind her by a pair of plastic handcuffs. Beyond the observation deck she could see the long entrance road and the gate on the highway, all empty save the dust. The drive to The Sun from town had been uneventful. He remained stubbornly silent. She tried to ask two questions and got poked in the head both times with the barrel of the gun for her efforts. The first time she asked how he found out (about the affair), drawing a painful poke. She couldn't help herself – *how had he heard*, she wondered? Iraq was a long way from Alameda, New Mexico. It was unlikely that Charlotte had confessed in an email or otherwise given her secret up voluntarily. Perhaps someone had followed her to the Shack. Kevin? Was she his girlfriend too? Charlotte didn't seem like his type, though Bryce wasn't sure why she felt that way. You never knew. The second question she had begun to ask during the drive involved the two GO HOME messages, but he cut her off with another poke, though less painfully. What had been their purpose, she wondered? To keep her from finding the Shack, as Dale speculated? Was it a distraction? Part of a larger plan? Had he panicked?

They drove on in silence.

After parking in front of the house, he told her to look at the ground as she climbed out of the car. But halfway up the steps, she raised her head, having detected Seymour at the top of the stairs. He wagged. The gun poked her in the back roughly.

"Do that again and I'll shoot the dog," he had hissed to her.

He *was* scared. She heard it plainly in his voice. Maybe that's why he kept quiet, so she wouldn't detect his nervousness – or perhaps because he had no idea what to do next. His desperate framing of Estevan for Matt's murder had fallen apart. Abelard found Brunhilda. She found the Shack and the borrow pit. Dale found the body. He desperately needed a new plan. Bryce could see him standing outside the community meeting hall, fretting. A police officer appeared, followed shortly by Charlotte bursting out the side door – right into the officer's arms, stopping her flight as Dale had instructed. He watched from across the street or the far side of a parked car, his panic spreading. Charlotte would confess. One call to his unit in Iraq and they would know about his Leave. His goose was cooked. Bryce kept her eyes fixed on her feet all the way up the stairs. At the front door, she dropped the keys accidently. She flinched, expecting a poke from his gun. Nothing happened. Inside the house, he pulled out a chair, bound her hands and ordered her to sit in front of the glass door.

She sat.

Bryce heard a sound behind her. It was metallic, sounding vaguely military. What was he doing back there? It stopped and the house was silent again. What was Dale up to? Surely, she had been missed. Dale was probably kicking himself. But it wasn't his fault she had become a hostage. The guy had been lucky. There was another sound behind her, this time the shuffling of paper. He was probably looking through the various police materials that had been left on the table from the morning's meeting. Or else he was surveying the big map of the ranch that she had used to find the Shack. She heard a sheet of paper scoot along the table top, sounding like a map. There was a pause.

He knew now how she had foiled his plan.

"What's your name?" she said suddenly, surprising herself.

"Be quiet," he ordered, his voice unsteady. "Ben," he added after a moment.

"How long have you and Charlotte been married?" she tried.

There was movement behind her. He was going somewhere. To the kitchen? The bathroom? No. There was shuffling sound near the table. He was looking at the other papers, probably trying to figure a way out of his dilemma.

"How did you find the cabin?" she ventured.

"I followed her, how do you think?" His tone was harsh.

Bryce swallowed. It probably wasn't productive to remind him of the affair. Was it the first time she had been unfaithful, she wondered? Was his rage at Charlotte for her betrayal sudden or cumulative? Bryce twisted her hands. The plastic handcuffs were biting into her skin. What was Dale doing?

"How long have you lived in Alameda, Ben?"

He greeted her question with silence.

Not long, Bryce guessed. No one had recognized him as he followed his wife, and herself, around town. Was Saturday night the regular rendezvous date for Matt and Charlotte, she wondered? Bryce imagined the young woman heading out from town under the cover of darkness, her seething husband following on his motorcycle at a safe distance. She saw Charlotte fumble with the lock at the gate in the woods, cursing the dark, checking the road behind her, not knowing that he had pulled over, lights out, to watch.

"Did you know my uncle?"

"I said, be quiet!" Ben ordered, sounding scared again. "He was an idiot. Everyone thought so."

"Did you know I had inherited the ranch? Did I surprise you when I arrived?"

There were more shuffling sounds. He was moving around again.

Bryce took a deep breath. She imagined Matt and Charlotte's parting. The door to the Shack opening. The fresh air on their faces. A stretching of arms. A kiss on the porch. A hug. A laugh. The tinkling of keys as Charlotte walked to her car. The engine turning over quietly. A wave goodbye. Matt watching her drive off, smiling. Ben grabbing a pipe from the pile of debris near where he hid.

The shuffling sound stopped.

"Why did you put the Go Home message on the BBQ grill?" she tried. "So you could scare me by triggering the gate alarm over and over?"

Silence.

"Why couldn't you shoot the horse? Did you grow up on a ranch? Or a farm?" She waited. "My grandparents were farmers in Nebraska, though I never got to see their place. My mother didn't like farming at all, or farm animals…"

"Shut up!" he interrupted loudly, sounding like she had touched a nerve. "I couldn't do it, ok? I couldn't shoot her like that. I should have, but I didn't. I figured she would die on her own."

You figured wrong, Bryce said to herself.

"Did you mean to kill Estevan, Ben?"

He was moving around again. "No," he said simply. "He was down at the tank. He called the bastard on the radio. I heard him. Sounded like there was something wrong with the well. He wanted help. I was afraid he was going to come up and find the body."

"That's when you got the idea to frame him."

Ben didn't respond.

"Did you come back from Iraq intending to kill Matt?"

"No."

There was more clinking behind her, louder this time. Guns, she assumed. He was getting ready to do something.

"But then you saw them."

"Shut up," he barked, sounding nervous again.

There was a ruffling sound now, as if he were putting on some article of clothing. He was wearing a sweater when he abducted her, but had apparently removed it after he made her sit in the chair. Was he putting it back on now?

"How did you find out?" she tried again.

"I got a note," he replied, surprising her. "In the mail."

"From who?"

"Didn't say."

Bryce heard beeps close behind her. Ben was dialing her cell phone, having demanded the device and its key code earlier. There was a pause.

"Dale Archuleta?" she heard him ask.

Suddenly the phone appeared in front of her face, resting in a gloved hand. He held it up to her ear.

"Hello," she could hear Dale say, sounding far away. "Bryce, it that you?"

She felt the muzzle of the gun against her neck. "Tell him you're fine," Ben hissed.

"Yes. I'm fine Dale," she lied.

"Where are you?"

She felt another nudge by the gun. "On The Sun" she said as calmly as she could, staring out the glass door. "At my uncle's house," she added almost casually.

There was a pause on the line. "Ok," Dale said.

The phone disappeared, as did the gun muzzle. "We want a helicopter," Ben demanded. "Now."

Bryce slumped as she listened. A helicopter? Where were they going to go, Mexico? Could a helicopter even make it that far?

"I don't care!" Ben shouted suddenly, sounding very scared.

Suddenly, Bryce realized he had moved to a point in the room where she could see his blurry reflection in the broken glass door. His sunglasses were gone. He was a kid! He was clean-faced, had close-cropped brown hair and wore dark clothes from head to foot. He was medium-sized but skinny and had a military bearing, reminding her of Earl. She couldn't make out his eyes in the blur, which seemed appropriate.

He paced. "You heard me. We want a helicopter!"

There was a motion on the observation deck. It was Seymour. He had come up the narrow stairway and now stood at the glass door, his tail wagging, wanting in. He whined. She waggled a foot at him as carefully as she dared trying to shoo him away.

"No excuses!" Ben shouted suddenly. "And no tricks! Or she dies."

A bolt of fear shot through her. Wait! Bryce realized that only her hands were tied. She wasn't bound to the chair by anything. It would be fairly easy to rise and run. True, Ben had a gun in his hand, and true he was a highly trained marksman, and true the front door was closed and possibly locked. Opening it would be difficult. What about the garage? If she could reach the wall button and open the door...

She heard a beep.

Ben hung up the phone and moved out of reflection range. She half-expected him to say something about his plan. Instead, she heard the metallic sound again. A rattling this time. Had he broken into her uncle's gun safe? He probably had the skills to do so, though she doubted he needed the extra weapons. There was more rattling. Did he expect a firefight? The prospect terrified her. That's probably why he placed her in front of the glass door. As long as Dale and the officers could see her, they wouldn't attack. She stared out the door at the grasslands beyond the observation deck, trying to remember that first day on the ranch...

Seymour whined. She waggled her foot at him again, more aggressively this time. He got the hint, turned and trotted off. What a good dog!

"Do you like wine?" she asked suddenly.

The metallic sound stopped. She waited.

"What did you say?" Ben said finally, sounding surprised.

"Do you like wine? There's two hundred bottles down in the cellar. Help yourself." It was worth a try, she figured.

"Shut up." He grunted. "What kind of wine?"

"All kinds. Red, white. Fancy stuff, mostly. There's an empty bottle on the kitchen counter, take a look for yourself."

Nothing happened. Then she heard the soft tapping of shoes as he crossed the floor to the kitchen. There was a glass-on-tile scraping sound, followed by more silence.

"It's all down in the cellar."

The wine bottle clinked on the counter top. She heard more shoe tapping sounds. Then silence. Where was he?

"How's the war in Iraq going?" she asked, testing to see where he was.

More silence. Had he gone down to the cellar as she hoped? Should she run for it? Bryce sat up straight in the chair.

"Did you kill a lot of people?" she asked.

Nothing. Run! She was about to stand up when she heard a footstep, following by the clink of a wine bottle again on the counter. There was a squeaking sound, followed by a pop! He had snuck down to the wine cellar and back too fast! She silently cursed.

Her phone rang.

"It's for you," Ben said. "A doctor."

She sighed. Not now.

"A Doctor Thomas," he added.

Bryce blinked. "Is it a Chicago area code?"

He grunted an assent.

Bryce's mind ran. Why was Meili calling her? "It's about a very sick patient," she said. "It's important. Let me speak to her."

The phone had kept ringing, urgently it seemed to Bryce. Then she heard the beep. A moment later the phone suddenly appeared next to her ear again – but far enough away that he could listen.

"Hello?" she heard Meili ask.

"This is Doctor Miller," she said, using her best office voice.

"This is Doctor Thomas," Meili said, equally officious. "I'm sorry to bother you on your vacation Doctor Miller, but I thought you'd like to know that the test results you ordered have come in."

Bryce frowned. *What test results?* "And the prognosis?" Bryce said, trying to keep her voice calm.

"Mixed, at best," Meili said. "There's been some progression in the liver tumors, but also some degeneration, particularly in the kidneys. And the condition is worsening quickly. We're not sure what the next course of action is exactly. Give me a call when you get back. That sound ok?"

"Yes," Bryce replied.

The phone disappeared. It clicked off.

*The condition is worsening quickly...*What did she mean? *We're not sure what the next course of action is exactly.* Why had she said that? Dale was behind the call, Bryce was certain, but what was he trying to tell her? That they didn't know what to do? That wasn't very encouraging. But why would they go to the trouble of calling her? Bryce heard a shuffling sound behind her, somewhere in the kitchen, followed by the clink of a glass, followed by a splash of liquid. He was drinking. Maybe that hadn't been such a good idea after all. She tried to think. Something was happening, that's why Meili called. But if it was good news, why didn't she say so? Why say the test results had been mixed? There was another clinking sound from the kitchen. He was refilling the glass.

"Do you like being a sniper?" she asked.

The glass clinked sharply on the counter. She waited.

"No."

"Then why did you become one?"

"Because I can kill things from a long ways away," Ben said, a bit proudly. "I grew up hunting with my dad."

"Where?"

"Idaho."

"Did the Army make you into a sniper against your will?"

"Shut up!" He made more splashing sounds.

Yes, they did. Could she use this knowledge somehow?

Bryce suddenly became aware of a different noise – low and distant. Was someone driving down the entrance road? If so, why hadn't the Mozart alarm gone off? She tried to peer through the glass door at the road, but the glare was too strong.

"I didn't want to go into their program, just so you know," Ben said, sounding angry. "They made me do it."

"Who made you do it?"

"The Army. We just got married. I needed to support Charlotte," he said plaintively.

Bryce frowned as the rumbling sound grew louder. "How did your dad feel about you becoming a sniper?"

"I didn't ask."

"Had he been in the military too?"

"The First Gulf War."

Bryce searched her memory – didn't Earl say Dale had served in that war? Saddam. Kuwait. Oil. The rest was fuzzy. What was the year? 1991. She had been nearly twenty years old and not paying attention.

The rumbling sound kept growing.

"Was your dad in the Army too?" she asked.

Ben didn't respond. She waited. Did he hear the sound as well? Yes, of course he did! Bryce suddenly recognized the noise.

It was the sound of a helicopter flying toward them.

The glass clinked sharply on the counter top. She could hear him walking swiftly toward her. At the same moment, her phone rang again.

There was a beep.

"Chief Archuleta," she heard Ben say very close behind her. A moment later, she felt the muzzle of his gun on her neck again. "You don't say? That is good news."

He was trying to sound calm, Bryce thought.

"Where do we want to go?" he said loudly. "That's a good question. Wouldn't you like to know? That'll be a little secret between the pilot and me."

Bryce's heart sank.

There was a beep. Then silence – except for the growing

thud of the helicopter. He removed the gun muzzle from her neck. She heard footsteps. Should she run for it?

"Are we going to Mexico?" she asked, testing his location.

"Shut up," he said from somewhere deep in the living room. "Keep your face straight ahead."

The helicopter sounds were loud now. Her mind raced. Did the police normally let hostage-takers go? Weren't they supposed to negotiate first? Why was it happening so fast? Were they making an exception for her? Was it an Army helicopter? Had Ben been given a pardon for his crimes by the Pentagon? Wait. What had Meili said? *We don't know what the next course of action is. The test results were mixed.* It wasn't a police helicopter.

It belonged to Stanley Richards.

There were more metallic sounds behind her, mixed with a scooting noise. He was pulling his gear together, she guessed, preparing to leave. Seymour suddenly appeared at the door again, wagging. He wanted in. She waved her foot at him, but this time it didn't work. He looked at her forlornly through the glass, as if knowing a tempest was about to descend on them. Where would they put the helicopter down? In the parking area again? What about the car? The space was too tight! She waggled her foot at the dog. The thudding grew louder. She looked up. There it was in the sky! A big black dot to the left of cardboard patch covering the bullet hole in the door. Bryce turned her head to the right to look at the front door. Should she run for it? Then she heard the sound of a gun being cocked.

"I told you to look straight ahead!" he yelled nervously.

"Please let the dog in!" she yelled back. "Before they land."

"Better if I just shoot him now."

"No!" she cried, wagging her foot madly at Seymour, shooing him away. He flattened his ears and turned away.

The helicopter was very close. As she watched, the black machine drifted out of her view, preparing to land in the parking area. Bryce stared at the entrance road through the glass glare and the rising dust, but it remained empty. No Calvary troops coming to the rescue. Dust began to swirl in waves, filling the air. The house began to be engulfed in a brown shroud. She could hear bits of rock pelt the windows near the front door. Slowly, everything outside turned opaque, lost in a maelstrom of noise and flying dirt.

She closed her eyes. She heard the timbre of the helicopter's engine slacken a tiny bit. It had landed. The muzzle of the gun suddenly pressed against her neck.

"Get up," he ordered.

She got up. Without waiting to be told, she turned and began walking toward the front door. The muzzle followed. The engine sound continued to diminish outside and she could sense the volume of dirt and dust in the air falling as well. Ben's hand grabbed the door knob, twisted it and opened the door for her. For a moment, the muzzle disappeared from her neck. Then it returned, pressing harder than ever.

"No tricks," he ordered. "And no talking."

She stepped onto the porch, squinting to keep the dust out of her eyes as the helicopter's blades continued to slow down. Somehow, the pilot has artfully wedged the machine into a narrow space directly in front of them. The adjacent seat was empty, she noticed. Where was the bodyguard?

"Stop!" Ben barked.

They halted at the top of the stairs. There was a latching sound and the main door to the helicopter suddenly opened. The blades continued to kick up some dust, blocking her view of the helicopter's interior. The square, black hole remained stubbornly empty. Why was no one coming out? Were they supposed to go down?

"What do we do now?" she asked.

"Shut up," he said harshly, scared. "That's what you do now."

He was standing directly behind her, using her body as a shield. There was movement inside the helicopter. Someone was emerging, doubled over so she couldn't see who it was at first. It didn't look like Kevin, however. The person stepped heavily to the ground, his hands set firmly in the pockets of his long dark coat. He straightened up.

It was Stanley Richards.

"I'll be damned," she heard Ben mutter behind her.

Richards stood at the open door, immobile. He was watching them, coolly, waiting. Waiting for what? Ben began to chuckle in her ear.

"This is better than I expected," he said. "Let's go."

He pushed on her neck with the muzzle, urging her to go down the steps. But she resisted. She wasn't sure why she did it, except she was tired of being told what to do, not only now but in general. She was going to stand her ground, she decided. It was foolish, probably, but she didn't budge.

"Move," Ben hissed.

She refused. The gun pressed harder into her neck. She stared at Richards, realizing that he was watching *her*.

"I said *move!*" Ben ordered.

She refused, tensing all her muscles stiffly.

He placed his hand on her back and roughly shoved her forward. She stumbled onto the first step, lurching forward slightly, inadvertently creating a small space between them. Suddenly, there was bright flash of white from inside the helicopter. Then another. Followed by near simultaneous sounds of two gun shots. Bryce flinched reflexively, feeling like her heart might explode.

When she recovered, she realized the muzzle of the gun no longer touched her neck. She heard a loud thud behind her and felt the wooden planks of the porch shudder. She turned. Ben had been shot twice in his chest. Blood was spreading. His eyes were open and he seemed to be breathing, but barely. Bryce turned sharply back to Richards – who hadn't moved a muscle. He was still watching her. The blades of the helicopter began turning faster and the engine began revving up. Dust began to swirl, filling the air again.

Richards turned and climbed into the helicopter.

An unseen hand slammed the door closed behind him as the blades and the engine continued to wind up, whipping more dust and dirt. When it became clear the helicopter would lift off soon, she turned around and looked down at the gunman. He was dying. She kicked his gun away and fell awkwardly to her knees beside him. Blood flowed across the porch. Her hands were still tied behind her, which was incredibly frustrating. She strained against the handcuffs, wanting to help Ben, but they wouldn't break. She could see his breathing become swallower. She tried again, hurting her wrists as she strained. No good. She leaned over the gunman and twisted her torso until her right hand could touch his wrist. She felt for a pulse. It was fading.

Dust became dirt as the helicopter reached lift-off speed. She removed her fingers, shut her eyes tightly and bent over the young man, trying to shield him from the flying debris. She felt the sting of the dirt and rocks on her arms and neck. She could feel the thudding of the blades. She lowered her chin to her chest, trying to keep the dust away from her face, looking, no doubt, as if she were praying over Ben, lying prostrate before her. In a way, she *was* praying.

Wind buffeted her body as the maelstrom engulfed her.

SUNDAY

The Mozart alarm chimed merrily in the air.

Bryce rose from the table in the office and crossed quickly to the video monitors, which blazed brightly. A solitary pickup truck drove steadily down the entrance road toward the house, raising a trail of dust. It was Earl, right on time. She returned to the table, which she had mostly cleared of papers, closed her laptop smartly and straightened up the medical files she had been reviewing all morning. It had been another rough night. After her hostage ordeal, she had been offered a room at the Saint Sebastian in town by the owner, which was very kind, but Bryce preferred to sleep in her own house, even with all the police equipment and crime scene tape everywhere. Dale and the police officers had poured into the ranch as soon as Richards' helicopter receded into the distance. There was nothing anyone could do for Ben Scott, however, other than close his eyes.

Praise and concern for Bryce poured in from all sides, overwhelming her finally. Some people drove out to the ranch despite Dale's attempt to keep everyone away. Meili gave her a bear hug as soon as she arrived and Earl choked up twice, which was saying a lot, Bryce imagined. Even the Mayor showed up. Not normally at a loss for words, Bryce suspected, the Mayor struggled to hold her composure together as she shook her hand. Then she gave Bryce a hug suddenly without saying a word. She seemed genuinely upset at what had happened. As they separated, the Mayor gave her a look. Bryce understood exactly what was on her mind: *the crappy things men do*. Dale kept other visitors away and when Bryce was no longer needed for police purposes, she signaled to Seymour and they retired to the office, where she was determined to return some semblance of routine to her life by opening up a medical file even though she had a ranch to run now as well. She'd think about that later.

The first thing she did after closing the office door, however, was cry. Bryce collapsed into the chair, covered her face and sobbed silently.

Earl's truck was halfway to the house, she could see on the monitor. Bryce didn't want him to reach the ranch Headquarters first, so she grabbed her vest from the back of the chair, opened the door and quickly crossed to the sliding glass door, ignoring everything else in the house, police-related or not. The door had been partially opened by Deputy Sandoval, allowing people to enter and leave the house without disturbing the scene of the shooting on the porch. Bryce stepped outside, followed closely by Seymour, who had not left her side. She pulled her car keys from a pocket of her vest. At the top of the narrow stairs, she glanced back at the triple lines of police tape that blocked passage down porch. She'd think about the shooting later. Bryce sped down the steps and 'beeped' the car open. She climbed in after Seymour, fired the car up – and then paused. They were going to a wake for Matt! She hadn't wrapped her head around this fact yet. Was she ready? Not really. Remnants of last evening's crying jag swam into her heart. She felt tears coming.

She gripped the wheel and pushed them away.

Bryce eased the car down the driveway. At the bottom of the hill, she turned right onto the main ranch road, heading for the Headquarters. Matt's wake had been her idea. She wanted to honor him before leaving later today to catch her flight home. She mentioned the idea to Dale and Earl, who quickly endorsed it. Soon, an announcement about the wake had spread across social media, thanks to Nate. There would be quite a turnout, she was told. Earl wanted to say a few words about Estevan as well, which was fine with her, of course. The leafy oasis of the Headquarters loomed ahead. On the right, she could see the foreman's little house and the windmill with the horse corral out back. The front door was still blocked with police tape, she saw as she drove past. Was it still a crime scene, she wondered?

Tall trees enveloped the car and a moment later she pulled into the driveway of the ranch office, which looked like it hadn't seen a car in a while. Weeds needed to be pulled. She parked close to the building and opened the passenger door for Seymour, who eagerly bounded out. She rolled down the car's window, killed the engine, and leaned back in the seat, closing her eyes. Birds sang in the trees. A slight breeze wafted by, feeling soft on her cheek. Had she really decided to keep The Sun? It didn't seem real. The applause at the community meeting had been hugely encouraging. There was no way she was going to pull this off without help – but would it be enough? She had the cattle herd and the cash that her uncle left her, plus her savings, though that had to be off-limits. She had her job, which paid well but required her constant presence – and her attention. She wasn't giving it up. Could she manage both? It would be difficult – but she'd think about that later as well.

There was something else to ponder: the McGrath report. It had disappeared from the community center after her abduction. Bryce asked about it immediately after Dale arrived at the house, telling him it was an essential medical file. Deputy Midas was dispatched back to Alameda to find it, but all he brought back was her pad of paper with the Pros and Cons lists. There was no accordion folder anywhere to be found. Bryce swallowed hard at this news, but kept quiet. Dale didn't ask any questions and she didn't volunteer any information. Besides, the police had plenty on their minds, they didn't need to worry about a thirty-year old event involving an obscure medical anomaly. Bryce was concerned about it, however. Who would steal the report – if indeed that's what happened? Maybe it had been tidied up. Maybe Nate picked it up on his way out of the building. She'd ask him casually today at the wake. Or perhaps the Mayor scooped it up accidently. Bryce would ask her too.

She could hear the whine of an engine approaching. She climbed out of the car and called to Seymour, who bounced over to her looking happy. What to do with her buddy had been quickly resolved, thankfully. Isaac said he could construct a dog-door at the house and Earl volunteered to teach Seymour how to use it, even if it meant employing cans of tuna. The dog would be fine, Earl reassured her, until she returned next time. When would that be? She had no idea at this point. Soon, she hoped. The engine whine grew louder and Bryce could see Earl's truck passing by Matt's house. Earl sat as erectly as always, both hands on the wheel. He had agreed to take care of Brunhilda until she found a new foreman, which was very kind of him, though he couldn't vouch for the horse's politics by the time she got back he said with a smile. They laughed.

Earl pulled up behind her in the driveway and killed the engine.

"How are you doing this morning, young lady?" he said as he climbed out of the truck, slamming the door. "Did you get any sleep?"

"Not much," she replied. "Hopefully, I'll be able to sleep on the plane."

"Good luck with that. Dale's right behind me, by the way," Earl said, jerking his thumb at the road. "I think he's got some news for you."

"About what?"

"About Iraq, I think. And he's heard something about Mister Nibble too," Earl said. "Malcolm, I mean. But I want to talk to you about your cattle. Are you still planning to keep the ranch?"

"I am," she said firmly.

He nodded. "Then I need to tell you a joke."

Bryce's eyebrows shot up. Tell her a joke?

"There's an old saying in agriculture that you ought to know." He paused for effect. "How do you make a small fortune in ranching?"

She shrugged warily.

"Start with a big one," he said, giving her a look.

She laughed. "I'm not starting with a big one," she protested.

"I know that. That's why it's not a joke, as your uncle found out," he said seriously. "It's something I want you to think about until you get back. Your uncle spent a lot of money on this place unnecessarily, in my opinion. I doubt you have that luxury."

"I don't," she conceded.

"I know you don't," Earl said, in a sort of growl. "My point is ranches cost money and right now those cattle are all you have as income. Think of them like gold coins. You will need every one of them if you're going to stay in business."

"Are they in danger?"

"No ma'am. I'm happy to help take care of them until you get back, but you're going to need a foreman soon. And a ranch hand. I can help with that too."

Bryce could hear the low whine of a truck engine in the distance.

"I'm telling you this to be helpful," Earl continued in a lecturing tone. "Your uncle didn't listen very well. He lived in a fantasyland of ideas and theories and wishful thinking, like most of you liberals. Luckily, he had Matt."

"I'll listen," she protested.

"I know that," he said, "and I don't mean to sound critical. It's just if you're going to run a ranch, you've got to live in the real world. There's nothing abstract about a cow. She needs grass and water, or she'll die. She can't eat a theory. You're a doctor, so you know what I mean. Sorry about the sermon." He chuckled. "I just wanted to say that up front."

The engine growl grew. Bryce recognized it as Dale's Bronco.

"I appreciate it," she said to Earl. "Really, I do. But there's nothing wrong in trying to imagine how the world should be, right?" she asked, giving him a look in return. "It needs to be practical, of course, but there needs to be room for dreams too. Otherwise, it's just drudgery. There has to be a vision."

"I agree," Earl said. "But your uncle was all vision. That was his problem. And it cost him a fortune. Luckily, he left you some money, it sounds like."

"He didn't leave me as much as you might think," she said with a sigh.

"The more reason to be practical," Earl said, sounding affectionate now, instead of lecturing. "That's all I'm saying. I'm happy to help you in any way I can."

"Thank you," she said sincerely. "I'll need it."

The Bronco turned into the driveway and pulled up next to Bryce's car. Dale was its only occupant. He killed the engine quickly and opened the door.

He waved. "Good morning Doctor Miller," he said, climbing out. "I hope you got some sleep last night."

She smiled. "Everyone's worried about my sleep. I'm alright."

"Good," Dale said. "There's a long line of folks coming from town for the wake. They should be here soon. Can I catch you up on a few things before they get here?"

"Of course"

"Do you want me to leave?" Earl asked.

Dale shook his head. "No, it's fine. You should probably know too."

"Alright," Earl said, folding his arms across his chest.

Dale grabbed a big gulp of air. "I spoke with Ben Scott's Commanding Officer in Iraq this morning. They searched his belongings and found that note he mentioned to you, hidden in his Bible of all things. Its language was rather crude, but it said his wife was sleeping with the foreman of The Sun ranch and he should do something about it. It was sent anonymously and probably can't be traced."

"Meaning what?" Earl asked.

"Meaning, someone deliberately tried to provoke Ben Scott into coming back to Alameda," Dale said.

"Hoping he'd kill Matt," Bryce added.

"Yes."

"Was it Kevin Malcolm?" she asked.

"I don't know," Dale with a sigh. "It could have been someone else in the area. I think Matt got around, though you'll be curious to know that I got an email from the Diamond Bar folks late last night saying Mister Malcolm no longer worked for them."

Bryce frowned. "Why not?"

"I'll try to find out but I doubt they'll tell me," Dale replied.

"Charlotte wasn't Malcolm's girlfriend, was she?" Bryce asked.

Dale shook his head. "No. I think he was seeing someone else, though last time I spoke with Kevin he denied dating a girl at all."

"Abelard might know. Have you talked to him yet" Bryce asked.

Dale made a face. "No. He still hasn't shown up. I've asked

around, but no one has seen him recently. He usually keeps in touch with his landlady at the mill, if nothing else. So, it's a concern."

"You said Kevin and Matt had their argument months ago," Bryce recalled. "Could it be possible that Kevin harbored a grudge all this time?"

"Possibly," Dale replied. "In any case, whoever it was took action when he discovered that Matt was sleeping with Charlotte. He knew how to get revenge."

"By sending her husband the note," Bryce said.

Dale nodded slowly. "Correct. Provoke the professional sniper. Let him do the rest. Pretty clever, if you ask me."

"Hoo boy," Earl said, shaking his head.

Bryce exhaled. "The perfect crime. Do you think it was Kevin?"

"Maybe," Dale replied with a shrug. "It might explain why Richards came in with the helicopter. I can think of two reasons why he might do something like that, to bail his employee out of the mess he had made or..."

He paused.

"Or what?" Earl asked.

Dale raised his eyebrows at Bryce. "Or he wanted to save you."

She considered this for a moment. "Whatever his motives, I'm pretty sure he still wants the ranch."

"And still I think there's something funny going on up there," Earl added, tilting his head toward the dark hills to the north. "And I think Matt knew what it was."

"You mean the Sasquatch-breeding program?" Dale said, teasing him.

"Not that," Earl replied gruffly. "I think they're making a weapon."

Dale shrugged again.

"What about Estevan?" Bryce asked, changing the subject.

The police chief sighed. "He had bad luck, it looks like. What Ben Scott told you was probably correct. Estevan drove up to the South Well on Sunday morning, found a problem and called Matt on the radio, knowing exactly where he was – just up the road. I suspect he knew all about the love nest. Anyway, the call alerted Scott to his presence who subsequently came up with his plan to frame him for the murder. We found Matt's radio in Estevan's truck, by the way."

"What about Seymour and Matt's house?" Earl asked.

Dale nodded. "I think Scott drove down to Matt's house after killing Estevan intending to rob something and make it look like Estevan did it. When he opened the door, Seymour escaped. I think he searched the whole house. Trouble is there was nothing to steal. Matt didn't own anything. I bet his panic level was pretty high at that point."

"That's when he saw Brunhilda," Earl interjected.

Dale nodded. "Correct. She was exactly the cover he needed."

"Except he couldn't bring himself to shoot her," Bryce said.

Dale nodded. "Right, or else he might have gotten away with both murders. And if it wasn't for Abelard, he would have."

"Did you know Ben personally?" Bryce asked.

"Not really," Dale replied, shaking his head thoughtfully. "They moved to Alameda about a year ago so Charlotte could take the job at the co-op. He was already serving in Iraq. I only met him twice when he came back. He was quiet and intense, as I recall."

"Where was he hiding? On the Diamond Bar?" Bryce asked.

"No, he was camping on The Sun." Dale pointed to the east. "Over there in a clump of trees near the borrow pit. Deputy Sandoval found his campsite yesterday. He followed motorcycle tracks leading in and out to the highway. That's how he knew about the pit."

"Are you going to question Richards about all this?" Earl asked.

Dale shook his head. "I'd love to but I don't think I'll ever get the chance. For one thing, the FBI has made it clear I should back off."

Bryce frowned. "Why?"

"They don't want us provincials snooping around."

There was a crackling sound from the radio at Dale's belt. He detached it and pulled it up to his mouth. "Yes?" he said into it before lifting it to his ear.

Earl turned to Bryce. "Are you going to say no if Richards still wants The Sun?"

"That's the plan," she replied quietly. "Bad idea?"

"We'll see," he said.

Dale lowered the radio. "That's Sandoval. He says they've turned onto the entrance road. He said there are about thirty cars. You ready?" he said to Bryce.

"Not really," she said with a small laugh.

She stared at the horizon for a moment. "You know, this doesn't resolve what Matt wanted to tell me. It might have been about what he saw on the Diamond Bar but it might have had something to do with my uncle."

"I don't know what it was," Dale said. "But that's a mystery for another day. Right now, I need to get these murders wrapped up. When does your plane leave from Albuquerque this afternoon?"

"Three," Bryce replied.

"And when are you coming back?"

Bryce looked at both men. A million things ran through her mind at once. "As soon as I can."

Dale nodded. "Ok. We'll hold down the fort for you in the meantime."

"That's right," Earl added.

The rumbling sound of cars approaching could be heard. Bryce glanced over her shoulder. She could see a cloud of dust through the trees.

"I have to do something," she said to them. "Just a moment alone, if that's ok."

She didn't wait for an answer. She turned abruptly and began to move toward the edge of the office building, aiming for the open space beyond it. She needed to think.

"Wait!" Dale called. "I almost forgot."

She stopped and turned. Dale was fishing in one of the rear pockets of his pants as he came forward, pulling something out. "Deputy Sandoval found this at Ben Scott's campsite. I thought you might like to see it."

He held up a can opener.

"Apparently, he needed it for his meals. All he had was canned food. Either he lost his or forgot to bring one with him. I bet he found it while he was searching Matt's house."

He held it out to her. "You were right all along."

She took the opener. "Thanks," was all she could think to say.

He gave her a nod before turning and heading back to Earl. "See you in a moment," he said over his shoulder.

Bryce stared at the opener for a moment before sticking it in a pocket of her vest. She resumed her walk. Soon, she left the shelter of the trees. Nothing but grass stretched away as far as she could see. She kept going. Behind her, Bryce could hear the slamming of doors and the faint murmur of voices. Someone laughed. She kept walking. The day was bright, warm, and beautiful. The ground rose slightly and she realized she was approaching the Alameda River. She could see its swale in the distance, looking like a low, green ocean wave. For a moment, she was on the catamaran again, sailing solo, this time across a sea of grass. She stopped and turned to look in every direction. Mountains and hills circled her, creating the sensation that she stood at the center of the universe. The Heart of The Sun.

It was still hers – blue skies and everything.

THE END

ACKNOWLEDGMENTS

Many thanks to my Beta Readers: Margaret Beattie, Gen Head, Ann Hume, Cynthia Kelley, Elisabeth West, and Olivia White. Thanks also to Fred Provenza, Joan Bybee, and Deborah Madison for their feedback and support.

My deep appreciation to Jone Hallmark, John Tollett, Anna Philpot, and Jacques Duvoisin for their skill and kindness in helping get this book into print.

I would also like to acknowledge – and deeply thank – the many amazing and inspiring ranchers, farmers, land owners, public land managers, agency employees, conservationists, wildlife specialists, range experts, riparian restorationists, researchers, scientists, educators, academics, artists, writers, journalists, media makers, co-workers, nonprofit directors, donors, legislators, mediators, tribal members, entrepreneurs, food activists, young agrarians, and members of the public that I met over the span of two decades during my unforgettable journey with The Quivira Coalition. This story was not possible without you.

UPCOMING

Sun Down

Someone is shooting cattle on The Sun...there is a mysterious death in the forest...a hunt for buried gold...a missing medical report...a Sasquatch sighting...or not? Can Bryce save the ranch? The next installment of the Sun Ranch Saga continues...

To be published in 2019

Consilience

A contemporary love story about time-travel, an uncertain future, and resistance.

Daniel notices a young woman behaving oddly in an upscale grocery store, where she marvels at the bounty of food. Thinking she must be a spy for a foreign government because of the high tech watch she wears, he strikes up a conversation – one that changes his life utterly. Jo *is* a spy, but not the usual kind. She's come from the future to secretly record information about today – a mission, Daniel eventually realizes, that is quite subversive. Though she won't divulge many details, apparently things have gone badly wrong in the future, a point driven home by the tasks she must undertake. Meanwhile, the authorities know of Jo's presence and as she and Daniel complete her assignments together they are relentlessly pursued. The danger and urgency bring them closer until they fall in love – despite the precariousness of their situation. After a brief parting, they become inseparable.

To be published in 2019

ABOUT THE AUTHOR

I've been creating 'right-brain' answers to 'left-brain' questions since I was thirteen years old when a long summer road trip through Mexico lit a fire that has never gone out. For over forty years, I have expressed my answers in writing, photography, and activism.

Born in Philadelphia, I migrated west to Phoenix at the age of six in a 'covered station wagon' with my family. Inspired by the prehistoric ruins I saw in Mexico, I became active in archaeology, including two memorable summers of desert survey as an employee of Arizona State University in my late teens. I pursued 'left-brain' questions at Reed College, earning a B.A. in Anthropology. I chose to express my answers creatively in books and photography as well as films made while attending UCLA's graduate school in filmmaking.

In my twenties, my deep love of the American West expanded through travel, camping, and conservation work for environmental organizations. While employed at UCLA's main library, I 'hit the books' in pursuit of a deeper understanding of the region, studying its history, people, and cultures. In 1990, on the centennial of the official closing of the frontier, I put my research to work when I embarked on a fine art photographic project documenting the modern West. Titled *The Indelible West*, the book earned a Foreword by author **Wallace Stegner.**

In 1994, my 'left brain' turned to conservation when I became active with the Sierra Club in response to troubling political developments in Washington, D.C. Three years later, I cofounded The Quivira Coalition, a grassroots nonprofit organization dedicated to building a *radical center* among ranchers, environmentalists, scientists and others around practices that improve economic and ecological resilience. I served as Executive Director for fifteen years before becoming Creative Director. I worked on the front lines of collaborative conservation and regenerative agriculture, exploring on-the-ground solutions to global issues, including land restoration, local food, and the storage of atmospheric carbon in soils.

Quivira was also a creative endeavor for me, involving writing, speaking, shaping an annual conference, and developing new projects. Over time, writing became an increasingly important 'right brain' activity. In 2005, **Wendell Berry** included my essay 'The Working Wilderness' in his collection *The Way of Ignorance*, a big endorsement that encouraged me to expand into book writing.

In 2014, I began a new 'right brain' project in my spare time: fiction. I was inspired by a distant cousin, William Faulkner. My first work, *Consilience*, is a contemporary love story about time-travel, an uncertain future, and resistance. *The Sun* is the first book in a mystery series set on an historic ranch in northern New Mexico during the tumultuous years of 2008-09.

I live in Santa Fe, New Mexico.

Made in the USA
San Bernardino, CA
28 November 2018